Chax

A Dolphin's Song

By Tom Yancey

A Dolphin's Song

By Tom Yancey

Text and artwork copyright © 2016 Tom Yancey
All Rights Reserved

ISBN-13: 978-0692636558
ISBN-10: 0692636552

To Jeanie, with love. For believing.

The LORD does whatever pleases him,
in the heavens and on the earth,
in the seas and all their depths.

—Psalm 135

Contents

Chapter

  1. Chax's first exploit. 1

  2. A good day to die. 7

  3. Help from the storm. 9

  4. In serious ways, an idiot...13

  5. A fine place. 17

  6. Where's Flipper? 21

  7. Into the blackness, briefly. 29

  8. Marine biologists, "black water" and the *Mary Lu*......35

  9. We like the same places. 51

10. Captain Pete gets desperate....................................55

11. Blast from the past. 65

12. Why this Boat?..69

13. Prospects brighten. 75

14. Chax lingers. 81

15. Kimbie finds her bliss...87

16. Popper is exuberant...91

17. Amazing. 93

18. This is unusual. 97

19. This is more like it. 99

20. Popper gets a story. 101

21. Played him like a fish..111

22. Men are poor swimmers..113

23. Aboard the USS Boise, SSN 764 115

24. The pod lingers. 121

25. The snorkel and the sub. 123

26. I believe you dropped this......................................129

27. Pirates! 137

28. What Bridget saw...145

29. Opie hears something...151

30. The dolphins bring lunch. 155

31. Dark of the moon. 171

32. Desperate measures..175

33. The pod hears, and sees. 181

34. Pirate control...183

35. "and his unfortunate crew ..." 185

36. If I get a chance. But … 193

37. Blood in the water. 195

38. Mid-rats...197

39. Adrift...203

40. Aboard the USS Boise. 207

41. A directed turn...211

42. Radio Watch..213

43. Inventory, reassurance..215

44. A 'Cold War' lesson. 219

45. First light...223

46. This must be why. 229

47. Can't just sit. 231

48. Ricky plays captain. 233

49. Pete sees..237

50. Second-guessing. 245

51. This is why,...249

52. White hulls. 251

53. Stay...255

54. Crunch time...257

55. Flares, even. 259

56. Low in the water..263

57. If memory serves...265

58. 'Whites of their eyes.' 269

59. The dolphins listen...273

60. Supplemental exercise. 275

61. Intervention..277

62. Mopping up...281

63. The songs are always right. Almost. 283

64. Sorting it out. 285

65. More good men..289

66. Debriefed, deposed, dispatched. 293

67. Unpleasant but necessary. 295

68. Deep-fried monkey..299

69. Mourn, heal, mend, plan. 307

70. Time to rest. 309

71. All squared away...315

72. Just to steal a nice old boat. 323

73. Up one coast, down another, home. 329

     Acknowledgements..333

1
Chax's first exploit

Sound travels fast in the sea, three times faster than in the air, and so do stories. Some stories go around the world underwater, without being heard above it. Unless they need to be.

The dolphin pod from the shallow, warm gulf of the green ocean (the sea men call Atlantic) like to sing about Chax. Chax has led them well. His reputation is known. His exploits are part of the pod's long song, the chirping song that tells the pod's story. The song reminds the oldest dolphins of what has come before, and informs the newest ones. Dolphins from other pods—even some birds—know parts of it. Chax has been everywhere, and done other exploits, but this was his first.

The song tells how Chax kept sharks from eating men that fell from the sky. This was long before he became a leader of the pod. Every dolphin in the pod can sing parts of that song, but no one knows it all, except Chax. He sang it the first time, tired and amazed to be alive as he was. A few terns had been there and added details. Part of it became part of the pod's song. When Chax became leader, it became more important, but it was already a good part.

Chax protected the men, so the story goes, because he was offered the opportunity, and because he admired one of them. Some men are admirable.

Chax had been swimming out from the pod on a hot day in spring. The pod was resting, feeding on mullet—slender, silver, oily, tasty, easily excitable fish. Mullet thrive in the warm water along the edges of what men call the Gulf of Mexico. Chax heard about the men from terns, who had heard from whales.

The leaders had said Chax could swim away from the pod if he wished. As a full-grown dolphin, growing into his place, he was ready.

Whales had seen the men fall. After Chax found the whales, he was guided to the men by a noise the whales told him about. He swam until he heard it. Eventually it stopped, but he found the bubble the men were in anyway. He asked gulls and terns and pelicans, and listened.

Sharks had found the men too. By the time Chax arrived, several had gathered.

Chax scanned the men with sounds he directed at them. From the echoes that came back, he could tell that the men rode what was mostly a bubble, covered with skin. Dolphins can send sound through the water, out of their soft foreheads—though it takes effort—and they can learn much from the echoes that bounce back. Much. Sound is intense under water, and full of information.

Chax could tell, for one thing, that the men were riding in something like a big bladder. The sharks did not know that. All they knew is that it was bigger than them. Dolphins say that all a shark knows is what he can taste, and what little he can see and hear. Usually, that's good, but when sharks are intent on eating, they're dangerous. Even to a full-grown dolphin.

The men had poured something onto the water. The sharks did not like the taste, so, in a half-hearted way, they tried to stay out of it. Even so, they were sure that they were going to fill their bellies. They had already tasted blood.

But they were wary. When they swam close, the men hurt them. So the sharks took turns. Not the organized turns that dolphins or bluefin tuna take, just rough, opportunistic turns. They made random passes close to the bubble, until it began to weary the men. Chax could tell that the sharks were afraid of the men in the bubble, because they never swam close under it. But they swam around it. Around and around and around and around it.

He ignored them and swam closer. The sharks didn't like it, but he was too large to scare away, so they ignored him. He showed no fear, for he felt none, but neither did he threaten them. So they still circled the bubble. Several about his size, or a bit bigger.

Three men bobbed in the bubble. Full-grown humans, as the whales had said. The whales were indifferent to the men, but they paid attention. Chax had never been where he could watch men as much as he wanted, not mature men, so he did. He was curious. For as long as he could remember, for longer really, he had heard that men are unknowable. Unpredictable. Not crazy exactly, but close. Unstable. Men are dangerous. They are also interesting. But they attract trouble, just as sure as they attract dolphins. Everybody knows that. His aunts had said it when he was small, and aunts still say it. The songs say it. Everybody says it. So Chax was wary, even if he was curious. He watched and listened as the men whacked the sharks. After he watched for a while, he saw that one of the men was smart.

One was hurt, too. He moved as little as possible, and when he moved, he showed pain. But he kept watch. Another was skilled with a long pole, a paddle so long it was almost an oar. He hit sharks with it. He stretched above the water to swing, or jabbed with it, and he hit hard. The sharks did not like it. He almost always hit with the narrow edge, not the flat part. Sometimes the oar cut.

The third man, the smart one, used his weight to keep the bubble upright. Chax liked that man best. That one took care of the others. He seemed to encourage them, too. He watched, always, and was smart.

Chax didn't move much, and the man with the oar didn't focus on him, though the watchful man looked at him now and again. Repeated hits from the blade of the oar made the sharks lose some of their interest. They swam off, but not far. They would be back. One would come, then others. Chax swam closer. The man with the oar relaxed. Chax could tell the man did not fear him, even before the man put his flipper in the water and splashed. It occurred to Chax that this might be a greeting, so he splashed back. The men made noises like laughter. He had not known that mature men can laugh. He knew babies can laugh, but not mature ones. These could.

The man splashed. Chax splashed. The man splashed bigger. Chax did too. The men laughed. Chax stopped to listen. He liked it. A man hit the water with his fist. Chax hit the water with his tail. He liked to hear them laugh. He marveled at the sound of it. Whatever he had to do to hear them laugh was worth it. He tried to do whatever they did.

Chax kept after it until the men grew tired, or remembered sharks, and stopped. Chax watched and listened. The sharks watched and listened too, from a distance, indifferent. The man with the oar lay down to rest.

Chax was more curious about men now than before. If men could laugh, what else could they do? He remembered the warnings, but his curiosity was strong. He sound-scanned the shell from underneath. He could scan the men right through the skin of the bubble in the middle, but not so well on the edges. Even so, he could tell that if one of the sharks bit the bubble that would be the end of it, and probably the end of the men too.

He surfaced. Not within reach of the oar, but closer. He wanted to know if the men feared. From their heartbeats, they did, though the heartbeats settled back down. Then a man began making soothing noises. Chax raised his head out of the water and listened—hard. He listened through his jaw and his ears. Dolphins have ears, but they're covered. He listened through the sensitive melon on his forehead. Listened with intent, and effort. He liked the sounds the man made. Perhaps it was a song, though it was not as deep or strong as whale songs, or as pretty. It was not as varied as dolphin songs, either. But he liked it.

He had heard stories about good men. This one cared about his brothers. He had a grin like a dolphin, a lean, flexible body, and good balance. He seemed helpless, with his tiny flippers, but he had fallen from the sky. He must have skill. Chax liked this one. He might like all three, though he was prudent enough to be wary.

Then a strange thing happened. The one who was hurt began to speak. Chax could not understand the sounds, but somehow he knew the man was talking to the Speaker of the Seas and Stars. The man dropped his head and raised one arm, with his little hand open. The other men lowered their heads too, but Chax knew before that. He had not seen much of men. Mostly he had only seen them at a distance, and he was not prepared for this. He had been surprised and pleased when they laughed. Now he was surprised indeed, and puzzled. How could men know about the Speaker of the Seas and do as they do?

But this one did know. Chax listened. He could not know what the man said, but Chax knew the man must be talking to the Speaker of Life. The man sounded as if he knew the Speaker. Chax marveled.

Not right away, but soon, Chax was sure he should stay by the bubble and keep the sharks from the men. This sureness did not come from the man. Everything Chax knew told him—urged him, directed him, offered him the opportunity—to help. The Speaker of the Waters and Land and Sky and all that is in them invited him. Chax had been told this could happen. He knew it was an honor. If he were ever asked, he had been told he would know to obey. Now he knew how right and obvious that advice had been. So he did. He would not have considered anything else.

2
A good day to die

It was the hottest part of the day. The sharks were back. They did not like it when Chax interfered.

At first they were only puzzled. Then annoyed. At last one, then two of them challenged him. He could not bite and tear as they could but he could evade them, even hit them, because he was smart and quick, and because they were still mostly focused on the men. The sharks didn't co-ordinate, except in the most selfish ways. But after a time they began to behave more like a pack. They took care not to bite each other, at least, and focused mostly on Chax. When one tired, another came at him, and another.

Chax rammed one shark hard enough to stun it, and was able to rest while the others argued about whether to attack their injured brother. When the rammed shark made a great show of being unhurt and strong, they turned back to the bubble.

Chax was still in their way. He was everywhere, and it made them mad. Chax was as engaged as he had ever been with anything. He trained every sense he had on the sharks. He watched them, probed for weak-nesses, bad habits, slow turns, anything, and stayed with the bubble. Sometimes he could anticipate where a shark would go, get there first, strike and be gone. Sometimes it seemed he had all the time in the world to bash and twist and thrust and stop and start again. He had not expect-ed, when the sky turned pink this morning, to be locked in the battle of his life, but that was what the day had brought. Now he fought not just for the men, but for his life.

Chax knew he had hurt the shark he rammed. He scanned and knew. If he could hit the same place again, the others might turn on their broth-er. That seemed the men's only chance—his only chance. Unless he fled, which he did not even consider. How could he? Where could he go that would be far enough? Besides, this was his first adventure. He had looked forward to this all his young life. The newness and intensity of it had frightened him at first, but now he enjoyed it, reveled in it, so much he had to calm himself.

In the confusion, the man with the oar hit Chax on his right front flipper. Chax knew it was a mistake, because the other men chastised the man for a second. The blow slowed Chax, but only a bit. He didn't look slow. Neither he nor the sharks looked slow, not to the men or to each other. The lean man had all he could do to keep the raft upright in the turbulence made by the twisting, twirling, hurling dolphin and the crazed sharks. When the men were not bailing the raft or holding on they watched, slack-jawed, as Chax hit shark after shark, again and again with his head, his beak, his tail, his flukes. It looked like he hit them with something they would have sworn he did not have. Shoulders.

Still, one of the sharks would soon take a bite out of him, or take an accidental bite out of the bubble and men. The sharks were crazed. The oar had made cuts. The smell and taste of blood in the water, their own and perhaps Chax's blood, made them crazy. They took more risks. Two sharks were knocked senseless when they crashed headlong into each other, but they came back quick enough.

"Eat! Eat!" they all said.

Chax knew he was slower than he had been. Soon he would slow too much—or misjudge. No matter. Sure as he was of anything, it was his duty and privilege to guard the men, even if he became the sharks' meal.

He was as sure of it as he was sure he was a member of the dolphin pod from the warm, shallow gulf of the sunset side of the green ocean. As sure as he knew the pod's job was to hurry fish along the rivers and paths of the seas. As sure as he knew this was his first adventure.

Chax was a good, brave, strong, healthy dolphin. Large for his age, and almost mature. He had been told, invited, allowed to do this. Now it was part of his song—short, brave chirps. He would die singing it, hearing it, whether today or a long time from now. Everything and everybody dies. Whenever he died he would be proud and grateful that he had been considered fit for this.

If he died today, he would die full of purpose. Purpose filled him as the sharks closed in.

3
Help from the storm

Far away, a whale sang about obedience and duty. Even the sharks heard it, or felt it. One mocked. The others looked behind them. Seeing this, terns dove at a small shark's head. The terns had pecked at all the sharks, but this time the small one flinched, fled. When it surfaced, the terns mocked more. When it bit the air where a tern had just been, they mocked worse.

The whale song helped Chax. Obedience. Yes. The terns cheered him. What strength he had left came from the song and the birds. And from being where he was, doing the right thing. From obedience.

He exhaled all the breath he had and rose to fill himself with air again, hot new air. As he dove he saw — right in front of him — the underbelly of the biggest shark. Without much effort, Chax hit it with his beak so hard that it stopped, turned and swam away. It did not circle back. Chax could not quite believe it was gone, but it was.

When Chax had found the men, the day had been bright, hot, and calm. He had not noticed a storm as it gathered. Now he could not help but notice. The sea was anything but calm now. Waves built on each other, until one rose so large it lifted the bubble high, and held it aloft. The same wave lifted Chax too, and the closest sharks — only to hurl them down. As Chax cleared his blowhole for a breath, another wave lifted him, dropped him. Another wave did the same, and another, and another. They seemed to come from every side.

All he could do was try to ride the power of the water. Wherever it went. Without any intent on his part, the water pushed Chax hard against a shark. All Chax could do was keep from being broken. The shark did not fare as well. As the wave pushed them both down toward the lowest swag of the surface, then below it, the shark crumpled. When Chax recalled that wave later, he remembered hearing yelps of joy, of exuberance. Only later did he realize they must have been his own. He and the shark were lifted back up, and dashed again. The dazed shark smacked the water hard, on its side, and was pushed deep. The shark swam further down, but it was bent, in a way the young dolphin had never seen a shark bend. Unlike the shark, Chax glided along the curl of the water and was pushed beneath it tail first, easy. He had forgot the men, but as he was lifted on the next surge, he saw them, still in the bubble. He watched them slide down the inside curl, gentle. It made him remember how his aunts had nudged him back into place when he was small and tried to stray from his mother.

Chax was filled with joy as he watched, as full as he had ever been. Joy came not only from what he saw, but because he was still here, and the men were still here, and the storm had come to help. Just in time.

One by one, waves overcame the sharks. One by one they lost contact with the bubble and swam down to calmer water. Hunger forgotten, they swam away.

Grateful, joyful, proud, Chax stayed with the bubble as long as he could. His heart wanted to stay even after his muscles began to tremble and jitter and spasm and work against themselves so he could not swim well. He had never felt anything like that. He had never been this tired either, or this full of joy. But at last he also had to seek calmer water in the depths, as the sharks had done, because the storm continued. Chax pushed out all his air, drew an enormous breath and took a last look at the bubble with the men still in it.

The men returned his look, tossed about though they were. They were too full of fear to really see, though, or to see that they had help. But as Chax watched the bubble ride the inside curve of that huge wave, with the men in it, upright, sideways, he knew.

He swam down like a newborn, short lunges, the only way he could. The current pushed him the direction the sharks had gone. He swam that way until an urge so strong he knew he should obey caused him to turn across the current at a curious angle. He pointed his short little surges in a direction that seemed brighter, and continued. After he turned, the going became almost restful. He surged and glided, surged and glided, surged and glided many times before he remembered to take a breath. He had never had to remember that before.

The end of the storm was as unnoticed as its beginning. The churning eased. The sun came back. He returned to the calm surface. The air was cool. Breath came easy. After a morning of easy swimming, he heard his pod. The pod had stayed deep under the storm. When the sun rose, and they rose to the surface, a flock of gulls gave them incomplete, bird's-eye accounts of what he had done.

When the others began to nuzzle Chax, to welcome and comfort him, he was amazed. Tooth scrapes were here and pits from teeth were there. A wedge bigger than his beak was gone from his flukes. The tip of his dorsal fin had a notch now. A flipper was scraped raw where the oar had hit. The same flipper bore a half-ring of tooth marks, deep holes. Except for the oar, he could not say how any of those marks had got there.

Chax squeaked out what he remembered. It didn't seem much of a song to him. No matter. The pod was rapt. Terns added to it. They had risked their lives to stay and help. They had dived at sharks. When two terns landed on his back in their excitement to repeat what they had seen, Chax let them. He smiled. He ruffled their feathers as he blew out his breath. Heard them laugh, felt them take flight to dry their wings, felt them land again. Relaxed. Tern stories are still part of his song.

Chax swam with the leaders that day, and the next days, though he was still not quite mature.

4
In serious ways an idiot

Captain Pete Gordon flipped a page in the log book and raked his fingers through his hair, frustrated. He needed to locate an entry about engine maintenance so he could schedule it again. If he couldn't find it in the log, he would have to go below and read it from the chart posted in the engine compartment. He flipped another page.

"Ahoy!"

He knew the voice, smiled. The captain turned to look aft, where a dab of orange caught his eye. Kimbie Barone, on the dock, orange shirt, next to a hand truck and boxes. Somebody would help her in a minute, so he went back to his log. Boat maintenance never ends. Tedious, difficult, sometimes, but maintenance could also be life-or-death important. Long ago he had taken the Coast Guard's credo to heart. Now it was almost fun. He had the ship's calendar open, looking for open dates when he could do semi-major work.

"Ahoy! Captain Pete?" Hmm. Pete stopped, put the cap on the Sharpie marker, raked his hair back again and stood. And grabbed the counter rail and wheel. His foot was asleep. He hobbled to the ladder and tried to shake life into his foot as he went. At the top of the ladder he waved, gripped the rails, stomped his tingling foot, easy, swung out and let his hands bear his weight on the polished brass. Gravity did the rest. His arms braced and his hands slid and he descended the ladder. The foot that was asleep registered what felt like an electric jolt when it hit the deck. It felt rubbery, out of contact. The other foot worked, though. He laughed at himself, glad he still gripped the rails.

"Hang on," he shouted, laughter in his voice as he shook his head. The deck at the bottom of the ladder was also the overhead for the boat's largest compartment, the salon. Captain Pete hopped a few more steps, shook his foot and glanced up. Kimberly was just ahead, above him, trying not to giggle. Wind-blown white curls surrounded her tanned face.

"Where's Digs?" he asked. He looked down to try to preserve a bit of dignity as he tried again to shake something other than needles back into his foot. When he looked up her smile was like sun on the water. He smiled back.

"Said he needed a haircut," she answered. The boat's aging first mate probably had friends to see, ashore, too, but Digs would be back by the end of the afternoon. With a story, most likely, plus stuff the boat needed, maybe even a haircut. Digby was his real first name, but when Kimbie had started calling him Digs a year ago, it stuck.

"What about Julian?"

"Schmoozing the foundation, tending his grant." She shrugged and looked up at the sky. He also looked at the nearly cloudless blue sky. "I think he was afraid I'd spill the beans," she said.

Pete snorted. "Ha! What beans? His naps?" Fat chance Kimbie would ever say anything that would not help the cause. If Dr. Julian Ping had any idea what was good for his grant, and his own reputation, he would take her everywhere, for her people skills and smarts. That was a no-brainer. But over the past year, as evidence accumulated, the captain had decided the professor was an idiot. Charming sometimes, high IQ, maybe. Well, okay, sure, very smart, well-educated, well-traveled, even likable sometimes. But in serious ways, an idiot. With a Ph.D.

Kimbie was still on the dock. "I just didn't want to drop this stuff in the drink, you know? I hate to bother you. Where's Fred?"

"Wandered off. Over at the houseboat with the girls, is my guess. It's okay. I needed a break. What *is* all that?"

Her head bobbed left to right. She did that. "Julian's mail. Fruit. Veggies. Food. Pink shrimp on ice!" She tilted her head, caught his eye and grinned. "I really don't want to drop it in the bay." She was pleading. Pete realized he was not helping.

"Okay, I'm coming," he said as he hop-skipped the last few steps. The tingle was going away. She hadn't laughed but Pete had seen muscles in her face twitch. Kimbie had dressed up to go ashore: pleated khaki shorts that came most of the way to her cute knees, a sleeveless blouse—orange, silky—that set off her nut-brown shoulders. Sandals, not flip-flops. She had gone all out, even a scarf. *If I were Julian Ping*, Pete thought, *I'd at least take her along as a distraction. And backup.* Ping didn't know it, but he needed her to finish his sentences sometimes. Connect the dots. Interpret. *The money people are missing out. Specially if they're guys.*

"Tell me when you're ready," she said, a tanned fist on each hip. "You seem a little ... spacey." She almost looked concerned.

Pete snorted. "Daggone foot went to sleep. Sat too long." Pete noticed more than he meant to about his partner's girlfriend—assistant—

whatever she was, as she kicked one dressy sandal into the boat, then the other. Her braided belt was exactly at eye level.

He forced his eyes to the deck, then to the sky, then to the stack of boxes, as he shook his almost normal foot one more time. "Okay. Hand me something."

She gave him a box and he turned and set it down on the open rear deck. When he turned back to the rail she had another box ready. She smelled nice, and he said so. "Thanks," she said, bobbing a curtsy that made him grin. Another box. "I thought I was going to have a nice lunch somewhere with the foundation people, so I girled up." She seemed disappointed. Another box.

"Their loss. What happened?"

"It was just three guys. He told them I wanted to shop. As if. So I went with Digs." She shrugged, but smiled and got the last box. As Pete took it, she steadied herself on his shoulder, stepped onto the gunwale and then down to the deck.

The open box in his hands had big ripe strawberries on top. He stuck his face down near them, took a deep breath and concentrated on their aroma.

"If you'll take the food to the galley, I'll schlep Julian's stuff to the stateroom," she said. "Or just leave it. I'll put it away." He headed to the air-conditioned galley with the berries. When he came back for another load she was up on the marina slip again.

"I'll stow everything after I take this dolly thing back." She wheeled the hand truck around and stopped. "I slipped on the ramp," she said, a different tone in her voice. She took a breath and frowned. "In those stupid shoes. Almost busted my butt and nearly lost the dolly. I waited because I was still shaky. Thanks, by the way."

"No problem," he said, concerned. "Two's always safer. Sure you're okay?"

She nodded, pushed the hand truck up the ramp, barefoot, steady, turned onto the pier, looked back and smiled. She looked like she was glad he was still a little concerned. Pete was embarrassed to still be watching, though, so he waved, and headed back up to the bridge.

It's none of my business, he thought, not for the first time. *But Julian Ping is a bozo.*

5
A fine place

This was still a fine place to be a dolphin. It had been better in Chobeem's memory, but it was still fine. Plenty of mullet to eat. Other pods near to help eat them. Plenty of men, too, but these do not seem to mean harm. They watch dolphins and sometimes chase them. They ride their noisy shells, but are easy to elude. They do not try to kill or catch, as some men do, other places.

Here, most men fish with hooks, baited with live things or dead things, odd things they must make. The men catch fish, but not enough to matter. That's what fish are for. Some men are not much smarter than the fish. They bunch together and put hooks in the water, all near the same place. But some fish are less smart than others.

Men have always caught fish here with small nets. A few. Not many more now that this is such a man place. Dolphins admire those men. They admire good fishing.

A good pod in the right place, like this place, can round up more mullet than they can eat. Will eat.

Schools of silver mullet—even slender ones—are something a creature as perceptive as a dolphin cannot miss. A good pod can chase them, drive them, scare and crowd and push mullet into a tight group, until the water boils and bubbles with them. Mullet are easier to herd into a cluster than some. A pod can work up an appetite that way. In the end each dolphin gets a turn, gets to crash through a tight column of fishes. Each dolphin, from the first to the least. Getting a mouthful is easy, but that isn't the point. A mouthful is not a problem for a dolphin, most of the time. What makes a boil worth doing is the cooperation, the controlled confusion, the excitement when it works.

Not every dolphin likes this sort of thing. Some dolphins disappear when a boil is talked about. Some only help in the early stages and wander off. Creating a mullet boil—any boil, groupers, sardines, anchovies—takes time and effort, and only results in some fish, after all. To some dolphins, there are more than enough fish to go around without a ritual.

But to most, especially the young, building a boil is the height of something good to do. The fun, or the value, comes not so much from eating, or even from driving the fish half crazy. Mullet are catch-able without a boil. Two dolphins can catch all they want. Mullet are content to poke along the bottom, to nibble at odd bits that grow there, or have settled there. It is a wonder they taste good at all, but they do. Somehow they get tasty.

And it's not like mullet are so easy to scare that a boil is simple.

Dolphins have to work at it, with sounds and thrusts, curtains of bubbles, tactical applied fear and confusion. If they coordinate it well — that is, if it is perfect, so no escapes are left open — it works.

What was just a big school of fat silver cylinders meandering along becomes something almost alive. Things like that are the dolphins' creations, their art and architecture. Nothing that takes that much effort to maintain can last, though. Boils are short. Disorder reasserts itself as soon as the dolphins let up.

But a good boil is not only fun, it is remembered, talked about. It strengthens the pod, helps its members work together and laugh. Members learn to follow directions, even anticipate them. Leaders learn to lead. Others learn to follow and help each other. Complicated fun and a meal at the same time. Making a good boil improves the grin of the pod that makes it, which is always a good thing.

Once, when a boil was in the works, a man was near. He seemed to belong there as much as the dolphins. As the mullet swam closer together, the dolphins became more and more intent. The man and his shell were never in the way. The mullet were fat with roe. The boil lasted long enough for even stragglers to plunge, if they wanted. Everyone was pleased, ready to brag, laugh, rest. They were about to let the boil scatter when a net landed on it. No dolphin was touched. Most of the mullet escaped. But the man hauled in a net full of fish.

The dolphins were stunned. The man handled the net, the boat and the small fish right, with no wasted motion. He laughed like shells moved by water. The man and a small dog in the boat seemed to understand each other. The dog was the color of brown sand, with hair that grew in all directions on its face. The man was the reddish-brown color usual for fishermen. He wore a sand-colored cap.

These dolphins lived most of the time in a place that had become a man place. They had heard laughter. They had heard the howl kind that goes with cruelty. And other kinds: courtship laughter, contentment laughter, ridicule laughter, hollow laughter.

They had even heard joyful laughter. That kind puzzled them. From stories, and from what some of them had seen, there was no reason for men to laugh that way. That was how this man laughed. The dolphins could tell he had known what they were doing. He knew that what he did would surprise them. And please them, because it was a natural completion of the boil.

His laugh and the way he looked at them told them all that. When he came across a mullet wriggling with life and just right to eat, he tossed it in the direction of one of the dolphins. They watched it hit the water and vanish. The man did not seem to care. He was lean. He would not expect them to gorge.

He continued to offer fish just right to swallow, and talked to the dog with his calm, gravel voice. At last, a mullet came through the air in such a perfect arc, with so much life that Marbi caught it, and tossed it straight up. When the small fish came down the right way, she caught it again and swallowed.

This pleased the man. He smiled and was quiet. The dog opened its mouth and cocked its head. The other dolphins saw nothing wrong with what she did. After all, these were mullet they had rounded up, the same as ones they had eaten.

But the dog took offense, with a sharp single bark and a low growl that tickled the dolphins, especially Marbi. The man laughed, and said something to the dog that stopped the growl. The dog hung his head, walked to the end of the shell-like boat, looked down at the water, came back, and watched the dolphins, silent. Sometimes the pod remembered that.

Chobeem had seen many times when mistrust of men was right. Prudent. He had seen men do bad things. He also had seen men do things that were not harmful, only puzzling, as far as he could tell. Over the years his attitude toward men had shifted slightly, but his aunts had taught him early that men are unstable, unpredictable, perhaps unknowable. Men attract trouble. Say whatever else you will, that is true. He always came back to it.

Chobeem knew that living near men could be precarious, but the places dolphins like best also seem to be places men like too. From the songs, this has always been true. Once there was more than enough for all. Not now, not always.

This pod had traveled to where waters were cooler, and to warmer places. Some places were just as good as when Chobeem was small, with plenty of fish and everyone healthy and curious. Curiosity mostly led to nothing but adventures and meals and pleasure and friendships and knowledge. But dangers exist now that he had not had to be warned about when he was small. And too many times now, food is hard to find, or not good.

There are things now that the pod no longer warns young dolphins about. Some of them are obvious. Others are inescapable and always there. Bad water. Too many boats. Too many fishermen. Nets that go on forever. Too much noise. The young ones have never been away from those things long enough not to be aware, and always wary. There are also still places men do not go, but not as many as Chobeem remembered from his youth.

6
Where's Flipper?

The white hull of Captain Pete's handsome old yacht cut the blue-green water, churning up frothy turbulence, rolling two flat waves in its wake. Just like the brochure.

The brochure had all but promised dolphins would surf the bow wave of the motor yacht *New Delphi*, an 85-foot Bertram sedan cruiser, twenty-seven years old but beautifully maintained and updated. Not this trip. No dolphin surfing had happened yet, but not for lack of trying. Captain Pete had made every effort to create what always before had been an ideal bow wave, the kind dolphins like to ride. But he had not been close to a dolphin for two days.

The passengers were signed on as temporary crew on a registered, sanctioned oceanographic expedition. They had paid handsomely for the privilege, and a few were impatient. On their second day out of San Juan, excuses about why they weren't seeing dolphins were tiresome. The captain wondered too. He had said so.

The galley fare lived up to expectations. Digby, that is, Digs, the first mate, cook and resident colorful character, got compliments, as usual. The two scientists, Kimberly Barone, M.S., and Dr. Julian Ping, were pleasant and knowledgeable, the passengers agreed. So were Captain Pete and handsome young Fred, the second mate. No one, as yet, had tired of the sparkling blue-green Caribbean or the Gulf of Mexico that surrounded them now. Or the tiny islands with white beaches and pastel houses they had cruised past, or the weather, which was travel-poster perfect.

Kimberly Barone, the pretty female scientist, knew a great deal about the sea and its creatures. Her enthusiasm was contagious. For the less scientifically inclined, sunbathing, frequent stops for swims and snorkeling, cool drinks and interesting conversations helped pass the time. Nearly everyone aboard found snorkeling off the mahogany tail platform of the *New Delphi* amazing, gorgeous, and fun.

They swam with fish of every color: iridescent blues and purples, bright yellow, intense red. Fishes of silver, brown, black, white, tan, even green. Schools of yellowtail, coppery snapper, dark grouper, striped sergeant majors. Big noisy drums and sheeps-heads abounded. They had seen flashes of silvery underwater lightning they were told had been tarpon. The startling sound and sight of huge croakers had alarmed them, and the silent glide of nurse sharks three and four and five feet long made some of them feel almost brave and adventurous.

They had learned how to catch lobsters, and eaten their catch. Tans were starting, or deepening. But no one could say for sure that a single dolphin had been seen, not close. The captain and crew thought it was odd.

"They'll show up," the female scientist assured everybody. Kimberly Barone, B.S., M.S., scanned the horizon, her tanned knees denting the white cushions of the seats built into the perimeter of the rear deck. "Sometimes they disappear for a while but they always come back." She swept the water with gigantic binoculars, her elbows resting on shiny mahogany not much darker than her arms. The field glasses narrowed at the eyepieces, the better to fit her small but capable hands.

By now the passengers realized that the Bertram, with its classic lines and real mahogany decks and trim, was a yacht to be envied. The *New Delphi,* or N-D, pronounced *indie*, as the passengers had learned to call the handsome boat, was smaller than some they had seen, but very nice. The cabins were comfortable, bright, fresh-smelling and well appointed. So was the salon, the old-school name for the boat's attractive "living room." Big sparkling windows and small spotless portholes let in ever-changing views. Every surface and corner was as clean, fresh-painted and as "squared away" as it should be, which was reassuring. They had encountered absurdly large yachts, newer and fancier ones, plus pretty sail yachts that were more stylish. But those who had not known it before were beginning to realize the snob appeal of "their" vintage boat, from the approving and sometimes envious glances they met. That was nice.

Everywhere they went offered plenty to see: white and pink sand beaches, forts and even piers made of coquina stone, the name they learned for huge, porous blocks of natural aggregate. Coquina stone is made by nature from the shells and skeletons of tiny sea creatures bonded together by calcium secretions. The Spanish built forts with it. The *indie's* passengers had swum with sea turtles, watched big scary eels back themselves into crevices, and caught glimpses of odd-looking creatures that didn't look like fish at all. They had seen and been told the names of more species than most had ever imagined. But not dolphins, not close. Dolphins kept their distance.

Most of the passengers were on vacation, for all their interest in ocean science, and they wanted to make the most of it. Snorkeling with experts who could tell the life cycles of what they saw was certainly fun, exciting even, for some. The first two days had been full enough that most of them fell asleep easily on the gently rocking yacht. Especially after drinks, an elegant supper and a spectacular sunset.

But they would be catching a plane in nine days, whether they swam with wild dolphins or not. No one was complaining yet, but some were counting. If their vacation was to provide the un-toppable stories, pictures and videos they still imagined, Flipper had better show up.

Then there was the leader of the expedition, Dr. Julian Ping.

Julian Ping, Sc.D., according to the brochure, was "a noted marine biologist, a respected member of the select handful of true experts on order *Cetacea*, especially genus *odontoceti*, the toothed whales, dolphins and porpoises."

Which he was. Lean, tanned Dr. Ping had written two books on marine mammals, full of gorgeous pictures he had taken himself. The brochure said in one breath that the books were based on "his own seminal research, conducted at virtually every depth in the multi-hued myriad of tropical and subtropical aquatic biomes that cover by far the majority of the blue-green planet so inappropriately misnamed Earth." Ping had taught marine biology at major universities, written articles and contributed chapters to other books and textbooks. He had a federal permit to study and interact with dolphins in U.S. waters, and United Nations permit that looked like a diploma married to a passport. Bound in leather, the document seemed to admit no limitations whatsoever on Dr. Ping's research or curiosity. It commended him worldwide, and asked UN member nations to "extend every courtesy." Casually left open on a table at the welcome-aboard party, it promised much.

Shiny dark hair crowned Julian Ping's head and curls of it sometimes hung in the professor's intelligent dark eyes. Underwater it became a dark halo. A trimmed, salt-and-pepper goatee and moustache framed dazzling teeth. When focused, he could be an entertaining speaker. At a conference, after he narrated a slide show about his dolphin research and talked off the cuff for half an hour, he was strongly encouraged to apply for a renewable grant to continue his studies of dolphins and their imperiled habitat. Ms. Barone had hounded him until he actually completed the paperwork. The grant came from a foundation that had not asked much from him so far except pictures, short non-technical articles, occasional VIP visits to the boat and the use of his name and pictures for fund-raising. It was the least pressure he had ever encountered with a grant.

Captain Pete's yacht had been hired to be Dr. Ping's research platform. Visiting foundation VIPs enjoyed it so much that they encouraged Ping to take potential donors aboard for a few days from time to time. With the foundation's blessing, he and Captain Pete formed a partnership of sorts and booked the other staterooms a week or a fortnight at a time. Ping was building a nest egg, and the captain wasn't suffering. In response to ads in eco-travel magazines, potential passengers received a brochure on recycled paper, a video (mostly undersea stuff, some of it very good) and Dr. Ping's welcoming note, handwritten (by Kimbie) on his letterhead. Photocopies of journal articles, some that he authored, others that mentioned his work, and an order form for his books were included.

The letter promised posh accommodations, and the chance to participate in important research. The *New Delphi* was plenty nice enough, and research was in fact taking place. Kimbie recorded data and collected samples almost daily. But those aboard had been all but promised a chance to closely observe and very likely swim with dolphins in the open ocean. They had been led to believe they could (possibly) interact with dolphins, under supervision, and assist Dr. Ping and his associates "in their ongoing studies and observations of inter-species communication involving marine mammals, though probably not whales."

Miss Barone and the first mate, Digby—Digs—met most of the passengers at their hotels or the airport. Beauty and the beast, Digs usually told them upon first contact. Slender and attractive, youthful in her late twenties, the beauty had startling light green eyes. Years of tropical sun had tanned her skin quite dark. Sun and salt had bleached her natural blonde hair almost white. She was not tall, about five-seven, with much of her height in her legs. Fit, strong for her size and naturally active, Kimbie was used to pulling her own weight. People who did not prefer extremely thin women liked her figure. The crinkles around her eyes were from smiles.

Digs, the beast by contrast, was even more tanned, but leathery. Of average height, Digs was thick and solid, with arms that looked like they could haul a heavy line all day, because they could. Shoulders to match. His black hair was only salted with gray, his dark eyes sparkled, and teeth were, as one startled passenger put it, "wolf-white." And quite large. He liked to smile.

The brochure said that, in addition to being Dr. Ping's research assistant, Miss Barone was co-author with him on a scientific work in progress. No mention was made of their shared stateroom.

Kimberly, as Dr. Ping invariably called her, had first-hand knowledge of every major island in the Caribbean, and could speak with authority about the waters around them. She was not as well traveled as Ping, who had been born in Singapore and educated in Australia and New Zealand. But she had been to several of the ports of Central and South America, had a working knowledge of the bays and depths of the Gulf of Mexico, and was familiar with the east coast of the U.S., especially from the Chesapeake Bay south.

Unless she needed a wetsuit, her "uniform" was a bikini, over which she usually wore a T-shirt, just now a soft pink one. "I try to stay covered up, honest," she said when someone remarked on her deep tan. "But when you live on a boat, and swim and dive for a living, it just happens." She wore sun hats or caps or visors, bought sunscreen by the gallon, used it and encouraged passengers to use it too. She put zinc oxide on her nose most days. Nothing else kept it from peeling. It was peeling just now.

She was much more outgoing and direct than Ping, and tried hard to put the passengers at ease. Most were charmed by her. Most men were a bit dazzled. She had gotten accustomed to that, but thought it was silly.

"Doctor P," as the yacht's two crew members referred to Ping, didn't seem to be aware of clothing. He might have on soccer shorts or tiny Speedos, over which he would throw whatever. Flowered shirts, military garb, team jerseys, garage-band T-shirts. He believed his devastating looks exempted him from any need to follow fashion.

Ping often seemed preoccupied, so Kimbie tried to stay close to help him focus and get him to explain, elaborate. Her admiration was obvious. When she suggested or asked or goaded, he usually come forward with an entertaining explanation or anecdote. But when dealing with non-scientists, which most days meant everybody except her, Doctor P could lapse into important-sounding strings of words and phrases that sometimes trailed off without making a point, or being a sentence. Ms. Barone happily connected the dots and answered questions that Ping didn't seem to hear. It made an acceptable package, but a few of the passengers already went straight to the helpful assistant.

The crew—Digs and Fred—preferred to deal with her. They knew she liked them, and did her slightest bidding. She kidded with them, never talked down to them. They teased her, but Digs treated her like a daughter, and made sure Fred treated her like a sister. Fred had a girlfriend of sorts at the marina, anyway.

Digs and Fred did not joke with Ping, who patronized them in an absent-minded way. They avoided him as much as life on a boat and courtesy would allow. On those occasions when Dr. Ping began to pontificate—a weakness he had—irreverent young Fred sometimes made circus-impresario gestures. Ping never noticed, and Fred couldn't seem to stop. His mop of sun-streaked dark hair would fall in his eyes as he gestured. He didn't try to draw attention. Some found this unsettling. Others were amused. Whenever Kimbie saw this annoying-younger-brother behavior, she would shake her head, raise an eyebrow and glare. Chastened, Fred would resume a stoic posture.

If Digby was around, he would use whatever was handy to quietly bop unserious young Fred. This also caused Fred to stop, and smile. Digs had reminded Fred more than once that Ping was "business partners" with their real boss, Captain Pete, "and that's enough said." In a lifetime on the water, Digs had never had a captain he liked better and respected at the same time. "I'd take a bullet for Cap'n Pete," he sometimes said. The captain would shake his head, tell Digs not to talk like that, and try to look stern. Digs would shrug and say, "I would." Digs always had Pete's back.

John and Ruth Zinser were aboard when the others arrived. Ping said John and Ruth were part of his "research family." Sixty-ish or better, they welcomed everyone. Of the six who had just come aboard, Melody was the youngest, a rising college junior. The next oldest, a married couple in their early 30s, were lean, earnest and attractive. The first evening aboard, Chip and Bridget had called themselves, very agreeably, "environmental activists, but more on a spiritual level now." Bridget was trim, athletic, with short, light blonde hair and golden skin. Chip was tall, with medium coloring and a brown ponytail.

Tanned, fit Sherry, a stunning Chicago marketing executive with a reddish blonde mane, was married to Mel, a banker with an easy smile, a squint in the sun, and cropped gunmetal hair. It seemed they had been everywhere.

Sarah, an intense paralegal from Atlanta, was tall, leggy, dark-haired, dark-eyed, and very fair, traveling alone. She spent part of the first day catching up on sleep from all the overtime she put in to get ready for vacation. She found, to her delight, that she slept like a log on the boat, even in her tiny berth below deck, with its porthole to let in the ocean air. The second day Sarah spent either underwater or in conversation with Dr. Ping and Kimbie. Ping was not her cup of tea. She wasn't sure she liked the way he checked out the ladies. His associate, or whatever she was, seemed to know a great deal about everything they saw anyway. Even better, Kimberly was nearly as enthusiastic about big schools of yellowtail as those swimming through them for the first time.

The white-haired Zinsers were native Iowans, he a retired school principal, she a librarian, but had long lived at coastal Del Mar in southern California. After retirement they sold their hillside bungalow with its garden and grape arbor, bought a condo with almost the same view and began to travel. They helped run a mission school in Central America until politics forced them to leave. They hoped to go back, but were happy resting up on the *New Delphi*.

John and Ruth had watched dolphins from their deck for years, and been regulars for lectures at the Scripps Institute of Oceanography, just down the coast at La Jolla. Now they were "following them around, and taking it easy for a while," Ruth said.

Sarah Cale liked the Zinsers. On the other hand, Sherry McRae, the red-haired marketing exec, was as pushy a person as Sarah, who worked in a world of lawyers, had encountered in a long time. Sarah was sure she had been dropped from Sherry's list as soon as it became clear she worked for an hourly wage.

Mel McRae wasn't pushy at all. He listened, answered and asked questions without trying to impress. After a tour as a young Navy officer on a plywood boat along the rivers of Vietnam, Mel had found banking a piece of cake. He counted himself lucky, and looked younger than his age. Mel never apologized for his wife in so many words, but his comments improved the situations Type-A Sherry created. It was obvious he adored her, and she was easier to like when Mel was around.

Chip and Bridget Strewsberry-D'Mer seemed nearly as young as Melody Molinari, the undergrad. Pony-tailed Chip had just left the Washington staff of a New England congressman. After two terms and three elections, he had been unhappy with the "restrictive grind on the Hill," as he put it. He and Bridget, a yoga devotee and sometime instructor, met while wreaking havoc with the tuna fleet off the coasts of California and Mexico. They had stopped because it was "so confrontational, so edgy," she said, "and showboaty."

"Not how we might approach it if we were in charge, but fun at times, and important," Chip had said, agreeably. Bridget nodded, but did not quite concede the point. After the election they had spent the winter in Colorado, skiing. "Since the ocean is so essential to who she is," Chip said, they had flown out to Grand Cayman to see his dad, who was there on business. Happening to hear about Dr. Ping, they had flown over "just to see," and here they were.

"I think being here is going to be important," Chip said as he perched on the boat's aft rail, arms outstretched. He reminded Sarah Cale of a large bird.

Melody Molinari was vacationing by herself because a college friend backed out at the last minute. Kimberly, the boat's unofficial social director, tried to pay extra attention to Melody, the youngest person aboard, and so did the Zinsers. Sarah, traveling alone after ending a relationship that had gone nowhere too long, joined them in that. Melody was sweet and pretty, a little overweight and embarrassed about it. She almost never took off whatever dusty pastel "Life is Good" T-shirt she had on until she slipped into the water. Sometimes not even then. But she volunteered for everything, mopped the deck, helped Digs and Fred clean fish, everything. "This is so great!" she said, often.

7
Into the blackness, briefly

Chax did not like the sound of this place—there wasn't any. He didn't like the way it tasted or looked, either, but those things did not bother him as much as the quiet.

The ocean is rich with life, and with sound. Clicks of shrimp, croaks of croakers, the groans, drumbeats and bleats that different fish make with their air bladders are always in the background, not to mention dolphin clicks and chirps and the ocean-filling songs of whales. The ocean is full of sounds. Men add to it many places, but not at this place. Here Chax heard no sounds at all, let alone noise. No clicks, screams or crashes. It was hard to hear dolphins that were close by. Chax had long ago learned to ignore sounds that don't matter and focus on those that do. He could do that, most places. This place seemed to soak up sound, or eat it, or kill it. Maybe scare it away. He could not ignore that.

This lack of sound almost scared Chax, and he is brave. Chax had been to places so noisy that he could not echolocate, where he had to depend on his eyesight. Eyesight is a help, but it does not tell a dolphin as much as sound. If you can make your own sound and interpret what it tells you when it comes back to you, the way a dolphin can, sound tells plenty. It was rare for Chax to have to depend on his eyes. And here, even good eyes were little help.

This place was black, and dead quiet. It was not oil that made it black. Chax had been around places where oil oozed from the bottom or floated on the surface, or both, often enough to know. This was something else. He had been to one other place this dead, if not this black. He got sores afterward. At that place he had turned around immediately because of the terrible smell and bitter taste. This place had neither.

The huge brown dead place that comes and goes in the Gulf of Mexico is not as bad as that place had been, and it is bigger. That big brown place is unpleasant, bad-tasting and smelly, but not this quiet. Not all of it is dead, either, but most that isn't dead is dying. That big brown place off New Orleans has sounds, even though they are muddled, muddied, unhappy. Chax had seen other big brown dead places like it, and heard of others. They come and go. When big storms stir the

Gulf of Mexico, the huge brown place gets smaller. Sometimes it goes away. When storms don't stir it enough, it gets bigger. The ocean has stories about such places. They're bad. Usually they offer nothing to eat. Nothing live. Nothing a dolphin can eat. Nothing a healthy dolphin will eat. Chax avoided that place, and others like it.

Once the ocean did not have so many dead places. The pod's song told of that time. Now, the ocean has too many. Part of this pod's long song tells of when the water turned bad in the pod's home waters. The oldest dolphins—Chobeem was one—first heard that song from older dolphins who had lived it. The water had not turned muddy, or black, only sour. Men piled sand between islands called the Florida Keys. The sand blocked routes and changed currents the pod had used since the oldest songs.

Men put a railroad on top of the sand. For too many seasons, the train ran on it, thumping the sand, until hurricanes undid much of what the men had built. The huge storm re-opened blocked channels and created new ones, as the biggest storms always do.

But until then, for most of a dolphin's lifetime, the water in the bay behind the islands was not as good. Behind the big barrier that men ran the train on, currents flowed odd directions, or not at all. Growing things and living creatures choked and starved in some places and flourished oddly in others.

After the hurricanes, men started again, but they did not connect islands with sand and block passes as much. They pounded poles in the water, season after season, but they left the passages open. That was better. They built bridges on top of the poles, and many more men came. Many stayed. They still come.

There are many fishes in the water of the Florida Keys. Fish like the water near marshes and tidal mud flats and mangroves, because small creatures thrive in them. Fish like the small creatures. Men like the fish. Fish also like the reefs on the sundown side of the islands, for the same reasons. So do men.

But even here the pod did not find as many fish as before. Chobeem, though only about forty winters old, could remember when many more fish swam these waters. More than the youngest members of this pod had seen. He had songs about that. Things change. Songs tell of changes. Elders of Chobeem's first pod sang about things they saw and ate that he had not seen or tasted. Chobeem knew those songs. Chobeem's song told of fishes he had eaten or chased that the young ones had not seen at all, or had not seen in large numbers.

But this was still a good place to be a dolphin, even if the pod had to share it with so many men.

Chobeem knew songs that told of things the young ones almost could not imagine, songs about strange creatures. Songs of men who fought on the sea for days and seasons. He had heard those songs from elders he knew and trusted. Some of those elders had seen and heard and lived with what they sang about. Or heard them from elders long gone that they the elders had trusted. Some of those songs were almost too strange to believe.

He believed them. The pod knew Chobeem was trustworthy, and a good judge of others. His own story, the story of his terrible captivity and escape was almost beyond belief, but they believed it too. If Chobeem had learned a song from old ones he trusted, and they had learned it from older ones *they* trusted, then the pod trusted those songs. Trust is essential. Not to trust is a concept dolphins do not understand.

Some of the oldest songs always left the pod slack-jawed and full of awe, but the pod did not doubt them. Doubt is a concept dolphins do not understand either. Except as something a twisted dolphin might do. One that doesn't listen. A bad thing.

Trust is as natural as breathing, and as necessary.

A dolphin would never bother saying that. It's too obvious.

Trust holds the pod together. When the leaders said to swim into the black dead place, the pod followed, only to turn around and swim back out, when Chax turned around. No one criticized Chax or the leaders. The leaders did what they saw as best.

Chax and the leaders had earned the pod's trust. If the pod did not trust them, did not follow them, it would cease to be a pod. A pod is necessary for life. Few dolphins are big enough, or brave enough, or foolish enough to want go it alone. Every dolphin in the pod could remember times when they had needed the pod to stay alive. Even the biggest and strongest knew they could not survive without the pod's protection, or food, or help, or wisdom, or just companionship. Dolphins they had affection for, respect for—dolphins they trusted, who trusted them— needed the pod. So did they.

Besides, a pod cannot do its work if it isn't a pod. No single dolphin can chase fish in the right direction for long. It's hard for two or three. With a pod, it's not so hard, it's fun. And less dangerous.

No dolphin would say something as obvious as that, either.

A pod's job is to swim the paths of the seas. Its job is to chase fish to where they need to be, to eat some of the fishes along the way, and to enjoy each other.

Fish have small brains. They have strong drives that can make them want to eat certain food or spawn at certain places at certain times. But fish can be confused by conditions, or trapped by circumstances, or by predators. Dolphins have big brains. They also have stamina, and are more resourceful than most fish. They have the pod, too. Dolphins listen better and make better choices. All that is as obvious to a dolphin as the need for another breath.

Not that dolphins cannot be misled, or confused or harmed by conditions, or circumstances, or predators. Or men. It happens. Too much noise is disorienting. When the water is too full of noise, it's hard to talk, or listen. It's harder to understand what's going on around you. Sometimes that's bad.

Too many men close by can be disorienting, distracting. Too many sharks can too. Sickness is disorienting. Bad water is disorienting, and unhealthy. Water stirred full of sand and silt is confusing. But healthy dolphins in a healthy pod do not get misled as often as you might think.

Dolphins can become ill, though. Then—especially then—they can become disoriented, frightened, confused. A healthy dolphin can "see" a thin wire, swim right up to it, look at it, and swim around it. That is, she can echolocate it with sound, by effort, or hear the water move past it and become aware of it without much effort. But a dolphin that is ill will blunder into anything, and sometimes cannot flee. A dolphin that is ill sometimes cannot find her way out of a heavy net, even when the net has an opening a healthy pup could find. That is, if that pup were not too fearful or too confused.

Even a pup can jump high. A dolphin that is ill cannot.

A dolphin lives in a world bound at least in part by its senses. But like us, sometimes a dolphin cannot understand all she sees, or hears. A dolphin can see a net, and perhaps can even see water on the other side of the net. But somehow, most of the time, most dolphins cannot combine what they know about nets with their ability to jump high and re-enter the water some distance away. Men can put that together. Dogs can too. Deer and horses and lions can. Dolphins can't, though they can be taught to. That's that.

Chax did not like this place. His duty was to guard the health of the pod. This was not a healthy place. Dead quiet. Dead. Quiet. Water too thick for sound.

He had taken the measure of the dead place. After leading the pod a short way into it, he led the pod back out.

8
Marine biologists, "black water" and Mary Lu

The way Captain Pete had it figured, if the black water turned out to be smelly or something, he would just turn around. People said different things about it. He wanted to make up his own mind. Let Kimbie get a sample maybe. If it was nasty, he planned to just take a quick look and leave. But he wanted to see it. Black goo covering the water for miles was something he had never seen. It was new in his neighborhood. He had heard about it for weeks. Now he was close and wanted to see it.

Kimbie Barone wanted to see it too, he knew. Out of professional curiosity. Or just regular curiosity. Both were strong. Her boss and sort-of boyfriend, Dr. Julian Ping, didn't. He thought the passengers would see black water as an unpleasant distraction. And icky. "Dolphins are our focus, not some random event," Ping had said. Not that they were focused in a very organized way just now, but he was right in thinking the passengers expected dolphins, even if they hadn't seen any yet. Ping had heard that dolphins stayed steer clear of the black water, as did every other living thing, apparently. He wanted to do the same. He reasoned, and had said, that going to see "black water" would most likely be another day without dolphins. The passengers might be repulsed. Or ask a lot of questions. Nobody had answers. He didn't. Either way, he didn't like it.

But Ping had not categorically ruled it out. Not technically, Kimbie told herself, again. Not letter-of-the-law. And just now Ping was taking a nap. So she meandered up to the bridge, where Pete was.

"I've been thinking about the black stuff," she said when she got there. Aloud, but more or less to herself. She looked out from the bridge. Captain Pete nodded.

"The area it covers is twenty-some miles across," she said. "From what I've read, it's not smelly, but it might turn the passengers off for swimming. *I* sure don't want to swim in it." She shivered. Pete smiled.

Like a terrier tugs at a lead, she continued. She had read that the layer of black water was not oil, not even oily, but some accounts said it was slimy, viscous and thick. Unappealing, at best. She had seen no chemical or biological analysis, but it was all over the news, and much discussed around the marina. "I can't get it out of my mind. People keep comparing it to red tides, but I don't see much similarity."

"Go on." Pete's eyes were on the horizon.

"Well, fishermen say the black goes right to the bottom. A red tide isn't like that, of course."

Pete nodded. *Strange, if true,* he thought. A fast boat splits red tide and leaves blue-green water in its wake. Apparently she knew that too. The news said even big, fast boats didn't move the black stuff out of the way. People who had lived along the Gulf any amount of time and paid attention were aware that red tide is a "bloom," a growth-surge of a certain kind of algae, and floats on or near the surface. Pete knew something most do not: a red tide—any algal bloom—is alive. It "inhales" carbon dioxide and "exhales" oxygen, like a green plant or a tree, and it needs sunshine to live, like plants.

They both knew red tides are smelly and toxic, and kill fish. Red tides have been observed in the Gulf of Mexico for at least as long as records have been kept. Captains of Spanish galleons noted them in their logs, hundreds of years ago. Red tides come and go, too. Nobody Kimbie thought was credible had ever been able to predict one, or define a cycle, exactly, but red tides are common, and recur.

Fishermen on TV said this black water leaves its dead on the bottom, where they are not found. How anybody knew that, she wasn't sure. Dead fish usually float. Fish kills had been noted in reasonable proximity to black water, but that wasn't conclusive. Unless you believe the stories about dead fish being dredged up.

Kimbie didn't. She knew that fishermen like to tell "fish tales." She tried to keep bar talk and wild assertions separate from what she considered plausible. She wanted to see for herself. "It's not that far," she said.

Pete saw her hopeful look. "What say we cruise over and take a look?"

She had misgivings, mostly about Ping's reaction, but nodded agreement, as if it had been Pete's idea. She smiled like a conspirator.

People with asthma have trouble breathing around red tides, but as far as she knew, this black water did not affect people with respiratory problems. Her curiosity was killing her. She could not believe Ping could be indifferent to this stuff. Staying focused on dolphins was not reason enough to stop a marine biologist from at least taking a look. Not one like her, anyway.

Captain Pete took his bearings and nosed the yacht southwest a few degrees. In a few minutes he turned southwest a few more degrees. Kimbie smiled at the gentle turn. Apparently neither of them wanted to alert anybody, especially Doctor P. A sunbather on the foredeck noticed that the sun was coming from a different angle and adjusted her hat, but no one else seemed to notice. The diesels droned steady on.

Its appearance was sudden. One minute everything was blue-green and gorgeous, next minute, the horizon to the east and south was black. Kimberly's jaw dropped. Her eyes grew wide. She shielded them with her hands for a better look.

Pete eased the throttles back a bit and made a slow turn to starboard. He wanted to run along the edge of it, not into it, and in a moment they were headed almost due south. "You can't see the end of it," she said, incredulous. "I knew it was big, but ..."

"Ugly," he said, stating the obvious.

To port, the entire Gulf was shiny black now, and seemed flatter and more calm than the blue-green water to starboard. As if the blackness subdued the chop. Pete didn't smell anything out of the ordinary, and said so. Kimbie didn't either. Digs soon came up the ladder. Chip and his pony tail were right behind him.

"Black water," Digs said, staring out over it, pushing back his cap. Digs had lived all his life on boats. His skin was creased deep, but his dark eyes were sharp.

"The name fits," said boyish Chip. "Is it oil? I hope not."

Kimbie thought before she answered. "It's not oil. I've heard several explanations for whatever else it is, but so far, they don't convince me. Theories range from sewage or agricultural runoff, to some natural phenomenon, sort of like red tide, only bigger and more rare, like the every-hundred-years occurrence of something," she said. "I'm still trying to educate myself."

Chip nodded, and kept staring. "Wow," he said.

Kimbie usually trusted Occam's razor, the idea that the simplest explanation is probably right. Unless proven otherwise. Despite that, the theory that intrigued her most was complicated.

For the past couple of years the U.S. Army Corps of Engineers had been raising the water level in the Everglades. The level had been allowed to drop for decades, as the need for drinking water grew in south Florida. More recently the Corps had changed its collective mind, and the current strategy was to conserve. Water levels rose a bit each year and flooded land that had been dry for a long time. Some areas were submerged that had been farmed or grazed for decades. The rising water level had forced adjustments by individuals, farmers, Florida DOT, marinas, even whole towns.

According to this particular "black water" theory, the higher water level was "flushing" stuff into the Gulf from places that had been high and dry for who knew how long.

"The problem with connecting that to this is the lack of debris, and lack of a bad smell," she said. "Whatever's being carried into the Gulf should decompose and decay, too, and it should stink, but I don't smell anything. Do you?"

Chip shook his head, intrigued. "Attorneys must be salivating over this stuff, though." Then he chuckled at what he had said. "So to speak."

Kimbie made a face, but nodded. "Lawsuits were filed to try to keep the Corps of Engineers from raising the level, but they got to go ahead."

"Sure," Chip said, nodding. "Going to court to prevent something is hard enough," he said, thinking aloud. "Stopping Uncle Sam is another thing entirely. Almost impossible."

Kimbie gave him an appraising glance. Digby studied the boyish-looking passenger out of the corner of his eyes, too. She could see that Digs was maybe chewing on his tongue. She smiled.

Still looking out to sea, Chip mused, "I'll bet lawyers who know about this can't sleep for wondering who's being damaged, who's doing it, how to prove it, and how much it's worth."

"Fishermen are being damaged," Kimbie said. "If this doesn't go away, the tourist industry is next. Can you imagine this stuff hitting a beach, or being carried up the East Coast by the Gulf Stream? Why, that would be … bad for tourism! Nothing's worse than that!" She was trying not to laugh so Pete laughed for her, and she smiled.

"Why isn't that happening?" Chip asked, chuckling, inquisitive at the same time.

"Prevailing currents, I think. This part of the Gulf is shallow. The Continental Shelf is only a few hundred feet deep here and hundreds of miles wide. On this side of Florida, the surface currents are weak and go different directions." She looked to Captain Pete for confirmation. He nodded, so she continued. "What's called the Loop Current circulates in the Gulf, but mostly it's west of here, where the water is deeper. The Gulf Stream is a combination of the Loop Current and the stronger

Florida Current. It gets strong off the tip of Florida and moves warmer water from nearer the Equator up along the East Coast. This stuff is sort of local, in sort of in an eddy, in terms of really big currents. And from what I've heard and read, it's breaking up."

Chip looked thoughtful.

"Anyhow, most water in the Gulf isn't as warm as water from the tropics, but some tropical water gets into it from the Loop Current. Out in the middle where it's deeper it mixes with cooler water from undersea springs. There's a theory that says not much water from the Gulf of Mexico actually gets into the Gulf Stream. Oceanographers argue about it. What I just said is well known. Still, there's plenty nobody knows. Which is what makes what we do ... what I studied to do ... so interesting. Nobody knows all of it."

Kimbie looked thoughtful. "There's another big dead spot, well, really a huge dead *zone*, northwest of here, off New Orleans, but it's not like this at all. It's way bigger, if you can imagine, about the size of New Jersey sometimes." Chip looked startled, and she nodded. "Really. It's huge, it stinks—literally, it smells—and it's there almost all the time, unless a hurricane disperses it. It's brown, it's full of debris, and it definitely stinks. The Loop Current has an effect on it too, but you can get an argument going about just what, if you get a few oceanographers together."

Pete laughed, but it was a grim laugh. He had seen that ugly brown watermark. "People don't like to talk about it," he said, "and they don't have to, because it's out where nobody goes unless they're looking for oil. Fishermen and cruise ships avoid it, even freighters. It's hidden in plain sight." He shook his head. "I've heard ... well, some experts I've heard about say the big brown zone includes runoff from farms—fertilizer, manure—and general runoff from cities. Which makes sense. All of that gets into the Mississippi River—'Big Muddy,' after all. I've got to think sewage is part of it, too. As Kimbie says, it stinks. Natural decay could account for the smell. That and fertilizer. Whatever. It's unreal huge."

Chip's world was rocked. "New Jersey? Seriously?" He shook his head.

Kimbie and Pete both nodded.

"Could climate change be a factor?" Neither one answered. Kimbie was thinking. "Maybe not in all that, but in this?" Chip asked, frowning now as he looked out at black water as far as he could see.

Kimbie bobbed her head back and forth. Pete always had to smile when she did that.

"Some say it is," she said, "but since nobody knows exactly what this black stuff is yet, I'm skeptical, or maybe agnostic is the right word. I don't know. Could be. Same with the currents. They change some, from year to year, but people argue about why." She looked serious. "Whatever the reason, there are 'dead zones' like the brown one in oceans all over the world now, at the mouth of most big rivers, more than ever. And there are gigantic floating garbage areas, gyres they're called, where whatever floats is collected by circular currents. In every sea, all over the world.

"The big brown place in the Gulf is a gyre, more or less. The gyres that are getting noticed lately are mostly plastic stuff, zillions of throw-away cups and bottles and containers and wrappers, tiny and not-so tiny pieces of plastic, plus wood, any stuff that floats. People are starting to know about the big one northwest of Hawaii, but there are others. Plastic's everywhere and it takes forever to break down completely. Even when it does break down, that's not good, because little tiny fish and other tiny sea creatures see the tiny pieces of color as food, and eat it. Some of it gets into their flesh, or their fat, and bigger fish eat the little fish, and so on, *ad infinitum.*"

She giggled. "It's like the nursery rhyme: '*Great fleas have little fleas, upon their backs to bite 'em, And little fleas have lesser fleas, and so, ad infinitum.*

The great fleas themselves, in turn, have greater fleas to go on, While these again have greater still, and greater still, and so on.'" Pete laughed heartily. She curtsied, which made Chip laugh. "Fleas, fish, same difference. Thus endeth my classical education."

Chip and Pete and even Digs applauded. Kimbie smiled and looked embarrassed at the same time.

"And dolphins are some of the biggest fleas in the ocean, guys. No offense to any dolphins in the vicinity. That's where the fun stops. The higher up the food chain you get, the greater the chance of poisons or toxins or just non-food accumulating. Non-food meaning plastics. It's called bio-accumulation, but you don't need a brain like Einstein to see how it can work. Of course, big baleen whales do not eat big fish, they strain tiny stuff out of the water, krill and plankton even, and tiny fishes, so bio-accumulation doesn't affect them the way it does dolphins. And guess who else is at the top of the food chain, eating big fish like salmon and tuna and tarpon, hmm? Grouper and snapper? When's the last time you had some of those? Hmm? Think about it."

"I've heard something about that, actually," Chip said. "But I love tuna and salmon. I love all of the above."

"Bingo," she said.

"Wow. I thought the black water was a buzz kill, but it seems tame compared to that." Chip looked gob-smacked, for a former congressional staffer and tuna terrorist. Kimbie noticed.

"Sorry. It's kind of a big deal, but most people don't have a clue. They're starting to though. Better surveillance technology accounts for some of the raised awareness, Google earth for a major example, satellite photos and so forth, but remember, sailors publicized it first. Maybe we should too. All I know is this, Chip. See if you don't start to notice how much trash is floating wherever we go. See over there? That bleach bottle, or whatever it is? Somebody may have put a hook on that and lost it, but more likely it just got blown out of a dumpster or trash bin. I bet it won't be long before we see something else. Not in gyres, usually, not like off Hawaii, but plastic trash is everywhere, in every backwater for sure. That huge gyre northwest of Hawaii is getting a ton of publicity, and that's a good thing. Hey, maybe we ought to go to Hawaii! You up for it, Captain Pete? Huh?" He smiled.

Kimbie was on a roll. "The main thing is, way too many people still think the ocean will always be able to absorb—hide—handle, make whatever crud, chemicals, garbage go away, whatever we put into it. I guess that's sort of understandable in some parts of the world. Places where they can't afford to deal with their waste in good ways. But in our country, it's crazy. And believe it or not, we do a better job than most of the world."

Pete nodded slowly. "People I talk to say floating trash is everywhere there's people. The Indian Ocean. The Philippine Sea."

Kimbie nodded, emphatic. She was well into lecture mode now. "Influential people who should know better still think the ocean is infinite. We all should have known better the first time a space shot sent back pictures of the little blue ball we live on. But noooo. We all marveled for a minute and a half, but most of us didn't get it. Some still don't." She ducked her head a little, hunched her shoulders. She smiled almost apologetically.

Mel McRae had joined the group and now scanned the black stuff with binoculars. He looked concerned. "I read about this stuff, and wondered if we would see it."

"There it is. Big as life, twice as ugly. Sorry," Kimbie said. "It's not much of a travel poster, is it? I got on my soapbox just now. Sometimes I get carried away."

"Don't apologize, sister," Chip said, putting his arm around her shoulders. He made eye contact when she turned and drew back a little. "I asked, remember? I thought you'd know, and you do. Don't back down, sister, preach it!"

Kimbie tried not to blush. Pete laughed out loud, and nodded. Digby clapped his big hand on Chip's shoulder, hard, turned Chip toward him and said, "You're right, boy, she's the smart one." Chip almost lost his balance, but grinned.

When Digs steadied Chip and let him go, Kimbie hugged the aging first mate's neck. "Thanks, Digs," she said. Digs patted her on her head like a proud papa. Digs was a teddy bear where she was concerned, but his large, wolf-white teeth still always surprised her.

She took a deep breath. "Okay. Stop me if you get sleepy, guys. This black water seems to be a new thing. Black water events have been short-lived, but this has happened a few times now. It's like some strange growing thing, except that ...guess what? From what I've read, it also meets the criteria for being dead. Does not react to stimuli."

Digby looked like he was chewing on his tongue again. She took a breath. "It needs to be studied. We used to do marine research in a lot more structured way than right now, in a more rigorous way. We do our best to observe and study wild dolphins, and we'll keep doing that, but I want to get back into ocean research too, and soon. At least dolphin habitat, which is the entire ocean, after all." The firmness she heard in her voice surprised her. I have to think about that." She smiled. "Captain Pete wants to learn more about it too; he just doesn't know it yet." Pete chuckled softly. "Captain Pete's been studying the ocean all his life, but he's never seen it as study, or written much down, except in his log. He's obsessive about his log, though. Check it out. Have I said anything that surprised you, captain?"

"Well, yeah, some," he said, not quite defensively. "I've avoided the big brown crud place for a long time. The first time also was the last, I hope. And yes, that's in the log. But everybody I know is trying to figure this black stuff out, and you've thought more about it more than most. I always learn something when you get on your soapbox."

She liked the compliment. Digs grunted. "The cap'n knows his business, and keeps his log like he should, is all she's sayin.'" He grunted for emphasis and disappeared down the ladder, faster than Chip or Mel would have guessed he could.

"See? Digs knows," she said.

Pete smiled. "I'd be ashamed not to keep my log the way I learned long ago is the only right way. Digs just has my back."

Kimbie picked up the log. "Look at this: weather in detail — storms, tides, wind — see here?" She held the big bound volume open. "Boat problems, other problems, where he goes, what he does, what fish are running ..." She flipped a few pages. "Who he sees, all the daily stuff, plus anything unusual. If it's in this log, you can take it to the bank." She looked out to sea when she added, a bit softer, "Or put it in your dissertation." The boat was nearly at the well-defined edge of the blackness, so she handed the log to Mel and followed Digs down the ladder.

Pete was surprised. Kimbie had never said anything like that before. He liked it. He used his telescope to try to find something in the middle of the blackness to focus on, but it all looked the same. Mostly he just tried to take in the size.

"I've seen — and logged — some strange things over the years," he said to Chip and Mel, "but nothing just like this." With the big brass telescope to his eye, he said, "Why no dead fish? Why no smell? They say it's not oil, that it's not even that slippery, and I'm sure they're right. If it was oil, we'd have heard plenty about that. We may know a little more in a minute."

On the rear deck, Kimbie knelt next to a box of wide-mouthed bottles. A spring-clamp fixed to the end of a long pole was ready for her to use to dip out samples of the black goo, from out past the edge. She yelled for Pete to slow even more and get as close as he could stand. Pete had already let it be known he did not want to suck this stuff into his sea-water-cooled diesels, not at all. Kimbie understood.

Fred, the junior crewman, stood by with the pole. He shook his head. "This is way worse than the pictures!"

She nodded. "Yup. How are the passengers?" she asked, quietly. Out of earshot because of the burble of the diesels, two women perched on the cushions and passed binoculars back and forth. One took pictures.

Lowering his voice, Fred said, "They're okay. I wonder if this creeps them out though. It does me. Maybe you could talk to them."

"In a minute. Let them watch first."

The boat settled into the water as it slowed, and Pete didn't have to yell. "Fill as many bottles as you need. We'll cruise along the edge a bit, see if it looks different down the way. Then we can head toward the coast, try to find something more fun." She gave a 'thumbs up' and smiled.

Bridget and Sarah came close and asked questions. Kimbie found herself repeating some of what she had said topside. John and Ruth Zinser came from the salon to hear. John added tidbits. The *Naples Daily News* had reported the black water story for weeks, and John was an avid newspaper reader. This goo was in the paper's back yard, so to speak. Reporters had interviewed scientists, who were cautious, and fishermen who mostly weren't. Other papers picked up those stories. Pete took a southerly course, close to the edge. The passengers did not seem to mind. Instead, they seemed energized. She wondered why Ping was still asleep, but was glad.

Kimbie moved her informal lecture into the shade of the salon after she filled three bottles. After a brief reprise of what she thought was plausible, she mentioned a few of the more speculative theories. Everybody laughed when Ruth suggested alien spacecraft bilge.

When the questions slowed, Kimbie asked the group if they were okay with being here.

Mel McRae took a reading from his smiling wife. "Well, isn't this what we signed up for? You're marine biologists, and this is happening in your bailiwick. With no dolphins to watch just now, if I were in your field, I might be doing the same thing you and Pete are doing." Murmurs of agreement were heard and heads bobbed all around. "I think we're fine." More nods.

As they headed south, Digby pointed out a good-sized fishing boat off the bow, maybe a mile away, stopped. When they got closer, Pete thought he recognized it. An older craft, big black hull curved up at each end, deep draft, with low, wide gunwales. The boat looked a lot like a tug, except it had a square stern and was rigged to handle nets, with a broad, uncluttered working area aft and booms overhead. A serious utility fishing boat, it could go after crabs or bluefish or shrimp, and was big enough to use a crew of three or four. A large white wheelhouse, with a flat, rear-sloping roof and wraparound windows on the front sat forward on the broad deck, much like a tug. Its rail was about knee high and looked stout. Wide enough to walk along, if you were steady, and sturdy enough not to be damaged by a heavy net or much else in terms of equipment or cargo.

Pete got his telescope. He did know the boat. He had crewed aboard the *Mary Lu* as a teenager. She had been home-ported at Marathon then, plying the blue-green waters from the Keys to the Ten Thousand Islands and beyond. Apparently she still was.

Mary Lu had always had good lines, and didn't look that much the worse for wear, though she had not been new when Pete was a lad. The deckhouse was different, somehow, but it was the same boat. He slowed to a crawl. Pete didn't want to get in the way of a working boat.

In a minute, the *Mary Lu* gave two toots of her whistle. Pete did the same with his horn, throttled back to nothing and idled toward her. The *Mary Lu* was stationary, so it was easy to pull alongside. Fred caught the line thrown by one of her crew, snugged it to a cleat, and heaved a line of his own. Pete noted with relief that the *Mary Lu* used proper white fenders now, not the car tires she had sported back when.

"Ahoy, Pete, I thought that was you," came a booming voice from somewhere. Andy Grinell's voice.

"What's left of me," Pete yelled back, still looking for Andy. "I heard you hit the lottery and moved to Palm Beach."

Andy came from behind the deckhouse, a rag in his hands, a grin from ear to ear. His sun-browned face sported stubble that looked whiter than last time. "Not yet," Andy said, chuckling. "You know how rumors get started." Andy wore a khaki baseball cap and cutoff khaki pants. On his arm was a tattoo of a very fetching mermaid.

"I might have known you were responsible for this mess," Pete said, indicating the black water with a wave of his visor.

"Some of my better work, doncha think? If I can keep this glop around long enough, the price of snapper will go through the roof."

Pete laughed and nodded. Andy's eyes squinted against the sun, bright blue and alert. His tongue had to be shoved way over against the inside of his cheek, from the look on his face.

"I'm just about out of Jello, though," Andy went on. "Any chance you could wire money to this food broker friend'a mine? He's got a container-load of blackberry stashed up the coast, but he won't front me any more 'til I cross his palm with silver."

Kimbie almost choked. Controlling her face, she said, "I was thinking how much it looked like Jello. Blackberry, huh."

Andy nodded. "Mostly. We had ta use what we could get, black cherry, a little root beer, but mostly blackberry. No sugar, though. That would be bad for the *environment.*" His voice crackled with melodrama. Pete, still very pleased to see his old shipmate, lost it, followed by Digby, who guffawed. It was contagious. Kimbie finally dissolved into giggles.

"It would draw flies, too," Pete said, trying for deadpan, despite the broad smile spread across his face. Then he remembered the others.

"Andy, 'ol buddy, this is my … um, my partner's partner, Kimberly. I know you know Digs." Digs touched the bill of his Greek fisherman's cap, grinning. "That good-looking kid is our second mate, Fred. John and Ruth here are ship's company, just about family, and we have passengers too." John's white-haired wife had joined him at the rail, and waved.

Pete noticed how John and Ruth smiled at being called family. Addressing everybody, he said, "Folks, this is the legendary Andy Grinnell, the last honest fisherman in the Gulf, and his historic boat, the *Mary Lu.* I crewed on this fine old craft in my youth. Andy was already old then."

Andy swept his baseball cap in front of him with a cavalier's flourish and hint of a bow. Putting the cap back in place with both hands, he saluted Pete with a couple of fingers. "My pleasure, ladies, gents, but— please—keep that 'honest' stuff to yourselves." He paused to let them respond, which they did, pleased to get a close look at a real working boat, and its entertaining captain.

"And this is my crew: Curly, Moe and Larry." Raising his voice a little, Captain Andy continued, "I got them from the state home for the mentally insufficient, when it closed. They're good lads, mostly."

Andy's crew had wandered over, grinning pleasantly and nodding agreement. All three had what looked like oil or grease on their hands and arms.

John Zinser asked, "Is that the black water you've got all over you?"

"I wish," Andy said. "Our transfer case jammed. We had to take it apart, realign everything. Pete, you remember the drill, I'm sure. It still does that, once in a while. Needs new bushings. Should'a put 'em in *before* it jammed. Nope, it ain't black water, unfortunately."

Pete remembered hours in the heat, fetching tools for those who knew how to fix the balky transfer case, waiting for the gears to be un-jammed. He nodded. "You need anything? A tow? Some ice?"

"Not really, but thanks. I've promised the lads beer when we get this thing whipped, but I don't want to distract 'em just now."

"Want us to tow you away from this stuff, Andy?" Kimbie looked concerned.

Andy looked shocked. "No way, ma'am! Haven't you heard about its wonderful anti-fouling properties? Pete, you might want to take a run up through the middle of it yourself, just for the sake of your pipes."

"You pulling my leg, ol' buddy?" Pete smelled something fishy, and it wasn't the water.

Andy laughed. "Some chowderheads swear it cleans their hulls, and their cooling passages too. Me, I'm skeptical of anything a fisher-man says, if he's not drunk. I don't believe half even then."

"Got that right," Pete said.

"I think I read something about the anti-fouling thing," John said.

"I'm sure you did," Andy said. "This black water has gotten more fishermen on TV than anything in years. And if you want to keep the reporters interested, you need good stories for 'em ..."

"You wouldn't know anything about that yourself, would you, Captain Andy?" Kimbie asked, all innocence.

Andy laughed, a hearty, rolling laugh. "I have been known to spin a yarn, when it suited my purpose. That's why I'm sure that about a third of what you hear is just fishermen being fishermen, seeing what they can get away with. Maybe another third is real; pick a number. The rest is just speculation, science fiction. And a dash of ignorant."

"That flesh-eating part's real, Andy, you'll not deny that. You've seen that yourself." It was one of Andy's crew that spoke; he looked and sounded serious.

"I've seen it, Larry. You're right. That's some bad stuff. I don't know if it has anything to do with this black goo, though. I don't know what's connected and what's not."

"That's the problem," Kimbie said.

Larry smiled at her. Captain Andy nodded. "Right. One thing I do know is, you can't treat the ocean like a dump and not have problems. Just like you can't catch all the fish, dredge up the bottom and find plenty next time. As to what's going on with this black water, I'm not sure." He saw Kimbie nod.

"Have you been out in it, Andy?"

"I went a ways into it the first time I saw it, after some said they saw big fish kills in the middle. We didn't find any. And no, it did not eat the crud off the hull, or make the engines run cooler. Or hotter, for that matter."

Larry, who had been serious, laughed.

"What did it look like in the middle?" Kimbie asked. Out of the corner of her eye, she saw Julian Ping among the passengers on deck. He yawned.

"All we saw is more of what you see here. In places it had bigger blobs, and little stringy things laced through it. The strings ... threads, whatever they are, have no strength, though. They're just there. Spider webs, some call them. They look like the veins on a leaf to me. The blobs seem to be the same stuff as the rest; maybe thicker. Maybe pushed up out of the water by waves or bubbles. Maybe gas that's released by heat the stuff absorbs, whatever."

"It ain't pretty," said another of Andy's crew.

"No dead fish? Hmm." Kimbie asked.

The entire crew shook their heads, Andy too. "Not in it. Not even near it. Some guys say they dredged up dead fish in the middle, but I've got my doubts. For one thing, who would intentionally put a net in this stuff? Nets cost money. We've seen fish kills this year, of course, same as you. There've been some, but not here."

Pete and others nodded. "I hear nobody has caught enough mackerel to sell," Pete said, a question in his voice.

"We sure haven't. We've caught grouper and red fish, blue fish and roughy. Snapper and bass, some, and the usual trash fish. People who go after marlin and big trophy fish are getting them, but nothing special."

"We heard that too," Pete said. "What are you guys after?"

"We fell into a little crabbing, to pay the bills. You do any fishing, Pete?"

Pete tried not to laugh. "I have a bamboo pole somewhere, and a cast net. Digs is the fisherman on this boat."

"That's what I thought. You never did like hard work." Andy grinned.

Pete laughed and smiled at his old friend. "Ha! Kimbie has thought of all kinds of scientific labor you guys never heard of. See these blisters?" he said, holding up his hands. "Do these look like the hands of a riverboat gambler?"

Andy laughed so deep that Kimbie for the first time understood laughter like a rolling barrel.

"Your boat looks good, Pete," he said. "You needed a partner like Kimbie all along." He turned to her, smiled even more than before, and said, "Do you have any sisters, honey?"

Kimbie could feel herself blush, but she could not take offense at what she knew was an innocent compliment. It had been a while since she had blushed.

" 'Fraid not, but thanks," she said, managing to look him in the eye and smile.

Andy shook his head and turned to Pete. "Maybe she could motivate these farm boys to finish the transfer case, so we don't have to paddle home."

Talk time was just about over, but Fred wanted to look at the *Mary Lu*, and Andy offered a hand. Fred and Pete went aboard, followed by John, Chip and Mel. Kimbie went to the galley and came back with a sack of fruit, which she handed across to one of the *Mary Lu*'s crew. The fruit was accepted gratefully, along with a pack of baby wipes. Andy quickly explained the transfer case problem to the boarding party. Once Pete was sure they could fix it, they exchanged cell phone numbers and radio frequencies. If the *Mary Lu* was not back in operation by late afternoon, Pete would come back and give a tow. Andy agreed, though he said it probably would not be necessary.

Julian Ping had given grudging, sleepy assent when Kimbie brought up the fruit. He shuffled over to the rail when she handed it across. Pete introduced Ping, told Andy that Ping and Kimberly were doing dolphin research, and said the passengers were aboard for a short stint to help out and learn. Andy nodded.

"We have not seen a dolphin in three days," Ping said, irritation in his voice. "Their being elsewhere because of black water makes it difficult to study them here." He frowned at Kimbie.

Andy raised his eyebrows. "At least you've learned they don't like this stuff," he said. Was that an edge in his voice? "Porpoises followed us into Everglades City yesterday. And out again."

"Dolphins or porpoises?" Ping asked, looking down his nose.

"Bottlenoses. *Tursiops truncatus*, I believe, twenty or so of 'em." Turning to Kimbie, he continued, "When I was a boy, everybody called bottlenose dolphins 'porpoises' around here. Some of us old timers still do." He smiled, and she smiled back.

"I'd heard that."

"Smileys is what I call 'em," Pete said, grinning at his old friend, who grinned back as Ping looked away.

When they parted company, Pete made Andy promise to "beam us up" if he couldn't get the case fixed in an hour or two. Andy said he would, either way, and made a point of telling "Miss Kimbie" he was glad to have met her.

Everybody wished everybody good luck and the *New Delphi* went her way.

9
We like the same places

Chobeem had long ago seen his mistrust of men confirmed. He also had seen men be benign or only puzzling. As best he could tell. Over the years his attitude toward them had changed little. His aunts had taught him early that most men are unstable and attract trouble. Whatever else he had learned, that was still the truth, and he always came back to it.

Living near men is not ideal, but the places dolphins like best also seem to be places men like too. Places with nice weather, good water, good food. He knew from songs that this had always been true, but in the old songs, there had been more than enough. Now that was not always true.

Chobeem's first pod had traveled to where the waters are cooler, and to warmer places, as this pod did. Some places, some not far from this place, are as good now as they were when he was small, with plenty of tasty fish and everyone healthy and curious. At those places, curiosity led to adventures and meals and friendships and knowledge then. But dangers exist now that Chobeem had not had to be warned about when he was small.

Worse, young dolphins do not have to be warned about some things now because they have never been away from them. They are always wary of cuts and hits from boats now, because there are so many.

Men in boats were around when Chobeem was young, of course. Boats, large and small. Most of the time that meant sport, riding the surge that fast shells make, laughing at men, men laughing back. Then again, he had heard stories, everyone had, about huge battles where men who fought and broke each other's shells and filled the water with dead. He had not seen that, but dolphins he had known saw it.

What he saw, now, was not battles, but many more men in many more shells, so many they cloud the water sometimes. Men had always put bad water into the good, but they did that more now. There is not much a dolphin can do about it. You live with the water because you live in it. Noise from more men makes everyone uneasy. Men love to chase dolphins. Most of the time this does no harm. Sometimes pods are scattered and feeding is disrupted, but men who want to chase dolphins are not a problem all the time. Some days they stay on shore. Other days men are crazy when they come to the water. On those days, some dolphins swim far out to sea rather than contend with them.

The old saying is still true. Men attract trouble. Where men live in great numbers, the water changes. Where once it tasted a certain way, or flowed in a direction or was a color, once many men gather beside the water, it is different. Sometimes it is bad. Some of the old ones become confused or don't want to hunt.

The old ones remember a place a certain way. When it is not that way, sometimes they cannot find what they need. Some dolphins cannot live with those changes, unless the pod helps. Sometimes not even then.

Sometimes not only the water changes, sometimes channels change. Big storms change channels, fast. Men are not as fast. Men put land where it has not been before, but it takes them time, and messes the water for a long time. Storms do that too, of course, but when a storm changes a channel, you can see the reasons on the bottom. In a day or two, the water clears.

When men change land or the water, there is almost never a reason, and the mess goes on. Men often make one thing better and three things worse.

There is no understanding them, and Chobeem did not expect to. But now that he was older, and was known for making good choices, Chobeem wondered whether men knew themselves why they do what they do. If there was anything he wondered about men, besides how they can laugh with what seems to be real joy, he wondered whether they know what they do. He did not know if men do things just because they can, the way a dolphin sometimes does something. It seemed that way.

All Chobeem could see was what they do. He could see that men prize some sea creatures. He could see the lengths men go to catch them. The effort men put into catching shrimp is crazy. They drag the bottom and tear things up over big distances. For shrimp! Other things make more sense. He had seen men swim under water after all manner of creatures. With tanks of air on their backs! Men seem to enjoy this. Catching fish is enjoyable, after all.

Other times he wondered. He did not try to judge how hard it is for men to make things. He could see that they prize things they make. Usually. Sometimes they don't, at least it looks that way from what men do, or don't do, with things at other times they seem to prize. Men are unstable, and probably unknowable. Everybody knows that.

It is the same the way men are with creatures. Just when Chobeem would decide that men truly prize some sea creature, to eat or look at or play with, that would be the time men would do something to drive those creatures away, or kill without gathering. Men are unstable, beyond understanding, troublesome. At least most are, maybe all. Almost.

When he was younger, Chobeem had chewed on this a great deal. Being captured gave him too much time to chew on things like that. He had wondered if it was good men that prize something, like shrimp or grouper, and bad men who harm them. Or perhaps it is the other way around. He had observed men enough to know there were many kinds of men. They are different shapes and colors, and like to eat different things, do different things. But they are all men. Some are strong, some weak. Some are smart, some not. Some are lazy, some diligent. Because he had swum the seas a great deal, even for a dolphin that ranges, Chobeem knew there were many, many more men than he had seen up close. In truth, he had seen only a few up close, and did not want to see more, now. But he had never been able to be sure which men stood for one thing, and which stood for another.

One day, many seasons ago, he saw that nothing good would come from more chewing on the subject, and stopped. He could see that, beyond what almost anybody knows, men are a mystery. That much, he knew. He had never known a dolphin who could explain them. Truth to tell, Chobeem had never met a dolphin who had been around men very much who saw them as less of a bafflement than he.

He had met one other dolphin who had been captured by men and then returned to the sea, as he had. That dolphin was crazy. Which had not surprised Chobeem at all. His own capture and captivity had been so crazy that sometimes the best way to remember it was not to remember it, if he could, to ignore it like a bad dream.

But he could not forget, always. Some young dolphin would ask him how he got the scars on his belly and he would remember.

10
Captain Pete gets desperate

Captain Pete Gordon, master of the *New Delphi*, eased the throttles back another notch. Maybe a different pitch of the diesels would sound better to the absent dolphins. It was odd not to see them at all for two days and nights. It bothered him, just as it seemed to irritate Ping.

Despite that, Pete could not help but smile when the twin Allisons responded. The purr was quieter, but also deeper and somehow harmonious. He had fallen in love with that sound years ago.

"That oughta suit the smileys," he muttered, laughing at himself. Pete had started calling dolphins "smileys" when he got tired of Ping calling them *Tursiops*. Pete knew that was the scientific name, just as Captain Andy did, but he had never liked the snooty way Ping said it. Ping had lectured Pete about how unprofessional and "provincial" he was to call them porpoises. That was technically right, of course. But Pete also knew fishermen who knew way more about dolphin habits than Ping, whether they knew Latin or not.

Pete didn't argue, he just started calling them "Smileys." That didn't please Ping either, but Kimbie giggled when she heard it, so that's what he called them.

The burble of the twin Allisons trumped his irritation. Pete had never gotten over the pride he felt from owning a boat powered by two of them. Diesels can be loud, but the engine room was padded, and they are less loud if maintained right and overhauled when needed, as these had always been. These could purr or roar. Or burble. Right now they purred.

For days the *New Delphi* had cruised waters that normally teemed with at least mildly curious dolphins, but the smileys hadn't gotten closer than several hundred yards. Turning toward them hadn't helped, even though Ping's license or whatever allowed it. In any kind of normal time, the dumb, smiley-face porpoises should have shown up and done their thing by now. Not that Pete thought they were dumb. He was just frustrated. And not just by the no-shows. It was a little more general than that.

To all appearances, Pete Gordon was master of all he surveyed, able to come and go anywhere in the world, as the mood might strike him. That's how it looked. He was in fact the owner and licensed captain of an enviable boat, with a crew of two. Technically two and a half, Kimbie being the half, though he didn't think of her that way. Pete never told her to do anything. Never had to. She seemed to read his mind.

He ate well. Fresh seafood whenever he wanted, smoked fish or a steak or burger for variety, wine with his dinner sometimes. His cabin was comfortable. He slept well in it, as sound as anywhere, ever. He was healthy as a horse, doing more or less what he wanted. The way he and the crew took care of the boat showed he was proud of it, wasn't lazy, and had some means. And he did. He seldom wore anything more elaborate than shorts, boat shoes and a polo, but he didn't have to. Most days he would have preferred a T-shirt, but as captain, it paid to keep up appearances. He didn't want the boat's dumb name embroidered on shirts, though. Ping bought ball caps anyway, with the name and a dolphin surfing. They looked good but Pete gave his to the first passenger to admire it. He owned and used a good pair of sunglasses. A hundred-meter stainless dive watch was nearly always on his wrist. But he favored a faded, salt-stained green visor. Kimbie regularly stole and washed it. Ruth Zinser bought him a new one just like it. He thanked her, but preferred the old one.

Of average height, Pete was strong, wiry and lean, with thick, brown hair he tended to comb straight back with the spread fingers of one hand or the other. He got a haircut when Kimbie or Ruth reminded him. He was more presentable since they had been aboard, he had to admit.

His captain's squint partially hid eyes the color of the Gulf of Mexico where it is a clean, luminous green. Ladies tended to forget themselves in those eyes, a phenomenon that mostly went right over Pete's head.

His reddish tan and pronounced cheekbones probably came from his Seminole grandmother. He smiled easily and liked to kid around, though he could go dead serious at the slightest change in the weather or the motors, or any real problem. He liked to relax in the evening with the passengers, if they were congenial. He would listen to their stories, if they had them, tell one or two of his own. He would have a beer with them sometimes, or just sip ice water.

He seemed to have no worries. The creases around his eyes looked more like the work of the sun than of worry.

That's how it looked. Mostly that's how it was. He had once been close to living his dream. He was thankful for being this close, and knew plenty of guys who envied what they saw. But the way Pete saw it, he made a somewhat precarious living now, running a vacation boat with a "business partner." He had money in the bank. Some. Plenty enough to pay what was owed for the last overhaul. Instead, he paid interest so that Ping had to help with the monthly installment. The arrangement was goofy, but Pete had a feeling that Ping might never get around to paying his share otherwise. That grated. Ping had to be prodded to do his share, more now than a year ago. Mostly Kimbie did the pushing, but it grated. Keeping the customers satisfied kept Pete from depleting his reserves. It was annoying enough sharing the boat with Professor Ping, sharing decisions and proceeds, even when things went well. When the watchable wildlife wouldn't cooperate … Pete's frustrations were closer to the surface.

Frustration was really too strong a word for what Pete felt. He was on the water, after all. As a boy, Pete began working on crab boats and shrimpers as soon he was big enough to talk captains of boats like the *Mary Lu* into letting him do scut work around the docks, then on the water. He worked hard, learned fast, remembered everything. Long before he could drive a car, Pete's services as a deck hand were in demand. Some captains took advantage of his good nature and love for boats, but he didn't care. He was learning. As long as he was on the water, it seemed a fair exchange. By the time he graduated high school he had been paid to crew aboard half a dozen working boats and could pick and choose, for decent money. Whenever he could talk his mom into it, that is.

After he saw the Florida Keys at fifteen, Pete never went home any longer than he had to, mostly just for school. He obeyed his widowed mom though, and gave her part of whatever he earned. She needed money and he didn't. His heart was on the water. The day he turned eighteen, he enlisted in the Coast Guard. He woke up smiling, worked hard and soaked up everything, as he always had. He had no life ashore to speak of, and became a diver, but after five years in uniform he chafed at not being his own boss, the way fishing boat captains are. So he didn't make the Coast Guard a career. After his six-year enlistment, he didn't have to talk his mom into anything anymore, but he still called her on Sundays and stopped by when he was near Port Charlotte harbor, where she lived. She had been out on the *New Delphi* a few times.

Mom Gordon, whose Christian name was Mary, had never completely understood how her Pete had come by the money for the boat. She knew he had bought and sold a little fish camp in the middle of nowhere. She had seen it once, right after he bought it, but how he had made enough money to buy it, or how he sold it for enough to buy a pretty yacht—was a puzzle to her. She was afraid to ask too many questions. Some of his boyhood friends had been caught smuggling drugs. Others had prospered mysteriously. She had warned Pete against drugs early. She had been a nurse, and he had never shown any signs of using them. She had hoped he might go to college on the GI bill after the Coast Guard, but instead, he showed up with the boat.

Pete had made his money the old Florida way, just as he told her, in real estate. As a Coastie, he saved nearly all the pay he didn't send home and kept his eye open for a little place he could buy. All he wanted was a dock, a bait shop and a few rooms he could rent to fishermen. He thought he had found it a few times, but his first efforts hadn't worked out, for one reason or another. He just kept looking, kept saving, and learned by trial and error how to negotiate, and how to talk to bankers.

Finally, he found a place he loved, and could almost afford. It was on an island just off the Intracoastal Waterway, deep channel. Nobody could get to it unless they had plenty of time and a boat. After so many turn-downs, he thought he was dreaming when the bank agreed to the loan. The fish camp was in terrible shape. You took your life in your hands on the warped planks of its pier. The former owner was happier than Pete when they closed the sale. But it was his.

With almost a year left on his six-year hitch, he let the same old guy who had run it for the former owner keep running it for him, though Pete gave the guy a heart-to-heart talk and a tiny raise. He wasn't quite breaking even, but he could pay the guy, buy fuel, pay the light bill—and the note—with what little the camp brought in, plus his Coast Guard pay. He spent the whole month of his annual leave fixing things. For the next year he headed to the fish camp with lumber or paint in the back of his well-used hatchback whenever he had a few days off. The old guy had to meet him with a skiff and ferry him over. For heavy loads they borrowed a bigger boat. The "regular" ferry brought supplies the second and fourth Tuesday of each month. Usually.

Keeping his dream alive meant he never had any money, or a decent spare tire for the Honda, but hey, the Coast Guard kept him fed, clothed and sheltered. He wondered if he was ever going to pay off his Visa card, or his tab at the lumberyard or the marine supply store. But the fish camp looked semi-respectable now, and business was better.

Five months before his six-year enlistment was up, he had a message waiting when he got back to his barracks one day. A car dealer from somewhere in the Midwest wanted to talk to him. Pete called. The man had a voice like an admiral. He had stayed at Pete's camp most of a week, fishing. He had enjoyed it, obviously knew the area well, and said complimentary things. Pete said thanks, and they talked a bit more. Before long, as if it were the most natural thing in the world, the man offered Pete more money than he had paid for the camp. Much more.

Selling had never crossed Pete's mind until then. He turned the offer down, as politely as he could. He was not used to talking to people like that. The 'admiral' said he understood completely, and didn't blame Pete a bit for holding onto it. But just in case, he gave the name of a man at his bank.

Pete tried to forget the call, but it nagged at him. He asked a friend from high school (now a banker himself) to look the other banker up and make sure he was legit. He was. Pete called. The banker. The Indiana banker said the man could afford whatever he wanted, within reason. In a few days, Pete got a letter from the banker thanking him for the call. The letter again spoke highly of the car dealer. The letterhead was impressive, the note, friendly. Pete stared at it a long time.

The 'admiral' called Pete a few days after the letter arrived. He upped his offer.

The money had been good before; now it was too good to turn down. Pete said he would have to think about it. He looked forward to running the place when his Coast Guard hitch was up, living there, working on it every day, being his own boss, fishing, getting an old boat to work on. Nothing fancy.

Two mostly sleepless nights later, Pete traded one dream for another.

The fish camp was still there. A new road and a bridge to the island came a few years after Pete sold. Though the old place looked mostly the same, it was kind of gold-plated now, if you knew what you were looking at. Sometimes Pete would stop by. The car dealer, who was semi-retired now, always treated Pete like a long-lost friend, and so did the old man who had once worked for Pete, now comfortably semi-retired himself. "The admiral," as Pete continued to think of the owner, topped Pete's tanks free, if Pete would let him, and wouldn't let Pete pay for food, or bait, or much of anything. Pete almost felt guilty pulling in because the admiral treated him so great, but the man always seemed glad to see him, made a point of telling Pete to stop anytime he was in the area. He seemed to mean it. Pete took the admiral out on the boat. He liked it and they enjoyed each other's company. The admiral took Pete for a scary ride on his airboat, bought him a great meal at a place on the water, and treated Pete like a friend, almost like a nephew. The way Pete imagined a dad would treat a son.

The admiral hated the bridge, and all the people and development it had brought to the island, even if it had made the fish camp worth more. Canadian investors were pressing him to sell, and he could no longer ignore them. They had talked to his wife. Now she thought selling was the right thing to do. The admiral had a beachfront home a couple hours on the other side of the bridge, and his wife did not care for fishing.

Pete was perhaps the only person not directly involved who knew all that. And while he got a chuckle out of it, maybe a painful chuckle, and could sympathize with his friend the car dealer a little, just a little, the bottom line was that if Pete had kept the fish camp he would have been rich. Or potentially rich.

But he hadn't. He had sold for what seemed like a fortune at the time. Even after he bought the boat, Pete had more money left than he had ever dreamed.

He had always kept his own counsel, so only a handful of people knew how he had come by the money, right out of the Coast Guard. Showing up with the boat raised eyebrows, but it blew over. His banker friend knew, and the banker was in Rotary with the sheriff. Some never understood how he had gotten his hands on the Bertram, especially old high school buddies who might have done a little drug running. But as long as it hadn't hurt them, as long as he wasn't competing, hey, they didn't especially care. In their world, too much curiosity was not a virtue. Whatever Pete had done, it looked like he had got away clean.

He mostly let people think what they wanted. The truth was, Pete resisted several offers to go into the smuggling trade. He lost 'friends' over it. Tough. He had seen too many shot-up, bloody drug boats as a Coastie, and heard too many stories of betrayal and murder.

He tried taking charter fishing parties out, but found he did not have the skill set—call it that—to put up with guys who wanted to get drunk and come back with trophies anyway. His expectations and habits had been formed on working boats.

Once, exasperated, tired of not working, and of not having an income, he had parked the yacht at a marina near his Mom's and worked on tugs on the Intracoastal Waterway. He had a captain's license, good references and a ton of experience. It was interesting, and challenging. But his boat, just sitting at the marina, cost almost as much as he could make away from it. It needed more maintenance sitting than running. Whoever said a boat is "a hole in the water, into which you pour money," was right. But he wasn't ready to trade it for a tug. So he began thinking about other ways he and the Bertram could work together. Besides charter fishing and smuggling.

Pete lived aboard. The Gulf Coast and Florida Keys were his neighborhood. He picked up his mail (what there was of it) at his mom's, or at Marathon, his favorite town in the Keys. He got a cell phone, but kept it turned off and checked it daily, almost. His mom knew she could reach him through the Coast Guard radio, nearly the same way she had when he was in uniform. She didn't abuse it. Reaching him might take a while, unless it was an emergency, but friends in the Keys or on the west coast of Florida generally knew where he was, or where he had been last week, or last month. Pete always called her on Sunday.

Once, not so long ago in months or years, he had cruised around the Caribbean and the Gulf feeling like an Arab prince. Those days were a memory now, but he had. He had thought about putting his money in the stock market, but he didn't want it tied up in something he didn't really understand. He parked a chunk in a "growth" mutual fund, after his banker friend explained the basics, but that was about as far as Pete went. When he was fixing up the fish camp he realized that the big-box home improvement store an hour away had to be making money, and bought their stock. After a year of growth and dividends, though, he realized he really didn't know enough about that business either. He sold just before the stock fell off a cliff. Dumb luck, but Pete trusted his instincts. Looking back was scary, when he calculated how much he almost lost. That soured Pete on stocks.

The boat was his investment. It was worth much more now than when he bought it, two or three times more. If nothing happened, his investment would be all right. But keeping the boat's value up, and keeping it seaworthy, took work. He didn't spend money or time on much else.

When he sold the fish camp, Pete traded the aging Honda for a little pickup truck, almost new, and bought his mom a super-quiet air conditioner and a top-of-the-line refrigerator. She let him add a nice little screened porch to her trailer, and buy some outdoor furniture for it, so she could sit and look at the water. But when he offered to buy her a Lincoln Town Car, she drew the line. Her Buick was only six years old, after all. It looked nice, had low miles and cold AC. When she wanted to go to church or the grocery store, the Buick was fine. He came by his frugal nature honest.

After a while, though, he got depressed watching his bank account erode from dock fees and fuel, food, marine insurance and just mainte-nance. So he began taking charters for day trips around the Keys. Mostly families. He let people snorkel or fish if they wanted, especially kids, but stayed away from serious fishing. The boat wasn't ideal for that any-way. It turned out to be fine for dive charters, which was fine with Pete.

During that period, the Bertram, a classic-looking yacht with a gleaming white hull and pretty mahogany decks and trim, was rented for a TV commercial. The commercial was a good experience, just a couple of days, and led to a movie. The money seemed nice, going in, and mak-ing a "film" was interesting to watch, but it was hard on the boat. Film crews were rough on decks and went around drilling holes in bulkheads if you didn't watch them. Pete didn't net as much as it had looked like he would. Glitz did not make up for it.

More dive charters. Then, through a happy accident, Kimbie char-tered the boat for a month. Ping needed a platform for some hurry-up research. It was crunch time on a grant update. Someone Kimbie knew had been diving with Pete. He and his boat were available. They got the data to complete the report, and Ping's grant was renewed.

A longer-term deal was struck. Dr. Ping and Kimbie moved aboard. Charters were booked ahead that Pete had to honor, but it turned out that his customers liked the idea of watching and helping with research. The grant people didn't object. Could foundation VIPs come along now and then, they asked?

Two-week "research cruises" like this one, looking for dolphins, had become Pete's bread and butter. He still had some money in mutual funds, but it had been a long time since he had felt rich. He was thankful to have clear title to the boat, some operating money and the truck. He also had a savings account he had created for his mom. Her name was on that account, along with his, in case he disappeared.

Pete knew he was in a position some people would kill for, so he tried to keep his profile as low as a yacht allows. So did most of the people he knew who had both money and good sense. The admiral, for example, dressed like a dock hand most days, and drove a five-year-old SUV most of the time. Pete took a page from him.

Selling the boat was not on Pete's radar. He would rather take a job on shore, but could not imagine what might force such a drastic change. The way Pete saw it, he was running in place. The view was nice, it was close to his dream. He sure wasn't complaining, but that's how he saw it.

The boat's log showed it had sailed the Third Coast from the Keys to Texas and Mexico, plus Belize, the Bahamas, Jamaica, Bermuda, Puerto Rico, Haiti and the Antilles. All under Pete's flag. He had sailed up the East Coast as far as Ocracoke Island, N.C., but saw little point in going farther "up north." As a Coastie he had enjoyed sailing the Chesapeake Bay and much of the New England coast, especially Maine. But the Seminole blood in him didn't want to live there.

Like most prudent Caribbean captains, he stayed away from Central and all of South America. At least now he did. On his first cruise as owner, Pete visited most of the Mexican ports, plus Venezuela and Colombia, both of which, looking back, had been stupid. Conditions in his neighborhood being what they are, he kept a matte finish 40-cal. Glock, the small-framed one, in the chart box, with a round in the chamber. He had some more intimidating guns on board, locked away. He practiced monthly. Once Pete had to fire the Glock at a former friend, crazy on crack or something. He did not want to, but push came to shove. Pete grazed the fat part of the guy's thigh to get his attention, then knocked him out. Didn't have to kill him, thank God.

Pete took his unconscious former friend to the hospital, and nearly went to jail for his trouble. If their paths crossed, they would speak, or nod, but any friendship was over.

11
Blast from the past

Pete squinted at the horizon. Where were the daggone porpoises? He had been daydreaming. He took a deep breath and flipped the radio to the Coast Guard channel for a reality check, but heard no chatter. For several minutes the radio was silent, as the diesels droned in harmony and pushed the boat northeast. In a few hours he would hit Florida.

A voice cut through the static. "Key West station, this is W-P-B -Kodiak, over. Do you copy?" Pete throttled down until the engines found an even quieter zone, the better to hear the cutter again try to raise the station. Pete did not recognize the Coastie on the radio.

"Go-head, Dubya pee-bee Kodiak, this is Key West base, over," came a much different voice, on a clear channel. Pete smiled. He knew that voice. More static.

"Base, this is ... um ... W-P-B Kodiak." A pause was followed by, "Uh, Key base, we were wondering how much longer the O.D. wants us to run this pattern, over?"

The reply was, "Dubya pee-bee Kodiak, yew want me to ask, over?" There was a hint of a chuckle in the voice.

"Umm, negative, base. We were just thinking ... um... we might change course for the next half-hour or so, before we head for station, over."

"One-four-nine-uh, you guys vote or something, over? If you're gettin' dizzy, sure, change course, over."

"Potter," said another voice, a tad exasperated. "This is Ensign Mosby, requesting the O.D.'s permission to alter course and proceed due east to intercept the archipelago and reconnoiter until the end of our patrol, over."

Pete Gordon found himself smiling. Ensign Mosby must have tight shorts or something. New guy, he guessed.

Then a feminine voice crackled over the radio. "Mr. Mosby, if you want to cruise the beach on the way in, why don't you just say so?" Though he had never in his life heard this woman's voice, Cap'n Pete instantly liked her. He pictured a tanned young woman in khaki, slender, perfect white teeth, big smile, sparkling eyes—green? No blue—shaking her head in disbelief. His old buddy, Communications Mate First Class Estil Potter, chuckled, probably sitting next to her.

"Commander Harris, we just wondered ..."

"Just do it, Mister Mosby," said the female voice, all business. "No problem. Anything interesting out there today?" Very pleasant.

"Nothing technical, Ma'am. No illegals. Routine stops. Some citations."

"And you want to cruise some beach on the way back? Is that all?'

"Affirmative, Ma'am."

"Well, don't scrape bottom on your way in, over," she said, nice as you please.

"Affirmative, Ma'am. Over."

Though he had no microphone in his hand, Pete Gordon tried to keep from laughing out loud, and mostly succeeded. He looked around, and steered a little to port, northwesterly. After a few minutes, he picked up the microphone, clicked it a few times, and said, "Key Base, this is motor vessel *New Delphi*, do you copy, Potts?"

After a pause, Potter's voice came back. "Motor Vessel New Deli, this is Key West Base, we copy, bro. When'd you get outta jail? Long time no hear. Over."

Pete had served with Potter when they were both very junior Coast Guardsmen at the St. Petersburg station. Estil Potter had sworn that Pete's mom's cooking—and her expecting that he would do what was right, same as his own folks expected—had gotten him over an important hump, and kept him from going AWOL. That was long ago, when he was homesick and miserable early in his first enlistment. Potter had made the Coast Guard a career, and didn't regret it a minute.

When Pete had told somebody his rich uncle had left him the money for the fish camp, Estil Potter, a tall, raw-boned Tennessee boy, hit Pete on the shoulder with the heel of his open hand so hard almost knocked him down. When Pete leveled with Potter about the fish camp, and showed it to him, his friend loved it. Potts spent a week of his own leave helping Pete fix it up, working all day, fishing all night. Potts had told him he was a fool to sell, but of course, he sold anyway. Potts only mentioned it now if he heard something about the place. They had been good friends, and still were, though they seldom crossed paths.

"Keeping the tourist industry going, Potts. We been following a polka-dot killer whale all day, thought you guys might want to see it."

"Riiight. Exactly where is this tourist 'traction just now?"

Pete gave his longitude, latitude, course and speed in the manner he had learned to relay it as a Coastie. Then he added, "No kiddin', I'm getting pretty desperate to see a smiley-face torpedo, with flukes." He looked around to make sure he was alone. "We all but promise dolphin contact, and we haven't even *seen* one for three days, except way out on the horizon, maybe. We're just about in breach of contract. I'd be glad to see a daggone manatee at this point. Or a killer whale."

"Dolphins all over the beach here this morning," Potter said. "You must not be livin' right, bro. Maybe you should re-enlist, do some honest work for a change." Potts chuckled. "Hey, I could be your boss! Ha! That'd be funny. How's your mama?"

Pete said she was fine. He was smiling when a big gray bottlenose dolphin popped out of the water thirty feet off the port bow, on a closing course. Before he could blink another one cleared the water, then another. The third one jumped higher than the first two. Another breached a short distance away.

"Ooooh, looook, dolphins! On the left! Port side! Port is left, right? Oooh! Look at them!" It was the college girl, who had been sunning on the foredeck. She looked like she wanted to jump in.

Tired as he might be of captaining a pricey excursion boat, Pete never got so used to seeing dolphins that he could even pretend to be indifferent. They were just too beautiful, and too independent. It was his long-considered opinion that there is really no predicting them. They do what they like. He maintained course and speed as the dolphins continued to breach like merry-go-round horses, ever closer to the bow.

Nearly all the passengers were on the port rail now, most of them on the foredeck. That woman with the crew cut, Bridget, was jumping up and down and squealing as much as the college girl. He had not noticed before, but now that she was happy, Bridget was really pretty. Suddenly Pete remembered the microphone in his hand.

"Potts, would you believe we just crossed paths with Flipper and his pals? You changed my luck, Bro! Over."

"Well, could be 'cause I said a prayer, bubba. You were desperate, right?" crackled the radio.

Pete raised an eyebrow. *Huh? Prayer?* He stared at the dolphins off the bow.

The radio crackled again. "Captain of the New Deli, you don't seem to require 'sistance, so if you have no other problems that need my 'ten-tion, we'll bid you good day, wish you the best. Fair winds, following seas. Tell your mama hey."

Pete grinned. "Roger, Key base, and thanks." Remembering how long it had been since he talked to Potter, he asked, "Hey, are your folks okay? You make chief yet?"

"Folks are fine, thanks. See 'em this fall. I'm an uncle again, prolly a future Tennessee Volunteer running back. Passed the chief test okay, but I'm way down the promotion list."

"You'll get there. Congrats on the nephew, Potts."

"Thanks. Tell your *mama* I said *hey*, hear?"

Pete smiled. "Aye aye, Potts, and thanks again, ol' buddy. *M.V. New Delphi* out."

12
Why this boat?

Chobeem the cappan had lived long enough and well enough that certain privileges were his by right. He swam with the leaders. He *was* a leader. In addition, dirty jobs that no one else could do were his. He accepted his lot with typical porpoise equanimity. It had been many seasons since he had to ponder his station. He had been shaped by his body, mind, and experiences. The pod had long known that Chobeem's almost automatic first actions or reactions were right.

He was not large, but he was quick, agile and brave. His reputation for tactics and even strategy over a period of time had determined his place in his adopted pod. His mate had been with him more or less exclusively for ten full seasons of long days, and he enjoyed her company. They had a daughter he was sure was his. A son had died while still small. They had accepted the loss and were happy, even by dolphin standards, which are high in the open ocean.

Because of his age and wisdom, Chobeem was called when a decision was hard to make. If time allowed. Chax, the acknowledged leader of leaders for a dozen years, depended on Chobeem. Chobeem had been captured by men, escaped and survived as a lone dolphin for a time. Perhaps for those reasons, he was shrewd. For whatever other reason, he was not mean or crazy. Sometimes his solutions were unlike anything anyone else might suggest. Chax liked to talk to him. Chobeem came right to the point. What he said was expressed so simply that his advice might have been overlooked if it came from anyone else. But Chax had learned to value what Chobeem said, and the pod followed Chax. They accepted that whatever Chobeem said had merit, even if it was not immediately apparent.

When a young one stopped eating, he was consulted. A young male, almost a baby, had shown less interest in straying from his mother and aunts than they had come to expect. At first this improved behavior was all too welcome. The young one, who had not said enough yet to have a name, had shown an abundance of curiosity about the world at as early an age as anyone could remember. His mother and even his aunts had to discipline him when most infants barely keep up. This one swam close to his mother only when he wanted to nose along her underside for the unremarkable slit that concealed her teat. Then he would push—hard, his mother told the others—until a stream of thick, rich milk started.

When his belly was full, he was off. The aunts had learned to watch him close. He could be the perfect serene baby one minute, and in the next instant chase a grouper bigger than him. Once he dove toward the bottom with all the speed his small, uncoordinated body could muster. He swam as if he expected to punch through the sand and coral as easy as he could burst into the air. An aunt got in front of him, but it took all she had. The aunts were sure his maturity would be exciting, because it was a challenge to watch him now.

So, when first he showed less interest in straying, they were pleased. When he did not nurse, they were concerned.

One aunt took up a station parallel to the mother on her left, with her right flipper all but touching the baby, and the baby touching his mother. Another aunt swam behind and below him. If the baby had been healthy, they would only have taken such positions in the face of a threat: sharks or orcas, or men. They might also assume such a formation as a disciplinary measure for a baby who strayed too far or too much. They had done that with this one a few times.

Now the baby swam without purpose or curiosity. When the four would break the surface to breathe, the baby's breathing was almost the opposite of what it should have been. Instead of a noisy blow, loud as a horse, followed by a barely audible intake of air, the baby simply let air go. When he drew air in, he made a gulping sound that upset the aunts. They discussed it, as they did everything else he did or did not do.

Flow was sure it was a bad sign, and said so. She expected the baby to die, but that she did not say. She was not as old as the other aunts, but she had come to this pod from another, and that pod had had many deaths. When she became part of this pod, she noticed its members did not feel the same about how often and fast death can come. So she stopped talking about it. There had been few deaths in this pod while she had been with it, and they were the kind anyone can understand.

She did not say she expected the baby to die, because the other two aunts would have made her sorry. It would have been bad manners to put something like that into sounds. Besides, the others knew how she felt.

The oldest aunt was Chobeem's mate. To Evie, death was natural and understandable. The reasons might not always be apparent, but she did not doubt they were there. She did not expect to know everything.

She had been an aunt a long time, a mother twice, and had seen the usual problems with injuries or eating. Her first baby had stopped eating. This one was still nursing. He chased fish, but no one knew if he had eaten one. Dolphin sonar can show digestive blockages, just as it can detect broken bones. An experienced dolphin like Evie probably could detect a blockage, if it was there. She knew what to do for the ill and injured. But she could see nothing wrong with this one, except that he was listless. Perhaps Chobeem would notice something, so she called him to her side.

Formalities had to be observed. Males were not welcome around young ones. Chobeem waited as the aunts, including Evie, drew close to the little one. They unconsciously took note of their surroundings—depth of water, current, obstructions, visibility.

When a male showed too much curiosity about a calf, the aunts sent him away with a little scolding, if they could, because at times, a male would show real hostility to an infant. Especially if its mother had rejected the male's advances. If this happened the aunts would take whatever measures they could. Sometimes a male would bother a baby so aggressively and with so much determination that it would die. This did not happen often in the open ocean, but Chobeem had seen it.

Preparing for the worst was instinctive. Chobeem made smooth approaches to the two aunts, touching them gently with his beak to reassure them. When all were satisfied that the cappan, the seasoned one, meant no harm, and after young Flow flirted a little, Chobeem asked Evie why she had called. She drifted away from the others, and he followed. They nuzzled until the aunts and mother stopped paying attention. They swam in a big circle, side by side, comfortable.

"It may be nothing," she said. Chobeem was silent. "You've seen how quiet the little one is. Little ones do that, but this seems different. This one has been full of life. Something isn't right. See what you can see."

Chobeem waited. There would be more. "The mother is upset. She hasn't been well either. If she sees that you are concerned, she'll assume the worst."

Chobeem understood. Evie was speaking out of experience. He trusted her. Whatever checking he would do would be quiet as a sea hare.

A quiet investigation can sometimes be a noisy business though. In the world of dolphins, there is noise aplenty. Not only do dolphins themselves make little effort to keep quiet, their environment is often a market bazaar of sound. Sound moves so much faster in water than in air, more than four times as fast, and with such intensity that the clicking of a shrimp when its oversized finger pops against some tiny, unsuspecting shellfish is transmitted over a surprising distance. Shrimps are seldom solitary, and the natural sea abounds with an abundance of percussive shrimp sounds where they are present.

They're barely noticed. Some sea creatures can sound like the underwater garbage collectors that they are, forever banging lids and turning over shells to see what happens. Sometimes the din from clams, rock lobsters, shrimps and even oysters can be all but deafening to a creature possessed of a sensitive listening device. And dolphins certainly have that.

Small creatures are not the only ones. Croakers grow quite large and can further distend themselves with air and water. When they do, a croaker can make a sound like a wet finger being dragged across a balloon. A croaker that weighs a few hundred pounds can sound like the world's biggest finger on the world's biggest balloon. Fearsome, in a word.

Drums also get their name from their sound. It is hard to ignore a school of drums. Without the visual huff and puff of croakers, drums still make a racket.

Imagine all these sounds as backdrop. Stir in sixty or seventy dolphins from several pods when they have not seen each other in a while. Remember that dolphins are gregarious by nature, and that they use sounds not only to talk, but for navigation and maneuvers that have nothing to do with communication, at least as humans think of it.

If a room full of humans enjoying themselves gets loud, imagine how noisy the room would be if every person's every glance or studied look produced an audible click, or chirp or squeak—or burst of them. Put all that together and you have some idea of the arena in which Cappan Chobeem began to make quiet inquiries.

But remember also the sophisticated information-gathering equipment at his disposal.

Like all dolphins, Chobeem was born with a sonar receiver capable of discriminating differences in objects that humans need sophisticated electronic measuring tools to verify. Remember also that as a seasoned dolphin, Chobeem, or any mature, healthy dolphin, is experienced and skilled at using that bionic sonar echolocation system over respectable distances, on the run, underwater.

Add to that his vision. Chobeem's vision was better than average for a dolphin, underwater or above, and most dolphins have good vision. He had also acquired the habit of focusing on what is important, the way a skilled politician picks out the important stuff from the seeming chaos of a legislative floor session.

Remember that the cappan was an old campaigner. He had led large groups of dolphins through the best nets and snares men can devise, around sharks and through whirring, sharp, noisy propellers, past shallowing shoals. In the black of night, sometimes in water clouded with silt. The cappan could juggle all that, and be aware of who in the pod was keeping up and who was not. He could keep track of who was weakening, who was anxious, who was too far ahead. He could do all this and still probe for what to do if thus and such set of circumstances were to present itself.

Certainly the cappan could look into a small matter like a small dolphin a bit off its feed. And because he was aware that he was at least in part responsible for any dolphin not as able as himself, he did.

13
Prospects brighten

Pete didn't know why dolphins had showed up, but he was glad. Now the professor could pull his weight for a while. He fished his brass telescope out of the chart box. These days everybody uses lightweight binocs with glare-cutting coated lenses, but Pete's telescope made him smile.

He scoped the lingering dolphins. Three were close—a big, alpha-looking one, young; a small, high-mileage one, dark with whitish scars; and a smaller young one, maybe a female. Another big one had been with them before, but not now. Without the telescope Pete swept the water. On the other side of the boat he saw it. But ...

"Son of a ...."

Hanging onto the big dolphin, the one he had seen first, doing maybe fifteen knots, was a ... mermaid. That's what he thought for half a second, but no, it was a dark-haired woman. Sunlight played off her shiny hair. Her long hair, her white arm holding onto the grey dorsal fin, and her white shoulders—against the dolphin—made quite a picture. Where had she come from? Pete had looked for a mermaid since the Coast Guard. Usually he pictured her blonde, or with seaweed hair. He had dreamed about both. He had to laugh. At himself, but not the situation.

With the eyepiece, he brought her into sharp focus. It helped that the dolphin stopped. Clearly a woman. Black bikini top.

Whats-er-name, the one Digby called the schoolmarm. Sarah. He hadn't had a clue she was in the water.

Man! What a dumb trick, he thought, and started to get mad. Mad at her, at himself. What if he had left her? He probably wouldn't have, but had anyone else noticed? They hadn't said anything. Everybody topside was looking at dolphins on the other side of the boat. Digs maybe saw. But no, he was up there too.

As casually as he could, Pete took the telescope from his eye. Without turning his head, he took stock. Everybody on deck was watching the dolphins to port. Even Ping. The mermaid was to starboard. And somebody was on the ladder behind him. Kimbie. Dangling her gigantic "field glasses."

He put the telescope in the chart box and took a breath. It would be all right. But man, was he glad nothing bad had happened. He shivered. It was involuntary, but he rolled his shoulders intentionally, to shake it off, shake off the willies. Stuff like that was scary. Somebody probably would have seen her ... but. A captain who lost a passenger through negligence could be prosecuted. Negligent homicide would be a hard conviction to make, but a review of his license—and most likely a lawsuit—would be automatic!

Kimbie's face was a question. "You okay?" He took another breath, nodded, forced a smile. She trained her field glasses on the dolphins.

Pete had not expected trouble out of the schoolmarm. He tried to remember her name. Sarah ... something. Sarah Spinach. No. He laughed to himself. Some kind of greens, though. Not turnips, creecy, collard, mustard. No, it was kale! Sarah Cale. Sarah Cale had slept in, much of the first day. She spent the second day snorkeling, and talking to the learned doctor. She seemed nice enough, went along with the program, seemed to be enjoying herself. Goes to show. Women!

But no harm done, he reminded himself. Pete took another intentional breath and relaxed a little. Maybe she slipped off the stern while everybody was watching the other dolphins. But how did she catch hold?

The schoolmarm had kind of cut Ping off at supper, now that he thought about it. He wanted to cut Ping off too, often. Those stories were good the first time, even the second, but ... Pete had to remind himself that passengers hadn't heard them at all. Except for the Zinsers, who were too polite to mention it. Have to give this Sarah Cale woman a little credit. After he straightened her out.

"How did she get out there? Who helped her? Kimberly? I cannot fathom why, but they've taken up with her. She didn't seem that interesting. Or that good a swimmer." Ping was clearly frustrated, ticked off, puzzled, and coming up the ladder.

Pete almost chuckled. So, the professor doesn't like it either? In a heartbeat, Pete changed course. "You didn't send her?" he said, offhand, unconcerned.

But Kimbie Barone had seen him shiver. She cocked her head and raised an eyebrow. Without him saying a word she had known Pete was mad about something, or upset. Now she knew it was the swimmer, Sarah. She had gone in alone, without telling anybody. Pete had freaked, too, she had seen it! And she had seen him shift gears when Ping piped up.

Boys, boys, she thought, and bit the inside of her mouth to keep from laughing.

Pete noticed. *Good thing Ping can't see her face*, he thought. He hoped he didn't laugh himself. Pete was too tickled to be embarrassed. Kimbie knew what he was up to. Ping was plenty smart, but he could be tone-deaf. Not her.

Doctor P needs her around to keep his limey self from being ridiculous, Pete thought. *Whether he knows it or not. And he doesn't*. Pete tried to stay professional about the two of them, but it was tough. Not that long ago, Ping had been all business. If he had been distracted by the passengers, it was clear he wanted to get on with his research. Pete could understand that. The people *are* a distraction, but they help pay the freight, too. Means to an end. The paying passengers made it possible for Pete to charge Ping less for the charter and still do okay. Too much less, maybe.

But also lately, in addition to repeating the same spiels too often, Ping had slacked off, lost focus or something. He seemed to have stopped relating to the passengers as people. Pete tried to treat everybody the way he would like to be treated if the situations were reversed. He even tried to treat Julian Ping that way. *Maybe I need to have a talk with him*, he thought.

Pete had wondered whether Ping's old girlfriend, the one he said was in Australia now, had helped him stick to business. Kimbie clearly thought Ping was great, for all his faults. With Ping more or less drifting, she either could not crack the whip, or would not. She worked harder than Ping, unless Ping worked when others slept. And on a boat, that would show. People would know. Ping slept. Lately, Pete could not see why Kimbie stayed with him, but she did. She clearly liked him, and they all liked Kimbie. So, bottom line: Pete didn't make fun of Ping the way Fred did, but it wasn't easy sometimes.

It was funny. Kimbie could jerk Fred back in line with her eyebrow, and did, sometimes. But she seemed not to mind a joke at the doc's expense. *She isn't stupid, she can see that the man has flaws*. Pete knew Kimbie cared about Ping. There are few secrets on a boat. He also knew she realized—because it was obvious—that Ping has an absent-minded-professor streak a mile wide. Even Digs saw that. So did Mary and John, though nobody ever said anything. Well, Fred.

Kimbie either liked Ping's goofy absent-mindedness in some way, or put up with it, since it was part of the package. Sometimes the professor could be so oblivious—give him the benefit of the doubt—it was almost comical. She could laugh at that, up to a point, then she would help him, defend him, save his bacon. It had been a while, but there had been times.

"Want me to motor over and pick her up, Doc?" Pete drawled as Ping started back down the ladder. The boat had long since lost forward motion. The only sound was an occasional wave slapping the underside of the stern platform. The dolphins and Sarah were at least a hundred yards away. The swimmer would disappear from time to time, behind a swell, but from the helm, Pete could keep track of her.

"I should say not, Pete," Ping answered, humor in his voice. But as he shielded his eyes from the sun to look, Ping clinched his teeth and his shoulders tensed, Pete noticed. The professor was clearly in a pickle. Something very cool was happening, and he had had nothing to do with it. He had missed it. He needed to get control.

"Just think, an actual inter-species interlock, in the open ocean. Unforced," mused Bridget Strewsberry-D'Mer, loud enough for everybody to hear. "Why do you suppose they chose her?" Bridget's expression was rapt. "Would you think, say, if Chip and I swam out, they would accept us too? Or maybe it's a woman thing. She's ... um ... Sarah is ... kind of intense."

Her comments were directed to one and all. Chip gazed at Bridget with the adoring look they had all grown accustomed to seeing. Chip only had eyes for Bridget.

Melody Molinari, the ex-sophomore, was excited. "This is so great!" She had stars in her eyes too, for the dolphins.

"No one is going in just yet," said Ping, in a too-curt classroom voice. Faces fell. He tried again. "This is unusual, as Bridget has alluded—unusual. Clearly. Something is affecting these *Tursiops*, these dolphins. That much is obvious, but until we understand ... we must observe a while longer." Kimbie cocked her head but didn't speak. What was he thinking? *Sure, Sarah broke a rule and is out there ahead of us, and he's out of the loop just now. But this is fixable. Wonderful, in fact. Those three dolphins are watching us!*

But Ping continued to dig. "We will proceed deliberately ... and cautiously." *Why is he flustered? He's usually so much smoother.*

Mel McRae usually knew when somebody was backing and filling. "Just how unusual is it, Julian? I thought this is what we're out here for."

"Indeed," Ping said, shielding his eyes, massaging his temples as he watched Sarah and the dolphin. "You're correct. This is indeed what, as you say, we are… here to do. Ideally. Quite right, of course. A rare opportunity. But one doesn't jump off the pier until one is sure the boat is going … in the right direction, does one?"

"I'm not sure I follow." Mel almost chuckled.

Kimbie looked through her binoculars as if she were not listening, but Pete, next to her, saw her jaw muscles twitch. She was trying not to laugh, he was sure. He could feel a big grin spreading across his own face. As Kimbie turned and started down the ladder, he saw her shake her head.

"What I'm trying to say," Ping continued, still trying, "is there are ways … right ways … of proceeding … " he trailed off. "What has happened is not …" But his voice failed him. Sarah was being pulled directly toward them, at maybe ten knots. All eyes were on her. Melody, the rising sophomore, gasped audibly.

The dolphin turned away, swam a short distance and stopped. Jaws were still dropped but Ping continued. "This … is … fortuitous. But we may not be get … the maximum …"

"Oh!" said Melody, who now had somebody's binocs. "Maximum interaction! She's like *talking* to them." She could not decide whether to relate to Ping as professor or tour guide. Either way, she didn't see him as an authority figure. She just said what popped into her head.

"Indeed, but we … are not. Kimberly, fetch snorkel gear."

Kimbie had already done that. She also had inflated a raft, with Fred's help, and now sat on the stern platform holding the raft's tether line. Her T-shirt was gone, replaced by a pink inflatable vest. It contrasted nicely with a lime green bikini. She adjusted her facemask and waited for Ping.

"I think she's anticipated your request, Julian," said Mel, who was enjoying all this, along with something cold and clear, with a slice of lime.

"Just so," said Ping, as he made his way to the stern, struggling out of his shirt and shorts, eyes on Sarah Cale and her dolphin. Fortunately, he wore Speedos under the shorts.

"What should we do?" asked Bridget, following him. "Should we be ready to dive?"

"Yes, ready to dive. Snorkel. Snorkel gear. Yes. Though we don't exactly … Certainly, ready yourselves." As he passed the salon, Julian flipped his shirt through the opening, an easy lay-up. He kicked his shorts into a corner, without breaking stride. Pete chuckled to himself and shook his head. Maybe the professor was back on his game. Sometimes he was sort of likeable.

Kimbie held a snorkel and mask at the ready for Ping. His flippers were beside her. She slipped in the water and waited. Ping joined her and they swam toward Sarah, with the raft trailing by a line attached to her tanned ankle.

14
Chax lingers

Chax ignored the boat. The pod needed to eat, and rest. After that they would swim to colder water. Not now. They were tired. Here they would eat, rest, heal, fatten and enjoy. This was a good place for those things. It had been good as long as the pod remembered.

The water was warm. The sun was hot almost every day. The only difference between days might be a storm. Every day, pelicans ate mullet. Dolphins teased and splashed them. Big fish—tarpon—often came to see if the mullet were guarded. Dolphins challenged them. In the confusion, tarpon would eat stray mullets and leave.

At night turtles came. Dolphins pushed them around. A nearly mature dolphin, Kip, had already learned a painful lesson about big green turtles. Now she had a small notch in her flipper. It would heal. No snaps had found their mark since. Turtles do not eat many fish, and they're fun to push around.

Now and then men would net fish. Dolphins would move them. That was all it took, most days.

The boat changed its sound. Chax heard. It sounded better. Now the boat would slow. He had not been able to hear much today. Warm water is good for sound, but cloudy water is not as good. This water was clouded from yesterday's storm. There wasn't that much to hear anyway. This was a food place, and a rest place. Chax remembered when this place had had fewer people, fewer boats, better water and more mullet, but it was a good place, even now.

Chobeem, who was the oldest in the pod, could remember more birds here. More than he had names for, and he knew many. Bird stories from the long song of the pod are some of the best parts. Songs about clouds of big pink birds, of white birds that flew so thick they hid the sun. He had not seen that, but believed it, even thought the song about it is like a dream.

Chax also liked birds. He didn't tease them, as some dolphins do. Neither did Chobeem, most of the time. Birds seemed to know. Chax's first exploit had been seen by birds and told first by them, after all. Birds liked Chax, and he liked them. He always learned from them.

He swam to the surface, blew, took in air and floated, with only his fin and blowhole and forehead exposed. Gulls came. Looping and circling, they got his attention and told where the storm had gone. They talked about a garbage dump, not far inland, that was worth the flight. Chax said he had not known. They knew that and laughed. He thanked them for news of the storm, and expressed polite interest in the dump. Gulls will eat anything, but it would not be right to criticize their tastes.

A young gull of their acquaintance had been careless that morning, and was almost eaten. An enormous mouth and teeth—a gator—had missed by a few feathers! She was unnerved. Chax did not laugh, which was appropriate. The birds did not laugh.

He asked about mullet. The gulls said the ones the pod guarded were quiet now, feeding over a huge underwater meadow, where the pod had left them. The gulls asked what he knew about the boat. He knew only that it was more interested in dolphins than most boats that do not catch fish. The gulls knew that men on this boat throw tasty food overboard, and never hurt them. Sometimes these men let gulls eat undisturbed, right on the boat.

Chax said that was good to know.

He had heard this boat before, and had never heard of it hurting dolphins. Some of the people who rode on it tried (and failed) to grab them, with their tiny, bony flippers. They want rides. Sometimes all the people did was squeak, put noise in the water, laugh and try to get dolphins to eat things.

Chax knew all he cared to know about this boat. The people on it had not seemed to mean harm, but you never know. Some humans are twisted. Some dolphins are twisted, for that matter, but the few twisted dolphins Chax had met, all got that way from being around men. The old saying was an old saying for a reason. It is true. Men attract trouble. It follows them. They create it.

Chax wished the gulls luck and listened for the pod. After he listened for a while he would return to them. Instead, all of a sudden, he wanted to swim to the boat. He was sure. He felt urged to go there. So he went.

As he swam the boat slowed. Chax was sure he should swim near. He needed to call some others. So he did. He whistled. Dolphins whistled back, and soon were beside him.

As they drew near, Chax surfaced fast enough to break out of the water, fully, instead of just enough to blow and inhale air, so the others did too, up and down. The surface was smooth. Popping and diving isn't a fast way to swim, but with something to look at, like a boat, or the shore, or birds, it's nice. So they wove along like that, tight little arcs above the surface, long ones below. Soon the top of the boat was covered with people. Weaving the air and water always draws people.

At this speed, the boat's bow wave helped, and Chax rode it. Though he had felt urged to the boat, he still had no intent other than to swim alongside. The others followed him. When the boat made a long, graceful turn, he turned. So did the others. The space between the dolphins and the boat was less now. He could see the people well. Many. Some looked old, as he had learned to judge people. He saw no babies.

Long ago, he had encountered two small humans floating next to a boat. Not really babies, but small, with their mothers and aunts. He swam close. The aunts were not afraid, and the young ones were not either. He enjoyed that. Noises from the small ones reminded him of porpoise babies. Hearing very young dolphins squeal and laugh was one of his favorite things, and still is. He swam near the man-babies, and stayed. The babies bobbed like coconuts, or the floats men put on nets. The aunts did not try to drive him away. He let the babies rub his beak and head. One of them patted his eye. The little flipper was too soft to hurt. The small human squealed with delight. It meant no harm, and caused none. He had squealed back, but not loud.

The pod had only one baby now. Not long ago another had died before it was born. That happened too often now. The aunts could remember when a mother's first baby was sure to be the biggest, healthiest one. Now, so often that it was remarked upon, a female's first baby died, before it was born, or soon after. Sometimes the babies that died were misshapen, or too small. Sometimes they did not grow into babies at all. Always this was difficult for the mother, and the aunts. Even the father.

When a female birthed her second baby, usually it lived and thrived. This was a new thing. Chobeem was first to notice. Now all did.

Chax still popped into the air. So did the others. The boat slowed more and settled into the water near a sand island, the kind that is revealed at low tide. Perhaps the men would fish, or rest, or swim. The boat was so slow it took effort to stay by it. Chax continued in the same direction, turned, slowed, swam fast, slow, turned again. The boat cut its motor, settled low in the water and drifted.

Chax still was sure, somehow, that he was to stay near, so he dove underneath to see what he could see. The bottom of the boat was smooth. Almost nothing grew on it. He could hear small noises from inside, now that the big noise was gone. Scrapes, bangs, clangs. He could hear and feel pings in the water. Fishermen ping when they do not know where the fish are. Perhaps they were going to try to catch fish. They should try somewhere else.

Chax hung under the boat. He could hear men, hear their bones hit the boat's shell, hear squeaks. He surfaced, and a mature female human looked right at him. Close! Her mouth dropped open, and her eyes grew wide. Chax expected she would call others, but she didn't. She slid down the side of the boat into the water, under it, slow, smooth, feet first. As soon as she was in, she pushed away from the boat and swam toward him. Underwater. Chax felt no need to flee, so he watched and waited. With one twitch he could be out of her reach, and knew it.

She swam in lunges, like a big frog. Chax almost laughed. He had seen big frogs, and she reminded him of one, with legs too long and white. She was bigger, of course, and had tiny flippers, not big frog flippers. He swam toward her and watched. She swam underwater better than most men. He studied her.

She was not fearful, he could tell, though he heard her heart race with excitement. Her torso was small, and her arms were long and white like her legs. She watched him too, but was not tense. She seemed to mean no harm. He liked the way the sun reflected on her dark hair, and the way her legs shone like the belly of a frog. Her torso was iridescent white and covered in places by black and blue cloth that danced in the filtered sunlight from the storm-clouded water.

He closed the distance to her.

She stopped. Her feet went down and then came up in front of her as she pushed and pulled herself back with her arms and hands. Her white face was still close, so he rolled to point one eye at her. She let out bubbles, sank, smiled. He saw her relax, first her face, then the bigger muscles. She extended her arm to him.

Except for the mothers and aunts and babies, Chax had never been this close to a person. When others swam with people, he stayed back so he could watch not only them but the surroundings. Now he was alone and close. And safe. He had not been afraid then, and was not now.

But he was alert. He knew where the others were. He knew no one else from the boat was in the water. They might watch, but he was relaxed. He wondered if this was how men tricked dolphins, until he remembered how wary and apprehensive he had been other times when men were near. He felt none of that now, and moved almost imperceptibly to place his head against her hand.

The hand was soft, slightly warm. The pads on of her long, bony fingers felt nicer than he expected. Not slippery, not rough. Softer than a dolphin's skin, smooth, but not slick. Not as smooth or soft as the human babies, but nice. She pushed the side of his head, easy, near his ear but not on it, as if she knew where it was. As if she had felt a porpoise's skin before, and remembered.

She slid her hand to the base of his dorsal fin, and gripped. Not hard, but firm, a firm but careful grip. She wanted him to pull her through the water, that was plain.

Her grip did not hurt. She smiled. Without even considering whether it was a good thing to do, he twitched his flukes and the two of them surged forward and up. When they broke the surface, he heard her gasp, to exchange air. She held on and no longer gasped, so he dove. She trailed along with him, tumbling in the flow, smiling like a porpoise. When he paused to look at her, she relaxed, changed hands. Now her back was to him. Swimming with a burden was tricky, but not difficult, because she let herself stream back from her arm like a piece of seaweed. She was small, compared to him, too. He could tell she tried to keep her legs out of the way of his flukes, at least a little, but it was difficult, because they extended behind him. She tumbled against him in the turbulence, but it didn't hurt. It felt good. He knocked against her with his flippers and flukes until he figured out how not to and still go. When he just ignored her, as if she really were seaweed, Chax was able to move forward well.

She wanted another breath, wanted him to surface, so he did, and she gasped again. They were no longer close to the boat, so he turned toward it, slow, on the surface, to reassure her. The others swam to meet them, squeaking questions. As he got closer to the boat again, people were still all over the top of it. Instead of going close, he turned when he met the other leaders he had called, swam away from the boat a short way and stopped.

All she did was change arms again. And smile. She smiled at him, and at the others. Most men talked. Chax had heard them. He had heard the mothers talk up close, too, but she didn't make any sound. She knew how to float, and did, but did not let go, except to get a better grip. Chax let her move him.

The other leaders were less sure about this than Chax, but they were not afraid. It was unusual to see Chax take up with a human. Chobeem, the storyteller, was first to approach close, and nuzzled her foot with his beak as she floated. She had one hand on Chax, face up, back arched, toes down. She pulled her foot back when he nuzzled, but when she saw him, she relaxed and made contact again, gently, on his flipper.

"She is not in distress," Chobeem said.

"No. I surfaced in front of her. She got in. She touched me."

"I feel no fear," Chobeem said.

"Nor I. If I had, we would not be here now."

"Right. The others may come for her," said Chobeem.

"Yes. I don't know if they can see her. Can they?"

"Who knows?"

"Indeed."

15
Kimbie finds her bliss

Kimbie swam steady, with the raft tethered to her ankle, and stopped perhaps fifteen yards from Sarah. Julian had strayed. He chased a large, young-looking dolphin that kept just beyond his reach. Julian hadn't said anything to her, just veered away.

Sarah floated on her back, breasts and belly oddly out of the water, eyes closed. Her arms and legs dangled. Underwater, Kimbie was amazed to see a dolphin with its beak and head under Sarah's spine, to support her. She could hardly believe her eyes, and wished Julian could see.

After she watched a moment, in a calm, even voice, she said, "Sarah, it's me, Kimbie. Can you hear me?" Sarah didn't, with her ears in the water. But she opened her eyes after a bit, and saw.

"Oh," she said, moving mostly her eyes, hoping the dolphin would continue to support her. Her expression reminded Kimbie of a child caught eating cookies. "You found me," Sarah said in a guilty little voice, much different from her usual matter-of-fact tone. The big dolphin let her sink and surfaced, facing them.

"Yup," said Kimbie, treading water, pushing the raft forward. Sarah took hold of it. "You're the main attraction. I'm jealous. We all are." The dolphin turned to inspect this second female, and Kimbie inspected him. He was big, eight feet at least, fully mature, with some scars, but he was healthy, no lesions she could see. He made no move to leave. She could not quite believe this. *You never know what a day will bring, do you?*

"He was so close. When he looked at me, I just had to see," Sarah said, taking courage from a flicker of a smile that had crossed Miss Barone's face for a second.

"It's okay," Kimbie said. "I might have done the same thing, but ... seriously." He voice turned stern. "Seriously, I mean this, swim with a buddy! A *human* buddy. We could have left you. I don't think we *would* have, but I'm pretty sure Captain Pete freaked. I'm pretty sure he was scared when he noticed. He probably expects me to give you grief, so ..."

Sarah's face fell, but Kimbie smiled, impish. "I should. But let's don't and say we did." She closed her mouth as a small wave smacked her face, but still smiled. "I've never seen anything like I just saw, and I'm not going to lecture you for it. But you better act chastised when we get back, or I promise you a real lecture. Really! I will! You took a dumb chance. It's a long swim back." She all but giggled, but managed not to, and Sarah smiled, relieved. "Julian's mad, and Captain Pete was mad at first," Kimbie continued, treading water, "but mostly I think Julian's jealous. He went that way," she said, gesturing with her head, "chasing another dolphin. You okay?" She pushed herself up on the raft for a better look around.

"Wonderful," Sarah said. "Did you see him pull me?"

"Did we ever! I told you we're all jealous. This is ... real unusual in the wild." There was a question in her voice. "And that thing just now ... when he held you up; I've *read* about stuff like that, but never seen it, outside of a pool or a tank. I don't think I believed it until now. Definitely cool. Did he do that on his own? Of course he did!"

Sarah held on to the raft, nodded and smiled. "I was pooped, and floated. He just got under my back when I did."

Kimbie kept her eyes moving, and settled on several dolphins squeaking and blowing. The dolphins were still around. She decided they must be interested in something about Sarah, and didn't seem to mind her own presence. Two of them were almost motionless, twenty feet away. Another, probably a young male, swam big circles, jumping, close. He kept an eye on them. She suspected that one also had an eye on Julian and the big male he was after.

"Want to rest in the raft?"

Sarah did. She was exhilarated, but tired, and cold, despite the warm water. "I'm more out of shape than I realized."

Kimbie nodded, and steadied the raft so Sarah could push up, kick and roll in. Once in, she lay on her back, feet dangling for a whole minute.

She noticed with surprise that Sarah trembled, shivered. Out of the water, the sun would warm her. "Rub your upper arms, hard," she said. Sarah did, and tried to scoot to a sitting position, and almost tipped the small raft over. She still kept her eyes on the big dolphin that had pulled her. He had his face toward her, out of the water, but watched Kimbie too. So did the others.

Kimbie eased away from the raft and breast-stroked quiet and slow toward the big dolphin. When she was close enough she put her hand next to his left flipper, but didn't grab it, only rubbed. He rolled from side to side without moving the flipper away, as if he enjoyed it. This was awesome! These were not tame dolphins, if Kimbie was any judge, but she had never seen wild dolphins this laid back, either.

This one is battle-scarred, but not old, she thought. *He's been in some scrapes with sharks, that's plain enough. Too big to be a female.* She touched what looked like old, deep, tooth marks on his pectoral fins, and marveled. The old scars were smoothed over so well that they were only shallow indentations now, but they must have been deep once. A few of the dips were white at the bottom. He flipped her hand, gently.

"I'm going to see if he will swim with me," she said, making eye contact with Sarah. "I say 'he' because he's so big. Just chill in the raft." When Sarah nodded, her teeth actually chattered. Kimbie stifled a sympathetic laugh. "Umm—I mean, warm up, if you can. The sun will help. Rub your legs too, but don't tip over." Then she turned serious. "When Julian comes, remember: we could have left you,. None of us saw you go in. We probably wouldn't have left you—scary thought— but we could have, and it scared Captain Pete, seriously. Me too, when I thought about it."

Sarah nodded, embarrassed. Kimbie adjusted her mask and let go of the raft. She ducked and pulled at the water and kicked her feet up to start forward and down. Dolphin-kicking with her huge flippers, she swam straight down for a count of five Mississippi, leveled off and looked back. The dolphins had not followed.

She swam back toward them, stopped, looked intent at them and circled down in a slow spiral. The one that had jumped so much, the young one, squirted down and fell in beside her, six or seven feet away. She rose and dove again. So did the dolphin, so she headed back up on a course a little away from him. He followed. When she stopped, he stopped. When she rose for breath, so did he, except that he jumped clear out of the water. *Wish I could do that*, she thought, marveling as the dolphin cut back into the water and returned to his post beside her, six or seven feet away.

Kimbie felt a thrill like she had not felt in a long time. She had been fortunate enough to swim with dolphins a few times, in several places, and treasured each time, remembered it vividly, but nothing exactly like this had ever happened. Wild dolphins often showed curiosity and passing interest in people, or boats, or birds, but generally they were skittish, prudent, tentative. After a while they moved on, kept going. A few inshore dolphins she knew about were regular beggars and would hang out with divers. But usually, in the open ocean, wild dolphins only broke stride for a little while to interact with people. At least that had been her experience. After a short interaction, or a slightly longer one, they continued whatever they had been doing. It always looked like the dolphins had better things to do. A mission.

This was different. These dolphins weren't going anywhere just now. Among friends, she would have sworn—speculated at least—that the big one that had held Sarah up had also told the younger one, the jumper, to take a turn. And he had, obedient, but wary and tentative. That's how it seemed, anyway.

16
Popper is exuberant

The woman pulled at the water and used her big, fluke-like flippers to turn herself and swim straight down. She swam well, for a human, leveled off and looked back. The dolphins watched. Clearly she tried to swim like a dolphin, and wasn't bad, in short spurts. She swam a few meters toward them, stopped, gave them a look and retreated, spiraling down slow.

Popper was curious. "What is she doing?"

"Follow her," Chax told the young porpoise, who wanted reassurance. Or permission. The sun-darkened female with the white hair was closer to Popper, but he hesitated.

"Me?"

"Perhaps it's a game," said Chax. "You can see she does not mean harm."

"Yes." Popper was off. He followed, and gained on her. In seconds he realized he had never been this close to a human, and paused. Still, he felt no threat. Chax watched. The leader was relaxed, so Popper fell in beside the woman. He tried to mimic what she did, but did not get close enough that she could touch him. He swam the same course as the female, but parallel, beside instead of behind. If she turned his way, he maintained the same space. If she got too close, he spurted off. Only to return.

As Chax and the others watched, she rose a few feet and descended again. So did Popper. She headed to the surface on a course away from him. He followed. When she went down, he did too. When she took a breath, so did he, though he also jumped clear out of the water.

The woman swam toward Popper. He squirted away, but turned to face her. As she continued toward him he maintained the same measured distance. When she stopped and retreated, he moved with her. Not in a menacing way, more like a dancing partner, or a shadow. The woman seemed pleased. Like the other woman, her heart raced, but not in fear.

Every time she broke the surface for breath, he jumped high. The shadow dance went on with endless variety. She swam loops and somersaults. So did Popper. In her excitement, she squealed. Apparently she surprised herself, for she looked embarrassed. She also looked pleased. Popper made a sound like hers, and released bubbles, as she had. The woman almost choked, laughed into her snorkel. She surfaced, more pleased than before. But tired. She swam one last loop toward him, produced the same response from Popper, and stopped. She looked tired as she turned and took the direct way to the raft. She hooked her arms over it and pushed her mask up on her head. For a time she just breathed, and laughed. Panted. Began to talk to the other woman.

Chax had watched. When he saw young Popper's natural exuberance appropriately moderated by caution, he turned to Chobeem.

"We are to stay with them," he said. "I am sure."

"Yes. I was not sure at first."

"The pod is safe, happy, eating."

"Yes. We need to eat too, of course." Chobeem was hungry. Mullet was his favorite, a treat meal he always liked. His first fish had been a mullet, not far from here, many seasons ago. So he had been told.

"We will. These men are not going anywhere. They may follow us to the mullet."

"Yes. Will we let them?"

"I don't know," Chax said. "They may stop here. The sun is low. We're supposed to be here."

"Yes," said Chobeem. "She is a good swimmer, strong. Tired now."

"Yes. Tired but strong. Not bad," Chax said, as if looking at a checklist. "A human, female, strong of heart."

"The other is better."

Chax looked at the women, scanned them. "The other may be better. Not a better swimmer."

"No. But good. She is why we're here."

"Perhaps," Chax answered. "She knows how to reassure us, but she may not be why. The boat is full."

"Oh. Yes. Many. Right."

"Yes. What about the male?"

"Puffed up. Band played him the way a female plays an immature male." There was mirth in Chobeem's voice.

"Ah. Yes. Puffed up. A fair swimmer. Lean. But puffed up."

17
Amazing

Kimbie marveled at how the dolphin could jump. Every time she broke the surface for breath, he did too, but he popped high, as if to say, "Betcha can't do this!" She was envious, but couldn't stop smiling. The shadow game went on, and she wanted to take advantage of it while it lasted. 'Playing' with them like this was so unusual that Kimbie didn't realize how tired she had gotten, how much she had swum. She turned to see if seaweed or something was caught on her flippers. Something was hung on her calves, too. They felt heavy. But there was no seaweed. Kimbie was in good shape, great even. She swam every day and had plenty of stamina. But she wasn't a dolphin, even if Captain Pete said she was. She had enjoyed this one so much that she almost forgot Julian, not to mention the group back on the *Delphi*. She was close to Sarah in the raft though. This was just way too cool to stop, just because you were tired.

Almost. Her legs dragged. She had to think about swimming. She knew that was not good. With reluctance, she broke off the game. Just too tired. If she hadn't been, what she really wanted to do was see if the dolphin would take a turn being "it." She had thought about how to initiate that.

Not that she could have kept up. Kimbie was pooped. She did a slow turn, underwater, to see if she could see Julian. To her delight, the dolphin did the same thing. This was too good; Kimberly Barone the experienced, impartial observer of nature squealed underwater, involuntarily. The squeal broke out of her mouth in an upward cascade of bubbles.

She waited to see if the dolphin would mimic her. No.

Then it did, making a sound much like hers and gargling bubbles. She almost choked, pulling water into her snorkel as she laughed and broke for the surface, where she cleared the tube, grabbed a breath and looked around again. She couldn't remember if she had ever laughed like that underwater. This was too great! She could see the raft, see Sarah in it, and thank goodness, still see the Delphi.

But Julian? Wasn't it just like him to go after something interesting and forget about her, forget what they were doing? Swim with a buddy, my foot! They *both* were supposed to be going to get Sarah, after all.

Oh well. Julian knew *she* was dependable. He depended on it.

Ping was a recognized, published authority in her chosen field, but Kimbie had known he could be a spaceman when she went to work for him. Everybody did who took his classes. She had taken most of them. But she had not really known he could totally zone out until she put him on her thesis committee. He knew plenty about dolphins and the ocean, of course. That was why she had always gone to his public lectures and taken his classes. She had even listened in the hall to his other classes sometimes. He had a way of making them varied and fun, but still full of content.

Not long after she finished her masters, he got a contract to write another book. She congratulated him. He spontaneously asked her to lunch. And paid, which had flattered her. All the girls thought he was good-looking. He thought so too, but Dr. Ping had always been careful about not dating students. He didn't even hit on them. He was involved with another professor. For that matter Kimbie could always find enough guys willing to take her where she wanted to go, when she had time.

With her masters completed, though, Kimbie could not find a job. She wasn't sure she wanted to go for her doctorate yet, mostly because she wasn't sure about a topic, let alone a specialty, or how she would pay for it. She had almost decided she was going to have to start anyway, when Ping's lady, who studied coral reef colonies, changed jobs. Within months his girlfriend was in Australia, and Ping was trying to figure out how to start his book research, alone. The girlfriend tried to motivate him via email for a while, but it wasn't working.

Long story short, Professor Ping hired Kimbie as a research assistant. The pay was crummy, but it was real, research on a topic that interested her, and a job. It would do while she figured out her next move.

Almost immediately, she realized Ping mostly needed a keeper, somebody to keep up with his schedule, maintain his dive gear and lab equipment, buy his supplies, remember his obligations, pay his bills. Keep his life running, academic and otherwise. Remind him about his outline, keep him focused, nag a little. That kind of thing, except the nag part, which did not come easy for her. She kind of liked the research on dolphin home ranges they were doing. She still found Ping brilliant, charming and interesting, in an absent-minded-professor way. She was learning. He knew stuff she didn't, had seen parts of the world that she hadn't, and treated her like a colleague. The research might lead to something. And Dr. Ping *was* good-looking.

After she worked out an agreement to use Pete Gordon's boat, they moved aboard. Kimbie had to intervene when negotiations stalled, because Ping and Pete were from different planets. The three of them worked it out, finally. Though she had to mostly suggest, ask, propose, hint, and let Ping lead.

For her efforts, Ping got a nice airy stateroom, big enough to spread out in, with two windows, and she got a tiny berth below deck. Her space was a really crew berth with a door. It had a narrow bed (Digs called it a "rack") built into the wall with storage compartments under it, and a sink. No desk. She shared the micro-bathroom with the crew, meaning Digs and Fred, but they were both nice about it. They always gave her as much privacy as the cramped situation would allow. Neither of them snored, which was fortunate, since only five or six feet and two thin doors separated her from them. And they kept the bathroom surprisingly clean, for guys.

Ping's big stateroom, on the other hand, had a small desk, a full-sized bed, a wall-mounted TV and a compact but private bathroom. It doubled as their workspace. Sometimes they worked late. One thing led to another. After a month or so, she moved in. There was no discussion. One night she fell asleep up there. The next day, she went below and filled a drawstring bag with bathing suits and stuff. A few books. She was initially flattered that he found her physically as well as intellectually attractive. She thought she was attracted to him too, at first.

The attraction didn't last, though, not from her side. She didn't make a point of it, and he didn't seem to notice. They still did their research, and got along fine. Fine enough, anyway. She still admired him, and appreciated the job. It would look good on her resume. She was not sure what moving out would mean, from a work standpoint. Once in a while, if she was in a mood, she slept below deck in her little crew berth, but she never stayed more than a night or two. She tried to keep the relationship stable, even if it wasn't going anywhere. She wasn't proud of it, but there it was.

She kicked the short way to the raft, hooked her arms over the side, and pushed her mask up off of her face. She had to take several breaths, grinning like a crazy person, before she could talk.

"This is the most ..." and she had to gasp for more air before she could say "amazing ... thing." Sarah nodded and kept the raft level.

"They're always great, but..." Kimbie stopped again and panted, took a really deep breath and composed herself. "But I've never ... me, personally, Kim ... seen ... never seen them act like this ... hang out like this." She stopped for several deep breaths. "Usually their attention span ..." She shook her head and just breathed. "Their attention span, where people are concerned ... is about that short." She shook her head and closed her eyes. She had to just breathe for a while.

"I know," said Sarah. "I worked with them at an attraction a few years ago, in big tanks. It had a big closed lagoon too. I've read some about them, but not in a long time. You're right. This is amazing."

"Really?" said Kimberly, shocked. Sarah hadn't mentioned working with dolphins. "Yup. Over the top. We'll have to talk." She dropped back into the water and began to kick toward the boat. Then, raising herself on the raft again, Kimbie asked, "Where's Julian? Dr. Ping? You see him?" She had forgotten about him, but then, he had forgotten first. Swim with a buddy! She was really tired.

Sarah shook her head. "No. But the people on the boat keep looking over that way, and back here. He must be what they're watching."

"Mmm," grunted Kimbie, still kicking, mouth in the water. She was still grinning from ear to ear. After a minute, she stopped, held on with one hand and rolled onto her back to rest. "It was," and she paused for breath, "incredible." A minute later, between breaths she said, "I really think he would ... play tag ... if I had the energy ... but I'm jelly."

Sarah laughed, and tapped Kimbie's arm. "I've rested. Why don't you get in, and I'll push you?"

"Oh," said Kimbie, looking at the raft, making herself vertical, bobbing her head back and forth. "No, but lookit, if you could swim ..."

"No flippers. You need a break." Kimbie didn't argue, so they traded places. Sarah, who had been mostly tired in her arms, put on Kimbie's enormous flippers and began closing the distance to the boat.

18
This is unusual

Two more females got in the water. They did not bring a bubble to ride, but they had air bladders tied to their bodies.

"This is unusual," Chobeem said to Chax.

"Yes. Pleasant."

"Yes," said the wizened old storyteller. "I am drawn to them. One is newly mature, if that. Almost a baby."

"Humans take many seasons to mature," said Chax. "Like us."

"Yes. These mean no harm."

"No," said Chax. "They are playful. Pitiful swimmers."

"The dark one swims well for a human," Chobeem said. "Did you see her take her flukes and give them to the other?"

Chax almost laughed. "Popper was startled. When first I saw a man take flukes off, I was startled too."

Chobeem nodded. "Yes."

19
This is more like it

It seemed Sarah Cale was none the worse for her solo swim. She was pushing Kimbie Barone back in the raft. Those watching did not know why Kimbie was flopped face down, and were relieved when she waved.

Dr. Ping had swum back into the picture too. The crowd on the foredeck had almost forgotten him, watching Sarah and Kimbie. Sherry McRae had made up her mind: Ping was clueless. He had obviously gone off to pout, she said, jealous of the Atlanta woman's rapport with the dolphins. Why they were interested, Sherry could not understand, but obviously they were.

John Zinser defended Ping in calm, mild tones. He wondered what Ping's reason might be, but Zinser had seen the man so caught up he would forget basic courtesy, forget that most of the people aboard had paid for the privilege of vicarious participation in his research.

Bridget Strewsberry-D'Mer told herself, and others, that they each had their mission, and in time everything would make sense. It helped her cope. She wanted to be in the water with the dolphins. Now. Only her husband's gentle persuasion and diplomacy kept her from slipping over the side as Sarah had.

Bridget was sure, after seeing Kimbie Barone's face through binoculars, that this was far out of the ordinary.

Melody Molinari was impatient too, and so excited that even Bridget felt the need to calm her. With Chip's encouragement, Bridget grasped Melody gently by the shoulders, raised the girl's chin and said, "Sweetie, you and I need to calm down and be patient. I'm impatient too, but I'm sure we'll all get a turn." Melody continued to fidget, but was calmer. Helping her helped Bridget too.

Captain Pete noticed. He asked Melody and shirtless young Fred to fetch another raft. Lean, tanned Fred, who had dropped out of Johns Hopkins at the end of his junior year only a few years earlier, had teased Melody about college since she had come aboard. She was charmed. Helping Fred helped her too.

Mel watched it all with great interest. Coated lenses on his binoculars cut much of the glare and let him see a bit of what went on under the water, if the sun was in the right place. He had seen the big dolphin with the huge tail flukes play the professor like a fish, so to speak. Dr. Ping took the bait every time.

Now that he thought about it, Captain Pete was mostly just glad the dolphins had showed up, glad that nothing bad had happened. From the way Kimbie waved, it looked as if she was only pooped, overextended in her enthusiasm. Another educated guess said Doctor P. had just zoned out. Again.

Near Naples, Florida, Ping went off with some fishermen "for a few hours" and didn't come back for two days. And although he was the one who had gone missing, Ping was angry at Pete and Kimbie. He had to wait on the dock for an hour because they had saved the day by finding offshore dolphins in the open Gulf, accompanying a big school of grouper. Pete had defended Kimbie, and what they had done, until she said maybe they should have waited. The passengers who watched his tantrum were so mad at Ping they had to be placated with champagne and discounts.

Compared to that, Sarah's swim was a blip. Pete thought she looked embarrassed. He allowed himself a pleased smile. Kimbie's smile was ear to ear.

And daggone if the dolphins weren't swimming escort for the raft, like destroyers flanking a tanker. Ping was bringing up the rear. This trip was getting better!

20
Popper gets a story

Dolphins like stories. Old ones and new. They also like what they can taste, feel, hear and see. That's what they care about. Stories, and now. Now and stories. Songs, actually. Their stories are in their songs, and they enjoy them when they can.

Sometimes a dolphin has a reason for a song, but sometimes the reason is just entertainment. It helps that dolphins listen actively, most of the time, and that they have good memories. Story songs can be as much fun, in their way, as the adventures they celebrate. Often story songs are more fun than whatever the pod is doing or resting after, swimming to, or away from.

Not all the story songs are old. Dolphins that have lived even a few seasons have had adventures. Most have witnessed—or participated in—heroic acts, narrow escapes, bold attacks, prudent retreats. They have stories about them.

Every pod has its own, and every pod has the old songs. The old songs help dolphins understand their place in the oceans, and help them keep track. Even on the fly. Dolphins don't need a campfire to put them in the mood for a story. Which is, of course, fortunate.

Most stories are sung on the go. Some are an ongoing narrative. A sound track, if you will. Sound not only travels faster in the ocean, it travels a long way. Stories travel too.

Dolphins are mostly happy, if the water is decent and the food is plentiful and fit to eat. Those who are still alive have either made mostly good, brave, obedient choices, or else they have not been born very long and have had their choices made for them. Bad things happen, but life goes on. With fish to chase and eat, and friends to share the swim, life is good.

But sometimes young ones are impatient.

"I'll tell you a story, one you may one day need to hear," said Chobeem, addressing Popper. Popper was almost mature. He had lived ten summers. Compared to Chobeem, though, Popper had not been born very long.

Popper was so happy right now, so full of fish, he had forgotten that he had asked the cappan for a story that afternoon. He stopped doing backward loops and gave Chobeem his full attention. He moved closer too.

Popper appreciated the small honor of being addressed directly by one of the most important members of the pod. He really did. His buddy Band, who was close to his age but bigger, moved closer too. Band didn't want to miss any story Popper might need to hear. He might need it too, so he assumed a similar position and attitude. Kip, who was smaller than Band but a tiny bit bigger than Popper, and beautiful, moved close too.

Chobeem took note, but let himself drift, until he did not quite face them. They would hear anyway. They were fixed on him. So were several others. Chobeem was a leader. He was a trusted strategist, and a survivor. If he was going to say something to the young ones, anyone near would give him at least part of their attention.

He rose to the surface. The air tasted good today, and so did the water. The water was clear, but had the taste and tint of tannin from mangrove roots. Good water.

"We live in the sea, the best part of the world," Chobeen chirped. "Water is better than land. It feels better. Everyone knows that. Even you young ones. You have rested on the bottom. Did you want to stay? You may have scraped the edges of land too, though from the looks of you, you haven't. If you did, you remember."

Kip and Band only listened, but Popper squirmed. A few summers ago, chasing an elusive yellow fish and not watching much else in a place much like this, he had banged into mangrove roots hard enough to scrape and bruise his beak. Had nearly torn his eye. It didn't show now, but yes, he remembered. And when he was very small, he had strayed from his aunts into water so shallow he scuffed his belly. He was stuck on the rough bottom for what seemed like a long time, until he wiggled backwards and retreated without incident. And without telling.

He remembered. Perhaps because of that, he always seemed to sense, better than most, where the nearest dry land or rough bottom might be, and stay well away. Popper did not like how this story had started. He shivered.

"You young ones have seen the dry land, but seeing it is not the same as being there," said Chobeem. "When you jump above the top of the ocean you fall back into it. It feels good. But young as you are, it has been a long time since you have jumped where you might come down on rocks, or the edge of land. If you did, of course, you would hurt yourself." Chobeem waited until he heard agreement. It came.

"You have all let your body sink to the bottom. It can be pleasant. Most places, the sandy bottom will not hurt you, if you are careful."

As he squeaked, Chobeem expelled more and more air until he was only a few inches from the bottom. The others watched as he settled onto the sand. Some of them squeaked a giggle when he stirred a tiny cloud of sand and silt.

"But I will tell you something I know that you don't. Above the water, even if you could pick a smooth, sandy place, and by some awful miracle get there, you would not like it. Resting in the air and sun in that place would hurt. I know.

Chobeem checked to see if he had their attention. He did.

"A breath would not feel good. With air all around you, you would miss the pleasure of a breath. You would breathe, but without joy.

"Your skin would feel strange. At first you might like it, because at first the feeling is warm and different, but soon your skin would change. Skin that feels so good now can get big bubbles under it, as big as your eye. They hurt. If you stay long enough, the bubbles tear. Like seaweed." He grimaced. With the slightest movement of pectoral fins and flukes, Chobeem moved off the bottom and glided up for a breath, as all watched. Talk, even high-pitched squeaking, takes air.

"Have you ever seen these marks on my flanks, and under my mouth?" he asked as he returned.

They all had, of course. Popper had noticed the jagged, smoothed-over marks. They were hard to miss just now, as the old one swam past. They all had seen them. They looked like scars from a fight.

Now Popper wondered if the scars had come from land. He found it hard not to swim away. Though young, he had heard a bit about this before. He had not wanted to chew on it. Now it seemed he must.

He remembered what the old porpoise had said before he started the story. He might need to hear this. Did Chobeem know this would happen to him? He shivered.

Chobeem saw that Popper was swept up in the story. Good.

"If nothing happened to put you back in the water," he said, "you would sicken. You would imagine strange things. You would die."

Popper could contain himself no longer. He was troubled. It did not help to notice that those lolling near the speaker did not seem to be.

"But why?" Popper blurted. "Couldn't you just—just flip back into the water?" In his short life Popper had not yet encountered any bad thing that his aunts, at first, or his pod, or his own strong flukes could not fix. Flipping and wriggling had worked when he was stuck where the water was shallow. He saw no reason why the terrible land above the edge of the water should not be the same. He stayed away from it. He had never heard of land coming after anyone, as men sometimes do. Does it?

"Listen," said Chobeem, sometimes called "Chobeem of Many Swims." He liked it when a story got this kind of reception. "Listen" sounded like a command the way he said it, not just a word to get their attention. Popper listened. They all did. They heard a boat in the distance. They heard croakers. They heard small waves strike the shore. Two dolphins some distance away, chasing fish, cooperating. "This is one of the things I don't understand, but accept. When you are out of the water, flukes can do very little good, and may do harm. Good movements may produce bad results."

He paused and looked around. Some of the older ones nodded. Younger ones looked respectful, expectant, though a few looked puzzled. Except for Popper, who was the picture of fear. Chobeem wrinkled his forehead to try to read Popper before he started again.

"What did I do?" Chobeem asked, pausing until everyone wanted to know, until all watched and listened.

"I gave a mighty flip, I flexed my body and flukes as hard as I ever had. That's what I did, Popper. I flipped myself up high—came down hard. My beak dug into the sand. I hurt, and was no better off. But I tried again. I tried several times, and I felt worse after every try. I hurt.

"I tried until I was exhausted, injured, then I came to myself. I listened. I listened until I remembered that was what I should have done first. So I listened more. I listened until I knew. I knew I should lay still. Still. I hoped the water would come back before an enemy found me. I hoped the water would come back before my skin tore open, before my life ran out into the sand. I hurt, and felt sick. I was confused, but I waited. Because I listened."

Even Kip and Band looked fearful now. Dolphins know how to wait. Wait for day, wait for fish to come or weather to change, for fish to tire. Wait for enemies to lose interest or sickness to pass, or death to come. Wait. Swim. Wait and sleep. But to wait on land ...

They tried to understand. Chobeem saw this and it pleased him. What had happened to him had been odd and hard to understand.

"I waited and waited, and became confused, and sick, and vomited, to tell the truth. But I kept quiet. After a long time, men came. Was I afraid? Yes, I was afraid—you know why. But they did not hurt me. They put cool water on my skin, and rubbed the bubbles and torn places with something like milk. It smelled odd but felt good. I would have been very afraid if I had not listened, and if I had not been sure that I was to wait. They helped me, and they made comforting sounds."

"I had seen men before, but had not known they could comfort, as well as hurt and kill and kidnap. I was amazed—and thankful—because I had fallen into the hands—this time—of good ones. They put a sail between the sun and me, and kept me wet."

Popper and Band and Kip gave each other amazed looks. They made little exclamations of near-disbelief, almost disbelief, though of course they believed Chobeem. They would never have considered doubt. They believed him.

"I rested a long time, until the men rolled me onto a thing they made. It hurt, but I could tell they tried to be gentle, and did not mean harm. I was still fearful, and sore and confused, and sick, but I was not crazy. I lay still, as I had been told.

"Then they lifted the thing—and lifted me—above the sand. There was nothing to do but lie quiet and let them. By then I knew thrashing would have hurt me, and probably hurt them too. Small as I am, I was bigger than them, and more solid. They walked to the water. I could hear their little flippers dig into the bottom, feel it too. They walked in until water rolled over me, cooled me, until I could breathe easier. It is hard to breathe outside the water. I hope you never have to learn that for yourself, but if you do, at least you will know one thing."

"They put a cold, dead fish in front of my beak—sideways! I just looked. What could I do? But then they offered me one the right way, head-first of course, and I ate it. It was like ice inside, but I ate it, and another. I had not eaten for a long time. That's another story. I went too close to land because I was hungry and young and alone and was not wise.

"The fish they gave me were frozen, but they were good. I had eaten frozen fish before. That's another story, for another time. You can eat frozen fish if you have to. I ate them, as I rested on the thing the men carried me on.

"This made them happy. They hugged each other and made sounds of joy! After I rested they picked up the thing and carried it, and me, into deeper water. Deep water was a problem for them, because although they breathe almost like we do, their breath holes are in an inconvenient place, next to their mouths. When they swim, their breath holes and mouths are on the bottom of their heads, not the top. Mostly. They can turn their heads better than we can, and can swim on their backs. Not well, but at least their breath holes are on top, then. I don't know how they see where they are going." Kip giggled. "When they carried me, their breath holes were close to the water, even under it sometimes." The other listeners giggled. "It's true," Chobeem insisted, laughing with them. "Watch them. They have to move their heads to breathe when they swim. That's one reason they are poor swimmers, one of many."

When the giggles subsided, Chobeem went on. "When water almost covered them, they lowered the thing until I floated loose from it. It took me a minute to know I was free. As soon as I could swim off of it without hurting myself, or them, I did. I did not go far at first, but far enough. That seemed to make them happy too. My skin still hurt, but not as much. It was like after a dream. I still felt bad, but after a moment, I swam. Away. This also seemed to please them. I tried to thank them, confused as I was. I don't know if they understood. I wanted deeper water and something to eat that wasn't frozen. I did not find anything right away, but later I did. I did not see them again. But there are some good men. I have seen other good men since, a few."

He looked around, and measured reactions. Band was slack-jawed, Kip was chewing on what she had heard, Popper was … upset. Worried.

"I looked for my pod many, many new moons, but did not find them. They were gone. I do not blame them. I didn't listen. I was away a long time. That's another story, as I said. Some terns told me about this pod. Your pod. Our pod.

"That happened to me, before some of you were born. It is why I am here to tell you this story. When I tried to get myself back in the water, it only hurt me. Then I listened. What I heard was that I should be still and wait, and not try to thrash or flip. After that, what else could I do? Only a stupid old loner would disobey."

The other dolphins, even the older ones, giggled. A loner or a stupid dolphin might disobey, and might be stubborn enough to keep trying something after it hurt him. But nobody had ever heard of a loner that was both old and stupid. The idea was impossible to picture. Stupid loners do not get old; few loners of any kind do.

"The only thing I could do on the dry land was to listen, lie still, not injure myself, and wait. I waited for the water to come back, but water was not what came. But waiting was good, that time." Chobeem paused and looked around. They were focused on him.

"I have often chewed on this. It was right for me to wait then. But the most important thing was to listen. Trust. It was unusual for men to help. Others might have eaten me, or made me a slave. I know about that. It is true that people are unstable, unknowable, and attract trouble. I know that. Everybody knows that, but I have known a few good ones."

Popper tried to chew on this. He chewed so hard and so long that he wrinkled his forehead in a most un-porpoiselike way. Chobeem noticed.

"Popper," the old one said, "You look like you've been out on the land too long yourself. What's in your head?"

Popper had many things in his head just then, but nothing he wanted to say. Now he had to. The story had upset him because he still was not sure whether or not it had been told for his sole benefit. It seemed like it was. Whether it was or not, he had taken it to heart.

"I am confused, Cappan," Popper said, using Chobeem's title instead of his name. "The men that helped you must have been good. I do not know if they were unstable, but they did not bring trouble to you. Why do I need to know this?"

The young porpoise said this with so little humor that Chobeem cocked his head. Then he read the reactions of the others again. The older ones had already gone back to what they were doing before the story. One couple nuzzled and nipped in playful, amorous ways. They were not upset, that much was plain.

To his right, a mother and two aunts clustered around the baby that Chobeem had been asked about. The baby swam this way and that, close at his resting mother's side. He did not venture away. The aunts were there to watch, in case he should be distracted, and to prevent anything or any other porpoise from getting too close.

The aunts had listened with intent only moments before, and even the tiny one had seemed to listen, at times. Once, when the baby quivered with delight, it nearly caused Chobeem to lose the stream of his story. He was pleased to see the baby show interest.

The others that had listened were untroubled now.

"What do you fear so much, Popper? Look around you. Do you see fear in the others? Look at Band and Kip: if they are fearful, they have fooled me."

Band and Kip had been as attentive as Popper, and Band had been slack-jawed several times. Now they turned their attention elsewhere. At the moment, they moved a dark green mangrove leaf around in the water with their beaks. The shiny leaf was fresh and rigid. When they pushed the leaf it moved. When they quit it hung motionless. They jostled like puppies with a ball, except they were more graceful than puppies. There was still some puppy fat to their shapes, but they were both becoming mature and beautiful. Popper recalled that they had wanted him to join them, but he had not been able to stop chewing on the story.

With all the courage he could muster, Popper said, "They have no reason to fear." He forced himself to face Chobeem. "You did not tell Band he needed to hear the story, you told me."

Chobeem saw the trouble now.

"It was one we *all* need to hear, Popper. I could have told Kip the same thing. Most of the others knew; we are all dolphins." Watching Popper close, he went on. "I addressed you because you had asked for a story. Remember? What I said is not what must happen, but if it does, you will know. It may also be that if something like that happens, and you listen, you may be told to use your flukes, not to wait. Who knows? The important thing is to listen. And obey. You may need the story one day. You may not. Band may. Or Kip. But if you live long enough there will be times when each of you will have to listen until you know. Listen now."

Popper listened. He heard squeals and squeaks, and pops of shrimps. He heard fish noises, made with air bladders. Peaceful sounds. He heard a manatee grunt, and a motor, going away. He listened to the sounds until he could listen between the sounds. As he did, Popper relaxed. Chobeem noticed. In a few moments he said, in a much gentler tone, "Someday you may need to know more about men. You asked. You may need to know soon. But you need to know about dolphins first. You did not know this story, so I told it. I was not lucky enough to learn it in a story, but there is no need to fear it, only to remember.

"Men are a threat. More than when my father was young. You know that, of course," the old one said, gently. He remembered something about Popper's father he had forgotten until now.

"When few men ventured into the ocean, we were glad to share it. We still are. We enjoy their company, and even help them. But more men mean more trouble, and now there are so many ..." Chobeem's voice trailed off, as if he too were unsure about something.

"But before men came to the ocean, dolphins were here. You need to know about being a dolphin, the paths we swim. If you were the only young one with fears, we would just laugh and jostle you until you forgot them, but you're not. You have not had an easy time. I know about your father. He was my friend. But I notice more fearful young ones. It troubles me. I see things you are too young to notice, because you have not seen what I have. But even you young ones, must see we still have little to fear, except from men." He grimaced. "Bad water is bad, but we live where we live." He paused.

"That is another story. Except for man, what do we have to fear? What has less to fear than we do? The great turtles, once they grow to any size, have less to fear than us. Small sharks will pester a young turtle and kill her, sometimes, and turtles have suckers that bother them, but mostly they just feed, rest, swim, rest, play a little—you've seen her. She's secure all by herself, except from men. Men eat many turtles other places, but they do not bother turtles here, except to watch them.

"Except for turtles, sharks, and the great whales, what has less to fear than a dolphin? Maybe crocodiles." Popper looked puzzled, and Chobeem laughed to himself. "Some day ask me about crocodiles. For now, remember this: as long as we stay together, and do the things we learned long ago to do, and listen—especially if we listen—we have almost nothing to fear. What shark would venture into a pod of dolphins? What fish, even of our size or bigger, can hurt us?

"Man can hurt us. We try to avoid them, mostly, interesting as they are. They attract trouble. But worrying about men is like worrying about being hit by a falling star." Chobeem nodded to himself. It can happen. They fall. There is a song. But stars also help him find his way.

Chobeam twisted half sideways, and gently touched Popper's forehead with his own. For an instant, they did not move, then Chobeam nudged the young one gently, with just his soft forehead. Both of them laughed as they parted. Popper felt honored.

"We live with much that gives pleasure and contentment. We have tasks, we do them well, and have little to harm us. We are blessed above all sea creatures, except of course the great whales. Chew on that."

Popper was much cheered by all this. Even though there was little of it he had not heard before, it was good to be reminded. He was relieved not to have been singled out for some horrible fate. That comforted him, and Chobeem's assurance was a comfort too. He was honored that Chobeem had spent so much time with him. Chobeem had touched his forehead as Popper had seen fathers do. In all his life, that had never happened to him. Now it had. In a second he had known a great deal about the cappan, and a bit more about himself, though there were no words for it. Chobeem had been his father's friend, and remembered him with affection. They had fished together, sought mates together, protected each other. Like all dolphins, Popper could hear best through his forehead, and that was what he had heard, somehow. He was sure the cappan knew all there was to know about him, somehow, and liked him. He liked the cappan more than before, knew more about him. It was good to know.

"Right! Thank you, Cappan." Popper reigned in his exuberance and spoke with grateful respect, for once. He liked the sound of it. He was more than a little surprised at the honor a private talk with the Cappan, who now had drifted or swum a short distance away.

Popper watched to see if the old one would nod, or in some way acknowledge what he had said. With a turn and thrust from his crusty old flukes—so quick that Popper did not really see it—the aging porpoise hurled toward him. All Popper could do was gulp. He tried to twist out of the way, but knew he could not. As Popper tried to go limber for a crash, or at least a bad thump, the cappan hit him, nearly flipper to flipper, left to left. But instead of a thump, the cappan hit with the kind of light slap a man uses to brush dust from his hands.

Startled, relieved, Popper twisted just enough to see the old one's grin as he went by. And kept going.

Popper was able to squeak after the old one. He scanned as hard as he could. From that, he was sure (almost, not quite, but almost) that Chobeem, the Cappan, saw that Popper might just become the right sort of dolphin after all.

21
Played him like a fish

The big dolphin with the oversized flukes led Dr. Julian Ping away so well that he did not realize he was farther from Kimbie and the boat than was prudent, sensible. The dolphin swam what seemed to Ping a random, zig-zag, pattern. Almost exhausted, Ping still had the impression that he and the dolphin were close to both the boat and Kimberly.

But they weren't. The dolphin had maneuvered him some distance from both. When he took his bearings, he was at least a hundred and fifty meters from the boat, maybe twice that. He could not see Kimberly, or the raft. Where had she gone? *She should be right here.*

Then he remembered Sarah Cale. Kimberly probably had done the right thing. Gone to Sarah. He had not.

He cursed himself. And for a second, Ping panicked. He had been irresponsible. If anything was wrong, his dereliction would be obvious. *But this young dolphin is such an amazing specimen.* Big, young, huge flukes. A splendid *tursiops*, almost as willing to play as Sarah's dolphin. The whole time he had followed it, at every turn it seemed that it would now allow him to catch hold, as that woman had done.

Almost.

But it still hadn't happened, and now Julian Ping was not where he should be, and tired. He was envious of how the dolphins had interacted with the Cale woman. Jealously and desire to duplicate that interaction—top it, he hoped—had made him forget his duty, which of course was to make sure the woman was all right. He had also forgotten to conserve his energy, and to stay with Kimberly until they found and returned Sarah. He needed to find them.

Sarah is fine, he reasoned. *She was not distressed. Kimberly is dependable. In Kimberly's good care, the woman is no doubt already on the boat, regaling everyone with stories.* He grimaced at the thought. But at the same instant, Ping's confidence, never really in full retreat, began to swell. He began to be a bit angry with Sarah Cale again. He had sense enough to be concerned about her too, and prudent enough to start back. Using the position of the sun and the boat as his references, he swam toward a spot he guesstimated to be halfway between the boat and where he had left Kimbie.

It will not do to return clueless, or to find she is still in distress. After several minutes of purposeful swimming, with pauses to look about, he noticed the big young dolphin still was behind him.

Good, good. Follow me for a change, big-fluked tursiops, there's a good lad.

He spotted the raft and both women as they neared the boat. Kimbie waved. Relieved, he turned toward them. Over his shoulder, thirty meters back, hovered a gray hulk. *Good, good*, Ping thought. The dolphin kept its distance.

22
Men are poor swimmers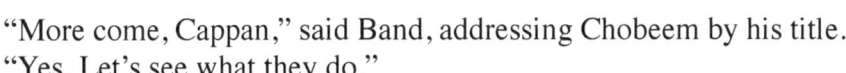

"More come, Cappan," said Band, addressing Chobeem by his title.
"Yes. Let's see what they do."

The two dolphins separated, and came at the two swimmers from either side. Chobeem did not want to let them see him. He had long ago learned that men do not see well from the side. He wanted to watch them before they saw him, if he could.

He saw a male and a female, good swimmers for land creatures. One pulled a small skin-covered bubble.

With effort, with echolocation , he learned that the male was tense, almost angry, but the female was calm. She seemed pleased, was the better swimmer, and kept pace, despite the bubble attached to her. The man pounded the water with clinched fists a few times before he settled down.

The female was more observant, as well. She looked around often, as she swam. Chobeem saw her point out Band to the male, who turned in the young dolphin's direction. Chobeem watched as the female stopped, bobbed and spun herself around, saw him, and swam away, toward Chax and the other human female.

She showed no fear.

Chobeem swam toward Chax too, and outdistanced her. The first woman, the one with white legs, had let go of Chax, but was near him. She put her hand on his side or his fin now and then, as if for reassurance. He did not move away.

Chobeem knew the woman was tired. Chax knew too. As she floated with her face up, Chax put his forehead and beak under the middle of her back and lifted. He raised her until her face and breasts were out of the water. Her head lolled back, relaxed. Arms and legs dangled. Her chin pointed almost straight up, and her shiny hair spread behind her like a black fan coral and caught sunlight in a way Chobeem liked. She looked and sounded happy and comfortable. Her breath came easy.

She even made a contented noise, a hum, like, "Mmmmm." Then she laughed.

"The other female comes," Chobeem reported. "She is pleased. The man chases Band. He was angry. Now he just chases. Band is always just beyond his reach."

23
Aboard the USS Boise, SSN 764

Master Chief Petty Officer Stan Schuermann smiled his tight-eyed, confident smile, the smile of a man who had, over the years, learned how to make a nuclear submarine run better than almost anybody. No brag, just fact. Schuermann knew the *USS Boise* inside out, knew her missiles, her torpedoes, her battle systems. He understood her propulsion and navigation systems, her awesome capabilities, and her quirks. Because of his wealth of experience, Schuermann had helped choose and design her electronics, and had proposed and helped get engineering and command approval for modifications the Navy copied on other subs. Though not a commissioned officer, he knew her every space and what was in it, knew what she needed, and how to provide it. Though not an engineer, he had watched her being welded together, and knew how to take her apart. He could draw you pictures, good ones.

Schuermann was the ranking enlisted man aboard, which showed in the title Chief of the Boat, COB for short. Everybody called him COB (pronounced like corn on the cob). It was correct to say "the COB," as in, "The COB said" this or that. Off the boat, someone from another boat might call him "Chief," or Master Chief, or Chief Stan if they knew him, Chief Schuermann if they didn't. But aboard the *Boise*, officer or enlisted, he was "the COB." No one doubted that the COB knew more about more of her systems than anybody aboard. She was his boat.

It was not uncommon for new crewmen on the *Boise* to be set up by their saltier buddies for an eye-opening introduction to what was expected of them. The drill was simple: tell the new guy—the "newb" in Navy parlance—to ask the COB how to perform some maintenance procedure, and watch.

Schuermann, the COB, who knew the drill, would proceed to describe the activity down to the last left-threaded screw and color-coded wire. He would tell the new guy—the Newb—what he could expect to see under each seal and cover plate, at each step, in amazing detail.

Schuermann could picture it all in his mind, and describe a maintenance procedure as if he were watching a movie. This was a gift, honed by experience and effort. Because he had always been able to do it,

Chief Schuermann's gift did not seem all that unusual to him. But gifted or not, in order to become submarine-qualified, entitled to wear the two dolphins device on their dress uniform, every new guy eventually had to be able to do the same thing. A newb on a sub has an enormous amount to learn.

In the nuclear Navy, the smartest sailors with the best attitudes and the highest test scores are hand-picked for submarine duty. They are trained and study until they can not only do their own jobs, but also the most critical parts of the jobs of just about everyone on board. Submarine-qualified sailors have to know how to operate *every* system, including the nuclear power plant. How to shut down *every* system and start it up again. To earn their dolphins, new submariners have to sketch the important features of *every* system, including propulsion, weapons, hydraulics, electronics. From memory. The sketches must show the location of every hatch. Every escape route. Every control box. Every wire. Every pump. Expectations for these young men—some still in their teens—are high. To stay, expectations must be met.

They know this going in, but young sailors, even some with multiple surface cruises under their belts, have been known to get physically ill as they watch Stan Schuermann, the COB, describe some obscure operation in patient, good-natured, mind-boggling detail. In irritating color.

That the Cob knew all that, and expected them to know it too—soon—hit some young sailors like a wave of nausea. When the crew saw that look on the new guy's face, it made their day. It gave everybody something to razz the newest newb about, something to talk about at chow. It was their way of saying, "Welcome to the *Boise*." In the same sense as "Welcome to the NFL."

The *Boise* was humming, figuratively. All systems were operating within expected parameters, and the COB liked the way they hummed: Silent.

The boat was a day and a night out of Cape Canaveral, on a verification and training mission. Now it was running up the shallow part of the Gulf of Mexico to give the crew more appreciation for the luxury of deep water, as well as some hands-on familiarity with underwater charts, navigational systems and whatever traffic they might encounter. Continual training and retraining is one reason submariners can sleep.

When a submarine is on "cruise control," if you will, it likes to operate either at periscope depth, or else about a hundred and fifty feet down,

just below the thermocline. Thermocline is the name for the demarca-
tion between warmer surface water and colder deep water. Cold water is
more dense than warm water. Heat expands, cold contracts, right? At the
thermocline, the change in density is significant enough that it can trick
at least some airborne detection devices. The density change reflects
sonar waves from an airplane or a satellite back just enough to allow a
submarine to "hide" beneath it, to an extent.

With enough depth available, a submarine can cruise below the thermocline with relative ease and increased safety. But in the too-shallow,
too-warm, too-muddy eastern Gulf off Florida, there is no thermocline,
and usually not enough depth to make the man at the helm comfortable.
Especially not a new helmsman or planesman. The helmsman steers, the
planesman controls depth and attitude, that is, the sub's vertical angle.

The planesman was an experienced hand just now, but the COB had
put the newest guys on the helm today. He always put the newest guys
on the helm and the dive planes as soon as practical. Sweating at the
actual controls in real time is the best way to internalize a lecture, or a
training manual. There's really no substitute, and Schuermann knew it.
Driving a submarine is like flying an airplane, except that no one has
ever developed an "auto-pilot" for submarines. A team of highly-trained
people, not machines, must keep the sub moving, upright and pointed in
the right direction at all times, unless it is sitting on the bottom, hiding,
which is a desperation move.

The newbs were still nervous, but after steering "up" the Gulf
Stream—that is, after steering north along the west coast of Florida,
against and across the strong Gulf Stream—they were starting to get the
hang of the helm and the dive planes. It was sort of like getting the hang
of riding a unicycle. They were not comfortable yet, but getting better.

A secondary goal of this mission would be to expose rookie sub drivers to the underwater turbulence where the mighty, muddy Mississippi
River enters the shallow Gulf. The COB knew that the Mississippi's
turbulence usually is mild, compared to other rivers that discharge into
the sea—the Amazon, for example. But sometimes it's enough to rattle a
rookie. The *Boise* planned to play in that area, dodging oil-rig platforms
and heavy ship traffic off New Orleans for two or three days and nights.
Until the regular helmsmen and planesmen had rotated through several
watches.

Then, instead of cruising the coast of Texas and deep water off
Mexico, the plan called for the *Boise* to loop back south in the Gulf,

along the Florida coast again and ride the warm, saltwater river that is the Gulf Stream up the east coast, back toward Canaveral, Norfolk and beyond.

The *Boise* had a mix of experienced, "salty" sailors and rookies, because crewmembers are rotated. The sub had plenty of old heads aboard who had been to the deepest parts of the ocean, under both poles, and into underwater canyons that are not shown on most maps. Salty guys who knew the paths of the seas. Still, despite all that experience, the average age of the crew was about 21. Guys with many years of experience like the COB were the exception, though the crew contained almost a dozen really salty sailors.

For every experienced sailor in his late 20s or 30s, the crew included a new guy who was smart enough and squared-away enough to get a berth on a fast-attack nuclear sub, but short on experience. These new guys—newbs—were already excellent at their primary job, but eager to learn much more—and had to, for *Boise* to fulfill its mission.

Master Chief Schuermann, the COB, sat behind a third-class petty officer on his second turn at the helm. He made a comment now and then, a correction, or sometimes a joke. Schuermann had been in the undersea Navy so long he had a jibe stored up for almost anything that might happen. Many of these barbed comments he had learned the hard way. A few he had invented himself, as an instructor. He sincerely enjoyed putting submariners through these exercises. Making sure that training actually produces learning was a big part of his job, and he was good at it.

The new guy, Foshie, was starting to sweat just a little, on his upper lip. Foshie was operating near the leading edge of what he knew how to do as a helmsman. This was brand new to him, though he had not yet made a blunder he could not correct himself. He knew tons about nuclear propulsion, but on a submarine, everybody has to learn everything. Everything. Even how to drive.

The COB liked it when a newb was concerned enough to sweat. Especially a third-class. Petty Officer Third Class is the enlisted rank at which the Navy starts to hint at responsibility. Second class petty officers, one rank up, are salty with experience and responsibility. First class submarine sailors are … well, first class, in all respects. A petty officer first class has shown he or she can handle responsibility and is ready to move up to chief, as time and points and certifications and savvy accumulate. This guy, Foshie, was a brand new *third* class, recently promoted from seaman. His promotion had been earned in the surface Navy, not underwater. He was new to subs. He was smart, but he wasn't salty yet.

The COB periodically made his eyes sweep each scope, each LED readout and screen, and made himself think about its normal parameters, as prudence and the operating manual requires. Submarines have to be managed in a variety of ways as they move up and down and encounter changing conditions, to maintain neutral buoyancy. Otherwise, a sub can sink like a rock, or bob like a cork. Neither is recommended. Schuermann often sensed a problem with his hands and feet—or the seat of his pants—before any regular check of gauges would verify his suspicions. Before any electronic or mechanical warning indicators went off. But the COB still practiced the habit of sweeping his eyes over all the control panels in between actual readings. Readouts and gauges (many of them redundant, for backup) covered virtually every surface in the compartment, but because he was so familiar with the sub's systems, Chief Schuermann could sweep and just about know if something needed a closer look.

All the submarine's systems were well within tolerances, or on standby. There was no shipping close. No hostiles in the immediate vicinity, and not much friendly underwater activity, either. They had encountered a noisy Brazilian sub the day before. They knew a Russian sub had shadowed them as they left Canaveral, but they gave it the slip. They had been alerted about a drug sub that might be in the area, too, but had not heard it.

Stationary off to starboard was a surface vessel maybe seventy or eighty feet long, but unless it had big nets out, it was nothing to worry about.

"Opie, have you heard winches or anything from that close surface vessel?"

"Negative on winches," said the sonarman. "All I've heard out of them for an hour is a boom box playing Jimmy Buffett, and people dropping stuff." Opie paused to chuckle, then continued the report Schuermann had not exactly asked for, but wanted. "Hull is Fiberglas or equivalent, big diesel engines shipshape, not many rattles. I don't think it's a fisherman. Maybe a yacht, COB. Plenty of wood and carpet, sounds like. Maybe divers, swimmers, lots of folks. They're taking it easy. Dolphins around, too, squeaking like ninety."

Schuermann wagged his head from side to side a few times, like a bobblehead dog. With his brow furrowed, he smiled a bit, impressed. He could work sonar in a pinch, but didn't very often. In fact, he could *teach* basic sonar, but he continued to be impressed by somebody as good as Opie Simcox.

The officer of the deck was impressed too. The OOD was a lieutenant (junior grade) named Jake West. West was submarine-qualified, but was still accustomed to hearing someone else make the decisions. Right now he was sure the COB expected him, as the OOD, to do something. Though a junior officer outranked even the most senior enlisted man, West knew that the COB had stored up a wealth of knowledge in his twenty-plus years underwater. West trusted the COB's judgment.

Lt. (j.g.) West cleared his throat and watched the Cob's face as he spoke. "Helmsman, I want you to maneuver a loop. Left five degrees rudder, and come to a course that will head us back toward that surface vessel," said the OOD. On the COB's face he saw a smile.

"Left five degrees rudder, then close on surface vessel, aye," said Electronics Technician Third Class (nuclear) Jason Foshie, who hoped he would not be asked to get too close.

24
The pod lingers

The pod lingered by the boat. Chax was sure they should. Grouper abounded not far from here. The pod liked groupers if they were plentiful, but only the small ones were small enough for a dolphin to eat. Some groupers live as long as dolphins, and get really big, some as big as the biggest dolphins. The pod did not especially want to eat them, with mullet around. The grouper near here were mostly small though, and plentiful, more than elsewhere, so they ate some.

Men from the boat swam all day. They took turns, males and females The pod swam with them. Some were old, none were babies. All who swam with the dolphins were worse swimmers than the first three, except for one male. He was a strong swimmer for a human and could hold his breath longer than most. The man's skin was red for a man, and he was strong. One female with short hair and fluid movements for a human could swim deep, with no tank. Swimming with dolphins made her cry and laugh.

These humans treated the pod well. One young female tried to feed them odd things, but the others did not, and she was gentle, almost a child. She was a poor swimmer, even for a human. Chobeem took up with her.

In the middle of the day the pod chased some grouper to the boat and scared them into jumping. Men like to eat grouper and go to extremes to catch them. The pod wanted to see what would happen. Sure enough, one man got over his shock fast enough to throw a net. He hauled the net to the back of the boat, full of groupers, too many to lift. The man was old but strong, they could tell, though he did not get in the water. Netting the grouper made him silly, though he did not let the net go. He wiped tears from his face, happy tears, but did not let go.

That man and the young female that Chobeem took up with went through the fish and put the biggest and smallest back in the water, gently enough that most swam away in astonished delight. The old man and the girl kept only a hundred or so. The pod chased grouper to the boat again, just to see. This time the man caught almost as many, but let the net go slack after he brought it to the boat. Let them all go. He laughed until the pod laughed, as grouper skittered out of the net and away.

The men and women on the boat feasted, and the pod lingered.

25
The snorkel and the submarine

Supper would be late. Mel McRae watched the raft move back toward the boat and climbed to the bridge. Pete Gordon was there with his telescope.

"The trip seems to have taken a turn for the better, captain," McRae said.

"Got that right, suh," the captain answered with real enthusiasm, taking his eye from the glass for a second. He smiled. "Daggone travel poster." Remembering himself, he added, "Glad you're enjoying it." Pete Gordon had discovered that he and Mel shared a love of boats and an appreciation for good maintenance. The yacht captain liked this passenger's easy nature. But he couldn't help relating to Mel as a former Naval officer with combat experience. Captains both, in different ways, but in Pete's mind, Mel still outranked him, so he extended the courtesies.

They watched the swimmers and the dolphins that lingered, unwilling or at least unready to leave. Mel had seen dolphins before, odd-looking pale ones in the Mekong River, and spinners in the South China Sea that looked much like these. He had never seen them this close, for this long, and said so.

Pete Gordon had seen plenty of dolphins too, since his boyhood by the Gulf of Mexico, but not like this.

"You're right. I've watched them a long time in these waters, and you're right, they don't usually hang like this," Pete said. "I've never seen them this friendly. Maybe they like being around ... um ... Miss ...."

"Sarah Cale?" McRae offered.

"Right. Who knows? Could be." McRae laughed and looked to sea. Captain Pete continued, "In my experience, they're not predictable, except for showing up certain times of day in certain places, maybe, if they're in the neighborhood. Some will hang with fishing boats, but you never know if they're helping or hurting. Some fishermen hate 'em, 'cause it's more work to avoid them, or keep them out of your net. Others think dolphins are lucky."

He paused, saw Julian swim to the stern. "Professor Ping, there, says he can predict 'em." A wry grin twisted one corner of Pete's mouth. "Doctor P knows a lot about them, an amazing amount, but I personally don't think dolphins are as predictable as … most people. Less in fact. I don't think anybody could have predicted this."

Mel chuckled. "That's certain. It should be interesting to hear what Ping has to say. And Sarah, even more."

"Right," Pete said. "She's a surprise. I'll be curious what Kimbic thinks, too. Her thesis is on dolphins. Pretty interesting. Their communication. She might just be part dolphin, herself." It was said with admiration, McRae noted.

As the rubber raft touched the side of the yacht, several people reached down to offer Kimbie a hand. Half up now, on her knees, she smiled and waved them away. "I'm okay, just pooped." Unaided, she moved the inflatable raft hand-over-hand to the stern, got out and pulled one end of it up on the platform. She took a deep breath and seemed to relish the feel of the sun.

Kimbie was strong for her size, deceptively so, Pete knew. He caught himself admiring her firm little body and rationalized a bit. After all, he needed to know if she was too tired, see if she slipped or something. She had looked jittery on the stern platform, in fact. Still, Pete felt guilty for appreciating how great she looked. She had to be tired. Her legs trembled a bit.

Kimbie knew she had overextended herself, but this had been such an unusual opportunity, with the dolphins so playful for so long. She realized she was hungry too, and thirsty and a bit chilled. Certainly tired—but exhilarated. Her arms and legs were rubbery, and she could not keep her legs from shaking as she stood. Her rest in the raft had helped, but not much. She hoped Ruth had the teapot on.

A moment later, Ping pulled himself up on the platform and forced a smile. He was tired too, but tried not to show it.

Sarah Cale, on the other hand, was so worn out that she gratefully accepted any and all help offered. Her right hand cramped when she tried to grab the stern lattice, and her arm quivered at times. After she got back in the water to let Kimbie rest she had felt drained, but she could kick just fine.

When Fred leaned over the stern and offered help, she gratefully took the warm hand he offered and was glad when he braced his knees against the gunwales and gripped her elbow firmly with his other hand.

She grabbed his arm and thanked him as he helped her stand. He didn't let go when she turned around and sat unceremoniously down on the platform, bottom in the water, back against the stern. He still held her hand, and she appreciated it. The boat had treaded steps recessed into the outside of the stern, and after a minute she used them, again with Fred's help. She steadied herself on someone's shoulder as she was helped over. Digby, the older crewman, guided her to step on the seat, then the deck, and stood ready to catch her, just in case. He smiled, told her she was fine. Once she had both feet on deck, after Digby eased her onto the white cushions that wrapped around the afterdeck, Sarah drew her legs up and shivered. Her pale skin looked almost blue against the cushions, and it startled her, but maybe it was her iridescent swimsuit. From the bridge, Pete was a little concerned.

"Do you speak Dolphinese, or something?" asked Sherry McRae, deadpan, as she wrapped Sarah in a big towel and rubbed her back. Sarah shook her head. Everyone who had crowded into the rear deck area laughed, and so did Sarah, as she snuggled into the thick towel.

Kimbie handed the line tied to the inflatable to Digs, who hauled it forward to hoist it aboard. Then she stepped over the stern, sat next to Sarah and rubbed her shoulders and arms through the towel. When her own arms started to cramp, she asked Melody to take over. The young girl did, with enthusiasm. Ping lingered on the wooden stern grid without climbing aboard, spent. Digs offered a hand. Julian shook his head and looked away.

"She must speak something," Kimbie said, pleasantly, as she stood and rubbed herself with a thick towel Ruth brought, wrapped it around herself like a sarong and sat back down. Ruth nodded, rubbed Kimbie's upper arms to warm them and listened. After a few deep breaths, Kimbie said, "I've never in my life seen dolphins hang out like that … that long, and stay that interested. I've swum with them … near them … I don't know how many times, maybe hundreds, but I've never seen anything like it." There was a question implied in her comment.

Heads were nodding, and all eyes were on Sarah.

"I can't explain it," Sarah said, moving her shoulders around, shivering, hugging herself, enjoying the return of sensation in her arms. She thanked Melody, took a big breath and let it out. "But I loved it. When I saw him, I went in without thinking. I shouldn't have, and I'm sorry if I worried anybody. 'Specially the captain. I should have said something.

I thought he would swim away. He didn't, of course, he let me grab his fin. Then it was too late to tell anybody."

Kimbie thought about a 'swim with a buddy' lecture. *Not right now.*

"And you were off. Simple as that," said Bridget Strewsberry-D'Mer, questioning and accepting at the same time.

"I guess," said Sarah, who was really tired, but also excited. "He took me to the others. It seemed like they wanted to stay with us."

"They're still here," said Chip, gesturing with his head. His pony-tail underlined the comment as he turned to make sure. The two dol-phins that had followed the raft, and the one that followed Ping, hovered twenty feet away. Everyone could hear them chuff air and squeak now and then. One circled and jumped.

"I think somebody should get in the water with them," said Melody Molinari. "Me. Molly. Okay? Can we? Now?" Molly was a nickname she no longer knew whether she liked or not. No one had heard it until now.

Mel McRae laughed. "Indeed, Molly. Somebody." He looked around at the rose-tinted evening sky, breathed in the damp salt air, smiled at his pretty wife and mentally congratulated himself on being here. "What about it, Miss Kimbie?"

Ping was about to say something, judging from the way he pushed out his chest, but he hesitated. Kimbie nodded and winked at Mel. "As long as she's got a buddy with her that sticks real close," she said, giving Molly a serious look. "A *human* buddy."

Julian might be ticked off because she had taken the initiative, but hadn't he screwed up, forgotten about Sarah? The passengers might not want to hear from him just now. She was afraid he might take it out on them. This didn't happen every day and was just too good to miss. Ping surprised her by saying, mildly, "Certainly. With a buddy, as you say."

"I'm sorry about that," said Sarah, hangdog, looking at Kimbie. "I won't go without a buddy again." Ping nodded, silent.

"Bridget, you might miss tea time," Kimbie said, as she looked hopefully at Ruth, who smiled and headed for the galley. "But would you and Molly like to see if they'll swim with you? Seems you're both eager."

"Absolutely!" Bridget said, amazed to hear the word jump out of her mouth. Molly decided she really liked her nickname, if someone as cool as Kimbie used it. She nodded half a dozen times, eyes wide, a huge grin spread across her whole face. Kimbie smiled at Ping, who made himself smile. *Good boy*, she thought.

Ping had not quite figured out what his reaction should be to whatever was going on. The big dolphin had eluded him. He was chastened from forgetting Sarah, almost embarrassed. *This is a bit unlike Kimberly*, he mused to himself. *And not entirely a bad thing.*

"I'd tell you to slip in the water quietly any other time," Kimbie said. "But it doesn't seem to matter today. Go for it."

Bridget and Molly put on inflatable vests, climbed over the stern, sat on the mahogany grid and pulled on flippers and masks. They took no chances, eased into the water as they had been shown, and made no splash at all.

Chip leaned over the gunwales to help. There was teasing in Kimbie's voice when she said, "Two guys can get ready to go next, but they seem to prefer *girrrls* just now." She winked at Ping, who looked pained. *Good.* Obviously, his dolphin had not liked him as much as hers or Sarah's had liked them, and she couldn't resist. He had managed to do several things he always told the "untrained observers" never to do.

26
I believe you dropped this

Bridget and Molly breast-stroked in the direction of the dolphins, slow, as quiet as they could, and tentative. The dolphins took no apparent notice. Even with masks on, snorkels dangling, you could see that both young women were ecstatic. Molly put her snorkel in her mouth, but began to giggle and almost choked. "I can't help it," she said, as she shook water from it. "This is just so cool."

Bridget, who had been intense and serious about everything until now, laughed. "I know; I can't stand it." She put her head under water and laughed again. Bubbles collected around her ears.

"She's really enjoying this," Chip said to Digs as they watched from twenty yards back. "She hasn't laughed like that in forever." Digs grinned like a wolf. Chip grinned back.

When Bridget kept her face in the water, Molly decided to see how things looked. With beginner's luck, she kicked her flippers up and submerged like a pro. She was amazed to see that dolphins were watching. She was even more amazed at their size: huge! They had not looked this big from the boat.

Fear seized her, but then she reminded herself, wordless, "What do I have to be afraid of?" And answered with: "Nothing. These guys are nice. They were nice to Kimbie and Sarah." The smaller of the closest dolphins edged toward her. She glanced at her new dive watch, which showed 5:15, and noticed goose bumps on her arm, even in water that felt kind of warm. The dolphin came closer, tentative, slow, and she tried to swim toward it.

But when she kicked Molly went straight to the surface, which was not what she had wanted to do. She shook her head and took a breath, pushed at the water with her hands, bobbed up and sank. No points for style, but it was sort of effective. On the second try, she got far enough down to swim toward the small dolphin, which was actually a little shorter than she was, counting her flippers. It didn't scare her.

The dolphin turned on its side and swam by with its belly toward her. Molly turned her head to watch it, felt water rush into her left ear, and winced. The dolphin turned. Its eye looked straight at her ear. It edged closer. Out of the corner of her eye Molly could see its tail flukes move, but that was all. The dolphin came right up to her ear and she stared into its beautiful eye. Her stomach growled. She hadn't eaten since lunch, and not much then, because she wanted to be able to go in the water at the first opportunity.

Her dolphin friend immediately turned his attention to her belly, and let out a squeal of bubbles. The sound reminded her of a friend at school who always teased her when her stomach rumbled. Which it did often. Was the dolphin teasing?

The dolphin put its nose, or mouth—anyway its front part, beak or whatever—right on her belly and pushed. Molly tensed, but the dolphin didn't push hard, and then it eased off. This dolphin was kind of beat up, she noticed. It had old, smoothed-over, grayish scars. Under its chin were what looked like scuffs, and it had what looked for the world like stretch marks. Maybe it was a mommy.

She giggled, nervous, this time with only a few bubbles. The dolphin squeak sounded a bit like the giggle.

Molly couldn't believe her ears. Or her eyes. *How cool is this!* She looked around for Bridget. Bridget, underwater, close, held out her hands, palms up, in disbelief, astonishment. Her eyes looked huge inside her yellow mask, and she swam toward Molly. As Bridget neared, the battle-scarred dolphin swam around her, but returned to Molly. Molly was fascinated, but she needed air. When she surfaced, she forgot to clear the snorkel, sucked seawater in, and choked. She coughed and gasped and tore the mask and attached snorkel from her face. The mask floated a few seconds, then drifted down into Bridget's field of vision. Bridget started toward it, but she also saw Molly kicking and thrashing. As an experienced, certified diver, Bridget knew when someone was in trouble and kicked to the surface to help.

Molly was trying to tread water and clear her windpipe, still half choked. She needed a good breath but couldn't manage one. Bridget calmly told Molly to relax, got behind her and pushed her up above the surface a bit, which helped everything. When Molly quit coughing and could breathe well enough to float, Bridget showed her how to blow air into her buoyancy vest. Soon they both bobbed like corks, faces well clear of the water. They were maybe forty yards from the boat.

The small dolphin still swam around them, close, slow, sometimes on the surface, sometimes below. Bridget encouraged the young girl to rest and practice blowing air into her vest and letting it out, which she did. The vest wasn't adjusted just right, and Bridget helped Molly with that, too.

Once Molly was comfortable, and calm, Bridget said, "I'll try to get your mask," and dove. She wasn't optimistic. The water had to be several hundred feet deep. Still, she started down.

So did the dolphin. It matched Bridget's progress as she swam down thirty, forty, fifty feet. Bridget was a good free diver and could have gone deeper, even without weights, but with no mask in sight—and no bottom in sight, either—she leveled off. The dolphin stopped too, and looked at her. She decided to go just a little deeper, though visibility was decreasing.

The dolphin followed, but Bridget couldn't see anything, so she pointed down, and looked at the dolphin. She wondered …

But her lungs had had enough, and she began to swim toward the light, as slow as she could. She exhaled and tried to follow the bubbles up, tried to stay even or behind them, they way she had been taught. At this depth, pressure wasn't really an issue, but a good habit is a good habit.

At the surface, Bridget found Molly bobbing and now comfortable. The boat seemed farther away.

"Kimbie yelled and asked if we were okay," Molly reported, after Bridget pushed her mask up. "I told her we were. I didn't think we wanted to stop yet." Molly smiled. It was a question. Bridget nodded, waved to the boat, saw a wave back, and touched her hand to the top of her head, the diver's "OK" sign.

Kimbie waved again, and made exaggerated nods.

"I didn't get your mask," Bridget said, making a sad face. "It's gone. We'll have to take turns, unless we go back."

"Okay," Molly said in a brave little voice. She tried to smile. "It was Kimbie's mask, though. Mine leaked. Do you think she'll be mad?"

"I don't think so. You could offer to pay for it. I saw a trunk full of masks and stuff. She'll be fine. You can use mine while I rest."

But as Bridget started toward her, a bright blue mask and snorkel popped to the surface a few feet away, followed by the small, scarred dolphin. Then they vanished again.

Bridget and Molly looked at each other, wide-eyed, too startled to speak. Bridget pulled her mask down and dove.

Just below the surface she found the dolphin, with the mask in its teeth. She approached slow. The dolphin waited, and let her reach out and touch the mask, let her grip it.

But that was all. Bridget had a good grip, but so did the dolphin. After a ten-second standoff, she tried to pull. That was a mistake, because the dolphin pulled back, and it was no contest. They descended ten feet in a headlong rush. Bridget didn't want to tear the mask, or be dragged deeper, so she let go and surfaced.

"It won't let go," she gasped, just as the dolphin surfaced again, closer to Molly this time. The mask and snorkel were still in its mouth.

"There you are," Molly said, her voice so full of happiness it squeaked. "You brought me my mask, didn't you? Thank you so much." She extended her hand.

Molly had to dog-paddle to get to the dolphin and the mask. When she did, the dolphin released it without a struggle, and squealed.

Molly squealed back, a delighted mix of giggles and squeals, and patted the dolphin on its soft, rounded head, avoiding its eye and mouth.

"Now I won't get in trouble, and I won't have to waste any more of my daddy's money," she said, mostly to the dolphin.

"It knew it was yours," Bridget said, astonished.

Molly didn't seem to hear. Her cheek was against the side of the dolphin's head, but she beamed. The dolphin grinned too, or so it seemed. Bridget wished for a camera, and tried to memorize the scene. She could not remember when she had been this happy. Some of the salt water in her eyes might be tears. She turned to the boat, saw Chip lean out of it, holding binoculars, and waved. He waved back.

Molly adjusted the mask, put it on, and submerged. "No leaks," she reported happily when she surfaced. "I wonder if Kimbie would sell me this mask? This is just too cool."

After Molly let air out of the vest, they realized several dolphins were still nearby, and approached them. One showed polite interest. The small, scarred one had not strayed from Molly.

The dolphin Bridget approached did not allow itself to be touched, though touching did not seem to bother Molly's small dolphin at all. So Bridget stayed close to Molly and watched everything. When they dove, the younger dolphin followed.

That went on until all the dolphins—these two and others—turned as if they heard something. Molly and Bridget looked in the direction they looked, but she saw only a big cluster of dark blue, velvety-looking fish with purple fins, below them. The farther Molly tried to look, the more the light green water darkened.

Her beating heart reminded her of her need to breathe, so Molly surfaced, blowing bubbles on the way. Bridget surfaced, made sure Molly was okay and swam in a circle, face-down, while she breathed a half-dozen good deep breaths. Then she spit out the snorkel and dove. Bridget was a strong swimmer. She had held a SCUBA card for years, but she had hung back until now, watching Molly and the small dolphin. Watching them was pure delight. She frog-kicked down to where the dolphins hovered. They still gave their attention to whatever it was they heard, or saw. She looked in the direction they looked, but could see nothing, hear nothing.

The dolphins' mood seemed to have changed. She swam to where two of them hung motionless. They took casual notice but that was all. They were only interested in whatever they were looking at, or looking for.

Making the most of it, she studied them.

One was big and scarred. He was maybe the one that had pulled Sarah around. The other was even bigger, younger. A wide, faint band of pigment a different shade from the rest of its skin ran most of the dolphin's length. He was really something. He had to be a "he," she decided, because he was so big. His tail flukes were massive. He was really beautiful. Then there was the small, scarred one that had swum with Molly. It didn't look young. He looked like a "he," too. All three did. So watchful. They all were, but the scarred ones, big and little, seemed more so. They moved as if whatever they expected was closer. All of them moved their heads up and down, and slightly to the left. She didn't understand it.

Then she saw a shape, coming their direction. It got bigger until it was huge! A huge, dark ... shark! ... or whale! Deeper than they were, and fast. A huge black ... but no, it wasn't a whale either. It was a submarine!

Her heart raced! She could hardly believe her eyes. A submarine! Bridget turned her head to see if Molly was behind her, but she wasn't. Unless Bridget's eyes were deceiving her, at least a hundred feet below her, and maybe a couple hundred feet away, she saw a submarine.

Really. Her heart still raced. She had not quite gotten over her initial terror. It had looked to be the biggest shark she had ever seen. And she had been prepared to believe it was a whale for a second, until she saw the flat top of the … whatever it was, the part that sticks up from the main part of a submarine. Where the periscopes are, she supposed. Wow! The water was darker below, but clear enough to see it. And then it was gone. No numbers, no flags, nothing to distinguish it from the whale she had thought it was—except for that flat-topped thing. It had stubby rigid fins at the back end—submarine fins—and a round collar-like thing too. Where the propeller must be.

Now it was gone. Now she heard—no, felt—movement in the water. It hit her with force. It tumbled her around and left her even more startled.

Still stunned, she swam down in the direction she had seen it go. She expected to see … what? Bubbles? There were none. Perhaps it had been farther away than she thought. It had been a submarine, though, even if it made no noise, no bubbles. She hadn't seen a propeller either, but she was sure. She had felt the surge.

Or was she sure? Were there whales in the Gulf of Mexico? She hadn't heard about them. This one, if it was a whale, was huge, and the wrong shape. Pretty much the shape of a cigar, or a torpedo. Wasn't the Gulf was too shallow for whales? Too warm? Wouldn't it be too shallow for a submarine?

The dolphins were no longer as interested, though they were still more or less pointed in the direction that the submarine had gone.

At least they saw it too.

Realizing how much she needed air, Bridget surfaced. She had swum away from Molly. The dolphins followed her up. *Nice of them.*

"Chipper!" she yelled, and waved, and saw him wave back. Molly yelled too. Molly had worried when Bridget stayed down so long. She was ready to go back to the boat. Bridget started to tell Molly what she had seen, but panicked. They were never going to believe her.

Never.

Despite being almost humorless much of the time, Bridget was not always taken seriously. It was something about her attitude, her voice, her blonde hair or something. Whatever it was, lots of times she could say the most serious, real things, and people would laugh, or just keep talking as if she hadn't said them. Not Chipper. He believed almost everything she had ever told him. When they first were together, she made things up to test him, outrageous things. Even when he was skeptical, he had paid attention. To them and to her. She loved him for it.

Chipper would believe her, but was it worth it to tell the others? Would they even believe the dolphin had fetched Molly's mask? Well, yes, they would believe that, but only because of Molly. But a submarine?

In a second, she decided it was not worth being doubted. She would tell Chip when they were alone. They started back.

27
Pirates

"Fancy boats. Fancy women. We just watch. We could take any of them. *Easy*. Makes me wanta puke." The voice was bored, even whiny, but had a tinge of menace. "High-dollar boats full of money, women, drugs—rich people have *good* drugs, man—fancy liquor. Babes half-naked, supermodels, am I right? Everything, man. Some with wicked security, yeah, but some with none, or almost. When do we get off our butts? Watchin' the candy go by is *killin'* me."

Ricky's comment had been made into the air. It was not addressed to anyone in particular. Salazar almost laughed at him. Instead, he spit. Teddy actually did laugh, but he laughed at everything. Claiborne Chandler knew the comment was just short of a challenge. Eventually Ricky would go off in his face.

Claiborne's crew had everything they could need for a while—food, beer, fuel, spares, nose candy in Ricky's case, whether they turned a hand or not. They had no real complaints, but the natives were getting restless, some of them. It had been months since they had taken a boat.

They got a good price for the last one. Taken in plain sight, right under the man's nose. In Miami, people mind their own business. Ricky was right about that one. It had in fact been easy. There had not been enough mayhem for Ricky, but plenty enough drama for the rest, even Teddy. This boat, the one they lived on now, Claiborne had actually bought with the proceeds from that one. The price was a steal, for a reason, and this boat didn't sparkle like some they saw. But it was big enough, new enough, reliable enough, well provisioned, decently equipped. Its papers were impeccable. They were fakes, but any harbor cop would think they were unremarkable, and in order.

As for money, Claiborne could mentally count about twenty thousand U.S. dollars he had stashed various places on the boat. He had almost that much more in various kinds of island money. Some was locked in his safe. Some was even in a bank. He spent as their needs arose. The crew didn't have to worry about fuel or food. Nobody was suffering.

But the crew might not see it that way. Ricky didn't. Claiborne knew, more or less, that each of them had a few hundred or a few thousand—tops. Tucked in the bottom of sea bags, or otherwise hidden on board. Salazar probably had the most. Teddy and Ricky had the least. Not enough left to feel rich, not enough to impress any ladies they wanted to impress, next time they had a chance. Salazar didn't seem to need money, but held onto it. Teddy didn't need money either, not really. He gave his money away and didn't miss it, or so it seemed. Money went right up Ricky's nose. He, most of all, wanted to take another boat, to replenish his personal stores. And to relieve the boredom, if you got down to it. For the rush. Stealing was a rush to Ricky. Teddy could take it or leave it, but he got swept along sometimes. Salazar did not need the rush. Robbery on the seas was the life he had chosen.

Claiborne saw no need to steal for a rush. He liked to laze around the Gulf or Caribbean, snorkel, spear some fish or net them, cook them, eat them. Sometimes he liked to sit in a dockside restaurant and talk deals, tell lies, maybe hustle a game of golf. Or a boat. He could wait. He liked ease as much as he liked the rush of stealing. He could afford this attitude: his share was the biggest. He was good with money, too, and held on to it.

But then, Claiborne was smarter. He thought ahead, was quicker to act, when the chips were down. He saw the moment coming, too. That was why he was leader, why this was his boat. If he could keep it. That meant he had to keep the crew happy, within reason.

The paperwork said the boat was registered in Panama, but it had no name or home port on its stern. The name on the title was a corporate fiction, the address a mail drop, though Claiborne had bank letters of credit that said otherwise, and business cards with gold print. He could sell the boat anywhere, except maybe Panama. It didn't look that great, but good enough. He could sell it if need be. On the other hand, if the boat were abandoned or seized, the prepaid mail drop would be the end of the paper trail. No federal agent, no island police inspector, would track it to him.

Possession, they say, is nine-tenths of the law. So in reality, the boat was the possession and domain of Claiborne Chandler, and his home, just now. It had not always been thus. Claiborne had once been an altar boy up in Alabama. The silver spoon he was born with had chafed, as had the life his family had planned for him. Their plan included helping run two textile mills, a furniture factory, an oil distributorship and a large, showplace farm, known for purebred cattle and Arabian horses. And responsibility.

The last time he had run away from military school, Claiborne headed to New Orleans with two thousand dollars in birthday money. He returned home a year later with an unregistered airplane. The private school didn't want him back. Claiborne's aunt was on the local school board, but she thought some other solution might be best. He was sent to work on an uncle's ranch in Colorado. By fall, the uncle had used up years of goodwill and a chunk of cash to keep Claiborne from being killed, castrated or jailed.

Claiborne came home. His father and mother tried to find ways to keep him busy, but when he left again, nobody was too unhappy about it. His father had always warned Claiborne against falling in with the wrong crowd, but when it happened, he seemed to have found his element. The instincts and intelligence that had brought the Chandlers and Claibornes to prominence and gotten them through the Civil War and the difficult years afterward turned out to be helpful in his chosen field.

Claiborne's gift was his ability to size people up. He could find a weakness, and find ways to get almost anyone to like and trust and sometimes even feel obligated to him. Claiborne and his conscience were not well acquainted. He could have used this skill set in a number of legitimate ways, but somehow legitimate business, even purebred cattle and horses, did not hold his attention. The school board member's husband still thought Claiborne could be a crackerjack banker once he settled down, but his parents foresaw problems.

Aside from his flexible morals, bankers had to show up nearly every day and attend to the unpleasant as well as the pleasant. To be predictable and dependable. Things Claiborne had never got the hang of.

On the up side, he was audacious, smooth, tall and good looking. Not long after he left home the last time, he stole a small yacht, in what the former owner thought was a sale, in a white-tablecloth restaurant. By himself. The ex-owner even put the getaway fuel and provisions on his tab at the marina. The marina operator had taken the man quietly aside and said he didn't think this was a good idea.

"Nonsense," the soon to be former boat donor condescended to say. "This young man obviously is quality."

Claiborne had enjoyed that. He believed he could do it again, even if the Gulf and Caribbean were getting too small for him to count on charm over the long haul. He was next to the youngest aboard, but good with a boat, and the best talker and negotiator. Actually, he was the only good talker in his small band of pirates, smugglers and thieves, but one was enough.

Claiborne could walk in almost anywhere and strike up an acquaintance the others involved would see as potentially valuable. He was well-mannered, sure-footed and still looked youthful. What did not show was that he had lived two lifetimes in the world he had chosen, and had outlived several of his confederates. The crew believed he had killed three Mexican pirates. In fact he had killed one and shot another before the sun rose one morning. He liked to say it had been self-defense. He had once shot a rival in the face, too, but they were both high on mescaline mushrooms at the time. He did not shoot people for no reason.

He didn't use drugs often but he had smuggled them. Claiborne didn't really like smuggling, but he liked excitement and large cash profits, followed by periods of ease. For a time, that side of the pirate business held his interest. But drugs were not his thing. His drug of choice really was the Caribbean, a mostly legal drug. He had smoked marijuana until he found it annoying, because it took away his edge. He had tried nearly everything, really, but so far, all he really liked were deals, ease, boats, women, rum and island breezes. And high-return confidence scams. Not necessarily in that order.

The drug trade was dead serious now, but once he had actually liked selling marijuana to frat boys from Tulane or Tuscaloosa, though the logistics of something as bulky as weed were daunting and took teamwork.

The gun trade was lucrative, but he had sailed away from his only venture into that world when he realized the extreme strangeness of gun people, upline and down. Guns were as bad as marijuana, in that they were bulky and required you trust too many of the wrong people. Worse, really. Gun people were space aliens, once you stepped into their world. Not in a good way.

Once, when he happened to find himself in possession of a cigarette boat, he made a few fast runs to the Cayman Islands hauling men with steel briefcases chained to their wrists. Sent by an acquaintance, no questions. But those runs, though they paid well, were to Claiborne a lot like driving a bus: repetitive, with a schedule. Eventually somebody was going to rob you, or get nervous and try to kill you. After all, you're just the driver, and a witness. He saw no future for an independent.

He still tended to the fringes of the cocaine trade, mostly for the contacts, because his real interest was boats, and part of the cocaine trade still likes boats.

Someday, he figured he might move to Galveston or Tampa or somewhere and become a legitimate boat dealer, if he could get his hands on enough money to thumb his nose at his family and banks. That daydream had motivated Claiborne for a while now, but he was not ready to settle down and accumulate the money. What was the hurry?

Right now, he was too short on cash for a large deal. But something would come along. It always had. A boat, maybe.

This boat had been home for six months. This crew had been with him longer. Teddy, the longest, was a born sailor, the son of a son of a sailor, as the song says. Son of a shrimper, really, but Teddy had got in trouble and left Florida a long time ago, and burned his bridges. Burned down the pier, actually. Without meaning to, which was how Teddy did most things ashore.

Teddy had grown up in Fort Myers, on the water. He was no rocket scientist, but as long as he was on a boat, around his family, he was a good crewman and a nice guy. He started getting in trouble—ashore— in his teens, and it turned out to be a pattern. Warrants were pending in Lee and Collier counties on the west coast and in Dade and Monroe counties on the east. DUI, assault, petty theft, drug and firearms violations. Police in Tampa wanted to talk to him. That was where Claiborne found him, anxious to be on the first boat out of the harbor. On land, Teddy was only a computer click away from jail, so he mostly stayed afloat. He was loyal, not too smart, but good on a boat. Friendly and likeable in a goofy way, Teddy tended to trust everybody, which was not always the best idea along the waterfront. Claiborne had kept him out of trouble a few times, but wasn't sure he could do it again.

Teddy brought Salazar back to the boat. Olive-skinned and dangerous looking, Salazar wasn't a talker, though he always seemed to know everything he needed to know. He also seemed to know someone useful almost everywhere they had tied up since he signed on, not that anything had been signed. Salazar was strong, lean and agile. His hair was black. People had guessed his age from thirties to late fifties. If you pressed, he would say he had grown up in "the islands," but that was all he would ever say. He had an accent from somewhere, but no one had figured out what it was.

Salazar had decided Claiborne was worth casting his lot with because the boss understood money, was a smooth talker, was not especially crazy and was lucky. Salazar had been as loyal as anyone in Claiborne's position could ask. He counted on him. He didn't exactly trust him, but Salazar was useful. He could navigate and keep an engine running. He understood Spanish and French (though he never spoke much of either one), and he was a dead shot, without being trigger-happy. He took target practice every Monday morning, fifty rounds off the stern, popping floating targets. "Monday, got to go to work," he would say.

Then there was Ricky. Claiborne had little use for Ricky, but the boy had a few good contacts in the drug business. Teddy had brought Ricky aboard too. They both had needed to get out of Dodge. Ricky used drugs more or less all the time, as opposed to Teddy, who didn't drink, except ashore. Salazar never used drugs, and was disdainful of users. Ricky definitely did, even on the boat. First thing when he woke up, if he was holding. Weed, speed, cocaine, whatever. He liked to think he functioned better.

Claiborne attracted women, and he liked them, usually for short intervals, but he believed they were bad luck on boats. Any female attractive enough and smart and fun enough for Claiborne to want to take on his boat—and crazy enough to actually go—was the kind of girl who could get you killed, kill you, or incite a mutiny.

Claiborne considered himself lucky to have one or two out of his crew that were relatively stable, but Ricky ... wasn't. Ricky was afraid of Salazar, though, and of Claiborne, who could think several moves ahead of him, every time.

Fear, luck, money and mutual interests, so to speak, held this motley crew together, but Ricky was as mercurial as a squall, and antsy. He was also a good pistol shot, but not as good or as cautious as Salazar. To round out his improbable string of talents, once in a while Ricky cooked something worth eating.

The four of them took turns in the grease-coated galley. Turns in the galley was maybe the one democratic thing about life on the boat. Everybody looked forward to meals when Salazar or Teddy cooked, dreaded Claiborne's turn, and were never sure about Ricky. . Claiborne could live on food that would kill a normal person, but the other three still wouldn't let him out of cooking. Even though he was the boss.

That was the crew.

Ricky was restless. Sooner or later it would spread to Teddy. Teddy was the least ambitious person aboard, and could be talked out of anything Ricky could talk him into. But that would make things tense until Claiborne dealt with it. They had been through run-ups like this before. Rather than risk an actual confrontation, it was time to look for options. Long-term, the best option would be to replace Ricky, but short-term, a nice boat would do.

28
What Bridget saw

By the time supper was ready, everyone aboard was ravenous, and pleased with the day. Digby knew the passengers would eat anything, so he decided to make a buffet of leftovers, plus his special fried rice. The aroma from wok-fried onions, garlic, shallots, tiny cubes of pork and shrimp drove everyone crazy long before it was ready. Mel pronounced it a feast.

Captain Pete Gordon almost broke out champagne, but decided that formalizing the celebration might drive poor Ping over the edge. He had some smoked mullet saved for a special occasion, though, and brought it out, to Kimbie's delight. As confirmed marina rats, Pete and Kimbie both liked cold, smoked fish, 'specially mullet. A fisherman friend at Goodland, Fla., had smoked it just right. Digs and Fred liked the savory smoked fish too, as did John Zinser and Mel. It went great with the rice. Molly could not see the appeal, though she tried one nibble because Kimbie liked it. Sherry said no, thanks. Bridget said it was "interesting." Ruth squeezed Pete's cheek and said he should eat her share of anything he enjoyed that much. Ping always turned up his nose at Pete's smoked fish. Sarah Cale liked it; she liked everything tonight.

The places of honor went to Sarah and Kimbie, and everyone tried to sit near them. Slender Sarah ate like a refugee, though she remembered her manners and laughingly accepted being waited on. Kimbie was still almost too excited to eat. She had to be reminded that her plate was still half full, after she had disappeared the mullet and rice. She talked about how other encounters with dolphins did not quite compare with what had just happened. She spoke for several minutes with a shrimp impaled her fork, poised in the air. Pete struggled to keep from laughing. When he pointed, she ate the shrimp, laughed at herself, and at him.

Ping tried to explain why the day's dolphin encounter had been so good, but nothing was compelling. "We won the lottery," was Captain Pete's explanation. He wondered if his Coast Guard buddy's prayer had anything to do with it, but didn't voice the thought. At Kimbie's urging, Sarah talked about working at a dolphin attraction in college. Mel speculated that the dolphins sensed a kindred spirit. "Or maybe one of them recognized you."

That idea appealed to Bridget, and, actually, to Sarah.

The Zinsers took in everything—the food, the buoyant conversation and warm Gulf breezes—with smiles of enjoyment. Sherry McRae surprised everyone when she carried seconds and thirds of fried rice to Sarah. Molly piled up cushions and life preservers so Kimbie, her new hero, could rest her tired legs.

When Bridget told how the scarred dolphin fetched the lost mask and snorkel, Kimbie said the dolphins obviously wanted Molly to have them. No money changed hands, but Molly's smile was priceless. Kimbie hugged her. No one doubted Bridget's account of the return.

Bridget had not yet shared anything about the submarine, but Chip knew she was preoccupied. The pleased-but-perplexed look that flickered across her face at times told him. So did the way she seemed to want reassurance. Melody, who now asked everyone to call her Molly, was just glad to be having such a great time with such great people. Getting older was more fun than she had realized. She noticed Kimbie didn't eat much, and did the same. She was almost too excited to eat, anyway. Like her hero.

After supper, Mel and Sherry perched on the gunwales, the better to hear Sarah and Kimbie. From there they could also keep an eye on the dolphins. Every few minutes one would blow and chuff. Occasionally one would jump. Several stayed near enough that everyone was sure they would still be there in the morning. Digs and Fred said so, because this interaction was so unusual. Pete, John and Ruth agreed. Even Ping admitted he had never had the pleasure of wild dolphins as a backdrop for his evening meal.

The breeze was cool and steady. Coffee never kept Digs awake, so he ground some high-test Nicaraguan beans. The conversation continued into the starlit darkness. At dusk, Pete turned the running lights on and the salon lights off. Small red dots of light recessed into the steps and thresholds kept people from tripping, and didn't attract mosquitoes. The tiny red lights helped eyes adjust to the darkness too. Soon stars showed bright against the dark blue sky.

No one wanted the evening to be over.

But it had been a full day, and people began to fade. Digs turned in first, then Ping, who announced a big day ahead. Those who had skipped the strong coffee drifted below or up two steps to the staterooms, until only Bridget, Chip, Molly, Kimbie and Pete were clustered on the rear deck, aft of the salon. They were tired, but too wired to sleep. Chip fetched a bottle of red wine and five glasses. The sea anchor was out, off the bow, so the light breeze carried whatever they might say over the stern.

Twenty feet away a dolphin jumped high and made no re-entry splash at all. It gleamed in the starlight, and they all saw the water fluoresce at the entry point. No one spoke for a long time.

Finally Bridget broke the silence with a whisper. "Molly, did you ... maybe, I mean ... um ... when we swam, did you see ..." But her voice trailed off.

They had been over what they had seen and done several times. Molly only asked, "See what?" Bridget strained to see Chip's face. She couldn't, but felt his knee against hers. He reached for her hand.

"I really thought maybe, I mean, I saw something that I know ... you ... um, would have said something about ... if you had seen it."

"A shark?" It was a guess, a good one on Molly's part.

Bridget leaned forward. The others did too, until their faces almost touched. "I thought it might have been a shark, at first," she whispered. Pete almost laughed, but only rolled his eyes in the darkness. He was almost used to Bridget now, but this was a little much. Kimbie nodded encouragement.

"What was it?" Molly asked, ready to believe she had seen a giant squid, or the hole in the bottom of the sea, or anything.

"What was it, Bridge?" Chip asked, in his encouraging way.

"Well, I thought it was a whale at first," she said simply, in almost a normal voice. She took a deep breath, and let it out. "But I saw something that made me sure—and I'm really, absolutely sure—it was a submarine."

"You're not serious!" Chip said, surprising himself. "Bridge, do you think you were hallucinating? I've read about divers doing that. Mostly from bad air, come to think, but ... Really?"

Bridget was sorry she had brought it up. She tried to let go of Chip's hand, but he held tight.

Molly thought for a moment. "The dolphins watched something go by, I know, because they all turned at the same time." She had no disbelief whatever in her voice. "I saw them. That must have been it. I didn't see the sub, though. I can't hold my breath like you, Bridge. But that must have been it. I would have freaked. Are you sure it wasn't a whale?"

"Well, it had one of those conning tower things, on top," Bridget said.

"The sail," Chip said.

"Right," said Pete. He knew submarines operated in these waters, and had learned a fair amount a about them in his Coast Guard days.

Kimbie was puzzled. "Sail?"

"That's what they call it," Chip said. "Where the antennae and periscope and communication things are. And a hatch. Trim wings, too, on some. Trim fins, I guess they would be. Some sails have a little cockpit up top. The whole thing that sticks up is called the sail." Kimbie could just see Pete nod agreement.

No one spoke until Chip asked, "How deep is the water here, anyway?"

"Way deep," said Molly, meaning it.

"We couldn't see the bottom," Bridget said. "Not like yesterday at all."

"About five-hundred feet here," Pete said. "Maybe less. This is the shallow part of the Gulf, not too far off Florida, so it's in that range."

Chip was impressed. "Where's the deep end? Off Mexico, isn't it?"

"Off Mexico it's two miles or so," Kimbie answered. "The trenches south of here are really deep too. And it's much deeper than this in the middle."

"How do you guys know this stuff?" Molly asked. "Like, how did you know the top part of a submarine is a sail?"

"Studied charts. Picked it up," Pete said. "I've tied up next to submarines a few times. Was invited aboard one once, back in Coast Guard days. Kimbie knows because she's a scientist."

"That's so great!" Molly said, hugging her knees. "I wish I knew more stuff."

"I didn't know it was called a sail," Kimbie said. "I have a master's in marine biology, and this is my neighborhood, but I'm not exactly a scientist." She almost sounded embarrassed. "*Yet*. I'm still learning. Someday I will be."

"Sure you will," said Chip. "The captain's right." Others agreed. Kimbie almost giggled.

Captain Pete laughed, a relaxed laugh. After a pause, he said, "All right, Bridget. Say you did see a submarine. They operate in these waters. Why didn't you mention it earlier?"

"Right, Bridge, why not?" asked Chip.

"Well … and Captain, really, I appreciate you saying you believe me, really, I do, but the thing is … um … people don't take me seriously, sometimes."

"Please, call me Pete," he said, and she nodded.

"Would you have believed her?" Chip asked. "Think about it."

"I would have tended to give her the benefit of the doubt," Pete said. "Molly saying she saw the dolphins watch something helps."

"I believe both of you," Kimbie said. "I believed you about the mask."

"It *happened*, really," said Molly, reaching for Kimbie, squeezing her arm. "Thank you so much for my mask. It was the coolest thing that's ever happened. In my life! I could never lie about that. I lie sometimes, but I hate it." She sounded very young. "My great-grandma says God hates lies. Except when she lied to the Nazis to hide her friend. God was okay with that!"

"Wow!" Chip said. "You must be really proud."

"Yup. She's pretty great." Molly sounded proud indeed.

There were murmurs of admiration all around. In a minute, Kimbie took Molly's hand, and said, "I hate it when I lie, too, sweetie. I try real hard not to lie. Your great-grandma's right."

No one spoke for a while.

"Are you going to tell the others?" Kimbie asked Bridget.

"I don't think so, if it's okay. They'd wonder why I didn't say it right away."

"Then why'd you tell us?" It was Molly.

"I don't know. I wanted to. Just the right moment, I guess. The beauty of the sunset, the stars, the dolphins."

"The camaraderie, the wine," Pete said.

"Sure," said Chip.

"Besides, I wanted to know if you'd seen anything, Molly. You were great out there." Bridget reached across and squeezed Molly's hand. Molly squeezed back.

"Can we just make it our secret?" Bridget asked.

"I'd like to put it in the log," Pete said, "but if you don't want to talk about it, you don't have to. Free country. Your choice. I'm the captain, so I get to say." Kimbie giggled.

"Right," Chip chimed in. "And the captain has sort of an obligation to note it in the log, Bridge, to put down what you said you saw, anyway."

"Right, but nobody's going to hear it from Pete, or from me, or Molly," said Kimbie.

"No WAY," said Molly, sounding as if wild horses would not drag it from her.

"But I'm a little jealous," Kimbie said. "I've never swum with a submarine. Sounds scary."

29
Opie hears something familiar

"COB, I'm picking up a motor, well, two motors on a boat near us. I think I've heard it before. I'd like you to give a listen."

Master Chief Petty Officer Stan Schuermann, the Chief of the Boat, was ready to go to chow, but something in Opie's tone sounded interesting.

"Okay Opie, why not?" he said to Opie Simcox, his lead sonarman. Opie was actually Sonar Technician 1st Class (SS) Anthony Simcox, but he had long ago given up on being called anything but "Opie." His red hair and freckles gave him a passing resemblance to Opie Taylor, the sheriff's son on the Mayberry TV shows. Every submarine he had ever served aboard had a library of DVDs, and every library had the Andy Griffith shows.

"What's the deal?" Schuermann asked, settling onto a steel stool welded to the deck, next to the sonarman's ergonomic chair.

"Well, I heard this funny whine. It's not the yacht or fisherman we've been shadowing, but it's nearby and it bugged me," Opie said.

"So?"

"So I checked it against any known audio profiles, but nothing came up. It's definitely twin diesels, but I could have told you that the first time I heard it. I've been hearing two boats, both with twins, off and on for the last thirty-six hours. That's no big deal, but it wouldn't stop bugging me. I know this is like a training cruise, with plenty of rookies aboard, so I tried to put it out of my mind. But at chow, one of the newbs asked about other boats we've served on, and we got talking about crazy stuff we've done, and heard. I remembered motors I heard on drug interdictions about a year ago, little less, when I was on the *Asheville*. There was a boat mixed up in that with twin diesels, Allisons I'd almost swear, and I remembered it had an odd whine, like the one I'm hearing."

"Hmmm," Schuermann said, noncommittal. Opie wasn't finished.

"I don't trust my memory on stuff like that, COB; no one should," Opie said. He looked questioningly at Schuermann, who nodded.

"Can you think of a way to check it?"

"Well, when we surface, I could probably message somebody in Norfolk who could hunt down the *Asheville*, wherever they are, and they might have some record, whenever we would get it. Or the DEA, those guys might have something. But getting them to turn loose of it, and put it on the air . . ."

"We'd both be old guys swapping lies in some bar in Norfolk by the time that happens," Schuermann said. "What are you trying to tell me?"

"Okay, this boat wasn't in the profiles, but I'm ninety-nine percent sure that it's the one that got away. I can't prove it, COB, but I can't let it go, either."

Schuermann frowned—not at Opie, just at the situation—but only for a few seconds. *A drug boat in the vicinity of a training exercise. Hmmm.*

"Let's think about this," he said. "You still listening to them?"

"Nothing to hear now, but I know where they were when they shut down for the night. I can still hear a compressor and electric motors now and then."

Schuermann started to nod. He didn't stop until Opie counted five nods, with a pause after the first three. He was still nodding. That meant the COB was more than moderately interested, and processing. It was more positive than the side-to side thing when he's trying to make up his mind.

Opie had noticed long ago that he could tell a lot about the COB by his nods. It wasn't foolproof, but he had learned that several nods were good, one big nod followed by some little bobbles was most affirmative. Two nods was okay, but not certain. The thing you had to watch out for was half a nod, when the COB almost nodded, but stopped in the middle and looked at you. That was most negative. Opie had never said anything to anybody about it, but stuff like that was his hobby. It helped pass the time, and kept his mind occupied, which is important aboard ship, especially on a long deployment. Knowing how to read the COB had helped him get new equipment more than once, too.

"Fair enough. I'll take your word, for now." Schuermann said. He began to smile again. "You're right: this is a training mission. Almost what they used to call a shakedown, Opie. Remember shakedowns?"

Opie gave a half-laugh.

"Technically we're in pre-operational readiness testing and familiarization." Schuermann almost rolled his eyes. "Our main mission is to get some newbs certified in this and that. But the Navy encourages us to

… um, 'use actual events and circumstances that present themselves to enhance training whenever practical without compromising mission integrity or safety.' " He chuckled. "I think this fits. I don't see any reason not to tell the captain, and to suggest we linger in the area a while longer to take advantage of a more realistic exercise, should one develop. It's his call, but we do have a mix of newbs and experienced guys on board. All of us could use more real-world, real-time training. You and me included, Opie."

Opie nodded. Three times. And smiled.

The COB stood. "Way to listen, guy. Get me coordinates, and I'll pass this along when I go off watch. Be sure you brief your relief, not that I have to tell you that."

Opie cocked an eyebrow. From under the notepad in front of him he pulled a printout, with the coordinates and a brief description of what he believed he had heard.

30
The dolphins bring lunch

Dolphins were still near at dawn. Pete heard them blow and even jump a few times before daylight. But it was raining. Rain fell almost straight down, and steady. The morning sky was the color of lead.

No one cared. Swimmers were in the water by zero-seven-thirty. The dolphins stayed close. When the sun burned off some of the cloud cover, more dolphins appeared.

Ping got in first, but was unable to get close to them. When Mel and Sherry went next, dolphins swam right up, as if inspecting them. Sherry wouldn't touch them, and they didn't try to touch her, but she looked at one, face to face, almost touched it, and almost giggled. No one but Mel had heard that before. She clearly enjoyed the experience, though she had already told everyone she didn't like swimming in the ocean in the first place. Mel touched one, just to say he had. He patted it the way he would have patted a horse's neck, gentle but solid, with an open hand. The dolphin reaction sounded pleased.

When the Zinsers ventured in, with Kimbie and Fred standing by, one dolphin stayed close for almost ten minutes. It hung so close that Ruth touched its side, its face and a flipper. It squeaked in what everyone took for affection. When Ruth got out, the dolphin stationed itself off the stern, a few meters away. Digby sat with her on the cushions, transfixed. "They like you, Miz Ruthie." Digs liked Miz Ruthie too: she helped in the galley, joked with him, and teased young Fred. Once in a while she fixed a meal all by herself, to give Digs a break. He usually drifted back to the galley to "pick up some pointers."

Chip had gone in the water after Bridget and Molly the evening before, with Fred, who was about his age, but they hadn't got close to the dolphins. This time, when Chip and Pete went in, they almost managed a game of "tag." It was random and hilarious, and looked as much like "keep-away" as tag, with the dolphins clear winners. Neither man had ever experienced anything like it. Pete spoke about the dolphins in much more respectful tones afterwards. Kimbie noticed this with some surprise, since he had always liked them. Ping was not pleased. Pete and

Chip had been able to get the dolphins to interact in ways he had not, comic though the contact had been.

"It's not us, Julian," Pete said as he tried to shake water out of his ear. He jumped and landed on his heel, hard, ear aimed down. He wanted to make Ping feel better. Pete knew Ping must be frustrated. "They just wanted to hang out, Lord knows why. They may have liked Chip's goofy game of tag, I don't know. I can't believe they're still here." Once the water drained out of his ear, Pete logged the exact location, and noted the unusual dolphin interaction, as he had the day before.

By late morning the rain stopped. Sarah and Kimbie and Bridget and Molly waited to get wet until everyone that wanted a turn had one. They got in the water as the sun came out, and the same dolphins that had swum with them the day before re-appeared. They acted like long-lost friends.

Which was what Sarah called them, from that moment.

Ping, relegated to the sidelines, took pictures, videos, and notes. He wrote down the weather, ambient and water temperatures, noted clarity as moderate to good, asked Pete for the location, estimated the depth and verified it from a chart on his laptop. Then he worked out the numbers of dolphins, as best he could. He photographed fin notches, documented scars, noted color and size, whether a particular dolphin approached, who it interacted with. His notes speculated genders and estimated ages. He wrote descriptions, made a spreadsheet, and described the types and duration of the interactions in detail. The passengers were happy to answer his questions. They were the 'experts,' in this instance, and this was the kind of para-scientific stuff some of them had hoped for when they sent their stateroom deposit. Kimbie was pleased. It was the most "research" they had done in a long while. Ping was fully engaged, if oddly frustrated.

Captain Pete and the crew postponed anything non-essential. They always watched as much of whatever was going on as their duties would allow, but this was special. As long as they had been taking people out to see marine life, they had never seen anything like this. The dolphins almost showed up in shifts, it seemed, and took turns.

Fred, a strong swimmer, assigned himself to "lifeguard duty," as he put it, with Pete's blessing. Digs said he had work to do, though he came out of the galley to watch every few minutes. For a while Digs climbed over the stern and crouched on the platform to be closer. Pete wondered, not for the first time, if Digs could swim. The old salt had spent his whole life on the water, but Pete had never seen him get in.

Ping had been careful to advise the passengers not to try to feed the dolphins on the first day aboard. Today, as an experiment, he said, he tried to feed them himself. The dolphins treated cold fish from the bait locker like toys, and tossed frozen flounder about until they disintegrated, without eating them.

However, after the sky cleared, the dolphins brought a school of grouper to the boat, perhaps to return the favor, or show what kind of fish they liked. No one had realized the groupers were near until hundreds jumped, all at once. It was so astonishing that Sherry and Molly, sunning on the afterdeck, were frightened.

Digs, amazed as he was, still grabbed his cast net. He kept it ready and used it often. On his first toss the net spiraled open perfect, and dropped onto the mass of fish. When he drew the net in, it worked almost too well. Digs pulled it next to the boat, but could not lift it. He was sure the net would break, even if he could have lifted it. So Fred scooped groupers out with his hands, several at a time. When that seemed too slow, he and Digs let down one side of the net, for a few seconds. Even then, it took all they could do to haul it up and over the side, into the stern well.

As soon as the net was aboard, the absurdity of such a catch was obvious. The whole rear deck was ankle-deep in wriggling, flopping fish. The boat had nowhere near enough bait lockers or coolers or freezer space to hold them. Digs and Fred put the biggest fish back in the water. Molly helped, then took over. On her knees, she worked with purpose to keep as many alive as she could. She acted as if she was having the time of her life. Digs showed her how to select eating-size groupers, just the size he wanted to keep. The rest, larger and smaller, went back in the water. All but one or two of them disappeared, unharmed. Digs shook his head in disbelief the whole time. "Never saw the beat of it," he said, over and over. No one else had either. When they were done Molly gave Digs a fishy high-five and a hug that embarrassed him, but made him grin.

With a somewhat dazed smile, he announced they had more than enough grouper for lunch, supper, and probably breakfast. Which was obvious. He even asked Sarah to thank the dolphins for the fish, only half joking. The dolphins were still near, on sentry duty. Sarah laughed and complied, orating like a Georgia court bailiff. "Oh yez, oh yez, be it known to all present... that the passengers and crew of the good ship *New Delphi*, being profoundly grateful ... and appreciative ... of the recent kind gesture by our dolphin friends ... do hereby offer ... our thanks. Thank you, onne and all!" She bowed to the dolphins. Digs doffed his cap. Molly bowed too.

Pete Gordon shook his head. He had heard of things like this, but had always wondered if they were "fish tales." He was as amazed as anyone.

Ping got the catch on video, but not the jump that preceded it. The tape showed Digby throwing the cast net, bringing it in full, trying to haul it in, laughing and grinning from ear to ear, unable to hoist it. Tears ran down his face.

Near normality returned slowly. The rear deck was washed down. The freezer was full, as was the fresh well and every cooler. Digs knew he could sell any he did not give away, back at the marina, if they were not eaten first. Before he hung his net to dry he threw it one more time, drew it to the stern, nearly full, and let all the fish escape. He laughed like a child, and wiped away tears with the back of his hand.

He had seen something almost like this once before, he said, as a boy, but had never expected to see it again, or to net such a catch himself. Now he had. "Whatta you know?" he said. "Whatta you know?"

Normally a man of few words, Digs sat on the rear deck cushions, something he seldom did, and told Molly about the amazing catch of pompano he had seen as boy. Everyone strained to hear, but no one else drew near, afraid to break the spell. Young Digs said he had been an astonished, unpaid member of the crew on his uncle's boat, right after the war. Pete had not known Digs had an uncle who was a captain. He listened the way he would have watched someone open a time capsule. Everyone did. Digs described his skinny, good-hearted Greek uncle. The boat sounded a lot like the Mary Lu they had just seen. His older cousins, who had been the real crew, were dead now. He looked out to sea and explained, when Molly asked simple questions about his family connections to the live sponge business around Crystal River "in the old days."

As a boy, Digs had been a sponge diver, which answered Pete's question about whether he could swim. When Pete admitted he had wondered, Digs said, "Aw, I can swim, but not so good. I was never good as my brother, or my cousins. Even some of the girls." He smiled his big, wolf-toothed smile. "It was embarassin'... so I asked my uncle if I could work on his boat. I was a good hand, even as a kid. He was glad, and I was glad, and that was that."

They worked up and down the coast, until he lost a girlfriend to a sponge diver who was home more. To get away from the situation, he took a job on another boat. That situation wasn't so good either. Instead of going back he wound up in Tampa on another boat. He worked for several captains over the years, and only went back to Crystal River now and then. He described boats and catches and a wide-open Tampa waterfront culture that was gone now. Digs said he had decided he was too old to be a full time sailor, and was almost ready to take a job ashore when he met Captain Pete. Pete needed an experienced hand who knew how to do things right, and would. They got along fine. Here he was. "Whatta you know?"

When Digs realized others besides Molly and Pete listened, he stopped in mid-sentence. He looked back out to sea. "Aw, that was a long time ago. Nobody wants to hear about that." Molly said she did. Kimbie too. Digs smiled, but turned his attention to the net. He spread and hung it up so it would dry, and nothing anybody said could change his mind.

A knot of people had gathered at the door to the salon to hear. Pete changed the subject. The grouper population was supposed to be way down in the Gulf just now, he said, probably from overfishing. Everybody up and down the coast pretty much agreed that the biggest ones were seldom seen these days, and the numbers were fewer. So did he. The state had new restrictions on commercial fishing for grouper, and talk of restricting even sport fishing. No doubt more was needed to protect them, he said, but here they were. It made him hopeful.

The groupers Digs and Molly kept turned out to be just the right size to fillet and fry in butter with slivered almonds and herbs, for sandwiches or not. All you want. Digs dug a big bowl of coleslaw out of the reefer, and iced tea. Perfect. The evening fare would be chowder, he said. Grouper, but different. "I garn-tee you'll like it." He smiled like he could taste it already.

Now everyone had stories, adventures, pictures, videos, suntans—or mild burns—and big smiles, even Ping. Mel McRae seemed to speak for everyone when he said the voyage was already better than advertised, even if they went home tomorrow. And they had a week left!

In the heat of the afternoon, the dolphins disappeared. They came back though, after teatime.

Late afternoon tea between 3 and 4 p.m. was a ritual to Ruth. The crew had taken it up too. Usually Pete would stop or slow way down for teatime. Fred put the sun shade up if Ruth wanted. Digs often supplied homemade cookies, oatmeal/raisin or chocolate chip, or hard ginger snaps he and Ruth liked. On special occasions, he baked scones.

Ping was hit or miss about teatime. Often he napped, but Kimbie was a regular. Ruth liked for Kimbie, Ping and the captain to join the group "to make it official." She usually asked Ping or more often Kimbie to start the conversation with a mini-lecture on some ocean topic. The serious part was brief. If it went too long, Ruth told a joke. She was not above "knock-knock" jokes, or groaners. Teatime got the passengers to talk and be silly together. Ruth tolerated anyone who wanted to bring a beer; the more the merrier. This time, though, there was little need to facilitate camaraderie. This group had bonded, and chattered like magpies.

When there was a lull, Kimbie said, "Sarah, you said you wouldn't mind telling us more about when you worked with dolphins. I know I'd like to hear about it." Others smiled. Several leaned forward. Molly nodded energetically.

"Well," Sarah began, "as I told Kimbie, my first job away from home was at a dolphinarium on the other side of Florida, after my freshman year in college. I was hired to sell tickets, usher and clean up. All I cared about was the beach, though I was just as pale ... as now." When the laughter subsided, she said, " 'Not pale, dear, fair,' mother always said. I made myself useful, ran errands, got food, whatever. The trainers let me hang out if I wasn't busy, and I and got to help them when tourists weren't around.

"I was supposed to go back to school in the fall, but when a year-round job came open, I took a semester off. My parents didn't like it, but they went along, because I didn't like school much then. Molly, that was not a good choice, by the way. Once you leave school it's harder to go back. Expensive too."

Laughter and underscoring followed. When Kimbie nodded, Molly said, "Okay, I get it. I'm going back." Sarah continued.

"I could not keep myself from watching the dolphins," she said. "And I didn't know what I wanted to study, yet."

All of the dolphins had been captured, she said. "We got two new ones that fall. The law was silent about how you got them then, and I understand it still is."

Kimbie nodded. "Mexico and most of the islands have almost no restrictions, except maybe mandatory bribes," she said. "Cuba. Sheesh." Ping and Sarah nodded.

"I was fascinated, and it was fun, but the longer I was there, the more conflicted I got." Sarah frowned, remembering. "The dolphins were treated well. We kept them healthy, and they got lots of free time in this artificial lagoon. It connected with open water, but a big steel net kept them from getting out.

"The thing was, we *had* to treat them well," Sarah said. "If the dolphins didn't get enough time to rest and play, they just stopped cooperating. Some got surly. We had to have enough of them so that at least some were in the mood to perform, all the time. They like to perform, if they're feeling good, at least it looked that way to me. Whenever they quit, we would put them in the lagoon and leave them alone. We fed them, of course. Eventually they would get bored and ready to work again. To do tricks."

"Was that what bothered you?" Molly asked.

"Partly. What really bothered me was when they would go to the net and kind of mourn. Sometimes a pod of wild dolphins would be out there, where we could see them. The ones inside the net would talk to them, long distance—it was obvious. That was always hard on the ones inside," she said. "Sometimes they would just wail, a sad kind of keening sound, like people sometimes do when they first learn about a death. It would break your heart. Faces around the circle grew serious.

"I remember one of my buddies said once, 'They're not people, you know. They're more like racehorses or circus animals. Sheep dogs,' he said. 'They do something for us, so we take care of them.' I tried to look at it that way. It made me a little cynical for a while."

"They're not people, that's true enough," Kimbie said. "But they're not fish either. At least I don't think so. A little like dogs, maybe. I've known a few really smart, really good dogs. We need a dog on this boat, Pete."

"*Of course* they are animals, Kimberly," said Ping, who leaned against a bulkhead, away from the group. "Very intelligent animals, of course, large brains, echolocation whatnot, but I've never seen them stage so melodramatic a scene as Miss Cale describes. She was quite young, and perhaps homesick."

"For maybe 48 hours I was homesick," Sarah said, and laughed. "I was having big fun, and I wasn't the only one to see what I saw. We talked about it a lot, among ourselves."

"I've seen something like that," Kimbie said. "I sat down on the side of a tank once, when I was an undergrad, and a captured dolphin swam up next to me and stayed. I guarantee that dolphin was sad. It looked healthy—I mean, to me, without much training yet—but I would have noticed skin ulcers, or if its eyes were cloudy. It looked better than most I see now, but it was just so sad, and it let me know it. I sat there with it until I started to cry. I swear, it knew I knew, too."

"How touching," Ping said, with obvious sarcasm. He made no attempt to suppress a derisive laugh. Ruth Zinser never said a mean word to anybody, but if looks could kill, Ping would have needed life support just then.

"I think it's sweet," said Molly. "And sad."

"Right," said Sarah. "I had almost the same experience." A sad look crossed her face. "Sitting by a tank. I stayed until spring. I was a trainer's helper by then. I got some insights into what they liked, didn't like, and could do. She would think through what she wanted the dolphins to do, and try to make it easy for them. She saw obstacles others didn't see."

Sarah's face brightened. "One day she got me to toss snacks to her, little chunks of cheese, and grapes, from like ten feet away, while she constantly looked left and right. She would catch them in her mouth, no hands! Seriously. She made notes. Said she needed to know what the dolphins would have to watch for. People thought we were nuts. Maybe we were."

Most everyone laughed. Kimbie just nodded.

When the laughter ebbed, Sarah said, "I learned useful habits from her, mostly to think several steps ahead. That helps in big law firms." She peered over the top of her sunglasses. Most laughed. This was a different Sarah.

"But by spring, I was ready to go back to school, ready to work at it. I no longer wanted to work with dolphins. Obviously, I don't object to studying them. Go for it. I don't have a problem with the Navy either. I'm sure you know they train them to intercept hostile divers. And let me tell you, mature dolphins can take care of themselves in the water. They're not gentle all the time, believe me. They can hold their own. They're not always like these have been."

Mel and John both agreed. Mel knew dolphins had guarded ships in Cam Rahn Bay, in Vietnam, and had heard stories. John had heard a lecture by a Navy trainer who worked with dolphins at Seal Beach in California. He and Ruth took the man out for dinner to learn more. People who did not know the Zinsers took notice.

Molly asked Sarah, "Do you think that's why they like you so much, because you knew the others were sad?"

Sarah smiled. "I don't know, Molly. Maybe. They sure haven't acted much like circus animals, have they? It seems to me *they're* the ones in charge here." She looked around to see Ping's reaction, but he was gone. "I know it's been more than fun. Swimming with them in the open ocean—with them free—wow. I don't know how to say this, but … it's helped me. Helped me come to terms with that time, years ago. Though I still have questions."

"*Tell* me about it," Kimbie said. She smiled and picked up Digs' basket, to hand out the last cookies. Pete waited until everyone either took a cookie or declined. When he took the last one, wordlessly broke it and offered half her, she accepted it.

After tea time, in her newfound enthusiasm, Sherry went in again, when her turn came. She was agreeable, helpful to everyone, even Digs, a working-class sailor if ever there was one. She was especially courteous to him. When she worked up enough courage to touch a dolphin, Sherry cried tears of joy. She more than won over anyone she had alienated the first days aboard.

The dolphins lingered. Swims continued through what would have been the cocktail hour, and then the dinner hour. No one seemed to notice. Bridget, Molly, Sarah and Sherry dried off for the last time as the sun touched the water.

Ruth, an adventurous cook, was skeptical when Digs peeled small round muscle masses off the sides of the "faces" of each fish and browned these "grouper cheeks" in garlic butter, right after lunch. Around them he made a stew. The grouper "cheeks" looked sort of like scallops, and were joined in a big stainless pot by onions, tomatoes, okra, diced potatoes, chunks of filets and bacon. He then threw in cayenne pepper, gumbo file' and a spice Ruth could not get him to name. He cooked it slow, and supper was late.

A hard breakfast biscuit was dropped into each bowl, "Spanish galleon fashion," Digs said. The chowder was as good as it smelled, and went fast. When it was gone Digs brought out a peach cobbler and vanilla ice cream. All were pleasantly sleepy by the time the sun "burned down into Texas," as Captain Pete put it. Most skipped the coffee Digs made to go with the cobbler and drifted happily to the sheets.

Kimbie, however, couldn't sleep. Her tummy was happy and she was tired, but she just didn't want to go down to the cabin she shared with Julian Ping. He had shown no interest in or respect for Sarah's experiences. He had been derisive and tried to change the subject, but no one would have it. After his sarcastic comment about melodrama he had wandered off. She made no effort to join him at supper and he had not come looking for her. On a small boat, she really didn't know where he had taken his chowder.

She knew Ping was jealous of Sarah, and even of Molly, but could not quite process it. No matter. She wanted to write down what had happened and some of what Sarah had said. No big deal, but it seemed like the professional thing to do. She wanted to remember. Pete kept pens and a notepad on the bridge, where he kept the log, so she climbed up, found what she needed and stretched out on the wide seat to write. It took twenty minutes, but she still didn't want to go below. So covered up her legs with a big towel and put her arms under her head. She could sleep up here. It would be all right, unless the weather changed.

She was somewhere between awake and asleep when she felt a blanket or something cover her. Turning to snuggle into whatever it was, her eyes opened. Pete smiled down. Half-startled, confused, a bit embarrassed, she tried to sit up. "Hey," she managed to say. She instinctively tucked the towel around her.

"I tried not to wake you," he said, quiet.

What she had thought was a blanket was Pete's jacket. He apparently had taken it off and covered her shoulders with it. "Thanks," she said. She tried to hand him the jacket, even though it felt good.

"Keep it," he said, as he folded himself cross-legged onto the deck in front of her. "Trouble?"

"Maybe. In my head, maybe." She made a face, trying to make it a joke. She flipped the warm jacket around her shoulders, drew up her knees and tucked the towel better. He smiled. "Actually, I wanted to write down some of what Sarah said, and what we did today." She found the wrinkled note pad and handed it to him. As he glanced at her notes, she tucked the towel again and leaned against the padded side of the cowl. The jacket felt good.

"She has some insights," he said, scanning the notes. "Interesting. Ping may not care, but I've always wondered what goes on at those places. I've always figured some are good, some not, some in between."

"Like a lot of things. And people," she said.

Pete smiled. "Duly noted."

"Not you," she said, shaking her head, wrinkling her nose. "You're one of the good guys. And you know stuff. Don't sell yourself short. Sometimes I wonder about Julian. I used to think he knew everything. And he does, but his attitude ... lately ... makes me crazy. Sometimes. Today, it did."

Pete thought for a moment. "He's not as curious about some things as I used to think he was. If I knew as much as he does about the ocean and was getting paid to learn more I would be super-grateful, and stoked about these dolphins. Being here, seeing them act like this is amazing. I put it in the log. Yesterday and today. Most of a page. I think I know what you mean. Sometimes ... it seems like he just does the routine. The motions."

Kimbie had to grit her teeth to keep from saying something ugly. She wanted to stomp, and yell bloody murder. Almost. Then a thought occurred to her: why hide what we both know is true? She nodded, then nodded again, and expelled her breath with so much indignation it was almost a snort. "Ya think! Just doing the routine! He's jealous of how much they like her! And me! And everybody. I want to smack him." This time, she really did snort.

She would have been embarrassed if Pete had not choked back a chuckle and nodded. He chuckled again though, almost silent, and shook his head. He was not laughing *at* her, just at the situation.

Pete took a deep breath. "I know. I have to fight against going through the motions myself. I never set out to run an excursion boat. Sometimes ..." He paused and seemed to correct himself. "Not this week, and definitely not the last few days, but lately I've felt like the skipper of the *Minnow*, doing 'three-hour tours' that last two or three weeks."

She tried hard not to giggle. Gilligan's Island and the *Minnow* had not occurred to her.

"Does that make me Gilligan?"

Pete chuckled audibly. "No, little buddy. Ping is Gilligan, though I guess he's also the professor." He breathed an inaudible chuckle. "You're definitely Mary Ann. And Ginger. Both."

"The movie star," she vamped, batting her eyes, posing, trying to look vacant. They chuckled together, if you can call prolonged diaphragm spasms "chuckles." When they stopped, Pete just looked into her eyes and smiled until she looked down and adjusted the towel again. What was this?

After a pause, Pete spoke. "The thing is, if I had a better idea ... if a better situation came along ..."

"Better than partnering with Julian?"

He nodded, raked his dark hair back with his fingers. "I can't see doing this much longer, to be honest. You make it bearable—you and Digs, and John and Ruth, I guess. But if I saw a good option, I'd have to ... well, at least consider it. We don't have a contract. I'd give him notice, time to line up another boat. I feel like I need to tell you that."

She tried to ignore how she felt, both about Pete parting company with them, but also about him saying she made it 'bearable.' Her and Digs and the Zinsers, true enough. But she couldn't. Didn't want to. Liked it. "Thanks. For telling me. I understand. I can't see me going on much longer like this either. We're just too unfocused." She had never said that to anyone, not to Ping, not even to herself. She was surprised to hear herself say it, but the thought had been forming for a while. She wasn't quite ready to follow that through, though, not here, not now. So she changed the subject. "Digs would sail into a hurricane with you."

"He would. Except I'd run from a hurricane—done it several times." He smiled. "I don't know what I've done to deserve that kind of loyalty, and trust. But you're right."

She thought before she replied. "Well, I'd say it's because you're *trustworthy*. I don't see that everywhere, and neither does Digs. Don't sell yourself short. I've heard Digs say you're not only a good captain, you're as fair and honest as anybody he's ever sailed with. I agree. You're the best captain *I've* ever sailed with, for sure, including some good ones."

She smiled that smile again. Sitting cross-legged on the deck, Pete had to swallow hard before he could say, "Thank you. Tell you what: you stop selling *your*self short, and I'll try too. Deal?" His upturned face looked like her answer mattered.

"Deal," she said, quietly, looking into eyes the color of the water in the Keys. She had not expected this. Or to feel like this. She knew she had been intentionally ignoring how she felt about Pete, trying not to compare him to Ping. She had been trying not to mess up a situation that …um … used to be good, sort of, but was starting to seem not so great.

They had never had a conversation like this, ever. Well, almost never. The closest had been on the first or maybe the second day after she came aboard, a year ago. She had been attracted to Pete, his direct ways, his modesty. Maybe he had been attracted too. For a day. The next day he was all business, nice, friendly, comfortable, but that was all. Ever since, for a year on a small boat, Pete had always treated her like a sister, or Ping's wife, or something. Until now. They had always had a good work relationship, but something had changed just now. She was pretty sure she liked it.

"Do you think I sell myself short?" she asked, not sure she wanted to hear the answer.

Pete took a deep breath.

"Maybe. I see you spend a lot of time taking up slack for Julian. Doing more work. Fixing his messes. I don't see you getting much credit, or moving toward being Doctor Barone, if that's a goal. But maybe I don't see the whole picture."

Kimbie looked at the ceiling, "the overhead," Pete called it. Fussed with the towel. Pulled the jacket tighter. Tried to remember the last time Julian had done something like give her his jacket. She couldn't. She wanted to put the jacket on, zip it up and pull her knees in and rest her chin on them. She would fit. She couldn't make herself, but she wanted to.

When was the last time she had looked at the timeline she had made for her doctorate? Goals, lists of things to do to get to the next place. She didn't even know where the timeline was, but she knew she was not tracking. It was in her sea trunk, maybe. And on her laptop. That laptop had gotten her masters degree, but it was almost too slow to use now. Except maybe to keep a timeline, if there was any progress to note. Julian had a fast new MacBook. He had said she could use it a few times, but she could not remember the last time she actually had.

Pete was right.

She nodded her head. "I think maybe you're right. You see the forest and I've been too busy with the stupid trees, or something." *How dumb was that? She almost winced.* "I want to think about what you've said." That's all she could say right now.

"Okay." He seemed deep in thought. He looked up, hesitated an instant, and did something he had avoided for a long time: put his hand on her hand. His hand was warm and dry. It felt good. She took it. Neither one let go.

Pete cleared his throat. "Listen, I meant it when I said Digs and I would not have put up with Ping as long as we have if not for you. Well, Digs would, if I told him we had to. He likes John and Ruth too, but I wouldn't have, if not for you. Do you understand what I'm saying? I'm still saying it wrong."

She did. She was very glad he had tried to be plain about it. "I do. At least I think I do."

"Try this: If we had another stateroom, you could have it, but you know everything's booked for a while, because you took the deposits. But listen, as soon as one is available, it's yours. I'll make it unavailable for passengers. I don't care what Julian thinks. If he gripes about money, I'll make that work. After you move, we'll talk. I wish we hadn't rented your berth below, but we did. You need a stateroom."

"Oh," she said. "Oh." How had the conversation gotten here so fast? She smiled, took a breath and tried to lighten things up, though she really wanted to kiss him, at least on the cheek. "I could sleep up here," she said, brightly.

"Or I could, and you could take my cabin. I've slept up here before; it's not bad, unless you roll off. But that might be more 'melodrama' than Julian can handle."

She made a face. "That made me mad."

"Me too. And puzzled me, after the last few days, especially."

"I wanted to smack him," she said. Pete smiled. He still had her hand, and she had his. Him on the deck, her on the seat. He had to be getting tired, reaching like that, but it seemed natural.

Finally, after what seemed like a long time, he said, "Okay. Now you know. We'll talk tomorrow, if we can, but I've got to get some rest." He rose in one motion, and didn't let go of her hand.

"Me too," she said. She let him help her up, and felt again how tired she was from swimming. She let go of his hand, but not his eyes. "Ping should be asleep by now."

He nodded. "See you at breakfast." His eyes were still locked on hers. "I'll look forward to it." Then he smiled again.

She almost sighed. "Me too." She handed him his jacket, folded the towel, picked up her notes, held them with her teeth. She faced the ladder like Pete and Digs did, instead of backing down like almost everybody else, gripped the rails and looked over her shoulder. The papers did not hide her smile.

31
Dark of the moon

Mel McRae got up if he woke up. Usually he read or worked. But this was vacation. Work could wait, and Sherry, asleep next to him, would wake if he read. So he padded barefoot to the galley in his pajama bottoms, found a carton of milk in the big refrigerator, and went to the afterdeck.

No one else seemed to be up. The boat rode easily on its sea anchor in a slight breeze. Irregular clouds blocked some of the stars. No moon, but the visible stars were bright.

He looked at the stars and listened to the quiet. After his eyes adjusted to the darkness again, Mel thought he could see a boat in the distance. Or perhaps a small island, maybe an oil platform. Something. It did not move, had no lights, and made no sound. Once in a while, a wave slapped the hull of the *N.D.* just right, the only noise in the otherwise still night. Perhaps that had awakened him. It had been a long time since he had slept on a boat. He thought of his plywood patrol boat on the Mekong River, and shivered. Not from the breeze. But the breeze was cool, and damp, so after he finished the milk and looked at the stars some more, Mel went back to bed.

Claiborne Chandler had expected the pretty yacht to head north, but it didn't. For two days now, it had lingered in the same vicinity, maybe so those aboard could snorkel or dive, though it did not make sense in water this deep. He was sure this was the same boat he had admired. He had stood next to it at a marina, had studied its fit and finish. He had heard it start, and liked the way its diesels sounded. He paid attention to its layout, asked how many crew it could carry, learned where they slept. The yacht was worth stealing. It would not be hard to unload, at a decent price. Especially if the parts that don't show from dockside are as cherry as the visible parts. Though it was older, it was a classic example of a once-popular type, and looked almost perfect. Priced right, he could sell it easy.

When he saw it again—or a boat almost identical to it, anyway—he followed, at a distance. When it stopped, he waited, even backtracked a bit. A reconnoitering trip in the zodiac that afternoon had established that the yacht was at anchor, but not in distress, with swimmers out. A dive flag was visible. He and Teddy stopped far enough away not to be noticed, unless the yacht had someone actively scanning the horizon, looking for trouble, with good binoculars. This boat had the same "old school" good looks as the one he had cased. Same lapped hull, very white, same dark decks and trim. Real mahogany if it was the same one. He saw two capable-looking men, or maybe three. The rest looked old, or female, or both. No children. Children complicate everything. Missing children, even rich kids, give the news something to get people hysterical over, which spurs law enforcement. Claiborne would not bother a boat with children.

He did not want to attract attention. In and out, nice and easy, if possible. At three or so in the morning, everyone would be asleep. His men could overpower the crew. Perhaps they would not need to kill anyone, or just one or two. Over the years Claiborne had noticed that the public does not get excited when civilian sailors die. Sailors are nobody anybody knows. Probably reprobates. It the whole crew died it would blow over. The Coast Guard and local cops would go through the motions, but something else would divert their attention away in a week or so. The trail would go cold. The ocean is big.

This boat looked to be well worth the small risk. Get the yacht without damaging it, and leave behind whoever's left in rafts. Unless the survivors were very unlucky, they would be rescued, or make their own way to shore. If not, they would just disappear. Another maritime mystery. If the yacht turned out to be as squared away as it looked, and if they didn't mess it up, he might not have to discount it much.

Ricky and even Teddy said it would be easy. Perhaps it would. At 2 a.m. they idled the sport fisherman in the yacht's direction, running without lights. They stopped when they saw the yacht's lights. With their sport fisher riding at anchor, they paddled the Zodiac the last leg of the way. When dolphins investigated, Claiborne took it as a good sign. At least he did after everybody who thought they were sharks calmed down.

To avoid the chance someone might see them out a porthole or window, they approached from the rear, and tied the Zodiac to the yacht's stern platform. From there they could get to the crew without alerting others.

Ricky and Teddy were antsy. Ricky had paddled all the way, and was still excited. Coked up, Claiborne was sure. He didn't like it, but did not want a confrontation just now, not with Ricky armed and primed. Salazar, calm as ever, had a silenced automatic pistol clipped to his waistband, and cradled his TEC 9. Teddy had an automatic weapon much like it, but cheaper. Claiborne's small 9mm was in the pocket of his shorts, in a flat leather pocket that hid its outlines. Ricky's gaudy, long-barreled chrome revolver dangled from a belt.

Salazar and Ricky went for the crew's quarters, as planned. Teddy, who had amazing night vision and was quiet as a cat on a boat, went forward. The plan was for him to take a position where he could control the staterooms in the unlikely event someone from there tried to help the crew. He was supposed to go topside and take a position by the hatch near the ladder, in the companionway between the staterooms and the salon. Claiborne had told Teddy where and how. Teddy had smiled and nodded. Now as Claiborne watched, horrified, Teddy strolled along the starboard rail past any number of stateroom windows and portholes. He was quiet about it, but sheesh.

Claiborne gritted his teeth and stayed aft, with the Zodiac, as planned. He watched Salazar and Ricky go through the hatch that led down to crew quarters. All he expected to have to do was watch—intervene if needed—and take over when the time was right.

For at least a full minute all was silent. Claiborne had not breathed since dumb Teddy had gone for his stroll, the wrong way. Now he exhaled, and willed himself to breathe. Teddy still had to make his way to the ladder Claiborne had told him to look for, drawn him a picture of. He must have wanted to stretch his legs after the cramped ride in the Zodiac, and seemed to have gotten away with it. Claiborne shook his head.

32
Desperate measures

Something was amiss. Pete could almost feel footpads that did not belong on the deck. He heard nothing, but he knew. Something had awakened him. It made him angry. And quiet as death.

Pete pulled on swim shorts in the dark. He wished for the small Glock, up in the chart box, shook his head and opened the drawer built in under his mattress for his second choice. Under some shirts was a blue-steel, snub-nosed .357 Magnum revolver with dark green custom Micarta grips. Big and intimidating, which was why he had bought it. But he wasn't comfortable with it. The Smith & Wesson .357 could make big holes, but was slow. Even cops used faster guns now. Bad guys used weapons that could spray a boat full of bullets — brrrrttt! — in a second. Somehow Pete knew bad guys were aboard.

A refurbished M-16 was mounted by strong spring-clamps under his desk. He had been able to procure it from the Coast Guard. It was mostly legal. He kept it clean and oiled, like everything else about the boat. The M-16 was light, tack-driving accurate, and fast enough. When no passengers were around, he fired a few clips at paper cups floating in the ocean, just to keep in practice. Getting it out of the clamps would be noisy, though, and it tended to alarm people.

He felt his way across the carpet to the cabin door. Finally he actually heard someone ... something. A creak. Maybe a hatch. Maybe in the space between the staterooms and the salon. He opened his mouth, took a breath and strained to hear.

Instead of another creak he heard a muffled scream. The whole boat probably heard it. It seemed to come from below, where Sarah and Molly and his crew slept. A woman. The scream was clear and terrified. He thought he heard a scuffle, then another noise that tightened his gut.. He knew the distinctive "piff" of a silencer. He had heard that sound a few times in the past. He was sure he heard it now. Twice. Three times. Heard what sounded like a bullet thudding into wood, too. Sweat trickled down his ribs and arm. He turned his head to where he had heard the creak in the deck, before the scream. It was full dark out, no moon.

Quickly he re-crossed the cabin to the long window on the starboard side, and pulled back the thick curtain, just a sliver. In a few seconds, against the starlight, a shape passed. A man with a gun. Either a big automatic or a small assault weapon. Maybe an Uzi or something like it, he guessed. A ring gleamed from his left ear in the faint light. The man strolled toward the bow on the balls of his feet, leaned over the rail. Now he headed back.

Something about the guy was familiar, but whoever it was, was up to no good. It took Pete less time to make up his mind than to say it. He drew the pistol from his waistband and pulled the hammer back, gently, until it caught. When the man was again directly in front of him, Pete sighted on the only target available. Probably the guy's hip bone. He squinted against the possibility of flying glass and pulled the trigger.

The noise and impact came before Pete was ready, but it was done, a fact. Just that quick. Cold, maybe, but he had heard the scream and shots. The small window did not shatter, but the impact of the bullet from the Magnum knocked the man into the water. Pete heard no cry, heard no splash either, only the ringing in his ears. Through smoke he saw a hole in the window the size of a quarter. Rings in the glass caught light.

More sounds came from somewhere aft. They seemed surreal, because the .357 shot still rang. Pete was amazed at how fast he had made up his mind and shot, but he didn't muse over it. There was more to do.

At the desk he knelt and jerked the M-16 out of the spring clamps. The noise was almost insignificant. He stuffed the pistol in his shorts and heard his heart pound in his chest and ears.

He checked the clip on the M-16—full—sent the bolt home, put the selector on automatic, stepped to the window and tried to focus. Gunpowder smoke bit the top of his throat. He crossed to the cabin hatchway. With the light rifle in his right hand, he opened the louvered door with his left. Sounds of alarm came from the staterooms.

Pete's wedge-shaped cabin at the tip of the bow was at the head of the passageway, up a step outlined with tiny red lights. He would have to pass four doors to get to the salon. A hostile could be behind any of those doors. But he doubted it.

He heard a tiny squeak. The door to Chip and Bridget's stateroom opened, and Chip's startled, pillow-creased face appeared in the red glow of deck lights. Chip saw the rifle and his eyes popped. Pete put his index finger to his lips and motioned him back inside. He pantomimed a turn of the lock. Chip nodded, backed up, closed the door. Pete heard the lock bolt slide into place.

The doors were teak, but thin. A film crew had broken a panel out by accident. But locked was better. Pete went to the opposite door and listened. He heard whispers,

"You okay?"

When he opened the door, Kimbie was behind it, in a fighting crouch. Both her hands gripped her dive knife, blade up. Ready to gut somebody. Loose T-shirt, feet planted shoulder width, knees bent. She looked fierce—and so cute—that Pete smiled. "'Atta girl," he whispered. The determined look in her eyes, and the set of her jaw startled and pleased him. He wanted to kiss her. Later. Ping peeped from behind her.

Pete pointed to the lock, pulled the door closed. Heard the bolt slide home.

Wow. What grit! He shook his head. The absurdity of the situation flashed on his consciousness, but he dismissed it. *First things first.*

The Zinsers' door was prudently locked, as he had expected. "Stay put, folks," he whispered.

"Okay Pete." It was John.

At the McRae stateroom, he whispered "Mel?"

Through the louvers, Mel answered quietly, "Yes?"

"Stay inside," he whispered, low.

"Aye aye," Mel whispered back. In the Navy and Coast Guard, "Aye aye" means, "I understand and will comply." *Good man*, thought Pete. The staterooms were secure at least, but it was a big, dark boat.

The passageway ended at three carpeted, ladder-like steps, outlined with more tiny lights. At the bottom was a hatch. Behind it was a small passage. Straight ahead, through a hatch, was the salon. To the left, wood steps with brass handrails on each side descended a deck lower, to a passageway past the engines. Back there Sarah and Melody—little Molly—were berthed in compartments that were nearly all bed. The rooms were smaller than a twin bed, and each bunk had drawers below. A tiny sink and mirror completed the furnishings. Digs and Fred shared a slightly larger space with two bunks. Once upon a time, all of the lower berths had been for the crew, but Pete had upgraded them as much as space allowed. Everyone below deck shared one tiny bathroom, with a toilet, a sink, and a phone-booth-sized corner shower. If he went down those steps now, anyone below would hear him and know where he was. He heard nothing from below. He again glanced up the steps that led to the bridge, and listened. Nothing. The hatch to the right opened onto the deck. He made sure it was locked and entered the salon.

Inside the salon, behind a bulkhead on his left, the starboard side, was the galley. Pete knew he could be seen better than he could see. The salon extended almost to the hull on his right, with big windows along the port side, on Pete's right, since he faced aft. Under present circumstances, assuming hostiles on deck somewhere, the salon was a dangerous place, but at least the wall had his back.

Where was his crew?

Three shots. Digs? Fred? Somebody else? Damn. Pete hoped not. He wanted to hope that the one and only pirate was sinking off to starboard. But a solo pirate could not have made all those sounds he had heard and be where that guy had been. If Digs and Fred were still alive, they would be making their way toward the noise of the Magnum shot. But they would have gotten there by now, probably before he got his M-16. If they were alive.

Digs had some wicked knives and maybe a pistol, but if Fred had a weapon, it would be a surprise.

He studied the salon furniture, the windows, anything his eyes could pick up. There was no one in here, but someone could be in the galley. He tried to use the faint light from stars to pick out shapes against the starlit windows, "winder lights," his grandmother would have called the large openings. Strange to think of her at a time like this. He shook it off.

The rear deck was clear. As soon as he was sure no one was in the galley behind him, Pete would go on deck. He peered under the pass-through, saw nothing, crouched and moved under and past it. He stayed low, crept to the end of the wall, looked around it and back. The galley door was closed, but the shiny deck reflected the lights from the coffee maker and microwave. He moved his head and eyes until he was sure no one was hiding in the galley, then pushed the door open to be sure. Clear.

He took a breath, but there was no relief in it. They could be on the deck outside or overhead. Or below deck. Or all three. The galley had a small window, but he could see nothing through it.

He could wait them out, but they could wait too. He could go back out the door he had just come in and climb to the bridge. Visibility out to sea was great, but much of the boat was obscured from there, except the foredeck, and some of the roof over the staterooms. From there he couldn't see much of anything else on the boat, or protect the passengers in their staterooms. Down here, he controlled—or at least could see—the entrance to the staterooms, the rails on each side, the passage with the ladders, up and down. But on deck, he might find them, or find out more.

Why was it so daggone quiet? Pete edged barefoot to his right. His eyes swept methodically. The most dangerous time would be when he came through the hatch from the salon to the deck and rail. He hadn't heard any noise overhead. He strained again to hear, thought about going back to his stateroom radio to make a distress call. He should have done that already, right after he shot that pirate-looking guy. He could have called it off later if things were secure. But he had just shot someone, for only the second time in his life. He was rattled, and hadn't. He had felt the need to secure the boat. Still did. *Where is everybody? Dang.* Got to assume somebody is dead from those shots. Digs and Fred, almost certain. They might be cowering in their bunks. But that was so implausible he dismissed the thought as it formed.

Pete reached the teak door, touched and gripped the brass knob and turned it quietly. The door would swing away and forward. He drew back the tip of the rifle so it would not precede him. He thought about the pistol, but needed a free hand for the door. He decided to push the door hard when he opened it, in case someone was behind it, and be ready to fire the rifle.

He had almost gotten used to the pounding of his heart, but now his breathing sounded—to him—labored, like a draft horse. The air that roared through his nose was not as loud as his heart, or the blood that pounded in his ears. He opened his mouth to breathe quieter and listened. He felt he should just stand there and listen, and tried. But just as keenly, he felt the need to move. *Damn*, he thought. He flipped the door hard with his left hand, across his body, shoved it until it slapped against the stop on the bulkhead outside and was held by the catch. He stepped out. The automatic rifle seemed to sweep his hand and arm with it. The Gulf was slightly luminous, but didn't help him see anybody. He could see nobody in the hatchway, nobody in front of the gun. Nothing.

With the hatch held against the stop he could look both ways along the deck. Nothing. Nobody. Either there was nobody else aboard, or they were on the other side of the boat. Or below. Or on the bridge, or the foredeck. Just not here.

Pete slowly let out his breath, and listened as well as he could, but all he heard, even out here, was the Gulf and his heart. Waves lapped the hull.

He took a deep breath. Could he smell anything? No.

If he went forward, there was little to be gained, and someone in a stateroom might decide he was a bad guy and shoot. That was probably wishful thinking, though. If he had given the Magnum to Kimbie or Mel, maybe. That would have been a good idea, now that he thought about it. But he hadn't. His mind flickered to the way she looked and he almost smiled.

He carefully closed the hatch and moved as quietly as he could toward the opening that would let him double back forward, or down. And remembered he had locked it. Locked himself out, at least from here. He peered through the salon windows to the other side of the boat. Nothing.

Thirty yards off the stern, a dolphin blew spray. How long ago had he watched Sarah and Kimbie with them? A long time, it seemed now.

He made himself think. Was there a boat? An inflatable? They had to have gotten here somehow. He had not looked at the water when he came outside, and did now. Nothing.

He heard a faint moan. A woman. As he cocked his head and tried to get a fix on it, a big, sweaty arm shot out, from behind, above. The hand grabbed the barrel of the M-16. Pete gripped it with one hand only, like an actor. He pulled the trigger without meaning to as he tightened his grip. Useless shots went into the air. Pete grabbed the front stock and the guy's hand. The guy was strong, but Pete thought he could use the gun and the guy's own weight to pull him off the overhead, maybe over the rail. He pulled hard and lunged back. The arm came with him too, but not enough, They guy still gripped. In the starlight, Pete saw a toothy grin. Up on the bridge, he thought he saw a long gun, pointed at him. Then he felt his head explode.

33
The pod hears, and sees

The pod still lingered. Chax was sure they should. Half were asleep. Half-asleep, one eye open. Grouper abounded. The pod liked them well enough, but most were too big for a dolphin to eat. Some groupers live as long as dolphins, and some get bigger than big dolphins. Others were too small. The pod did not need to eat these, not with tasty mullet near. But these were plentiful, so the pod ate some.

Humans had swum all day. Members of the pod swam with some of them. Some of the humans were old, none were babies. All were worse swimmers than the first three, except for one wiry male whose skin was red.

These humans treated the pod well. One tried to feed them odd things, but she was almost a child. Chobeem took up with her. She was a poor swimmer, even for a human, but joyful.

When the swimming stopped the pod chased grouper to the boat and made them jump. Men go to extremes to catch grouper, so the pod wanted to see what would happen. Sure enough, a man threw a net. He pulled it to the boat, full of fish, too full to lift. The man was old, and this made him happy. Tears ran out of his eyes, but he did not let the net go.

The young female Chobeem took up with helped the man put the biggest and smallest fishes back in the water. She was quick and gentle. Most of the groupers swam away, astonished. The pod chased more grouper to the boat again, just to watch. The old man netted almost as many, but didn't try to boat them. He drew the net close, let it go slack, and laughed. He laughed so much that the pod laughed back, as terrified grouper skittered from the slack net.

The humans feasted and rested. The pod lingered. In the middle of the night, when the boat had been quiet a long time, more men came, in a skin-covered bubble. They came from a noisy boat with slime growing on the hull. The pod listened and watched. Soon a bleeding woman, the one with white legs like a big frog, was in the water at one end of the boat. Soon she was dead. A bleeding, dying man, broken almost in two, fell in, sank and died. More bodies followed. The tough old man. The young female that had helped him. In moments, all were dead. The girl died as Chobeem waited with her. Another man. Sooner or later, men are trouble.

The pod lingered and listened. Chax was sure they should.

34
Pirate control

Mel McRae heard a door slap, heard silenced shots, and a scuffle. Heard something like potatoes tumble from a sack. Like a body hitting the deck. Mel had studied the boat's sounds in the last few days. The door slapped like the port-side hatch from the salon.

This was bad.

The captain had shot someone, or shot at someone, from his cabin. The noise was enough to wake the dead. Mel sat bolt upright, hugged Sherry, and pulled on some pants. He urged her to dress, and she did. He heard an M-16. He had learned that sound a long time ago. Who shot what, and who was hit, or not, Mel did not know. Whether the captain was dead or alive, he also did not know.

He had heard footsteps before the explosion, which is what the first gunshot had sounded like. He thought the footsteps were in the next stateroom. He was surprised to hear the captain's voice after that. Maybe he should have insisted on going with Captain Pete.

Mel took inventory. The crew might be alive, and might be armed. But those shots. The other passengers were not likely to be much help. Chip maybe. He was young, strong, brave, if Mel was any judge. But probably unarmed, just as he was. They had all flown in. The old man, John Zinser, was resourceful and nimble, maybe armed, but … old. Of the women, Kimberly might know how to take care of herself. He had seen her lug enough stuff around to know she was strong for her size, and had the confidence, maybe. She might have some kind of weapon too, a dive knife at least, but she was small. Oh, and Ping. Maybe he had a weapon, but would he use it? Ping did not inspire hope, and neither did Mel's inventory.

He sat on the bed, held Sherry, rubbed her back and shoulders. She hadn't said much. Not a good sign.

He continued his mental inventory. Molly was a kid. Chip's wife, Bridget, could not be counted on for too much, he guessed.

Counted on against … what?

And what should he do? Could he do?

35
'... and his unfortunate crew'

"Ahoy!" A strong baritone voice. From the salon, maybe.

"Ahoy, shipmates! This is the captain speaking. The *new* captain."

The voice was confident, well modulated, with cultured, precise diction. Southern. And it came from just around the corner.

"My men and I have possession ... of the boat." The voice oozed charm. "There is not one thing to be alarmed about. If y'all do not *resist*, you will not be *harmed*." The voice put emphasis on "resist," but drawled out the words "alarmed" and "harmed" with a broad "ah" sound. For effect, Mel thought. Creepy.

"Your captain and his unfortunate crew ... have left the boat," the voice said, matter of fact. Next item. "Be assured that we have *complete* control. But there was a scuffle and I have lost a shipmate, a good man. I am not happy about that, not at all. As a result, you all would be wise to ... behave yourselves and go along with the program. That would be very prudent."

Mel frowned. It did not sound like a bluff, and was consistent with what he had heard. What about the two young women?

"Now, I would like for you all to join me in the salon," the voice continued. "In fact, I insist. Right now. Don't bother to dress, come as you are. Once again, if you have heroic notions ... abandon them. Spare yourselves and us any needless ... additional ... drama. You should regard us as pirates ... buccaneers if you will... because ... we are." He let that sink in.

"You have one minute to come forward with your hands empty. That is not long at all. Don't make us come after you. Your minute has already begun. Count down from sixty. Fifty-nine, fifty-eight, and so forth."

The strange announcement was over. New game, new rules, all bets cancelled.

Mel went to the tiny bathroom and opened its small medicine cabinet. In his shaving kit he had a roll of quarters. Once he had slipped that roll into a sock and used it to brain a would-be robber at a downtown hotel. It had worked, but didn't seem enough in this situation. There was nothing else that might help, not even a pen knife. He and Sherry had hand-carried their bags on the plane. He turned on his cell phone, but the "no service" icon was all it would display. He used the john.

Sherry sat on the bed with a look of stark terror in her eyes. He sat and drew her close, stroked her hair. She was shaking.

John and Ruth Zinser were the first to open their door. They wore curious looks, but did not appear terribly frightened. Hearing their door, Mel opened his. Ruth immediately crossed the hall to comfort Sherry. Kimbie and Ping opened their door about the same time. Kimbie flipped on the lights in the hallway. Her dive knife was back under the mattress. It was too big to conceal under a T-shirt, which was what everyone seemed to be wearing, except Ruth, who had put on a denim dress.

No one said much, just whispers of confusion and alarm. When Mel motioned for Sherry she came forward, but clutched Ruth's hand.

Chip and Bridget wore inquisitive looks on their no-longer-sleepy faces. John Zinser gave them a small smile. "We'll be fine," he said quietly, as he moved to Ruth's side. Mel took Sherry's hand and led the procession down the short hall and into the salon. With his free hand in the air

They saw no one in the darkness as they crossed the T-shaped space at the end of the passageway. Mel walked into the salon as far as the passageway light fell, and stopped. Kimbie flipped on the salon lights and went about the room turning on lamps. They were all fastened to tables or bulkheads. Ruth ushered Sherry to a couch, helped the younger woman sit down, and joined her. Ping took a seat. The rest preferred to stand.

A large, medium-dark-skinned man, clean-shaven, wearing a yellow bandana around his neck, appeared at one doorway, and a pallid, skinny, nervous-looking person showed himself at the other. Both had at least one gun. The first man, who carried a compact, exotic-looking automatic weapon, looked strong and menacing. The skinny one, who brandished a large, shiny cowboy revolver, looked scared, but also cocky, dangerous, maybe a little unhinged. Sweating heavily. The pirates wore shorts, dark T-shirts, and canvas deck shoes. They took positions like guards.

Then Claiborne Chandler walked in, showing no gun, in clean khaki cargo shorts, a black polo—collar popped—and expensive-looking boat shoes. His sun-streaked chestnut hair was longish, but trimmed and clean. Tanned, fit, he carried himself as if he had just come from some fashionable watering hole. His expression said nothing at all, except for traces of a sneer.

Then he smiled, and Sherry McRae, at least, responded involuntarily with a smile of her own. She didn't want to smile, and tried not to, but could not seem to control her face.

"Please, let's all take seats and try to make the best of this," Claiborne said cordially, and smiled again. Chip and Bridget sat, though John Zinser and Mel did not. Nor did Kimbie, who wore an intense expression they had not seen before. She seemed relaxed, though. Ping looked as if he might become ill, but still carried himself with his customary confidence.

"Now then," the smiling pirate began. "Your situation. We are going to keep this boat, and anything of value on it. We have *already* taken it. Your crew ... has prudently abandoned ship," he said, without a trace of irony. He clinched his jaw for a second, and a look of dread (or was it distaste?) flicked across his face, only to be replaced by a cold, determined look. "The captain as well. I believe."

Kimbie's face did not move, but she went pale despite her tan. Ping looked down.

"But enough history," the polo-wearing pirate said, all business. Next item.

"You people present a problem, but it need not be an ... *insurmountable* one." He spoke carefully, paused and looked from face to face, eye to eye, and smiled with what had to be menace. "That is, if you cooperate. Completely. I sincerely hope you will. For your sakes."

He paused long enough for them to think, and was about to speak again when Kimbie asked, "What about Sarah and Molly?"

"Below deck? Didn't catch their names," he said, with a look most in the room read as distaste. The pale, skinny pirate almost laughed, but his leader cut him off with a hard look.

"Abandoned ship, as I said," Claiborne Chandler repeated. Mel noticed a smear of what looked like fresh blood on the side of the skinny pirate's knee, and on his calf and shin.

Kimbie glared at the pirate chief, but did not speak. Ping looked even more ill. It was contagious. Bridget appeared stricken. So did Chip. Sherry began to sob and looked plaintively at Ruth, whose eyes were closed. John put his hand on Ruth's shoulder and tried to smile at Sherry, to reassure her. Mel reached for Sherry, but she seemed not to notice. Were there only eight of them left?

In a steady voice, John asked, "What do you propose?"

The pirate leader smiled an ironic, crocodile smile. "Good sir, what I *propose* is that you be put adrift, with food and water, your meds if you need them, life jackets, whatever will fit, even flares. I am not a bad man. Very soon, in a day, two at most, you will be found. We will be elsewhere. You will have an exciting story to tell your grandchildren."

"That would be a great risk to my wife's health," Zinser said. "You could put us ashore."

The man in the black polo shirt with the alligator logo looked John Zinser in the eye. "Hear me, old sir: we're not *negotiating* here." His tone was suddenly ugly, menacing. His lip actually curled as he said, "negotiating." Then the pirate chief recovered himself, took a breath, exhaled, and said, almost congenially, "Life is full of risk. Putting you ashore would be a risk we are not willing to take. The raft is nothing, like traffic, which I hate, and avoid. That's my proposal, my offer, old man. My only offer. You would be wise to take it."

John Zinser said nothing. Mel McRae realized that his jaw was clenched, and made himself relax it. If he could get close enough, Mel still thought he could overpower the skinny gunman, maybe even the bigger, stronger-looking guy with the assault gun. If he got lucky. One or the other. That might give the others a chance to act.

But he still had not seen a gun with a silencer, and he had certainly heard one. That could mean another man, outside in the darkness somewhere, had a silenced gun trained on them through the windows. That would help explain Mr. Smooth's confidence. Mel drew a deep breath and sat, quiet.

The silencer was at the bottom of the Gulf. Salazar had used it to kill Fred and the younger girl. Fred had lunged for Salazar and the girl tried to help. Somehow, in the haste to dump their bodies over the side, the silenced gun was lost.

Mel was having a hard time believing that these guys were going to release people who had seen their faces. Not after killing ... how many? Five. Nobody would do that in Chicago. But this was not Chicago, not even the States, exactly. At this moment they could be in U.S. waters, or not. These men had any number of options open to them in the Caribbean, or the coastal countries of Central and South America.

"When?" asked Chip, as matter-of-fact as he could.

"Shortly," said Claiborne. "As soon as we get organized. Each of you can take a few things you'll need: hats, glasses, meds certainly, food, water, of course. We are not uncivilized. Come to think of it, breakfast might be in order before you shove off. Who can cook?" He sounded inappropriately cheerful.

The passengers looked at each other. Until now, Digby, who had made the last meal they had eaten, chowder, had cooked nearly everything. Digs was "gone," so the man in the black polo had said.

Ruth Zinser took a deep breath before she broke the silence. "If you're serious, I can certainly scare up breakfast. Who can help me? Could you, dear?" she asked, turning to Sherry. Sherry, who was sniffling, nodded, but made no move to get up. "I'll help," said Kimbie. Her voice still sounded odd, unlike herself. She moved to put her hands on Sherry's shoulders. Sherry stood.

"Very good, ladies. Do that, while we put together everybody's little survival kits," said polo man. He passed Chip a yellow legal pad and pencil, and asked everyone to list what they absolutely needed.

This is surreal, and this guy is goofy, Chip mused as he wrote "prescription sunglasses, flop hat, wallet, long-sleeved shirt, khakis." *This guy just killed five of us, but he wants the rest to be comfortable.*

"Good sir," Ping piped up, "I am afraid I shall have quite a list." Claiborne's eyebrow arched, but Ping's sense of self-importance was apparently undamaged. "As it happens I am a scientist (he paused here) of international reputation. I have research data aboard that are priceless to me and I dare say to science, that are of no use to you, I'm sure. And instruments much the same." After a plaintive start, Ping now sounded condescending. Mel was glad Kimbie was in the galley.

Claiborne Chandler's eyes widened. He almost laughed, but instead snorted derisively. "That's helpful, old chap," he said, not trying to hide his amusement. "What kind of research?"

"Zoology, marine mammals," Ping said, one colleague to another. "I am considered," and here he paused again, "one of five or six real experts on the order *odontoceti* in the world." He sounded more Tory upper class than anyone remembered when he said "in the wuhld." When Claiborne continued to stare, expressionless, Ping added the English translation. "Toothed whales. Dolphins."

Claiborne's eyebrows rose and he nodded deferentially. "Ah. And the name?"

Ping told him, and even added "Doctor of Science."

Mel McRae shook his head. He couldn't help it. Now he had seen everything. Some of Ping's actual colleagues were dead or dying, these guys had killed them, and he was trying to impress their killers with his credentials. Mel mentally reprimanded himself for thinking such an un-productive thought at such a moment, but he could not have helped him-self. He resumed his study of the gunmen, out of the corners of his eyes.

"Excellent," Claiborne said, deadpan. "No doubt there's a market for the equipment. I don't think a raft would hold much of it, do you, old chap? Really? Or your records, for that matter. It's a small world. Perhaps you'll be able to buy it back."

The olive-skinned pirate actually laughed, and raised his free hand at Claiborne in a tip-of-the-hat gesture. His other hand held that menac-ing automatic weapon.

"But ..." Ping stammered, "My good fellow, surely you wouldn't ... Don't you appreciate the scientific value?" Ping stammered.

"Perhaps not, English, but I appreciate you mentioning it. It may help us unload it. Anybody else have anything specially valuable we should know about?" He had said "English" the way he might have said "slimebag." No one else spoke.

When Mel's turn with the pad and pencil came, he asked for his favorite watch, why not? A loose, longsleeved shirt, his Cubs cap and long pants.

Kimbie came back with a tray of fruit and left again. Claiborne, who had not taken much interest in the list, picked up an orange wedge and looked around.

"Everybody, eat, please," he said. He was oddly gracious about it. People moved toward the tray.

After he picked up a handful of fruit for Ruth, and gave some to Sherry, John Zinser sat down, bowed his head, as inconspicuously as he could, and prayed silently. He began to eat.

The pirate in the alligator polo noticed. "That's a habit," he said, catching John Zinser's eye, "my mother was never able to develop in me." It was almost a threat.

John picked up a kiwi slice and said, softly, "Good habits are worth developing, at any age." Claiborne was oddly contemplative, but the youngest gunman suddenly reappeared, clutching hats and clothing to his chest, gun still in hand. He seemed agitated.

"I don't like this shit," he said, too loud. Somehow the young pirate looked sallow, almost sickly, despite obvious exposure to the sun, as he waved his shiny gun around. "I keep seeing these eff-ing geezers in some courthouse, pointing at us and saying, 'That's them right there, judge.' I say eff'in waste 'em, feed 'em to the eff'in fish."

No one breathed.

Calmly, Claiborne said, "Ricky, as we have discussed, boats that don't have a lot of blood and bullet holes sell better." He spoke as to a child. "This is how we do it. You'll never see them again."

The skinny one dumped his burden on the carpet, but said nothing. Claiborne kept eating his orange. "What about coffee? You have coffee?"

"They're probably making some. If they can find it," Chip answered. He looked at the windows. There was no light outside, yet.

"Coffee would go good," Claiborne said.

Chip didn't know whether he should go inquire, so he just nodded.

"I think I'll see if they made coffee," Claiborne said. "*Fresh* coffee."

And he strode into the galley, not a care in the world.

Mel brought grapes to Sherry, who was back on the couch . The fear in her eyes hurt. It had occurred to him that the captain probably had more weapons in his cabin, or on the bridge. He considered the idea for a moment, stood, and walked over to the olive-skinned man, now clearly on guard. Salazar moved the menacing gun in Mel's direction as he approached. Mel stopped at least five feet away. Leaning as close to the gunman as he dared, Mel tried to look embarrassed, pained. He said quietly, conspiratorially, "I need to go." The gunman shrugged. "To the bathroom," Mel added.

The man almost laughed. His expression was not sympathetic.

Mel ducked his head in supplication, tried to look distressed. The pirate did nothing.

Mel could read neither yes or no, so he asked. "May I?"

"I don't trust you, so no. Sit down. Cross your *legs*." The man's accent sounded part Spanish, part Caribbean, part something else. He snorted a laugh, and almost looked away, bored. But he also pointed the barrel of his assault pistol a bit more intentionally in Mel's direction. Mel backed away.

That was that. He had tried. That was that, for now. In a way, it was a relief. If he had been allowed to leave the salon, and then found a weapon, that would force a hard choice. Having a gun would almost obligate him to use it. If he had got within springing distance, he would have had to decide about that, as well. But he hadn't. All he could do was watch a bit longer. As time passed he grew more hopeful. With all this fuss, it seemed possible they really were going to be put adrift. Land might not be far. Boats had been seen each day. They could be safe before nightfall.

But until then, their lives were in the hands of the least stable of these fellows, probably the skinny young one. And Mel continued to suspect another was still out there in the dark, with a gun trained on them.

When he sat down, Sherry whispered, "I thought you went to the bathroom."

"Nervous" He tried to smile.

Sherry took a deep breath. "It'll be okay." She put her hand over his. Despite eyes red from crying, she looked as if she believed it. That was better. He hoped she was right.

The up-tick spread to Bridget, who still looked sad, but hopeful.

Chip was tense. Mel had chatted with the young man a few times since meeting him but there was no real mutual understanding to draw on, except for their unspoken need for each other's help now, should an opportunity arise.

But without a plan, and without weapons, active resistance—if there was going to be any—would have to be dictated by circumstance and individual opportunity. Resistance did not look promising to Mel.

He studied his fellow passengers. Chip wore a bathing suit, a loose khaki shirt and dive shoes. Chances of a weapon seemed slim.

John Zinser, in walking shorts, a sport shirt and canvas shoes, looked as if he had been awake, waiting. Probably no weapon.

Ping, in a Hawaiian shirt, shorts and sandals, studied the carpet. The baggy pockets in those shorts could hold anything, but Mel did not think they held a weapon, unless Ping was a better actor than had been shown so far.

Kimbie, on the other hand, was in the galley, full of sharp knives. She might know how to use them. For all anybody knew, Ruth Zinser was putting poison in the eggs. Mel smiled. Somehow the thought cheered him.

36
If I get a chance. But ...

Nothing to do but stay alert and watch. Their captors looked bored. The menacing one with the accent and the Uzi, or whatever it was, looked relaxed at least, like he'd done this before, but the young one's face was sweat-covered, and he seemed as agitated as ever. Worse, he kept shifting his attention between the windows and Sherry.

Not surprising. Though she probably was old enough to be the pirate's mother, she didn't look it. Sherry was very attractive, with a big mane of reddish-blonde hair and an hourglass figure only partly concealed by a designer sweatshirt and shorts that came nearly to her knees. There was really no hiding her. She had ignored the shiny pistol and the man/boy holding it since before the leader had squelched him, but the guy had not ignored her.

Whose blood is on the guy's leg? Mel wondered. *His own? Molly's? Sarah's?* Sarah had been attractive too, in a quieter way. Mel tried not to think about her in the past tense, but that was probably reality. Molly too. The captain. Digby. Fred. Probably all of them.

Mel tried to figure out what time it was. It had been about 3 when he heard the first shots. Could half an hour have passed? An hour? Ten minutes? He honestly had no idea.

He saw a watch on Bridget's wrist, but couldn't read it. He didn't want to call attention to himself, or to the watch, or to her.

He didn't have to. Kimbie came to the door and announced that breakfast was ready. The only clock he had noticed except for the one on the bridge was mounted on the galley wall.

Kimbie's eyes were dry but they were red, like Sherry's. Her movements were purposeful.

John Zinser rose and followed Kimbie to the galley. No one challenged him, so the others followed. Mel eased Sherry away from the nervous young guy, and they made their way without incident. The guy in the black polo faced them, relaxed at the table where they had eaten breakfast twice since coming aboard. He had both hands around a big, steaming white mug decorated with a gold Coast Guard shield and anchors. Pete's mug. The clock said 3:36.

"Great coffee, guys. Fix you right up," he said, as if he were their bartender.

37
Blood in the water

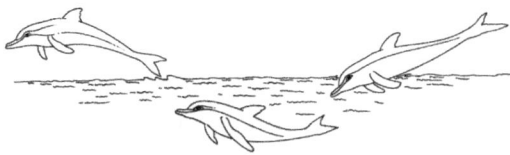

Blood had attracted sharks. They were frenzied.

The pod was some distance away, and quiet. Chax might move them, but just now he focused on the swimming man.

The man was smart enough to stay calm and swim like a turtle. For that reason the sharks had not found him. But he was not far from the blood, and bloody himself. He would be part of their meal if they noticed.

Chax took Band and Popper to the man, and sent Chobeem and the rest to guard the pod. They would be safe unless something worse happened.

Earlier that night, Chax had heard another boat. He had watched a small bubble from this new boat go to the first one. Soon dead and dying people were in the water. Then one began to swim.

Chax had swum with the dying. He recognized the young female Chobeem had taken up with. Chobeem had taken his place at her side soon after she hit the water. He could not help her, but would not leave. Another body came from the other end of the boat, badly broken, soon dead. Then the female that had reminded him of a big frog. Dead when she hit. She had been gentle. The tough old fisherman. He had been full of joy over fish the pod brought to the boat. Skilled with the net. Another male who had tried to get Chax to play.

Men had killed them. They had not killed this one, but sharks might get him yet. It did not surprise Chax. He had been around men. Men kill without eating, and kill their own kind. Men are unstable, unknowable, attract trouble. He found himself chirping the old nursery lesson, leader or not. What he knew did not free him of the obligation to stay. Or the desire to stay. So he chirped about obedience, which improved his mood.

The killings made Chax see more, understand. He remembered what he had heard. He had been given the opportunity to stay. That had not changed.

Popper joined Chax in chirping about men being unstable, how they attract trouble. Chax noticed. He took time to remind Popper not to jump. Popper, who loved to jump, had been pleased to be chosen to help. He answered with respect.

Some of the dead sank, others floated, others dangled. One of the females floated just below the surface until the sharks came, the other floated at the surface, alive, breathing. The young one. Chobeem went to her, but she did not respond. Not with fear, not at all. He kept sharks away until she stopped breathing and her heart stopped. Then he left. Sharks found and rolled and tore them all.

38
Mid-rats

Ruth had performed a miracle. While she comforted and directed Sherry and Kimbie and prayed for all of them, and herself, she fried sausage, scrambled eggs and made toast. Her helpers found fruit, washed and cut it up, set it out. Then they set out bread, butter, jam, juice, coffee and tea. Activity dried their tears. As she rummaged through the refrigerator, Ruth remembered Pete always called any meal in the middle of the night "mid-rats." Midnight rations, she supposed. These "rats" had shown up in the middle of the night, too.

Mid-rats indeed, she thought. *Pie-rats.* She smiled at the bad pun in spite of herself. Pete would like that one. Then Ruth shook her head and said another prayer for Pete, for Digby and Fred, for young Molly, for Sarah, for all of them. She trusted and hoped. She even prayed for the pirates. Once upon a time, they had been someone's little boys, she reminded herself. They needed God as much as she did. Ruth hated what they had done, but she didn't hate them, she pitied them. She knew they were killers, but she couldn't hate them. *There but for the grace of God go any of us,* she thought.

No one was hungry, except the pirates, but everyone ate and drank anyway. It seemed like a good idea to think about fuel and fluids for whatever might be ahead, as Chip quietly put it. Even Sherry ate, with a little encouragement.

John thought about giving thanks aloud, but decided against it. He noted that Ruth bowed her head, and thought perhaps that Chip bowed his too, though perhaps Chip was just thinking. Claiborne, the new captain, looked thoughtful. Then he laughed, and nobody liked the sound of it. The pirate chief dug into his breakfast, and toasted Ruth, called her "your fine cook." Toasted her with Pete's mug. Ruth gave him a sad smile in return.

The skinny boy with the big pistol, Ricky, didn't bother with a plate. He roamed the galley and helped himself from the platters on the counters and table. Several times he picked up a chunk of scrambled egg, tilted back his head and dropped it into his mouth.

Claiborne, the chief, used acceptable manners, Ruth noted. He still held no weapon, yet he was totally in control. The one with the Caribbean accent and the high-tech pistol or whatever sat with his back to the corner of the galley, put his gun in his lap, and ate quietly. Somewhere he had learned European table manners, knife and fork together, which surprised those who noticed. The skinny young one, Ricky, on the other hand, picked his teeth with greasy fingers. He occasionally wiped his eating hand—his left—on his shorts while he held the gun with his right. Ruth offered him a napkin. He took it, wiped his fingers, put it on the table and walked away. Several times he stopped next to someone as they ate, and stood too close. Only Kimbie allowed herself a glare, which he returned with a leer.

He moved away from her though, only to move on to Sherry. He seemed to be trying to provoke something. He looked down at his own greasy fingers, and reached toward the shoulder of Sherry's dusty rose sweatshirt.

"Ricky," Claiborne said as he looked up from his coffee and shook his head. "You need to get over this power thing you've got." Mel clinched his jaw but said nothing.

Claiborne laughed, almost a real laugh. His tone with Ricky had scolded, but also mocked, teased. Ricky fumed, but did not move away. Then the leader began to use a tone the passengers had not heard—soft, pitched high, insulting. "Idiot child, are you trying to provoke them, or me?" Skinny Ricky stared into space. Kimbie could see sweat on his forehead.

Salazar looked in Ricky's direction, snorted, and laughed. It was a rumble so low that some thought they imagined it. Ricky looked down, looked back up. Chastened, he backed away from Sherry. He tried to make the move look unintentional.

Claiborne's voice was more normal when he said, a moment later: "For what I hope is the last time, the plan is to get hold of an almost cherry boat, not one messed with bloodstains and bullet holes. I know how you like to trash things, but ... that is *not* the plan."

Then Claiborne took a drink from his mug, saluted the table with it, and said, quite pleasantly, apparently to everyone, "Good coffee."

Silence followed, but in the moments that followed, some of the passengers ventured hopeful glances at each other. No bullet holes, no bloodstains. Ricky picked at sausage. Kimbie stared at her plate. The exchange had not helped settle stomachs, but it did seem to indicate that at least one of the pirates did not plan further bloodshed. John Zinser urged everyone to eat. His few words encouraged those who had not tried.

Claiborne rose and walked to where Salazar was seated, took care not to block the gunman's view. After they put their heads together, Claiborne stood and announced that the passengers were to be put off in rubber rafts. The inflatable the pirates had arrived in was tied to the stern. It was dirty, nasty really, but mainly too small. Plus it had a small outboard motor. They left it tied where it was.

The Delphi had a little inflatable somewhat like it, a Zodiac boat with a Mariner outboard motor. It was nicer than what the pirates had, but it was never considered. Getting it out of the locker and into the water would be a chore, for one thing. Plus, its motor could let them hightail it to shore, relatively speaking, and it was valuable, part of the package they planned to sell or trade.

Ricky grumbled. Salazar said nothing. Claiborne did all the talking. No one asked questions.

Kimbie thought she saw dolphins when the pirate leader started the *indie's* diesels and burbled into the darkness. Lights appeared ahead. The lights, lit by a remote the pirate leader carried, were on a sport fisherman, it turned out, about the size of the N.D., a bit taller, maybe not as long. Nasty orange bilge stains ran down the side. The dolphins kept their distance, but Kimbie saw them. They seemed to watch. This encouraged her, somehow. She wondered how much the dolphins could understand. It had only been a few hours since everyone had swum with them. If Sarah and Molly were dead, as she now assumed, they had at least had an amazing last few days. Those free swims topped anything she had ever imagined. Could that have been just hours ago? And Pete...

Salazar ordered Ping, standing off from the others, to grab the hull of the pirate boat as he brought the N.D. alongside, next to a smelly stain. The leader then yelled down from the bridge, "English! Fenders!" When Ping was did not move, Kimbie placed two white neoprene fenders, tied them off, and tied the boats together with lines from the N.D. Claiborne, the leader, then directed everyone to climb over to the pirate boat. Kimbie jumped over. She and Chip helped Ruth and John first, then everyone. Once they were all assembled in the deep rear deck well, Claiborne told them they would be allowed to go to "the head,' down below, one at a time. The menacing pirate went first. When it was Sherry's turn to go below, she was sorry. The "head" was wretched.

Ricky stayed on deck and kept his gun on the passengers, who bunched together. Salazar stood in the passageway at the bottom of the ladder, outside the head, with his assault pistol. He looked so grim that no one loitered or attempted anything. Besides, bathroom privileges seemed yet another tangible sign that the pirates really were going to release everyone unharmed.

But as Sherry climbed back up to the deck, she tripped on the high threshold of the hatch-like opening at the top of the ladder, fell forward, and sprawled onto the deck. She would have landed on her face, with a sandal still hooked on the threshold, if she had not put her hands out to catch herself. As she fell her sweatshirt rose and the deck lights illuminated her lean torso and a lacy black bra. Before she could react, Ricky grabbed her waistband and hauled her backward, in a clumsy move that pulled her shorts low. One leg slipped back down the ladder. It looked like she might fall further. Mel, who reacted to help her when she tripped, saw part of Ricky's hand disappear inside the back of his wife's shorts. Off balance and angry, Mel skidded toward the hatch on one knee. Afraid he might push her down the hatch himself, unarmed, eyes full of fury—Mel stopped in front of Ricky. In less time than it takes to blink Ricky pistol-whipped him to the deck. A quick forehand motion caught Mel hard on the temple, and a backhand motion swiped his head as he fell. The big chrome revolver made an awful sound, especially on the first lick, and knocked Mel nearly senseless. But Ricky let go of Sherry and pointed the gun at the stunned watchers.

Blood ran down Mel's face, and he swayed as he tried to get back up but he still tried to help her stand. Her eyes grew wide, horrified. Sherry gasped.

Kimbie and Claiborne Chandler were in Ricky's face in the same instant. Kimbie glared wordlessly as Claiborne calmly took Ricky's gun. Ricky let him take it, but looked as if he might be sick. Salazar climbed partway up the ladder and rested his weapon on the non-skid ridge of the high threshold. With his other hand, Salazar steadied Sherry by her elbow. She turned from Mel to stare at his hand.

"I'll take care of this," Claiborne told Kimbie, almost gallantly, as he waived Ricky around the corner of the bulkhead. Ricky went. Salazar had control, though Ruth was still below, in the head, behind him. With a jerk of his exotic assault pistol, Salazar directed Kimbie to move back to the others. She did, but began to shake. John and Bridget each moved to support her. Salazar reached down to help Ruth back up the ladder. The only sound was water that lapped up between the two boats, and bits of the reprimand Claiborne was giving Ricky.

John gave Sherry his handkerchief. She helped Mel press it to his temple and from somewhere produced a handful of tissues and began to wipe blood from his cheek.

Chip realized he was holding his breath, and put his arm around Bridget, who now was being comforted by Ruth. In a few minutes, at Claiborne's direction, Claiborne and Ricky dragged a bundle to the rear deck. It began to inflate itself into a large rubber life raft. Apparently it had not been used before. Chip and Julian and Bridget slid it into the water. There was no mention of another raft. When Claiborne gestured toward it, all eight of the survivors from the *New Delphi* helped each other get in, clutching whatever they had brought. Nothing else was said. No instructions were given otherwise, so after a minute Chip and Bridget pushed the raft away from the stern of the pirate boat. It bobbed away from the dim running lights, toward the darkness.

The big raft bobbed in the faint glow of the running lights from the two boats, but stopped drifting away and seemed to hover. No one in its canvas confines could keep from wondering, as seconds ticked into minutes, whether the pirates might, despite all the leader had said—despite everything—just shoot them and let their memories and bodies sink with the raft. They watched the three pirates huddle together, but could not hear. The N.D. diesels still burbled. The raft was still less than a dozen feet from the pirate boat. The yacht was tied on the other side. Bridget was sure that she was not the only one who realized that shooting up the raft now would kill everybody without blood or bullet holes, not in the yacht or anything else. No chance of resistance. Going over the side only meant a slow death. Silent, desperate prayers were raised by people who had not prayed in a long time. Kimbie had never seen starlight so bright, or her vision so acute.

Then, as abruptly as they had come, the pirates started the diesels on their own boat, let them burble for what seemed like no time at all, and unceremoniously motored away. Slowly. Those in the raft were afraid to react, and too tense to even feel relief. They had half-expected a speech, if not gunfire. Neither happened. When the boats were perhaps thirty or forty yards from the raft, they each increased power and began to put distance behind them. The roar of four diesels took over the night, but soon began to fade.

The last thing anyone in the raft saw as darkness enveloped them and they strained to watch the boats was the glint of a bright light that came on and went off. Mel McRae was sure it had to be the searchlight on the bridge of the *New Delphi*, hitting the skinny guy's shiny revolver. Whatever it was, it reflected the last light they saw from the boat that had been their vacation home.

They listened as the noise got farther and farther away. At last, everything was silent.

39
Adrift

The silence that followed was pregnant. No one wanted to talk if there was more to hear. No one wanted to miss the sound of diesel motors if they returned.

But finally, Sherry whispered, "They're gone."

Her voice, usually confident and well modulated, was tentative and small. As if she could not quite believe what had just happened. Some still held their breath as they watched where the red, green and white lights had grown small and disappeared.

"Thank God," said Bridget, just as small. "Is it too early to cheer?" Her voice seemed forced, childlike, but brave.

"I should say not," said Ruth, wedged between her husband and Julian. "Hallelujah!" Not loud, but strong.

At that, Sherry held onto Mel, twisted over on her stomach, and vomited into the ocean. No one spoke. Kimbie helped Mel hold Sherry's hair. Some fought nausea themselves. Ruth reached to pat Sherry's leg, the only place she could reach. "It's okay, sweetie," she said. "It's okay. We're okay."

No one else spoke for several moments. But Bridget all but whispered, "Wow. We're okay! We are." Then she buried her face in Chip's chest to muffle sobs.

Quiet, urgent conversations began. Lifeboat riders spilled observations, outrage, fear, relief, anger. Gratitude. Even laughter. Starlight sparkled on faces wet with tears of joy, sadness, frustration, anger, relief, gratitude. For some, denial, for others, the beginning of grief. For a few, real friends were among the missing, people they had eaten every meal with, shared life on a small boat with, for months.

Each felt different measures of sadness and relief, but also emotions they could not exactly name. They had survived. They were relieved, amazed. But they also grieved. Some already felt pangs of guilt. "It could have been me," said Kimbie, her voice childlike. "Maybe it should have been me. Why wasn't it?" Ruth reached as far as she could to touch her face. Kimbie took hold of the hand, not even sure whose it was, and pressed it to her cheek.

Things they had been afraid to say in front of the gunmen were said too, all at once. Everyone—everyone who wanted to—vented, or questioned, until they ran out of words. For now.

Mel McRae said little, as he held Sherry, who rested her chin on the edge of the raft, empty, quiet. Mel's head throbbed, and he was angry, but not as angry as he had been. Somehow being pistol-whipped had given release of an odd sort.

Ping, who mostly had studied his feet since the galley meal, had a lot to say now, most of it irate. Kimbie revealed a sharp little knife, a stiletto really, sharp on both edges. She said had spent every minute until she was in the raft looking for a way to use it. Any way that might look to have a decent chance.

"Good girl," said John Zinser, next to her. "I'm glad you didn't ... I'm glad you didn't have to use it, but pocketing the knife was brave and resourceful. Good girl." At this, Kimbie, who had been mostly in control, finally sobbed. Ruth wrapped the knife in a scarf. Others cried too, but not all of the sobs could be heard. The barbarity of what had happened since they had tucked themselves into comfortable berths a few hours ago overwhelmed. It silenced some, enraged others.

They had to assume that people they had gotten to know a little—or a lot—were dead. People they had learned to really like. Pushed overboard like refuse. Kimbie and Julian and John and Ruth had lost real friends, close associates. The rest had formed the instant bonds that can happen on a cruise, especially when intense experiences are shared. Bridget felt like she had lost a little sister she had just met. Chip could not comfort her.

John put his arm around Kimbie. She hugged him and laid her head against his chest. "If only ..." she whispered.

He didn't try to answer for a while. "We don't know why," he said, "and we can't change it. We can only remember and take care of each other, and in time, go forward." Kimbie heaved a huge sigh, and was quiet. As John held her, wisps of her sun-bleached hair tickled his nose. Try as he might to fight it, stifle it, a sneeze came. When he apologized, and said, "your hair," a tiny laugh came from Kimbie, despite her tears.

"Sorry," she managed to say, but hugged him tighter and didn't let go.

Ruth smoothed Kimbie's hair. "It's all right dear. I know. It's all right."

No one said anything for a long time after that.

Eventually eyes adjusted to the starlight. They could almost see each other, and see the gently rolling water, even where it did not sparkle with fluorescence, as it did sometimes when a small wave broke.

Before they could see that they had company, they heard. Three dolphins were about twenty feet away. They all heard them chuff and blow, but Sherry saw them first. Despite what they had heard, she thought they might be sharks, and was frightened. Kimbie disagreed, in a very soft voice. "No. Listen."

When one blew sent up a spray they could see, Bridget all but shouted, "It's them! It's really them! They're still here!"

This brought a mixed response. Bridget began to cry again. Kimbie stopped crying and laughed—soft, girlish laughter. She put her hand in the water, not splashing, just feeling the water.

"Hey guys! What kept you?" said Chip, apparently to cheer Bridget. He twisted toward the dolphins. "Hey, how far to Panama City? Or Clearwater, maybe? What about it, guys? How 'bout a tow? You might be on TV." Others chuckled. "All the Long John Silver you can eat. Hush puppies! You guys ever try hush puppies?"

"That is so disgusting, Chip," said Kimbie, who knew what he was doing. "Patronizing them like that." She made her voice stronger, and said, "Anyways, how do you know they're guys? You just assume. That's sooo sexist!"

Even Mel laughed, a deep, hearty laugh that made everyone feel better. This bolstered Sherry enough that she carefully backed into the center of the raft, sat on her feet, put her head in Mel's lap and wrapped her arms around him. This took up what room was left in the center, but allowed more room around the rim. Everyone shifted to get a bit more comfortable.

As they continued to joke and laugh the tension eased, and they grew quiet again.

Finally Sherry turned her head and asked, "What do we do now?"

"That's a very good question," said John Zinser. "For now, I suggest we sit tight. When we can see, I suggest we take inventory. Who knows, we may see land. I doubt it, but we might."

"We were several hours west of Florida, when we went to bed," Chip said. "I doubt if we can see land. We had a sea anchor out though. It could have pulled us a little, maybe toward the keys, or the Ten Thousand Islands, the Everglades." Silence followed.

Kimbie's voice was soft again when she said, "We're way north of there, Chip. As populated as the coast is, if we can't see lights, you and John are right, we're probably pretty far from land. I would guess northwest of Clearwater and St. Pete. But I could be wrong. It's possible that we're just too far out to see the lights, too low in the water. The current may move us closer."

"We'll know soon," Chip said. "And we'll know which way to paddle, if we have paddles."

"I may be sitting on a paddle," said Bridget.

"Try to leave everything where it is if you can, until daylight," said Mel, gently. "Unless it's really uncomfortable. I doubt if this raft was made for eight. We don't want to risk tipping, and we don't want to lose anything in the dark, either. Sunrise should be soon, in another hour. John's right. Sit tight if you can." Mel tried not to assume command, but in a vacuum, somebody had to.

"That's right," said Chip. "That's all we can do, for now. Sleep, if you can. It might be a long day."

Murmurs of agreement followed, then quiet. Several, starting with Bridget, rooted into sleep positions. Others craned their necks to face what they imagined would be a rosy dawn. Ruth was the first achieve a tiny, whiffing snore.

40
Aboard the USS Boise

Commander Fred Alvarez grabbed for his beeping watch, found it. Shut it off.

His cabin was dark. He stretched, put his hand up, touched only air, and swung his legs over the edge of the bunk, put his hand up again and sat up. He made sure he didn't bump his head from years of shipboard habit. He hadn't started out in command, after all. Alvarez had worked his way up through the ranks, which at first meant he slept in rope and canvas "racks" with very little headroom. His natural aptitude and the diligence he applied to whatever assignment he got moved him up the enlisted ladder fast. He qualified for special training and extra duties. In time he made the jump, was sent to college at Navy expense, graduated with honors and became an officer. Since then, the Navy had trained and retrained him, sent him to grad school for a masters in engineering. He was scheduled to go to the Naval War College at the end of this cruise. He rated a small compartment of his own now, the captain's cabin, including a bed with a mattress, not a rack. But some habits stick. Besides, there wasn't that much headroom, even in the captain's bunk.

The watch in his hand was the only light, except for a red glow to his left. He listened to the familiar silence of the *Boise* for a minute. The watch said 0400 hours. He flipped on the reading light. Sometimes, right after he woke up, he had to remind himself that he was the captain of a United States Navy nuclear submarine, at sea. He never forgot for long, not even in port, not even on leave with his family. Being in charge of a billion-dollar weapon is an awesome privilege, but it's also a huge responsibility that never quits. Alvarez had not known about that, not really, until he was given command. It had taken perhaps fifteen minutes to feel it in his gut. He was used to the responsibility now, but it never went away. He had always prided himself on not taking himself too seriously and he still tried, but he had to be serious about this job every waking minute.

As captain, Alvarez had the only private stateroom, and it doubled as his office. He picked up his phone, spoke to the chief of the watch and asked for coffee. Then he went down the passageway to the head.

A submarine is a remarkably fair, democratic place, exceptionally so for the tradition-laden, blue-suit Navy, but certain things are expected. Nobody else could have coffee brought up, and the crew expected him to exercise this perk, pun intended. Everybody understood that the captain has a lot on him.

Back in his cabin, Alvarez folded down the steel sink, splashed water on his face and brushed his teeth. After a tap on the door, the duty messenger set a cup of fresh, steaming coffee—black, no sugar, in a regulation mug—on his desk. The messenger, a seaman, said "Good morning, Captain," waited a few seconds after the captain returned the greeting to be sure Alvarez didn't want anything else, and left. The C.O. could have had a china cup and saucer if he'd wanted one, or a personal mug, but everybody aboard knew how the captain drank his coffee, even the new guys.

As coffee reactivated his brain, he thought about what he should do next. Two thick binders held a detailed checklist to be worked through. Every day, every watch, had tasks to be accomplished and documented. He also had work on his laptop. He swallowed more coffee, got his soap and brush and razor, and shaved. Seven minutes later he pulled on the dark blue coveralls officers wear when at sea. At 0419, Commander Alvarez entered the wardroom, where his executive officer and the chief of the boat studied a table of figures. It had been six hours since he had seen them.

"Morning, XO," he nodded to his executive officer, Russell Bean.

"Morning, Captain." They all knew each other's first names, of course, but "good order and discipline" called for titles when aboard. Though his rank was commander, his title was captain.

"What's up this morning, COB?" Captain Alvarez asked his chief of the boat, who had been in contact with the preceding watch.

"Mostly the usual, Captain," said the COB, Master Chief Stan Schuermann, who nearly always squinted from behind his grin. "We've been running patterns pretty much constant since you left the conn. The OOD ran us back into the current whenever he thought it would shake anybody up. A couple of times it did." He smiled. He did not mention suggesting the maneuver.

Alvarez nodded, imagining a "newb" sub driver with maybe a dozen hours of experience freaking out upon encounter with the slippery Mississippi River current. Hitting the current when you weren't expecting it could be startling. Only the right reactive measures kept the sub upright when that happened.

If the sub is going too slow, unexpected turbulence can make it fall like a rock. That calls for a set of buoyancy compensation maneuvers, and an increase in speed. If everything isn't done fast, right, coordinated well, it can get serious. A sub has no "automatic" devices to kick in for this; everything must be done manually, artfully, with intent, immediately. At the very least, "dropping" the sub is embarrassing for whoever is in charge, as well as those at the helm or on the planes that control elevation. Everyone aboard knows if it is not done right.

"Outstanding," Alvarez said.

Raised on a ranch, Alvarez had the understated, cowboy version of street smarts. They served him well in the Navy, along with his *cum laude* degree in hydraulic engineering from the University of Wyoming, and his nuclear post-graduate work. But he had always admired the way the COB, a non-degreed enlisted man from the streets of Norfolk, the son of a sailor, could put a crewman under sudden, controlled stress with a surprise or two, a few well-chosen words, a raised eyebrow. The captain suspected the COB had suggested what the OOD had had the helmsman do, and it suited the captain's purposes ideally. One of the main reasons for this leg of the cruise was to log helm time and planes time for rookie drivers. And not to just log it, but to make it real, intense and varied enough to produce experience and a measure of confidence.

"Much shipping?" Alvarez asked.

The X.O. answered. "The usual, Captain. About normal for New Orleans this time of year. Tankers, grain boats, a love boat. Freighters. Lots of small craft, fishermen, what have you. The Coasties worked late, stopping ships."

"Weather?"

"Calm from Beaumont to San Juan. Partly cloudy and dark. We ran at periscope depth until about an hour ago. You could hardly see the horizon. Mild wind farther south. Storms east of Florida, but nothing major enough to affect us, should we head that way later today."

"Outstanding," Alvarez said again. The Navy does not like "good," it likes outstanding. He did not like surprises, and apparently there had been none while he slept.

"You fellas have any ideas before we take a ride up the Gulf Stream?" he asked.

When Bean didn't volunteer anything, Schuermann said, "Most of the new guys have almost figured out the river, sir, but I'd like to let the next watch have to deal with it a few more times. I'd rather not leave the neighborhood right away unless we need to, captain."

"Very fine," Alvarez said.

"We've got guys aboard who have never been deep," said Bean, the XO. "What say we take a dip in the Cayman Trench on the way out, let the hull groan. Get their full attention."

"You for it COB?" Alvarez asked.

Schuermann nodded his head. "We've done the check-offs for that. No reason to pass up the chance for medium-depth maneuvers. Maybe some drills, too." His eyebrows shot up involuntarily as he said it, and he nodded several more times. "Meanwhile, Opie has been monitoring a surface vessel. He has reason to think it might be involved in drugs. That's another reason I want to linger a while, Captain, if that's not a problem. I'll keep you informed."

"Outstanding," Alvarez said as he picked up the log to read the previous six hours of notations. He swallowed coffee as he began to read.

41
A directed turn

The man swam steady, quiet, slow. He swam on one side, then the other, with his hands always under the surface. The water was calm enough that he floated on his back so long Chax thought he was asleep. Then he swam again. His bleeding had stopped. He had been swimming for hours. Chax was sure the man could swim and float like that for many more hours, maybe another day, if the water stayed calm. Perhaps a good boat would find him.

He swam toward the land, more or less, though it was far away. He didn't take a very good angle, either. Dolphins are good at herding fish, so they directed him. After Chax and Band and Popper took up their protective positions and watched him for a while, long before daylight, they turned him toward shore. The current was weak but the man didn't use it. He swam a little against it, like a baby. So Chax and Band got in front of him, but off to the left. They cruised like sharks at the surface, and didn't blow unless they were under water. Popper, whose fin was smaller, swam deep, and did not jump. With only stars for light, it took time for the man to notice the two large fins, but when he did, he turned away from them, quietly, slowly. Before he turned, they heard his heart race, a bad sound. They feared he might thrash and draw unwanted attention, but he didn't. They were glad, but silent about it.

The turn pointed the man toward where the pod rested, but he would not encounter them. Now the weak current was behind him, enough to help. He could make land faster, and not be as tired. If he swam like this for most of the day, this new course would take him close to land, maybe all the way to it. Chax hoped the man could swim to a place where other men could find him, or a place where he could walk on his own flippers.

The man swam the same as before, and turned like a turtle that has changed her mind. After a while, his heart settled down to match his swimming.

42
Radio Watch

The Coast Guard Cutter *Kodiak* plowed the Gulf at half-speed, with all but two of its crew of seven topside, eyes on the water.

Two hours ago, at 3 a.m., they had heard a garbled radio message about a shrimp boat with problems. It had not actually been a distress call, but they had lost contact. Now the Kodiak was in the area where the shrimper had reported taking on water.

The Kodiak's day had started when it intercepted a freighter from an unfriendly place, and delayed it long enough for port security to be ready. The crew also kept their "eyes" out for small craft that might be bringing in illegal cargo, human or otherwise. They were monitoring several. In daylight, they would intercept them, one at a time.

Such was the life of a Coast Guardsman. Most of the men aboard (there were no women currently serving on the *Kodiak*) would not have had it any other way. They took pride in being out in conditions that kept other boats in port, other aircraft grounded. They took satisfaction from being better equipped and better trained—and just generally better sailors and fliers—than almost anybody they encountered.

Communications Technician First Class Estil Potter was on radio watch at the station. He monitored the emergency frequencies, the regular bands that fishermen, shrimpers and crabbers use, the navigational channels, and all the Coast Guard's operational frequencies. It was easy, the way he had his radios programmed. Especially at this hour. But he had only been able to raise a handful of shrimpers in the vicinity, plus one farther out in the Gulf and another tied up at a dock up on the panhandle.

Nobody knew anything, but they would spread the word. Potter had also contacted land-based law enforcement and asked them to see if they could find the *"Lacy Janice"* tied up anywhere. She was supposed to be working out of Port Charlotte, so he had tried that area and Fort Myers, Cape Coral and Sanibel, just for drill. Nothing.

"*Lacy Janice*, this is Coast Guard one-four-niner, please acknowledge if you can hear me, over. Please acknowledge, over."

Potter didn't hear anything. He was beginning to wonder if this was a prank. It happened, though it is a federal offense to falsely report a ship in distress. Big fine, too. He had checked her registration, and tried the only phone number the computer listed. No answer. One of the shrimper captains he talked to knew the *Lacy J*, but had not seen her for weeks. So the mission continued. All Coast Guard vessels in the sector had been advised. The sector OOD saw no immediate need to widen the search, or bring in more help, not for a few hours.

But the *WMV-149* continued its sweep. On the bridge, a seaman with night-vision glasses scanned the horizon. Others manned the rail, and the radar. They would continue until called off. At daybreak they would interdict illegal aliens. They would check fishing boats for illegal species or quantities, contraband and/or drugs. They would monitor boats that might present a Homeland Security issue. That's what Coasties do.

43
Inventory, reassurance

Claiborne had decided to leave U.S. waters. Today. At daybreak. He was tired of the states, tired of questions. This had been too messy. He hadn't wanted it to go the way it had, but there was nothing to do about it now. Distance would fix it.

At first light they would paint the stern. He had been through much of the yacht's interior in the last hour, and sunk anything easy to identify, unless valuable.

By today's opulent standards, the *New Delphi* was not huge, and not what you would call luxurious. It had no "bling" factor, no gold fittings, no pool, not even a hot tub. Still, it *was* a beautiful classic yacht. It had nice bathrooms with showers and one real bathtub. Every surface and fitting was shipshape, and updated as appropriate. Everything he had seen was either pristine or had been re-done right. That was one reason Claiborne had decided not to shoot any more people. That, plus there were so many. He had not wanted to shoot anyone at all, but Ricky had put everything and everybody at risk for that woman. She screamed for help, which came, and forced the issue.

Ricky was a liability and getting worse. But they had scraped through.

Now they had this boat, in excellent shape. Once they got rid of its dumb name. According to the log, the diesels only had a few hundred hours since the last rebuild. He didn't need the log to tell him they sounded great, ran great. Much better than the diesels on their boat, the sport fisherman Ricky now piloted. Claiborne skimmed the log for a few minutes, mostly looking at where the boat had been recently, where it might be recognized. That done, he zipped the log into a monogrammed backpack, along with some dumbbells, and dropped the heavy package overboard.

As far as he could tell, the hull was sound. Everything he had tried, worked. Contemporary navigation gear, redundant electronics. Fish finder. Flat screens. The nice little galley had a gem of a five-burner gas stove, a serious refrigerator, lots of food, dishes, glasses, flatware. Table linens that fortunately did not have the boat's name on them. A most enviable boat.

Not new. But that was all right, Bertrams hold their value. Claiborne knew boats. But he also knew pirates, and he knew that just stealing a boat wasn't going to satisfy Ricky for long. Specially since his attempted rape had not worked out, and since Claiborne had stared Ricky down after he pistol-whipped that guy. It could have gone the other way. Salazar had reacted fast. Ricky had lost a lot of face in that encounter, but another confrontation would come, because Ricky never learned. As far as Claiborne could tell, Salazar was not the least bit sympathetic to Ricky's desire to take over. Ricky is a moron, to Salazar. But that wasn't going to stop Ricky from stewing and griping and kicking. And Teddy, dumb ol' loyal Teddy, now slept with the fish, blown away in cold blood by that tough captain. It was no consolation to Claiborne that the captain was fish food too. Teddy's death changed things. Claiborne was not sure how it would happen, but he either needed to replace Teddy or get rid of Ricky. Probably both. Soon.

Salazar was solid, but he was pondering, Claiborne knew, because he had not said much. With Teddy gone, Salazar would be reevaluating, just as he was forced to do. Claiborne wasn't worried about it, he just knew Salazar. Salazar thinks ahead.

As he scanned the east for the dawn, and continued to take stock, it occurred to Claiborne that all his weapons except the little pistol in his pocket were on the other boat, with Ricky and Salazar. For a moment he almost worried, before he caught himself. The pistol was enough. He took a deep breath and remembered the wiry little captain. That guy was well-armed. He probably had other weapons stashed someplace.

Claiborne checked his course, changed it just a little to veer more to the south, scanned the horizon for lights in all directions. He saw none, locked the wheel and throttle and took another look around the bridge. He rummaged through the compartments until he was sure nothing was there.

With the wheel locked and the other boat maintaining distance, he made his way down the ladder, through the galley to the staterooms. He bypassed the passenger staterooms and entered the captain's V-shaped cabin, in the bow. A pistol would be near the bed. He rummaged until he found a big Army model 1911 Colt automatic in a built-in drawer under the bed. Loaded, of course. A box of .45 cal. ammo with it. The clip only held seven rounds, with a trigger pull for each one, but it would do.

Claiborne relaxed a little with the big pistol in his hand. He had never shot one of these museum pieces. Perhaps he should, just to get the feel of it. Topside, from the salon door, he drew a bead on a whitecap fifty feet to port and fired.

"BAM!" The pistol jolted hard. Claiborne had his wrist rigid, but not his elbow. The gun had jumped toward his face and he hit the door jamb with his shoulder. "Damn," he said to nobody. "Damn." He had more respect for the vintage pistol, immediately.

Gripping with both hands, he locked his arms and fired again. The jolt was strong, but he was ready this time. The gun had a safety and he flicked it on, reloaded and made sure the chamber was clear, so there would not be another explosion. *Damn.*

He climbed the ladder back up to the helm, scanned the horizon and looked to see if the other boat was where it should be.

It was. It was possible they had heard the shots, so he blinked the running lights, once. They did the same. Claiborne smiled.

44
A 'Cold War' lesson

"Whoa!" Sonar Technician 2nd Class Alex Trabinsky grabbed the big leather-padded headphones that muffled out what little room noise there might be in the communication center of the *USS Boise*. The earphones, which he pulled away from his ears for a second, wired him into the sounds of the water outside. The volume was up high, filters off, because so little had been going on. In less than an hour, Ski would be off watch. Near the end of a watch, sometimes, a little extra headphone volume helped him concentrate. Helped him stay awake, really. He hadn't wanted too much more coffee until breakfast—pancakes today—and pancakes need coffee.

That was one strange sound, Trabinsky said to himself, just as it happened again. *Two strange sounds*. He had listened to two boats most of the watch. Yachts or fishermen, from the sound of their diesels and props. Word had been passed to monitor them. They were close, running parallel, slow. It had to be dark up there, at this hour. His ears had adjusted to the diesels when he had heard that too-loud "pizzzz" sound for half a second, like a torpedo. Now he had heard the same sound again. Nothing but a torpedo sounds like a torpedo, but whatever this was reminded him of one. Only it was too brief. Then it happened again. Now nothing, except the diesels. He checked the scopes. He had been dozing mentally before the first one, though his eyes had never even drooped. He was alert now, though.

The *Boise* had been way close to those two boats, still was. They were all headed more or less in the same direction—south, toward the Keys, Cuba, maybe.

Not that it was a problem, but he had not reported in a while, so he did. Ski pushed a button on the console in front of him and said, as nonchalant as he could, "COB, I just heard some weirdness from those two boats you're tailing. You *are* tailing them, right?" he said into the mic on the headphones.

"Duh," said the COB, a chuckle in his voice. "Sleepy, Ski?"

"A little, maybe. COB Stan, I admit I was less than on top of it but I was awake. It sounded—no kiddin'—it sounded like a torpedo, only it barely lasted a second, both times. I think it was small."

"Both times? What's the scope show?" Schuermann asked. He was glad for something to break the routine. Somehow the last couple hours before breakfast drag. Even underwater, stuff gets quieter.

He checked again. "Nothing, COB. Just those two diesel yachts. Twin diesels on each one. We following them?"

"Affirmative," Schuermann said. "We're their shadow. They changed course a while ago, and so did we. Like a little torpedo, you say?"

"Yes and no," Trabinsky said. "Want to hear it?"

"Why not? Tee it up." Something about a tiny torpedo rang a bell, and it bugged him.

In a minute, Trabinsky had found the noise, listened to it again and had it ready. "Here it comes, COB." Trabinsky patched the noise to a speaker in the console.

"Hmmm," the COB said when he heard the "zing" or "pizzzz" through the hum of the diesels. It faded quick, then there was another. "Definitely not a torpedo. Play it again."

"Hmm," Schuermann said to himself after the second run. He put on earphones. "Once more."

Trabinsky obliged. This time, Schuermann's ears and brain clicked, and he smiled, a smile of recognition.

"What do you think it is, Ski?" he asked. The COB's grin struck fear into the hearts of inexperienced submariners. Now it was pointed at Ski. He almost ducked.

"COB, I have no idea. But they were close."

"Too close," the COB said. "In fact, I would say they were ... launched by one of those surface vessels." He smiled more. "I think I know when it was, too. We got way too close at one point. They changed course and we were a tad slow to correct. Those things could have hit us, as close as we were. But all of us would have heard that."

"Say what, COB?"

"Don't you know what they were, Ski? Really? This one's easy. You don't even have to strain your brain."

"Stan, you know I can do an analysis, slow it down, maybe tell you how fast it spun, maybe get a direction, stuff like that. But *no way* do I know what it is. I mean, what they were."

"I do," Schuermann said. "At least I'm 99 percent sure. And I'm also sure you've heard that sound before. Think, Ski."

"Some kind of gas canister? Some relief valve? Chief, you know I'm guessing. You and I both know it doesn't sound much like either one of those, but is it maybe in that family?"

"Close, but no cigar. Gas, yes; canister, sort of. You were closer when you said torpedo."

"But COB, they were tiny, way too tiny for a torpedo, yet ..."

"You're getting warmer."

"My jaw is getting torqued, is what I'm getting." Ski un-clinched his jaws, took a deep breath and gave the Chief of the Boat an exasperated look.

Schuermann chuckled. "That's the trouble with peacetime," he said. "If you had ever been in a shooting war, you'd know right away, Ski."

"COB, I'm young, but I'm old enough to know you were never in a shooting war, not on a sub, bubba." Then, remembering himself, he said, "Um, I don't think. No disrespect intended, COB."

Schuermann laughed outright, but let Ski dangle. Out of the corner of his eye, the COB could see Trabinsky lean way out of his chair to try to see his face.

"Listen, youngster, just because they called it the Cold War doesn't mean it wasn't hot sometimes, if you were in the right places," the COB said. "The Rooskies and their subs never went away. The North Koreans? Jeez. Think, Ski! Grenada? Persian Gulf? Think back to your training, if you have to. The Gulf War was plenty hot, for a major example. Not to mention the run-up to it. Numerous times in the Sea of Japan, and in the North Sea. Pirates off India, Somalis off Africa all the time. Other stuff I still can't talk about. I stand by the shooting war comment." Schuermann smiled, because Ski was stumped.

Then Ski's face brightened.

"Shooting war ... awww," Ski finally said, getting it. Then very quietly he said, "That was a bullet, right? Two big ones? Some kind of big bullet."

"Sounds like it to me. The thing that threw you off, and me too for a minute, was hearing just two. And so close. Kind of out of context. Smaller, say, than the kind that comes from a strafing airplane, but it was a bullet. And they were damned close."

Ski had never heard a strafing bullet, not in real life, only training. He was impressed. "Probably some cowboys throwing beer cans off the stern and shooting at them," Ski theorized.

"They missed, if that was it," said the COB, his brow furrowed as he tested that idea. "Just the two shots, right? Nothing since? You still listening?"

"With one ear, 100 percent," Trabinsky said, as he nodded. "Correct, just the two you heard."

Schuermann smiled. "I love training missions." He stood, stepped through the hatchway into the operations center, where he nodded to the officer of the deck. The OOD had heard part of his conversation with Ski. Seeing the OOD nod back, the COB said to the helmsman, "New guy, you hang with those two boats until further notice, as previously instructed, but this is new: let everybody know if they split, or do anything squirrelly, anything at all."

"Aye aye, sir," said the newb, a three-striper just out of radio "A" school, where he had finished second in a class of forty. The new radioman was not submarine certified, but working hard on it. Not incidentally, he was still trying to convince himself that he was getting the hang of being underwater all the time.

45
First light

A faint glow made the horizon appear.

Mel and Chip saw it first. They had each stayed awake, but had not talked. Neither wanted to wake the others, or to voice what was in their heads. The rest, lulled by the calm Gulf and worn down by the tension of the night before, had nodded off, one by one. Chip's suggestion that sleep would help them be ready for the day had helped. He had not been able to follow his own advice, though.

More of the sky lightened. It was still too dark to read the time on Bridget's wrist, though Chip could see the wrist now, and the watch, and her face as she slept, serene. She had her knees against Ping, who had tried to give her room, without crowding Ruth. As a result, Ping was a pretzel. It was amazing that he could sleep.

Part of the horizon was rosy. Not red, as in "red sky at morning, sailors take warning," just rosy to the east. Chip looked at Mel. The expression on his face spoke more than Chip could take in. Mel looked older than yesterday, more serious, but also cheerful. Blood crusted some of his dark grey hair, and most of an ear. Kimbie had put an over-sized Band-Aid on the pistol-whip cut, in the dark, after glopping it with what she hoped was antibiotic ointment. It smelled right. Nobody had a flashlight, but she had done a decent job and covered it. The gash had stopped bleeding.

Chip, who had been measured and self-contained before and during the takeover, still felt angry and frustrated. Mel saw some of that, and must have registered surprise, because as he watched, Chip took a deep breath, and visibly relaxed. But he did not smile.

The sky was turning from rose below navy to rose gray now. The east was an intense pink at the horizon. Soon the sun would show. Sure enough, as they watched, the sun seemed to pop above the horizon like a buoy. In an instant, everything in the raft was bathed in warm, intense, reddish light.

John Zinser, whose face was to the east, opened his eyes and smiled. Rolling his shoulders, he pulled himself closer to an upright position and looked around.

"Good morning, my friend," he said quietly to Chip, who nodded. John looked from face to face. He stopped longest to look at his wife, nestled against him. As he looked at her, Chip saw concern, then calm. John did not try to really sit up. To do so would have risked waking her. But his eyes continued their inventory, and when he saw Mel was awake, he nodded a greeting and smiled. Mel returned both.

In a moment, Kimbie stirred, then others, until the only sleepers were Sherry and Ping. When Ruth awoke, she squeezed John around his middle and buried her face in his shirt. He stroked her hair. Bridget began to stretch almost as soon as her eyes opened. Wordlessly she begged indulgence as she carefully pulled one leg out of the tangle in the middle of the raft. She extended the leg, pointed and then flexed her toes. Then she threaded the other leg between two amused raftmates , stretched one arm behind Julian's head, then stretched the other behind Chip. Despite the cramped quarters she continued, catlike, until she was fully awake. Chip quietly explained to whoever happened to be in the way that she always did this when she awoke. Usually a lot more, he said, not to worry.

"I would too, if I didn't have on a skirt," said Ruth, who could not keep the giggles out of her voice.

When Sherry was awake, a council of sorts was held. Ping slept on. The first thing to do, everyone decided, was take inventory.

Sherry emptied a pocket and found folded bills, "About three grand" she had *not* been too hysterical to stuff in her shorts. "So I'm buying breakfast ... or brunch," she said.

"Eggs Benedict!" said Kimbie. From the pocket of her T-shirt Kimbie pulled a small compass, string, and a mushy Snickers bar. Chip had pocketed four "AA" batteries in a pack, though for the moment there was nothing to use them in. The gallon jug of water he had carried aboard was between his legs, unopened. Mel and Ping had also brought jugs, at Kimbie's direction.

Ruth showed five tangerines and a can of mixed nuts. "I ran out of time," she said, almost an apology. Mel had a medium-size Swiss Army knife. He also had a Visa card. "I wanted to bring a gun, but ..." Nobody said anything.

John Zinser had a tiny New Testament and two cans of sardines in mustard. "John loves his sardines," Ruth said, "and his Bible." He also had a warm six-pack of canned iced tea, sweet, with lemon.

From the bottom of the raft, Bridget sheepishly produced a big red ball that turned out to be a wax-covered cheese. Laughter and approval all round.

"Turns out we were a pretty sneaky bunch," said Sherry. In a zipper baggie were breath mints and a very small cell phone in a leather case. The phone was greeted by astonished looks, and murmurs of approval.

Chip grinned and produced a tiny pair of binoculars, good ones, and a nickel-plated whistle. "I didn't want to part with these," he said. "I've had this whistle since I was a kid. The binocs were from my granddad."

It took some shifting, but Kimbie had a flattened paper sack that contained an orange, packets of salt, four hard-boiled eggs in cracked shells, more string, fishhooks wrapped in a napkin, matches in a small waterproof case, seven tea bags, a pink silk scarf, cough drops, and a pink gold necklace and locket. "Picture of my grandparents. I figured, hey, all they can do is take it away," she said, as she continued to pull out one thing after another. She showed the locket to Ruth, who admired it and passed it around.

Kimbie asked the men to turn their heads and retrieved paper money from her bikini. She had openly carried a half-pound of beef jerky, triple bagged. What looked like a dozen big rubber bands of different colors were on her wrists. "I didn't know if they would help, but ..." she ended, sheepish.

"Why not?" said John Zinser, and hugged her, carefully, not shifting his weight.

Sherry's phone had raised everyone's spirits. Kimbie's cache had started a ripple of subdued mirth.

"That's pretty much the way I looked at it too," said Sherry. She produced a compact with a mirror, Ibuprofen gel-caps in a baggie, scarves, sunscreen (which she immediately shared), a tiny pepper spray, a nail file and polish.

"Silly, huh?" she said, matter of fact.

"Nice color," said Ruth. "One minute indeed."

"But a phone! We're saved!" said Bridget, bouncing, but careful.

"Is it charged?" asked Ping, who had been stirred awake when everyone started laughing. "Will it ... work out here?"

"Let's find out," Sherry said. She unwrapped it, held down the power button, and waited. No one breathed until she smiled and said, "One bar. And voicemail."

"I thought about trying to call, but I was worried the pirates would see it. And I didn't know where we were." She bit her lower lip. Nods and thoughtful looks told her it was all right.

"Should we call 9-1-1?" She looked from face to face. Mel nodded. The consensus was, "Why not?" So she did.

There was no sound for half a minute, then she heard a ring tone, and smiled. It rang three times before she heard: "Emergency 9-1-1, how may I help you?" It was a young-sounding male, loud enough for others to hear, and clear. Smiles spread.

"Okay," Sherry said, taking a breath, surprised. Trying to sound as serious and as sincere as she could, she said, "Um, I need help. *We* need help. I'm calling from … somewhere in the Gulf—I don't know where—and we need to be rescued."

"Ma'am did you say you're out in the Gulf of Mexico?"

"That's right. Eight people in a raft. Eight of us. We were some-where near the west coast of Florida … last time we knew. Maybe a few hours out from St. Petersburg, but north, or northwest. We really don't know. The captain and crew … we're pretty sure … and two passengers … we're pretty sure … were killed. Where are you?"

"Ma'am, this is Tampa Bay enhanced 9-1-1. If you're serious—and—no disrespect but you had better be—then I need you to hold on while I add the Coast Guard to the call. I don't understand how you got into our network, but you're here. You may be closer than you think. Did you say you're in a raft, ma'am?"

"Yes. A rubber life raft. Small. Eight of us, packed like sardines. And I'm totally serious," she said, eyebrows up, a little incredulous. "We were put onto the raft when our boat—the boat we were passengers on, I mean—was stolen. Hijacked. By pirates. The *New Delphia*." Several shook their heads. Kimbie waved her hand and said, "Motor vessel *New Delphi*, out of Tampa." Sherry corrected herself. "Last night—that is, early this morning. The captain … and crew of two … and two others … were killed, we're pretty sure. I'm as serious as a heart attack. My name is Sherry McRae, and I'm from Chicago." She bit her lower lip.

"Yes ma'am," the operator said. "Is your phone from Chicago? It's not showing up."

"Yes," she said, and gave him the number.

"All right, ma'am. This is so unusual that I've added operators from the U.S. Coast Guard on the line with us. You just told me that you and your party are in a life raft, in the Gulf. Eight people. Possibly a few hours out of St. Pete. Possibly north or northwest. You need to tell them anything you can. Are you in sight of land?"

Sherry looked, and asked the others. No land was in sight, and she told them. She described the yacht and what she could remember about the sport fishing boat, with help from Mel and Chip and Kimbie. She elaborated on what had happened during the night.

A female voice came on the line. "Sherry, we're going to start looking for you, but it will take time. Do you have a watch?" The voice was professional, reassuring.

She did, and they asked her what time she had. Then the woman asked her to call back on the hour. "And keep that phone dry." She said to call back immediately if she spotted a ship or plane. Instructions were repeated. Questions were asked and answered.

Sherry agreed, nodding, thanked them, and hung up. As she did, she noticed that her battery was low. She had meant to charge it, but wasn't sure whether the boat had the right kind of electricity, and hadn't asked. She had not thought of the phone since the dolphins. She turned it off.

When concerns were raised, she explained about the battery. "They said to call back on the hour."

46
This must be why

Chax was still sure he should stay with the raft. The people in it had slept. So had he, halfway, one eye open, as always. At dawn he visited the pod. They were content to stay. He did not want them right next to the raft, though. There was no point in that.

The people in the raft were resting when he came back. Awake but resting. He felt no need to go close.

47
Can't just sit

"Commander Harris, ma'am, I'd like to formally request to be part of the search."

Petty Officer First Class Estil Potter was already part of the search, on radio watch in the station command center, but he was land-based and restless. Potter knew a great deal about this part of the world, first hand, on water and land, and for that reason Lt. Cdr. Harris had already told him the first time he asked that he was probably where he could do the most good, at the comm center. Potter knew that was probably true. But he also tended to think everybody on station ought to know what he knew, ought to be able to do what he could do. He believed a new Coastie should not rest until he or she mastered everything they were supposed to know, the way he had, because that is their job. Potts also knew that a friend of his might need help, out there somewhere. Sitting on the beach wasn't easy, under the circumstances.

Harris leveled her gaze at him. "I know that Captain Gordon was— is—that he's an old shipmate of yours, Potts." She wished she had not said 'was,' and briefly touched his arm.

He smiled. "You ain't gonna let me, are you ma'am." said Potter, reading her correctly.

"Let's level, Potts. You're the best on station at three-fourths of the key slots. You probably know as much about this sector as anybody here right now—way more than I do, even though I'm catching up. You know which agencies will bust their butt to help us, and which ones only comply. I'm still new. I know you want to be out there straining your eyes, using your skills and instincts on a boat, but it's just not the right thing to do this time. It isn't in your friend's best interest. You're already helping him most by being here. Tell me where I'm wrong and I'll consider it."

Potts had thought it over, four or five times. The former base commander had sung his praises to the new boss-lady. At the time, he thought that might not be a great idea, even if it was true. She watched him like a hawk anyway, before she started to trust him without checking, but that had been almost a year ago.

She learned fast. He had trusted her for some time now, and had leveled with her on everything worth knowing locally. She knew her job, worked hard, and knew what she didn't know. She was right, since Chief White was on leave. If the chief were here, he would have put Potts on a boat as a search captain. But Chief White wasn't here, and that was that. Potts just wanted to do more.

"You ain't that new anymore, ma'am. You know where most of the deadwood's at," Potts said, giving it one more half-hearted tug.

She smiled at the compliment, but cocked her head and looked at Potts. "Thanks. I'm learning. But I still can't spare you. Matter of fact, I was going to ask if you'd stick close after your watch, and be reachable to help out if we need you."

"Okay, ma'am. Aye Aye," Potts said, using the sailor acknowledgement that means the hearer understands and will comply. "I was only going down to the beach with some binoculars. It's danged hard not to be out there, though. Gordo is ... well, at one time he was a daggone good friend. He pretty much still is, though he's a little stupid sometimes, and I don't see him much. He was a good Coastie, ma'am, almost as good as yours truly." She almost winced. "I know him better than he knows his dumb self. I know stuff about him that his mama don't know. I know his mama, too, that's the real hard part. I sure hope she don't call down here to see what I know. She and Gordo talked me out of going AWOL one time—me!" The lieutenant commander looked surprised, but he nodded. "I was gone quit and go home, way back when I was green as they come, a homesick, E-one stupid tadpole. That's how well I know 'em."

Lt. Commander Harris bit her lip. "Potts, honey, I wish I could."

Potter smiled. "I know, ma'am." Then he ducked his head and looked around like a thief. "You'd best not be calling me 'honey,' ma'am. That's fraternization. Shoot, these days that's harassment! I halfway feel offended, commander. Ma'am." His eyes twinkled. The corners of his mouth twitched.

"Potts, you ... you do no such thing." She shook her head, almost laughed and rolled her eyes. She was glad at least that he was okay with her decision.

48
Ricky plays captain

Ricky wiped his face with his T-shirt. His face dripped sweat, despite the cool night breeze on the bridge of the boat he was beginning to think of as his own. He was at the helm of the sport-fisher, while Claiborne was on the new boat with the snow-white hull. He could barely see it, off to starboard just ahead. At daylight, Claiborne would stop and tell him to scrape the name off its stern, pronto, paint it too, if they had paint. That was reality. But for now Ricky was in command. Of this boat, anyway.

Not that he could tell Salazar what to do. Salazar had told Ricky to steer while he messed with the engines. They were running too rich.

Teddy getting killed had changed things. Teddy had been close— that close, man! He was almost ready to go along with Ricky's plan to take over. If it had happened, Salazar might have gone along too. Maybe. If Ricky killed Claiborne, that would have make him the captain, no question.

If. Big "if."

Because Salazar was second in command. Nothing formal, but second, no question. Teddy had been third, according to Claiborne. If Ricky killed Claiborne, Salazar might leave on his own, but no way would Ricky cross Claiborne, or Salazar, and Teddy would never have either. No point in even talking to Salazar about going against Claiborne. Ricky had, once. Salazar laughed, called him "Junior." Whenever Ricky and Claiborne would get into it, Salazar would get this half-smile, and Ricky could almost hear him say "Junior" again. It made him crazy. Salazar better watch it, man.

Ricky could kill. He had before. For self-preservation. And this very night, in a rage of fear. Ricky liked to think he could be cold about killing, too, but he had not been cold about shooting that long-legged chick. Ricky had killed her only after he saw his own blood on that machete, and on his arm and hand when he reached back to where he had been cut, after Salazar dusted the old sailor. When he saw his hand covered with his own blood, felt it running down his back into his shorts, he thought the old man had cut him bad enough that he might die. It turned out the machete had hit the bulkhead when the old man fell, and had not cut him much. But the blood had scared him, put him in enough of a rage to shoot her, even after Salazar had killed the old man. She had some kind of wicked knife in her hand. Looked like she would use it, too. She didn't get a chance, though, because he shot her.

But he couldn't take Claiborne and Salazar both, no way. Maybe not either one. He had frozen again and let Claiborne take his gun. Remembering that made him shudder. Made him sick, if you want to know the truth about it. Ricky wanted to think he could, but he wasn't sure he could take either one, not if they knew what was up. And they always did.

Maybe he could just give Claiborne the slip, leave him on the new boat. This boat was good enough. The new boat was way too pretty and squared away for anybody to believe it was his, even with papers. Ricky didn't belong with that boat, no way. That was Claiborne's gig. Claiborne could look and act like he belonged on it, handle all kinds of people, papers, cops, harbor cops, customs, Coast Guard and that. He had that down. That was another reason Claiborne was the man.

But this boat was different. This one, Ricky was pretty sure he could pass off as his own. It didn't look all pretty, not ready for no boat show. It had bilge stains. Didn't look all spit-shined like the other one. Just a typical, deep-water sport-fishing boat. Tuna tower, dark windows, salt-crusted hardware, grungy seats and decks, grungy hull if you want to know the truth about it, stuff that needed paint. Faded flags. Which all kind of hid the fact that it was all there, and everything worked fine. *Like me*, Ricky daydreamed. Plenty of fishing gear in good shape, freezers full of food, tanks nearly full. Motors ran decent, most of the time. And Claiborne's money, man. There had to be plenty money in that stateroom. Maybe a couple hundred grand. Enough for anything, man. Claiborne was never short.

Thinking of Claiborne's money made him think of Teddy's stash. Maybe that's what Salazar is doing down there, man, going through Teddy's sea bag, finding his weed, and his money. Teddy never talked about what he had, but Ricky was sure Teddy had a little U.S. money and some island money, someplace. Mouse-trapped some weird way, bet on it. Wicked knives, from his shrimper days. But mainly Teddy had some good weed. Did have. He wouldn't smoke it at sea, didn't hardly ever smoke it, mostly he kept it to impress women, but Ricky was sure he had it. Salazar would throw it overboard. Claiborne wouldn't stop him. They didn't want Ricky to have it, and Teddy didn't need it now.

Thinking about that made him clinch his jaws. Made him sick, if you want to know the truth about it, but Teddy's gone. Reality.

Ricky thought about sneaking down there and surprising Salazar, blowing him away. It might work. Then he could turn off the running lights and boogie. Run due south to the Keys, then east to the islands, Bahama, Jamaica, wherever. Or Mexico, South America, someplace Claiborne would never find him. Yeah, Mexico.

Ricky smiled as he thought about catching Salazar with both hands in Teddy's locker. *Just dust him. Haul ass for Mexico. All that money, my own boat. Fine young Mexican cuties for a crew. Run a little cocaine into Beaumont or Galveston. Claiborne don't like those towns. Man, it would be easy.*

The first glow of dawn lit the clean white hull of the *New Delphi and* ended Ricky's pipe dream. Even in the dim first light, it was obvious that the yacht would be faster. Claiborne would run him down like a dog. Shoot him, cuff him to the wheel, open the scuppers, man. Sink this grungy boat and him with it. Claiborne would do that, no question, to somebody who had shot Salazar and crossed him. He was that cold, easy. Crazy cold. *Those people in that raft don't know how close they came, man.* Ricky shook as he remembered how Claiborne had talked to him after that red-headed bitch sprawled her fine self down on the deck. Took his gun.

Ricky's coke-stoked imagination, which had just taken him on a Mexican pleasure excursion, now raced down a paranoid path centered on Claiborne's vengeance. Ricky knew Claiborne would make his last minutes into living hell. He could easily imagine it. Could not help but imagine it. The confidence that had sprouted in him while he steered the boat was not even a memory.

When Salazar climbed to the bridge, Ricky almost cowered. Salazar noticed Ricky's sweat-covered face. He dripped sweat. *Thinking about Teddy*, he guessed. *That and nose candy.* Salazar had not thought too much about Teddy. He'd seen this coming, something like this. Teddy wasn't careful. He thought taking the boat would be easy, that people wouldn't fight. Now he knew. Poor guy. Live by the sword, man, it happens. Salazar crossed himself. It wouldn't hurt for Ricky to be more careful too. Use his brain. Not work stoned. Maybe he would. Not yet.

This whole thing has gone ragged, mon. We let those people go, to keep the boat all nice. Okay, that made sense, maybe, but it's a risk. Claiborne's call. That's the way it is. But Salazar had not liked it. If Ricky had not gone off like he did, Salazar might have said so, but even a stupid man knew better than to side with Ricky when things are tense. Ricky didn't need encouragement. He could flip out on you. Salazar was not stupid.

There was still time to go back and get rid of them. That was what Salazar wanted to do. Just business. For once, okay, Ricky was right. A stopped clock is right sometimes. Salazar would mention it to Claiborne—quietly, privately—when they stopped to take the name off the stern.

49
Pete sees

Pete Gordon was swimming when he saw the dawn. At least he seemed to be in the water. The pink glow in front of his face startled him. He didn't know what it was. It took effort to make his eyes see it. Eye. Only one seemed to work. Sort of. His mind only sort of worked too. It hurt, and didn't want to think just now. Still, he tried. He was swimming. Now that he thought about it, he had been swimming for as long as he could remember. If you could call it swimming. His body moved like a machine, an out-of-adjustment machine. His arms and legs felt like they were made of rubber. So did his head. He didn't know why.

With the daylight, though, it came back. A bit at a time. Once he realized what he saw, and sort of remembered where he was, he was so happy he lost track of everything else. He was so happy he was goofy. Crazy happy. He had never been so happy. So happy to see anything. To see the sun! He would have sworn he had been pointed south, after he turned away from those sharks. But he was pretty sure the sun does not rise in the south, and it was right there in front of him. The sun! That was good, right? He had to try to think. It hurt, but he tried. Just not too hard. If he tried too hard to think he might throw up. Can't do that. So he waited.

The sun in front of him meant he must be headed east. An old Grateful Dead song rose up to confuse him but he shook it off. The sun rises in the east. Yeah. He was pointed the right way! Had been since ... when? East of him must be some Florida beach. He had no idea whether he was five miles out or fifty. Thinking about it, though, thinking around the edges just a little, it must be less than twenty. Maybe ten. Maybe even five.

It was cold. Until now he had been balanced his need for rest against his need to stay warm. The sun would help. He still didn't know why he was swimming. Something bad had happened. He could not remember what.

His head hurt, he knew that. It was nearly numb, too. The way his head felt, he wondered why sharks had not smelled blood. In the growing light, though, he could tell pretty well from the eye that would open that his head was not bloody, just swollen. And rubbery. When he touched his face, he couldn't feel it. His fingers felt his face, but his face didn't feel his fingers. But his fingers didn't get bloody. That was good. He hurt all over. It hurt to turn his head, even just a little, but he did it. Pain helped him focus. He turned his head, turned it back. It kind of sprung back, away from the pain.

As pain began to clear his mind, he remembered something, before the sharks. Something or somebody had smashed his face. That must have been it. Maybe a bullet. Something. That much he could remember, but not why. He must have blacked out. Or something.

As the dawn brightened, he realized his left eye would only open a little, only a slit. He could close it, but he couldn't open it any wider. Still, it let light in. His other eye would not open at all. Not so he could tell. He couldn't see out of it. With his fingers he could feel, for pretty sure, that the orb was still there, the eyeball, but it was hard to tell. He didn't want to make it bleed.

If his eyes were that bad, his face must be bad too. It didn't feel right, didn't even feel like his face. Like it was made of rubber, that thing again. Somebody had been on his boat, but he could not remember why. It seemed impossible. Maybe later.

He touched his nose. It was there. He could breathe through it. On one side. He tried to feel the brow bone above his right eye, but couldn't. His nose felt flat. His finger could trace a cut across it. That must be where the blow landed. There and on his brow bone. Hard enough to knock him out. Duh. His head felt huge. A concussion, probably, because the bony arch that should have been above his right eye was … missing. Lower, crunched, whatever. Somehow, that was funny. Hard enough to mash my thick skull, but not enough to kill me. My thick skull. That's funny.

Almost. It must have happened hours ago, since it wasn't bleeding. But he had not thought about any of this until now. All he had thought about was breathe, swim and rest, breathe, swim, rest. Cold. Push 'til you get warm. If you call that thinking.

When he was little, maybe a toddler, Pete fell off a houseboat. Tied up at Port Charlotte, where his parents had lived. Years later his Mama said he was swimming when they found him, with his face out of the water, grinning, dog-paddling like crazy. It was a wonder that a 'gator or something hadn't gotten him, but just as much a wonder he could swim, small as he was. Maybe that was what saved him this time. Maybe.

He had prayed. He remembered that. When he was little he had been taken to church on Sunday. He had been raised to respect church, any church. Respect what people believe. It had been a while since he had been, but his Mom went three times a week, even now. He knew she prayed for him. Last night, or this morning, whenever, when he had been up against it, he had asked God to help him. That's a prayer, isn't it? It felt like a prayer. And it helped. It must have been a hallucination, but he had seen his mom at her kitchen table, saw her pray for him, real as anything. Like he was there, in the warm room.

He thought about that and peeped at the sunrise again. Marveled at it. You're not supposed to look at the sun too long, but he wanted to. He didn't but he wanted to. He had always liked sunrises, and sunsets. They're all good. They tend to run together in memory, even when his head was working right, but this one … was the one, really the one. What he could see of it was gorgeous. Rosy orange and intense rich yellow and deep blue, shading to white and pink and red like fire. Even through a slit it was gorgeous. Maybe because it was through a slit. No matter. He had to move his head and neck to see it, but the sight was worth a little pain. He would remember it.

As he swam, Pete tried again to remember how he got here. Who had he pissed off? What had gone wrong?

He had shot somebody. Good grief. The guy had looked like Teddy Barfield, but that was crazy. Teddy, poor old not-too-bright Teddy, was supposed to be in Venezuela or someplace. He had kind of liked goofy ol' Teddy, back in the day, when they had crewed together on a shrimp boat. But young as he had been, Pete soon realized that hanging with Teddy would get you in trouble. Teddy was a good hand on a boat, even if he was no rocket scientist. His instincts were good on a boat. He liked to have something to do and worked hard. But ashore, Teddy was always in trouble. He couldn't handle booze, or money, or teasing, or women. Or drugs. Or shysters. Or bad cops. Any cops. Around good people, Teddy was okay, but he was gullible. He didn't think ahead. It was uncanny how Teddy found bad situations, too. Like a magnet.

Pete had sure enough shot a guy that looked something like Teddy. The dude was trying to steal his boat. That was it!

His boat! Where was it? It was nowhere to be seen, so maybe somebody had stolen it. Not the guy he shot, though. Not that dude. Pete felt bad about it, whether or not it was Teddy, but … he had to do it.

His next thought was insurance. Marine insurance. It was more of a flash than a thought. He had a policy on the boat that would almost replace it. The insurance cost a fortune, twice a year. Nobody he knew believed he really, actually had it. A lot of shrimpers didn't. But that insurance was the only way Pete could sleep. A guy he had grown up with, a banker in Fort Myers now, found the insurance for him. Pete missed a payment once, let the coverage lapse past the short grace period while he was off in the Caribbean. When he realized, he could barely eat, much less sleep, until he paid it, got his buddy to pay it by wire transfer. He sat in port, tied up at a marina, until he got word that the coverage was reinstated. He had worked too hard, risked too much. He did not want to go back to a life without the boat.

His brain was starting to work now. The policy covered theft, but he wondered if it would cover piracy. It was supposed to cover "certain acts of piracy." That seemed like maybe what had happened. He hoped he would get to find out.

His next thought was for Digs. And Kimbie. He hoped they were all right. Then, with a sickening wave, he remembered the others. Fred, Ruth, John, Ping. Passengers, too. Lots of them.

The worst nausea and depression Pete had ever known came over him. It seemed to push him down. It sat on his chest, and he could not breathe. He stopped swimming, stopped doing anything, even thinking. Stopped even remembering, until he realized the light was getting dim. Through that slit, with his one good eye, he looked for the light. It looked like he was down a well.

Everything gone. The boat. His life. His crew, Kimmie …

As he looked up, he thought he saw a dolphin diving down toward him. It was swimming hard, but stopped a few feet from his face. It made a noise, and cocked its head. It looked puzzled. "Well?" it seemed to say.

Kimmie would like this one, he thought. Kimmie.

Pete wanted to take a big deep breath. Needed to. *"You're right pal,"* Pete said to the dolphin. Thought it, anyway. He had to be losing it, talking to dolphins.

He wasn't going to quit, though, that was stupid. That was chickenshit. He needed to breathe. So he kicked his way toward the light. What started as a parody of a frog kick turned into a half-decent dolphin kick. He had no bubbles to follow, just the light. He followed until he broke the surface and gasped, and gulped in the sweet air. It tasted so good!

Fresh, full of aromas and flavors and warm like the sun. There was no dolphin in sight. He turned all the way around with his hands, just to see.

He was beyond tired. In a while he would swim on his back, and float a while, to rest. He looked forward to it. But right now, he had to swim toward the sunrise, keep the pinkish-reddish-orange and blue in front of him. That sunrise was the one thing he had going for him right now.

They all had to be dead. Or as bad off as he was. But he couldn't think about that. He was alive. They might be alive too. He had to will himself to stop thinking about them, because thinking about that made the nausea come like a kick in the gut. Throwing up would be too dangerous. He didn't think he could throw up and not drown.

He thought about his mom, getting up about now, turning on the weather channel. Start coffee, toast a muffin, fish marmalade from the jar, get some rind in the spoon. Read her Bible, like she always did. Pray. Pray for her boy. Maybe she was praying for her boy now.

The thought stunned him. She probably was. Wow. He thought about that until his breathing was normal. It was light enough to see now, so he used his hands and feet to ride the swells and look around. Two turns around. Three. Nothing. Nobody. Water.

He remembered the passengers. Digs had called one of them "the schoolmarm." Sarah. She was quiet, but fun. He liked her. Hell, he liked all of them. John and Ruth are super. They had been with the boat so long, they were like an aunt and uncle. Are. Are. He made up his mind to at least hope. The teeny-bopper was, is, having such a big time, even though she can barely swim. He hoped she wasn't in the water, and his hope sank. For a few minutes, he just floated, despaired, forgot to think about something else. On top of everything else, it occurred to him that even if he were to be able to replace the boat, he would still be finished as a captain. The captain is supposed to go down with the ship. But he saw no reason it should sink. He wondered if he would ever see the boat again, wondered who had it, what they were doing to it.

With no boat, he had no business partner, no Ping. He almost laughed, but that felt wrong. A laugh would hurt too much, for one thing. Hurt his face, his head, his heart, too. If he had lost his crummy "partner," he had probably lost Kimmie. Not that he had her. Maybe she's okay. If he had to bet on any of them, he would bet on her. She could swim all day. *Can* swim all day. Can. Think positive. Can.

He should have kicked Ping's butt a long time ago. Offered her Ping's deal. Something. From the get-go, she had been more than half of what Ping contributed. She was easier to get along with, too. And to look at.

But things just plodded along and he let them. He had made a conscious decision not to try to take her away from that jerk. Why? He couldn't remember. She was too good for Ping, even if she didn't think so. Too late for that. Maybe. He had to focus, had to get his head right. He used his hands to bob up on the gentle swells for a look. After several tries he saw only more swells. So he prayed again.

"God, sir, help her. Please. Help 'em all." He took a deep breath. "Thank you for helping me. Thank you. I still need help, though. Sir." After he thought about what he had said, he added, "Amen." Pete had said more prayers in the last few hours than he had since his Dad died. A total of two, as best he could remember. They were short, but he meant them. He felt better.

Hey, he probably wasn't going to make it anyway. He hadn't seen any land when he did those turns, or any boats, not even anything floating. And his arms and legs were getting as heavy as his head.

His tongue was thick and his head had never hurt this bad, not even after the longest, worst drunk he had ever been on. Not that there had been many. Booze had never been his thing, not like boats.

He had to swim, though, hurt or not. No way could he make it. But hey, he had to swim. And not quit.

Pete was trying to remember if he had any bills due when an explosion—a volcanic eruption or something, happened just in front of him. It rocked him back, but it wasn't an explosion, or a volcano or any of those things. At that particular spot and that particular time a seven-foot dolphin chose to jump. Straight up. Then another one. And another, maybe bigger than the first. Right in front of his face. The splashes were so high that the pink rays of the sun made the water dazzle.

Once he got over being terrified, Pete laughed. It hurt, but it felt great, too. This is crazy, but ain't it great?

The more he laughed, the more his brain and the rest of him was flooded with gratitude, just for being alive. When one of the dolphins swam up to his face and stopped, all he could think was, "You know it, pal." So he said it, out loud, and laughed at the sound of his own voice. The dolphin cocked its head to look at him. Opened its mouth. Laughed.

Smiley faces. They weren't sweating it. Hey, life goes on. Pete began to swim again, into the sunrise. Slow and steady, toward Florida, the land of sunshine, with a three-dolphin escort. Or four, or two, he wasn't sure. Didn't matter. Hey, life is good.

50
Second guessing

As soon as it was light, Claiborne Chandler turned west and made a huge circle. As he turned he saw nothing but the blue-green Gulf of Mexico. When he was sure no other vessels were in sight, only smoke from a tanker headed away, he pointed the bow into the gentle breeze from the west, and stopped.

After putting out a sea anchor, he rummaged in the boat's squared-away lockers until he found a gallon of white anti-fouling paint, scrapers, a good trim brush, and sandpaper. He also found a boatswain's chair. Ricky could use the mahogany stern platform. He would not need it.

By the time Claiborne came back on deck, Ricky was alongside. Salazar put out fenders and tied the two boats together. They had done this before. For once, Ricky went straight to the task, even if he scowled and clunked around more than necessary. He rigged the boatswain's chair anyway, though it made little sense. He sat in it, feet wet, back to the sun, and scraped. The black-painted name began to disappear. Salazar boarded the yacht and went to the salon. He soon re-appeared with two mugs of hot coffee, and gave one to Claiborne.

"All the comforts." Claiborne grinned oddly. He cradled the Coast Guard mug with both hands.

"This is a million-dollar boat," Salazar said. "All nice. It will bring a good price. We could keep it. But it's ready to sell. We would not get near that much for ours, without much work."

"Too much work," Claiborne said. "Mostly paint and polish, but too much time. We don't want to deal with two boats long either, just three of us." By unspoken agreement they wandered up the port rail out of Ricky's hearing. Their backs were to the sunrise, and to Ricky. It was the first time they had talked since Teddy's death.

"We can't handle two boats that well," Salazar said.

Claiborne nodded, and his jaw twitched. He noticed the small round hole in the cabin window where they stood. *This is where that tough little captain shot Teddy*. He looked at the dark deck. Tiny shards of glass glinted there, now that he looked for them. Salazar saw the hole too. They exchanged a look, but said nothing. They could hear Ricky scrape, and swear.

"He's afraid. Those people saw him," Salazar said, quietly. "He stole motorcycles, sold drugs, got caught, locked up. He thinks they'll finger him, from some picture."

Claiborne snorted. "So what? He won't be there to arrest."

Salazar looked at him. "So nothing. Just saying. Won't happen. But …" His voice dropped low. "I wanted to get rid of them. If Junior had not got mouthy, I would have said. I didn't, not then, but even Junior is right once in a while. They got Teddy." Salazar looked over the side, looked at the hull, at the water. He looked at the window again.

Claiborne took a sip of coffee, looked at Salazar. "The one that got Teddy is fish food." He sounded irritated. "So are others. What's done is done. It's behind us. Maybe the raft leaks."

Salazar said nothing. His face showed nothing. Then he asked, "How far are we? Far enough?"

Claiborne looked at his expensive watch. "We ran for almost an hour."

"At what, half throttle?" Salazar asked, so casual it seemed insignificant.

"Not the whole time. I throttled back when I locked the wheel to throw stuff overboard."

"We couldn't find them," Salazar said, and let it lie. Claiborne dumped the rest of his coffee in the water. He looked at the mug with the gold Coast Guard anchors, turned it over, and tossed it too.

"Coast Guard won't be looking yet," Claiborne said, but there was no comfort in the statement. He had found a cell phone. It gave him chills. His stomach almost cramped now, at the thought of it. He had not thought of phones, or searched pockets. Sloppy. He hated cell phones. He had turned his back on them. Besides, they usually don't work out of sight of land.

Five Americans dead, he thought. *Eight rescued*. Headline news, eventually. *The dead are just crew, though. Nobodies*. Young women on the crew would make the story sexier, especially if the news had pictures. *Make them seem all sweet and innocent. Or hot. Works either way*. Claiborne seldom second-guessed himself, but with Salazar worried, now he did.

Ricky worked steady, as was prudent, if unusual. Even Ricky was worried.

In daylight, at full throttle, side by side a quarter of a mile apart, they could double back to where they left the raft in a short time. He could retrieve last night's GPS coordinates. It should be easy. If they saw a boat, they could turn around and keep going.

If not, they could sink the raft and leave. Quick. Ricky probably still wanted a woman, but no. Claiborne still did not want to kill all those people, but it would buy time. It would satisfy Salazar. And Ricky. He almost laughed that he was considering that. Almost.

"So, you want to go back, finish up?" Claiborne asked Salazar.

Salazar looked at him, unsmiling, but did not answer, so Claiborne asked a slightly different question. "Do you think it's worth the risk?"

Without hesitation, Salazar said, "No witnesses. It should not take long."

That was enough, though Claiborne did not like it. "Let's do it, then."

51
This is why

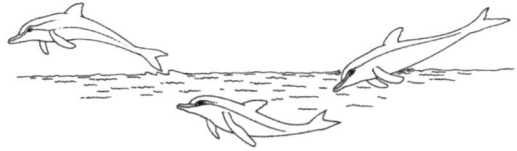

Sound not only travels fast in the ocean, it can travel far. Whales can send songs farther than dolphins, but dolphins do just fine. Chax had called. Answers came. Dolphins from several pods gathered. With nothing else to do they talked, raced, bragged, noted losses and sores, admired babies. Males chased females and generally enjoyed each other's company. The leaders gathered around Chax and swam a big, slow circle around the bubble. They agreed Chax had been right to call them. Still, they had no idea what the day might bring.

The pod told of those who had died in the night. The boats had left. That had been good, but now they were back. The bubble was full of people. Some were full of anger, and fear. Those in the bubble feared those in the boats. They would fight. It was as obvious as a gathering storm.

Some of the dolphins who came had said men were in a frenzy today, all over. Pelicans and terns and gulls confirmed it. Chax did not understand, but he did not need to grasp more than he had known all his life. Men make trouble. It follows them.

Now he was sure he had been right to call an assembly, even if there was nothing special to eat. The yellowtail had a bad taste. It was the wrong time to eat them. But shallow water near here teemed with mullet. They were right for eating, where the river pushed into the ocean.

If nothing bad happened, they would frolic. With this many pods together, it would happen. They could feed and rest and would not separate for a few days. That would be good, unless something bad happened. Chax expected something bad to happen.

52
White hulls

Chip saw them first. One white hull, from the south. Then another. The boats were not headed toward them, but were close enough to see, if they looked. He did not like it when he saw the second one. He gestured with his head to get Mel's attention, and handed over his small binoculars. Mel looked for maybe ten seconds.

"Sherry, it's time to get back on your phone. We see two boats. Nine-one-one said if we saw anybody, to get back in touch." Something in his tone caught her full attention. It would not have taken much.

The tiny phone was in her lap, back in the zip baggie. She got it out, turned it on and dialed 911 as soon as it cycled up. She tried to see the boats.

"Tampa Bay nine-one-one, what is your emergency?" came a voice through the phone, a mature-sounding male.

"My name is Sherry McRae, and I'm in a life raft. I called earlier."

"Yes, ma'am, I know who you are. We have people looking for you. How can I help you right now?"

Good question, she thought, but she said, "Well, I was told to call back if any boats appear, and two just did. They're within sight, but ... well, I ..."

"What kind of boats, ma'am?"

"What do they look like, Chip?"

Chip kept his tiny binoculars to his eyes. "Two white hulls, not small. Motor yachts, 50-footers or better, heading north, parallel." She repeated it.

Quietly, Mel added, "One of them looks like an 80-some footer, a traditional sedan cruiser. The other is about the same size, maybe shorter, but it's a sport fisherman with a tuna tower."

Chip nodded, and Sherry repeated this, trying to read Mel's expression as she did. Then, very calmly, she said, "We may be in danger from the boats." Chip and Mel nodded.

The operator, who now had a screen in front of him full of information about Sherry's earlier call, asked if she thought the boats might be the pirates. Sherry said she was afraid they might be. Then the operator said, "Miss McRae, I have the Coast Guard on the phone with us now. I want them to understand that you think you may be in danger because you see two boats approaching from the south ... that look like the boat that was stolen, and possibly the pirate boat. Is that right?"

Mel could hear the phone, and nodded. Sherry drew a deep breath and said, "That's what we think. We're trying not to panic here."

"You're doing fine, ma'am. Can you see land?"

"No, we cannot see land," Sherry said, as her eyes sought Mel's to make sure she was right. He shook his head. No.

"What are the weather conditions where you are?" asked a calm female voice, professional.

Sherry looked around. "Calm," she said. "Sunny. We can see a dark storm cloud ... off to the ..."

Sherry hesitated, so Mel said "southwest," and she added that.

"Waves are just gentle swells, less than two feet, tops, and not that many."

"Ma'am, we want you to stay on the line, and tell us as much as you can about the boats as they get close, if they do," said the female voice. "Considering everything, we do not want you to try to hail them. We have already put your earlier descriptions out on marine frequencies. Our broadcast described the sport fisherman the pirates used and the Motor Vessel *New Delphi,* as well. People are already looking for you, and some of them could be in white yachts and fishing boats, but right now, let's sit tight."

"Okay," Sherry said, as she scrunched down in the life raft. Others had already done the same, she noticed. *Better than nothing.* She was angry. *Keep it together,* she told herself.

For at least a full minute, no one spoke. Everyone tried to get small, even Chip. He watched the boats through his tiny binoculars but shielded the lenses from the sun with his hands, so they would not reflect it toward the boats.

"They're turning toward us," Chip said a moment later, as he craned his neck. Sherry repeated it into the phone. In a minute she asked if the boats were still turning.

"Looks like it," Chip said. "They're about a quarter-mile away. I think they've slowed." Sherry repeated this message as well.

"Ma'am, as they approach, tell them you're in contact with the Coast Guard, with law enforcement and the Florida Marine Patrol. Tell them you described their boats some time ago and that we now have your location. Tell them we are en route. Be sure to tell them we're close. We would be closer, but we didn't expect you to turn off your phone. We should have specifically told you not to."

"Oh," Sherry said. That one syllable, well, more like two, showed she was embarrassed—and horrified.

"It's okay, Sherry. You hang onto that phone, leave it on and describe anything and everything you can, especially the pirate boat, if it turns out to be the pirate boat. We found a good picture of the *New Delphi* already. Do you understand?"

"Completely. Chip, is there anything more about the pirate boat we can tell from this distance?"

"Sure," he said, as he peered through his binocs. "Um, the other one—the sport fishing boat—has big rusty orange stains on the hull, in two places on the side I can see—the port side. Bilge stains, one amidships and one near the stern. Dark green tinted windows. It's flying a pennant, sort of yellow or dull orange. The boat looks grungy."

After Sherry related Chip's observations, Mel said, "The sport fishing boat is smooth-sided, and the tuna tower is not real big. The yacht, on the other hand, has an obviously lapped hull, white over black, just like ours." He paused, then added, "I'm almost positive it's the Bertram, the *New Delphi*." Mel didn't have the binoculars, but he had sharp eyes, and Chip nodded agreement.

Sherry repeated it all. She could hear Ruth quietly praying, barely loud enough to be heard, not loud enough to distract. "They're several hundred yards from us, maybe three hundred, closing on us slowly," Sherry spoke into the phone. "Nobody on deck on either boat." It took effort to keep her voice from rising, but she sounded composed.

53
Stay

Chobeem was beside the bubble, where Chax had sent him at dawn. He gave a female human his full attention. She was fearful, and he stayed close. He had reported to Chax several times. So had some birds. Pelicans are normally standoffish, interested only in food, but these were curious about the dolphin assembly and the raft full of people. A few pelicans had settled on the water near the raft, even though no one fed them.

Chax knew the people in the bubble were not injured or dying. During the night, most of them had slept. They had not been this fearful then. Now all of them prepared for some dread. Perhaps they feared more death from the boats. Chax expected that.

He wondered why so many in the bubble were afraid of so few in the boats, but men always provided things to wonder at. One man can do much harm, Chax knew. He had seen that.

He no longer wondered why he had been asked to keep the pod close, or to call others. When people from the boat got in the bubble, he listened until he was sure he should stay with them. The people were the reason, not the boat, even if the boat was fun. The boats went away. Now the boats were back.

Chax listened. Not just to the dolphins, or the boats. He swam away a short distance, alone, and stopped. He listened.

A few dolphins talked, but not much. They did not make much noise, either, did not jump, did not chatter. Always before, when this many dolphins from different pods got together, with fish to eat and no threat near, a frolic happened. Not now. Men who had left in these boats had killed other men during the night. Chax's pod had liked the ones that were killed. The other pods knew. Now the boats were here again. Those in the raft were fearful. It was only prudent to be quiet, to watch and listen. Most dolphins did.

Men attract trouble. Men are unstable. Unknowable. Some men are wicked and create trouble. Bring trouble. School was about to be in session for the young ones. Real school. The young ones listened with everything they had. Chax had sent the aunts and babies away. Aunts from several pods were with all the babies an easy swim from here, with sentries posted. The aunts were on guard too.

54
Crunch time

Claiborne Chandler was sweating. Until now, the two times in his life he had killed had been in self-defense. To put a finer point on it, those killings had occurred when his position of control was threatened. To him it was the same thing. Each of those times his ... opponents ... had been bad guys, ready to kill him for what they wanted. These were not bad people. There was no way he could think they were. The thought of killing them made him uncomfortable.

Until now, he and his tiny band of pirates had been able to steal boats without violence, by trickery, a con, or simple theft. They had laughed each time. This time they had killed five people. They would soon kill eight more. Claiborne would do part of the killing. Not taking part would send a dangerous signal, even to Salazar. Last night, Ricky had killed two, a man and a woman. Salazar had smashed the captain's skull. He had also shot a tough old man who was about to decapitate Ricky, and the young female who tried to help.

Claiborne had to participate now. Everybody's neck had to be on the line. Teddy was dead. Ricky had caused it by deciding the plan included enough time for a rape, but that was history. The old man surprised Ricky with his pants down, with a gun trained on a leggy brunette. The old man had a razor-sharp machete. The brunette had a dagger. If the hatch had been wider, Ricky would have been dead right there. That was irrelevant now. The old man cut Ricky's back and butt with the machete before Salazar could stop him, but Ricky, sure he had been mortally wounded, terrified, furious, shot the screaming woman.

Claiborne had tried to go with the original plan anyway. The only other options then seemed to be to kill everyone aboard, or kill the men first and women later. He had not been ready to do either one, then. The bloodbath would have made the boat impossible to sell at a good price. That had been prevented, at least. It was bad below deck, but fixable. Crew quarters, after all. He also figured pursuit might not be vigorous if he limited the killing to unimportant people. He had seen that happen.

All his life, Claiborne had avoided things he thought of as unpleasant, things far less odious than this. Now, he was going to have to kill those people, in broad daylight, in cold blood. He could do it, but what they were about to do would cross a line. No amount of rationalization would change it. For a long time he had dodged this day, but he had known it would come. His gut told him his life was about to change forever, not for better. He had been headed toward something like this for years.

Ricky and Salazar were on the other boat. The only semblance of a new plan they had worked out in their haste to get the killing over with was to keep both boats on the same side of the raft, so as not to shoot each other. As soon as the raft started to sink, and it would, Claiborne planned to stop firing. The others would not stop, but it would not matter by then. Let them drown. Leave. But he had to shoot. He probably had to shoot first. He eased back on the throttles as he recognized faces.

55
Flares, even

Chip found a flare gun, unwrapped it. Loaded it. Read the instructions. Kimbie also had found tubes labeled "flare," several of them. Flares seemed to be the only "weapons" aboard, their only "shot."

The boats were stopped, side by side, a hundred feet away. They were loud, after hours of silent drifting. Above the din, Sherry told the 911 operator they planned to shoot flares at the boats when they were in range. The operator suggested they shoot one flare straight up to mark their position. "Do it now," he said.

"He says to shoot one now, straight up," Sherry fairly shouted.

Kimbie wondered whether she could aim the flares she had. They didn't look like a gun, the way Chip's sort of did. She had never seen dynamite, except in a movie, but these flares looked like that—round red tubes coated with wax or something, with a strip of waxy cloth that extended from under the wrapping. "Worth a shot," she said. She pointed it at the sky. The instructions on the side said to pull the cloth starter strip "sharply." She did.

As they watched, frightened and then astonished, the tube began to spew sparks and smoke. Kimbie held it as far out from the raft as she could, and as far up, pointed up. It did not shoot anything skyward except sparks, but it disgorged thick red smoke and then began to spew fiery, reddish sparks, even occasional flames, several inches from its end. It was certainly a flare, that much was certain. In the dark it would have lit the area, and was startling, even in the early light. Smoke poured from it. Red smoke filled the raft and spilled over the side, almost like a liquid. It spread, too. As everyone watched wide-eyed, unable to get away, a dull red cloud began to rise. Fiery light illuminated the cloud as it spread over the water.

Expecting to choke, Kimbie was relieved when the red smoke had only a little bite, nothing she couldn't deal with. Others coughed, especially Ruth, but not that much.

The tiny breeze tumbled the still-growing cloud toward the boats. The sun, which was orangey-red and still close to the horizon, helped the flare make the tumbling red ball of smoke look—from the boats, at least—like it had fire inside. The dark grey-blue storm cloud on the horizon behind the raft contrasted sharply with the fire-lit ball, and with the spewing torch in Kimbie's hand. Torchlight gave the raft and its occupants an unearthly glow, especially Kimbie. Her white curls looked like they were tipped with fire. Her arms and face looked like molten bronze, liquid gold.

From the raft, all this was obvious, understandable, but it looked different from the boats. From the boats, it was startling. But from one angle on one boat, the fire from the flare—and from the red sun still low in the sky—seemed to lick at the bottom and outer edges of the tumbling, glowing cloud with what looked like tongues of flame.

Ricky had found time—while Salazar went below to get his Kalashnikov and tweak the diesels—to snort a line of cocaine. He liked to get ready for an experience he knew was going to be intense, no matter what Claiborne thought. Coke sometimes numbed his fear, too. This was sure to be intense, and nobody was going to tell him not to do his own coke.

This time the drug intensified the fiery brightness of the flare and the low red sun. From where Ricky was perched on the tower, the red cloud looked alive, as it rolled toward him. Within it, Ricky saw a beautiful woman made of metal with her hair on fire, a strange, intense woman who shot fire from her finger and her eyes. Just out of reach of her freaky, fire-spewing finger Ricky saw a dragon raise its head. It shot flame from its mouth, back at her. But her glare scared the dragon, and it turned away. It disappeared. The fire tableau only lasted a fraction of a second, but it printed on Ricky's eyeballs, freaked him, and he screamed.

He screamed, and shook, and jerked the controls of the sport-fishing boat into neutral. He was afraid to look at the cloud again, but more afraid not to look. He was sure the woman and the dragon were still there, so he focused on the edges of the cloud.

As the cloud came closer to the boats, a bolt of lightning shot from the dark storm cloud behind it. The dark blue-grey of the storm looked like it was part of the red cloud. The smell of ozone mixed with the smell of the smoke, as the red-orange smoke tumbled in the low angle of the reddish sunshine. Fire that seemed to hover over the raft, and the close, blue-white lightning against the blue-grey-black cloud, in the magnified intensity of the cocaine high ... was too much for Ricky. Intense sensory inputs overloaded his coke-stoked ability to process what he saw, heard, smelled and felt, and he screamed again.

"Holy shit!" Ricky shook all over, and drew his elbows against his ribs. His arms spazzed and pressed into his sides as he jerked both throttles back, out of neutral into full reverse. The engines screamed without effect until he hastily pushed them forward to ease up. The roar deceased just enough to let the gears engage with a loud clank. When he heard the familiar groan of the reversing gear he sent more diesel fuel to the engines, which turned the twin screws backward, and they dug in. The reversed propellers dragged the boat backwards with a sideways lurch, aided by the rudder. The stern was pulled down and backwards fast enough to send a huge swell crashing over it. What looked like a great deal of water cascaded over the stern and into the rear deck well. For a second, the seat of one fishing chair was at water level, if not exactly sea level.

The rear deck had big drain slots, scuppers, but they were not big enough to get rid of that much water, which sloshed into the galley and, worse, through the open hatch that led below. From the hatch, water cascaded down the ladder into the bunk spaces, and the engine spaces half a deck lower. Trying to reverse like that was a blockhead move, a cokehead move. Ricky knew it, knew he had messed up, but he was still terrified, still feared the dragon-chasing woman. He could feel the weight of the water cause the boat to list to port. The lurch was exaggerated up on the tuna tower, though the angle was the same. Ricky held onto the wheel with one hand, braced his feet against the cowl so he wouldn't fall into the sea and throttled down so fast the diesels flooded, sputtered, died. When the screws stopped pulling, the boat more or less righted itself. When the bobbing stopped, though, it listed curiously to starboard.

Salazar, managed to hold onto the ladder with one hand. His AK-47 was in the other as water washed his feet from under him. Soaked halfway up his shirt, he let loose a stream of what sounded like cursing in some language Ricky had never heard. Adrenalin fought the cocaine to a draw, but neither let go. Ricky flooded the twin diesels even worse as he tried to restart them. Salazar cursed louder.

From the bridge of the freshly nameless yacht, Claiborne could see and hear enough to know that Ricky was being really stupid, and probably was stoned. From Claiborne's comfortable perch, twenty or thirty yards to the side, he could see the raft, and three sides of the red-orange cloud. He could see the pretty tanned woman who had got in Ricky's face a few hours earlier. Now she held a red flare out over the water, as far away from herself and the raft as she could, which was sensible. She looked fierce. Her eyes glared with a fire that he could not be sure was reflected. That look—and the lightning that coincided with it—got his attention. His vision was so sharp it was eerie. He wished it wasn't. Seeing those people that clear would not make what he had to do any easier.

Claiborne saw the water wash over the stern of the boat Ricky was trying to sink. He could not understand what had spooked Ricky, but this was not good. The pirate boat—his boat, bought and paid for—rode dangerously low in the water, and listed to starboard. The tuna tower hung at a dangerous angle, and Claiborne Chandler began to worry about his luck.

56
Low in the water

Everyone in the raft was positive 'their' boat was back. Sherry reported it to whoever was on the other end of the phone. The 911 operator said her precise GPS location, triangulated from the phone, had been relayed to all air and marine emergency channels in use in the area. Boats were on their way, and aircraft.

Chip waited for better range. He figured he would get only one shot with the flare gun. But just in case, he had two more cartridges ready in his lap. He felt good about the fuss Kimbie's flare had created, but figured another like it would not help much. His had to count.

The dolphins lingered, though only Bridget attended to them. From the time she realized the bad guys had come back, she concentrated all her attention on the dolphins. It was denial. She knew that, but couldn't help it. She could not, would not, look at the boats.

Claiborne did not want to fire the only shots, to do all the killing, one after another, which meant he could not, would not move until the other boat was in position. Its fuel-flooded diesels were probably also awash in bilge, too. It might be some time before they would start. He heard the starters churn, heard Salazar curse, saw him go below. The two boats pointed at each other about ninety feet from the raft. Close enough for what they had come to do, certainly close enough for an AK-47, but for the moment, the big guns were on the boat that sat low in the water, enveloped by a red cloud. Salazar was too busy to shoot and Ricky was too freaked. Claiborne shook his head. As he waited, his anger rose. Maybe it would help. But that was stupid; anger didn't help unless it was someone else's anger. He watched the rafts out of the corner of his eye and began to really sweat.

The little dolphin was close enough for Bridget to touch. "Guys, you've got to do something," she said, mostly to that one, the small, much scarred one, but also to the others not far away. Her voice was low and soft, childlike. "Those bad men killed our friends. They came back to kill us." She thought the dolphin looked like he understood. Ruth reached across the raft to take Bridget's hand.

Sherry spoke calmly into her cell phone. John prayed.

57
If memory serves

"Whatcha got, Opie?"

Master Chief Stan Schuermann, the chief of the boat, was back from breakfast. Sonar Tech Second Class Opie Simcox was hunched over his screens and controls, intent, intense. He held one earphone away from his head, looked at the COB and spoke.

"Something's up, COB. Ski loves his pancakes, so I relieved him early. Those two boats we've been shadowing were tied together for a while, doing maintenance or something. A lot of clunking around and scraping. I thought maybe they were fishing before, but I'd swear they're not fishermen, unless they're after tarpon or something. No winches. No fish finders. Heard hull noise too. Maybe they're trading cargoes." Melodrama in the way Opie said "cargoes" got the COB's attention, but he didn't laugh.

"A while ago they hauled butt back toward where they were during the night, side by side, wide open," Opie continued. "They ran zig-zag patterns, mirror tandem, like they were looking for something. A few minutes ago they stopped."

"Hmm." Schuermann was non-commital, but curious. What had Opie so excited?

"COB, it's weird. Just now, one of them did some goofy all-astern drill. They've got a bad reversing gear—it howls like a dog—so I knew. The guy stalled out, I think. Unless I'm crazy, he was turning about three grand in reverse until he stalled out, COB. I thought he was going to submerge."

Schuermann nodded, smiled, pictured some drunk helmsman.

"Anyway, he flooded the diesels or something. His starters make this unusual reduction-gear noise. Like uh-inch, uh-INCH, uh-inch. He's still trying to start them."

"Pretty good listening, Opie," the COB said. Maybe his best sonar-man needed some time off.

But Opie wasn't finished. "And COB, you know how I heard boo-coos of dolphins? It's like a reunion. Dozens, maybe more, just hanging out, near where the two boats are. Feeding, I guess, but ... I've never heard them like this. One will chatter, then all of them will go nuts for a second, and squeak so bad I have to put the phones on half-mute. Then they'll quiet down like they want to hear what's next."

"Cool," said Chief Schuermann, cocking his head. The COB had heard countless whale songs and dolphin clicks and whistles in his years underwater. He liked to listen to them. Whales fascinated him.

"Got that on tape, Opie?" he asked. The COB knew, of course, that everything the sonar and hydroscopes collected was backed up on digital "tape."

"Sure COB, but this is maybe the main thing. Since about daylight there's been unreal traffic up and down the coast, and out where we are, too. Either there's a search and rescue op, or a drug bust, or some high-security situation, because everything with a motor is running patterns." That got the COB's full attention. As Schuermann watched, Opie keyed up displays. Sure enough, he had recorded a sonar animation loop that showed somebody running a racetrack chain pattern between the *Boise* and the coast, another pattern to the north, and several to their south. This particular pattern was only ten minutes old.

"COB, one of them is only five miles from these guys. From the way it looks, somebody put the word out on something, big time. If I were the captain, I'd want to know what."

Schuermann thought the same thing.

"Opie, our two motor yachts may be what they're looking for. Then again, the yachts may be looking too. Except they're stopped. How far to them?"

"Two miles, COB, maybe three. Wouldn't hurt to turn to starboard forty or fifty degrees, so we can start to close, while you talk to the captain about breaking surface to listen up."

Schuermann frowned. "The captain gets to make that call, Opie." A reminder, not a reprimand. Opie smiled. The Officer of the Deck, Lt. (j.g.) Smith, drifted over. Smith, who had heard part of the conversation, asked just enough questions to make sure he understood before he called the Captain. The third-class machinist mate at the helm had heard too. His eyes grew wider by the second.

In less than a minute, the captain was in the control room. The OOD and the COB told Commander Alvarez the important parts of what the sonarman had heard. Opie brought up displays of search patterns on three screens.

Alvarez took in everything. "You think it could be the same boat, Opie?" The sonarman nodded.

"Most affirm, sir. If I know anything at all, Captain, it's one of the drug boats that got away when I was on the *Asheville*. I'm trusting my memory a little, but I'm almost sure. If we were running interdictions, I could verify it pronto, but we're not."

Alvarez stroked his chin. "How far?".

"Just over eight thousand yards, sir, and closing," the sonarman said. The OOD had directed a turn on his own initiative to close the gap, after he called the captain. The helmsman was afraid to look around to see the captain's expression.

But the COB watched. So did Opie, who hoped he could see the wheels turn his way in the captain's head.

"Take us up to periscope depth," Commander Alvarez told the planesman. Schuermann moved behind the newb at the helm, the better to see the displays. Alvarez picked up his microphone. "This is the captain. We're about to surface to periscope depth. Com center, monitor COMSUBLANT and emergency frequencies as soon as your radios will work, and let me know what you hear." COMSUBLANT, with the emphasis on the "SUB," is Navy-speak for commander, submarine force, Atlantic Fleet. When the radioman acknowledged with two clicks of his microphone, the captain turned to the COB. "I wish we had DEA frequencies."

Schuermann nodded. The time was 0728.

58
'The whites of their eyes'

"I think you'd better try another flare," said the 911 operator, as Sherry described the scene. "It sounds like the first one was a railroad flare. Use the flare gun this time."

"He says shoot your flare," she told Chip, trying not to shout, to stay calm.

Chip had reached the same conclusion. A shot now would give him a better idea about how to aim the next one. He had several. The longer the two boats sat there, one apparently dead in the water and the other … what? Waiting? He might as well. Chip sighted the horizon, pointed the flare gun as close to straight up as he could manage in the bobbing raft, and squeezed the trigger the way he had been taught.

When the crude trigger finally worked, the action reminded him more of the latch on his grandmother's garden gate than any weapon he had ever fired. What's more, the flare itself was more like fireworks than he expected. It spewed a few seconds, then took off like a bottle rocket. It reminded him of Moosehead Lake on the 4th of July.

The flare left behind a skinny, yellow-orange trail that seemed to cling to itself in the light breeze. It climbed maybe a hundred feet and made a smooth arc back down, to the south. The higher it got, the wider the trail it left. It tapered as it crested. The sun caught it beautifully. It would be visible for miles, except in the direction of the darkening storm. Chip was sure he could aim the next one. He knew he could hit a barn with it, anyway. Maybe a boat, if it was close.

He burned his fingers on the spent cartridge, cooled them (and it) in the sea, and dropped the empty at his feet. He reloaded and snapped the odd contraption closed. He no longer thought of it as a pistol, but it still might help.

Chip's flare provoked no reaction that anyone could see. The raft was still thirty or forty yards from the boats, too far for a flare like the second one to have much chance. Still, Chip figured it might be as close as he could hope for. He decided to aim at the big windows in the salon on the *New Delphi*. If he got a third shot, he would target any glass on the pirate boat. Unless an open hatch presented itself. If the flare filled a boat with smoke, it might create a diversion. If they were really lucky, it might start a fire. It wasn't much of a plan, but it was all he had.

Mel McRea was encouraged and said so. He gave a "thumbs up" to Kimbie, through the red cloud. She managed a grimace of a smile. The cloud was going away and the second flare gave no additional cover. Through the thinning smoke and mist, she could see the pirate boat against the sky. The men on it would be able to see the raft soon, too, if they couldn't see it now.

On that pirate boat, Ricky tried hard to settle himself down, something he seldom did. He understood, now, that the fiery cloud had been from a flare. He knew it, but his nerves still jangled and would not stop. Salazar climbed up to the helm, glared and spit on the deck. Ricky clinched his jaw so hard his head and shoulders trembled. Salazar had seen that before and laughed. Disgusted, he slid down the ladder and disappeared below. The engine room was still awash, but the bilge pump was working.

Ricky nearly hurled. He wanted to shoot Salazar in the back, but the man was too quick. He tried to think of something else. He was going to enjoy shooting those people. When Salazar opened up with his AK the targets would be spoiled, but he would still blaze away with his big revolver. If the raft didn't sink right away. Even if it did. That might give some relief. And if that damned Salazar got in his sights, he would …"

But he wouldn't. When it came right down to it, he was so afraid of Salazar—and afraid of dying—that the thought of actually trying to shoot the man made Ricky sick again. He could not go against Salazar.

Bridget was oblivious to flares, oblivious to boats, guns, pirates, to those next to her, everything but dolphins. The small scarred one was beside her. She could touch it. It wasn't alone, either. The raft was surrounded by dolphins, but she focused all her attention on this one. Chip touched her arm, but she didn't seem to notice, and he needed to stay focused, in case he got a shot. She would deal with this in her own way.

In her heart Bridget was sure the dolphins could help, and hoped they would. The scarred one kept looking at her, through its wonderful, deep clear eye, and she looked back. As long as she didn't let her eyes stray from its eye, fear did not overwhelm her. For some reason, her thoughts went back to when she had broken her back when her horse fell. She was in a body cast all summer. Her grandpa stayed with her, brought her movies, watched them with her, held her hand.

"I want to see my grandpa," she told the dolphin. She didn't care who heard. "The bad guys don't care. You have to do something. Maybe you and your friends can amaze them." Her voice was almost a squeak.

Ruth Zinser bit her lip and prayed.

59
The dolphins listen

Chobeem whistled for Chax. Chax was with the leaders of the other pods, but heard his friend whistle his name. In a flash he was beside Chobeem.

"The people in the bubble are distressed," Chobeem said.

"Yes. The men killed their friends. They may kill again. The people in the bubble have reason to fear."

Chobeem agreed, but saw no need to say it. He directed Chax to the female in the raft who did not take her eyes off him. They both knew she could swim underwater longer than most humans. If she hid, perhaps the men in the boats would not see her. But that would not help the others. Even if the men left, he might not be able to protect her. "I cannot see a way to help," he said to Chax.

"Nor can we. All we can do is stay and look for ways," Chax said. "And listen." He was as sure as ever that it was right to be here. If something else could be done, he wanted to be quiet enough to hear.

60
Supplemental exercise

"Officer of the deck, sir, you can tell the captain we hear all kinds of emergency traffic," said the communications tech on radio watch. "There's a search under way. Two rogue boats are believed to be operating together, a pirate boat and a yacht that the pirates apparently took by force, with loss of life. They're in communication with survivors, in a raft. As best I can tell, we're near the center of the search area. I have coordinates."

"Roger that," the OOD said, and quickly told the captain. *Pirates?*

The captain nodded. "How far are we from those two boats that are stopped, COB?"

Chief Schuermann checked. "Less than one nautical mile, sir, three—four-thousand yards, and headed right for them."

The OOD told the captain the search coordinates. The sub's coordinates were nearly the same. "Very fine. COB, it appears that the realistic training supplement you hinted at is about to happen," the captain said.

The COB nodded, grim. "It looked like a strong possibility, sir."

The captain told the COB to increase throttles to one-third bell. Schuermann relayed the order. The turbines responded with a silent surge. No noise at all, but for a few seconds, everybody looked for something to grip. The *Boise* could go a lot faster, but much more than one-third bell would tear away radio antennas, now fully extended, and maybe the periscope.

"COB, send a coded message to COMSUBLANT. Tell them we … only moments ago surfaced to monitor radio traffic … and find ourselves in the immediate vicinity of … what we think may be … the object of the search. Unless otherwise instructed … we plan to go into intervention mode … as soon as we are close to gun range … of two boats we were … already following." Schuermann nodded each time the captain paused.

Quietly the chief of the boat said, "Aye aye, sir," and stepped to the communications room, where he relayed the message to the radioman on duty. The COB settled onto a steel stool to proof-read it. The message was ready to go. When the captain proofed it, it was sent.

61
Intervention

Claiborne eased the yacht forward. He had made up his mind. Coming back had been a mistake. Once again, Ricky had made things worse. It was time—*past time*—to cut losses. Leave these people to be rescued, or not. It would happen. The Gulf is alive with people this time of year, this close to shore. There would be a search, but in a few months, it would be history. These people would have a great story to tell, he would sell the boat. Probably both boats. And lose Ricky.

As he steered to starboard, Claiborne's eye was drawn to movement on the port side. Almost idly he turned ... and saw ... what? ... a whale?

But it wasn't a whale that broke into the morning sunshine, it was the huge black nose of a submarine, pushing tons of water out of the way, still climbing. It was in fact a fast-attack, *Los Angeles* class nuclear sub, the *USS Boise*, SSN 764, though no names or numbers were visible. It surfaced so fast and rose so high and so close that Claiborne peed his shorts a little.

The sub dominated everything. It towered over the two boats and the raft. The spray it threw was awesome, frightening. The deck was still slightly underwater now, but sailors in orange jumpsuits, holding what looked like sniper rifles, were bunched atop the wing-like conning tower they called the "sail." Half a second ago that tower had looked like the fin of Mega-shark.

He wished it were. Claiborne tried to visualize the trajectory of the submarine, tried to figure whether it was going to hit this boat, hit either boat, whether an evasive move would work at his present creep speed, but his mind was jammed. As he tried to estimate the angle the sub would take, he flashed for a second on a big billiard table. The sub was the cueball, bearing down on him, with a leather pocket at his back. He had to shake himself. He was not the only one. From the corner of his eye he saw Salazar on the other boat. Salazar leaned out over the water, leaned away from the sub, as if he hoped to lean far enough back to dodge the terrible black submarine that changed everything.

Claiborne stared at the unfamiliar controls for a second, stared at his hands on the wheel. He knew how to drive a boat. These controls were almost identical to those on the sport fisherman. But his arms hung motionless. They awaited instructions. Finally, he made his eyes check the tachometer, and made his hands nudge the throttles forward, made them turn the wheel to point into the swell. The yacht turned, barely in time to avoid being thrashed, maybe even swamped. The other boat did not fare as well. It was pointed the wrong way, dead in the water. The swell from the sub caught it almost square in the stern, slammed the stern hard, and rolled *more* water over the gunwales and stern. The bilge pumps had only started to discharge the water Ricky had brought aboard, and the wave from the surge dropped the stained hull lower than Claiborne had ever seen it. Perilously low.

The sub's surge seemed to slip under the raft, though. The raft rode up and over it, but remained upright, almost undisturbed. All those dolphins nosed up to the raft probably helped.

Sailors bunched atop the submarine's tower pointed impressive long guns at Claiborne—at both boats. Serious-looking sailors, in blue jump suits and bright green life vests. Claiborne could see the big .45 pistol in front of him, in plain sight, sitting in a plastic-coated wire basket beside the controls. He wished it would disappear. He felt twelve years old. The submarine had gone past him now, but was on course to circle back in a tight arc. Its long deck was still barely under water, but not those guns. He wondered if it would ram him on its next pass. He had heard a story about a submarine that broke a ship in half, a much bigger boat than this one. He had heard the sub wasn't even dented.

Salazar's AK was not in his hands anymore, but Ricky had his big chrome pistol pointed at the turning submarine, a gesture beyond futility.

Time seemed to crawl. The sub's arc would bring it right back in a minute or less. It was slowing, but Claiborne was still under those guns. His vision was still unnaturally sharp. He could see individual sailors, see their mouths move, see their eyes. He read a name, Walker, on a jump suit. He could see details of weapons. At the top of the tower, a sailor reached down for what turned out to be an orange bullhorn, and handed it to a square-jawed man with bronze skin.

Stenciled on the bullhorn was "Boise 764." The bronze man raised it to his face. "Now heave to," the bullhorn blared, loud. The words were not crisp but they were clear. "I repeat, heave to. Stand by to be boarded. Lay down your weapons immediately, heave to, and stand by to be boarded. We are a United States Navy vessel responding to a call of distress. We have reason to believe that crimes—including piracy—

have been committed in U.S. waters. We will not tolerate any defiance. Lay down your weapons now, or suffer the consequences."

Claiborne saw Ricky's skinny arm flex, saw the big chrome pistol move down, then back up. Immediately, three wicked long guns pointed at Ricky from atop the submarine.

The swell had rolled through. The morning was unusually quiet again, but also much darker, as the storm closed in. Gulls screeched. Claiborne eased back the throttles and nudged the diesels out of gear. Within seconds, Salazar ignored Ricky's gun, pushed him aside, throttled back and took the sportfisher out of gear too. With the diesels idling, the pirate boat's bilge pumps splashed two noisy streams of water from the side openings.

"Don't be stupid, mon," Salazar said, loud enough for everyone to hear. Salazar had both hands up, and empty. He moved away from Ricky.

"Mister, you have a count of three to drop that pistol, or be shot," came the amplified voice. Ricky didn't move. "Marksmen, prepare to fire, on my count." Ricky looked at the pistol at the end of his arm.

"One ..." CRACK! Bolts of lightning hit the water half a mile away, and a nearly simultaneous boom of thunder overpowered the bullhorn and everything else for a few seconds. One of the sailors lowered his weapon slightly, but immediately shouldered it again.

"Don't, Ricky," Claiborne said, unable to believe Ricky still had the pistol raised. It inched toward firing position. Ricky turned his head a few degrees, enough for Claiborne to see more pure hatred than he could have imagined, even from him. Claiborne's jaw went slack. From the bullhorn he heard "two ..."

Ricky shrugged, sneered. With his arm still outstretched he turned his body and aimed at Claiborne!

"Three," said the voice in the bullhorn. Shots followed. Several, almost simultaneous with the count.

One bullet tore into Ricky's chest, right of center. Another ripped through the upper inside of his left arm. Ricky crumpled and spun clockwise to the deck. His knees hit first, then his head. The pistol spun away. A white chunk of the cockpit splintered into the air behind him.

The pistol clattered to the deck somewhere, and everything was quiet.

Ricky's one shot had hit Claiborne in the temple and shattered the clear plastic windscreen, sending pieces of it flying. Claiborne staggered but did not fall. Instead he dropped slowly to his knees, and gripped the helm chair. His other hand went to his temple. Blood ran down his face and arm. The hot smell of it mingled in his nostrils with the fresh smell of the morning and the sea, but remained separate too. From his knees, Claiborne settled onto his heels. He looked at the blood that ran down his arm and dripped to the carpeted deck and wondered when he would black out and fall over, when he would die.

62
Mopping up

Hard rain fell as the noise of the shots died away. It lasted about five minutes, long enough to wash away most of the blood. Then, as if the storm had not happened, the sky over the Gulf was blue again. Gulls circled, quiet and curious.

Those in the rafts were drenched, and silent. The raft was a floating puddle. No one cared. While the rain fell, Ruth closed her eyes and turned her face upward, raised her hands to the sky, perhaps to feel the rain, perhaps in praise. Bridget saw and did the same. Mel sat like a statue, ignoring the rain, smiling at his wife, who smiled back. Ruth and Bridget and Chip and John and Mel and Sherry could not stop smiling. From beneath a cushion held aloft, beneath a shirt or a hat, each of the eight variously registered shock, relief, strain, sadness, disbelief and fatigue, but smiles of gratitude reined.

Dozens of dolphins still lingered, though they did not jump. Everything had changed.

Claiborne's life had not flashed before his eyes when Ricky pointed the silver gun and fired. He wondered about that. The bullet hit hard enough to knock him to his knees, but did not enter his skull. It only plowed a furrow of skin and hair along the left side of his head. It loosed a flow of blood that was formidable, but it did not kill him.

Stunned, disoriented, probably in shock, he sat on his heels and continued to breathe, and see and hear. He did not die. Still, as he watched watered-down blood trickle down his arm and drip off his elbow, Claiborne knew that what had been his life was forever changed.

The submarine circled slow. Salazar stood rock still, hands as high as they would reach. Claiborne had an urge to do the same, but his left hand was pressed hard against his head, and his right hand pressed hard against the deck.

A dolphin surfed the submarine's smooth bow wave as long as it could. Others began quiet jumps. Claiborne wondered when he would feel pain, as he looked from one dolphin to another.

"Glory to God!" someone said from the raft, a woman, just loud enough to hear.

Not so much, thought Claiborne. *Then again, maybe*. He had never experienced this particular set of emotions. Defeat, shock, surprise, regret and anger swirled in the mix, but they were not exactly it. The one feeling that he could put a name on, oddly, was relief.

63
The songs are always right. Almost

"We are here to see this," Chobeem said. He and Chax and others had pushed the bubble away from the boats, but they had not pushed it far when they felt the submarine. The people in the bubble stopped being fearful when the submarine rose. Men from the submarine and one of the boats made loud noises. Two men bled. One was dead. Rain fell, and stopped. The people in the rafts were thankful.

"Perhaps," said Chax. "It was something to see."

"Yes. I had not seen an underwater boat rise."

"It made noise, on top of the water," Chax said. "It pushed water out. I was surprised. It was quiet until then."

"Except for the water it pushed. The men on the underwater boat may be good," Chobeem said.

"Many," Chax said. "Some may be good."

Chobeem knew what he meant. Many men. Unknowable men, with trouble sure to follow them, or to come from them. But he had scanned several of the men who came out of the underwater boat, and the other boats that came later. He did not find a bad one. They helped. "Some are good," Chobeem said.

"Yes," Chax said. "They did a good thing. Perhaps they are good. Some must be. The man that is dead was full of hate and fear. Twisted."

"Yes," Chobeem said. "He was twisted. Unstable. Full of trouble for himself and others."

"Twisted with fear," Chax said. He looked at the boats that gathered. So many now, in the middle of the western Gulf of the big green ocean, far from land. The people from the bubble were helped up into one. Men from the black underwater boat and others crawled over the two white boats the pod knew. They watched the dolphins, with admiration. It was something to see. "The songs were right about the one that died this morning. And the one that bled, and the one that didn't."

"The songs are always right. Almost."

"Yes," Chax said. "And the aunts."

64
Sorting it out

The Coast Guard and a detachment of SEALs from the submarine took possession of the *New Delphi* and the sport-fisher. The Florida Marine Patrol helped too.

In an excess of courtesy, each of the uniformed services deferred to the other, and especially to the submarine, now fully surfaced and stopped. A large round hatch in the deck of the submarine, just behind the sail, was open. At least a dozen sailors strolled the length of the sub's grid of a deck. Some wore or carried weapons, but like the dolphins, they were relaxed. They mostly took in the fresh air and sunshine, and the sights.

The captain of the sub, Commander Alvarez, had rank on everybody, but he remained atop the sail, and was only consulted occasionally by Lt. (j.g.) Billy Spears, the SEAL officer now aboard Claiborne's boat. Slung over his shoulder, Spears had a grey, fully-automatic assault pistol that outranked every weapon visible. The other SEAL, Chief Hospital Corpsman Phil Elliott, was a bit older. He wore a matte-black, plastic-looking pistol in a canvas holster, as he bent over Ricky.

"Doc" Elliott had already tended to Claiborne. A battle dressing slowed and then stopped the blood. It was thick with long strips of cloth attached to the corners. He carefully wrapped the strips completely around Claiborne's head, lapped them over the pad, and tied square knots to maintain pressure. It worked. When the corpsman examined Claiborne's pupils, they were the same size, appropriately constricted for the bright sun, and reacted equally to changes in light. A good sign. The SEAL chief made sure the wounded pirate knew the month, year and current president before he moved to the other boat, to re-check the man he already knew was dead.

After some negotiation, the Florida Marine Patrol took Claiborne and Salazar into temporary custody aboard their fast boat, and loaded the corpse as well. That left the Coast Guard to deal with the survivors from the raft. A second Coast Guard vessel circled the area, and warned away the curious.

The Navy's job was done. The sub had arrived first, and taken over. "Doc" Elliott confirmed that Ricky was dead, unofficially, since he was not a physician or a coroner. Not that there was any doubt. The submarine would soon disappear. Official accounts would mention the actions of federal and state forces, but public comments would be carefully self-edited by those making them. Any unnecessary mention of the timely arrival of the 360-foot black metal shark was avoided. The rescued civilians would be coached along the same lines. They were encouraged to say, if asked, that the vessels that came to their aid had been "Navy, Coast Guard and Florida Marine Patrol," and to express their thanks, but not to elaborate.

The Coast Guard took custody of the two boats. One was seized as a crime scene, the other as a pirate vessel. After a search and a safety inspection, Coasties in dark blue jumpsuits and ball caps were put aboard each, to bring them in. They headed for the Coast Guard's Southwest Florida station at St. Petersburg, several hours southeast. Kimbie made the Coasties promise to take the fish out of all the coolers and lockers. She showed them where they were and made them a checklist and note, and urged them to enjoy the fish and give away any they could not use. The two young Coasties who took over the now nameless *New Delphi* promised her they would empty and clean the lockers and coolers, even if they were not sure what they might be allowed to do with the fish. They invited her to visit the station any time, and said they hoped she would look them up. She hugged them both.

Kimbie and Ping and their passengers were put aboard a 25-foot Coast Guard rescue boat. It was snug, the only boat small enough to get to the nearest Coast Guard station. Ruth and John Zinser rode inside the tiny cabin with Sherry and Ping and the boat captain, a first-class petty officer who reminded Ruth of Pete. The coastie had not met Pete, but was sympathetic, and optimistic about his chances, especially after he learned Pete had been a Coast Guard diver.

Kimbie, Chip, Bridget and Mel wedged into the triangular open well in front of the cabin, and scanned the water all the way in. Kimbie held Chip's small binoculars up to her eyes almost the whole time. Bridget had gotten a little hysterical after the pirates were shot, but it turned out she was happy hysterical. When no one was looking she slipped into the water to swim one more time with the dolphins. The Coast Guard put a rescue swimmer in with her, a kind, good-looking kid who helped her regain enough composure to climb into the rescue boat. Now she was wrapped in a huge towel from the N.D., as they all were. Chip gave her most of his attention. When Kimbie had to rest her arms, Chip or Mel took over the binoculars, and scanned the water until she asked for them back.

When land came in sight, the helmsman turned south, as did the Marine Patrol boat. Both boats ran parallel to the coast for half an hour, then the boat carrying the two prisoners and the corpse peeled off and entered the mouth of a narrow river. The dark river passed under a highway bridge. Upstream from the bridge the river between the black banks was so straight it looked like a canal. The Coast Guard boat continued south, well off the coast.

Claiborne and Salazar were handcuffed, with hands behind their backs. On the ride in, sitting on top of a locker, Claiborne got as close to seasick as ever in his life. He was sure the bullet crease was not the reason.

Salazar did not seem to suffer. They did not talk; they would have had to shout, which would not have been allowed. The Coastie who had temporary custody sat between them. And what was there to say? The last part of the voyage, up the flat, nearly-black river, was slower, calm and quiet. The flat, marshy landscape was dominated by two huge cooling towers of a nuclear power plant, a landmark sailors in these waters and even motorists knew well. The water was dark as Irish beer, but teemed with life. Frogs retreated and fish jumped as they passed, but unperturbed cattle egrets only turned their heads, and alligators moved only their eyeballs. Claiborne could not picture himself making his way in handcuffs up the steep, slimy-looking, root-entangled sides of the river. Nor could he imagine getting away from the beefy, alert-looking sailors. Even if he did, then what?

In time the FMP boat pulled up to a medium-sized dock. The sign on the single small building said Florida Department of Environment and Natural Resources. The Florida Marine Patrol had once been an independent agency with a beefy role in the drug war, but not now. As a holdover from that era, the station had a small but stout holding area. Now it was used for storage,

A Marine Patrol officer and a state trooper helped Claiborne off the boat, then up the ramp from the dock and inside the little building, into the holding cell. An ambulance idled in the parking lot. Claiborne assumed it waited either for him or for Ricky's body. It turned out to be for Ricky.

Out of the sun for almost the first time since dawn, and out of the cuffs, Claiborne sat on the edge of a metal-frame cot with a piece of plywood on the springs instead of a mattress. He had slept on worse, but from what he overheard, they would not be here long. The plan was to take the prisoners to a proper detention facility, to await arraignment before a federal judge. Claiborne would be looked at by a doctor then. Though he was bandaged and bloody, he had not been treated as a casualty since Doc Elliott, the hospital corpsman chief, got back on the submarine. He was a prisoner now.

The Coast Guard argued by radio for arraignment in Tampa, for the convenience of the witnesses who lived there, and because the boats would be impounded there. But Orlando was closer. Someone got hold of a judge in Orlando, who agreed that Tampa made sense, and that was that.

Lunch was brought in while the calls were made. Barbecue. It smelled good. More than enough had been brought for the visiting law enforcement, but no one was concerned about the prisoners.

Not that either prisoner was hungry. The SEAL chief had said Claiborne should not eat until he had been examined by a doctor, and should only have occasional small sips of water. When he was given a small paper cone half full of water, he gulped it down. The water was so cold it made his head throb, something the bullet had not done. But it subsided. In time, they were allowed to use the toilet, under the unflinching gaze of a big state trooper, with a local deputy sheriff and the Coastie behind him.

Claiborne washed blood from his arm. He tried to splash tapwater from the bathroom spigot to cool his scalp and neck, but was told to stop. The deputy wet a paper towel for him, and reminded him to keep his bandage dry.

It turned out to be a good thing that he had not gotten too wet. Once they were in the back of the black-and-tan state cruiser, they discovered that the trooper liked his AC good and cold when transporting prisoners.

Claiborne could see the trooper's point.

Something about the morning had changed the smell of Claiborne's sweat. The sour smell reminded him of some acid that had made him gag when he smelled it at his uncle's chemical plant. Once upon a time, long ago.

Though he sat very straight in the back of that car as they rolled south, once in a while he would catch a whiff. It made him sick.

65
More good men

When daylight came, Chax left Popper and Band with the swimmer. He made sure they understood what was expected. He whistled about opportunities as he swam away.

Popper and Band were proud when they were chosen to swim with the man, when Chax swam with them. But now they were alone with him. They hoped they would be up to so much trust. The man still swam like a baby, like a turtle. He had swum this way since they turned him toward land by swimming in front of him like sharks. He was slow, but he swam. Floated and swam.

When they showed themselves in the daylight, the man reacted well. His fear was brief. Once he let himself sink, but when Popper investigated, the man surfaced again. They could tell he was glad they were with him. They also could tell that he was hurt, but he swam in spite of it, as they would have done in his place. He changed strokes, swam on one side, then the other. He rested sometimes. Floated on his back or his face. He would breathe deep as he rested, then start again. Over and over.

As the day grew hot, Popper feared that the man took too long between breaths, when he rested face down. Popper swam under him and rose, with the man on his back, as gentle as he could. The man seemed to be asleep, not dead, but let Popper support him. When Popper began to swim, the man held on, weak as he was. It was hard to swim with a man on his back, but Popper did it. Band was better at it than Popper. Band was not only bigger, he could move only his oversized flukes and make good progress, with the man draped over him. They took turns, and moved much faster than the man could by himself.

When the sun was at the top of the sky, the man seemed to come fully awake. They were not far from shore, and he resumed slow swimming, without help. He swam right into a sand bar. When he noticed, he dragged himself forward until he could lie down with his face out of the water. He rested a long time like that. It took even longer for the man to crawl a bit further onto the sandbar. He collapsed once his chest and head were out of the water.

The man did not move again for so long that Popper and Band feared he was dead, or close to death. They could not help, or even get close because the water was too shallow. They waited and stayed near, in water less deep than they were long. In time some men, young ones, appeared on the horizon, on noisy jet skis.

Popper went to try to bring the jet skis to the man, while Band waited with him. Popper jumped high but they did not see him. As the jet skis got farther away he jumped as high and as often as he could. He was sure they would not see him, when they turned. He continued to jump as they came back. When they got close, Band helped. It took a long time for Popper and Band to lure the jet skis close to the sand bar. It helped that the men—a male and a female—were young and playful, and did not mind doubling back again and again, to chase the friendly dolphins. When Band jumped as high as Popper had ever seen, dangerously close to the sand bar, the two on the skis finally noticed the man, and stopped. Popper could tell they were fearful, so he continued to encourage them by squeaks of approval and happiness, and more jumps. So did Band.

The young people stopped the noise of their shells and talked to each other. As they did, the swimmer made a noise, an odd noise, the kind a dolphin might make after eating many fish, or playing to exhaustion. He expelled breath in a loud way. It was like a groan and a question, and it was loud.

When the man did, the two young people waded to the sand bar, to him. They touched him, and he made another noise. Each one took an arm and pulled him up on the sand. They got his legs out of the water, something that had worried Band and Popper. The young ones held the man up, gave him something to drink from a bottle, laid him back down and let him rest. They went to get driftwood, draggled it next to him and shaded his head and shoulders.

Then the female got back on her noisy jet ski and roared away, hair flying. She circled the sand bar once, looked around several times, then did not look back. The male sat on the sand next to the man. When the sun was low, close to the horizon, a boat appeared. When it got closer, Popper and Band made a great show of welcome, with leaps and squeals. The young man did the same.

The same young female was on the boat, with others. They dragged the boat near the sandbar, picked the man up with care, carried him to the boat and took him away. Band and Popper stayed close enough to watch. When the boat left, the young male followed on the noisy jet ski.

But he did not leave until he had circled near the dolphins three times and waved his arms and looked at them with understanding and friendship and ... with love, they were sure.

Popper felt better about men after that. So did Band. They still understood that most men are unstable and attract trouble. There was too much evidence of that to ignore. But now he knew from his own experience that there are some good ones.

These had helped and not hurt. A mystery, but true. It's in the song.

66
Debriefed, deposed, dispatched

Near the tiny Yankeetown Coast Guard station, a couple of miles up the twisty Withlacoochee River from the beach, the rescued passengers from the *New Delphi* were put ashore and allowed to freshen up. A van met the rescue boat at a launch ramp near the mouth of the river and took them the rest of the way. There was no news about Pete or anyone else.

They would not to be allowed back aboard the nameless *New Delphi* until after a U.S. Marshal and an assistant U.S. Attorney took statements and depositions. Neither of the yachts came to the small Coast Guard station anyway; the river was too narrow and shallow. The station mainly served a wide section of the river farther inland. The big rescue boat was trailered to the station behind the van.

A federal marshal and a U.S. attorney arrived from Tampa while everyone was devouring fish sandwiches and hush puppies, washed down with gallons of iced tea, Gatorade, water, sodas and anything else the chief petty officer in charge of Station Yankeetown could find.

Mel was examined by a civilian doctor. The hospital corpsman from the submarine had looked at Kimbie's makeshift giant Band-aid, checked Mel over otherwise, and decided to leave her bandage in place, until Mel could get to a doctor or a hospital. "Nice job, ma'am. A-plus for in the dark, in a raft," the doc had said. That made her smile a little. The civilian physician agreed when he replaced it.

The marshal told them the *New Delphi* would have to be impounded while forensic technicians gathered evidence. But since nothing awful had happened in the staterooms, they were taken in another big Coast Guard van to rendezvous with the yacht at a marina, on nearby Crystal Bay. While the evidence tech and a Coast Guard petty officer watched, the survivors were allowed to pack what few clothes and personal items could be found. The Coasties tried to be helpful. It was grim, but they got it done. Not even Kimbie was allowed to go below deck, where the evidence techs worked. Ping didn't ask.

Vacations were not over, but the cruise was. When Kimbie tried to apologize, Sherry gave her a big hug. They both cried. Ruth joined the hug, and said, "Hush, sweeties. All we need is rest and time. We'll be all right."

The presiding judge for the district court at Tampa issued an order for the witnesses to be housed and fed at government expense overnight in the town of Crystal River, convenient to the marina. They were given nice rooms at the marina motel. During supper at the marina restaurant, the prosecutor left the table to take a call.

He came back smiling. Pete Gordon had been found on a sand bar, off the coast, alive. He was hospitalized but was expected to recover. Kids jet-skiing had found him. The prosecutor had been told that a young couple were attracted to the sand bar by dolphins.

Captain Gordon was at University of Florida hospital in Gainesville, being treated for a fractured skull, dehydration and exposure. Despite his injuries and ordeal, Pete was said to be alert and in good spirits.

Cheers — and tears of joy — greeted this announcement, but the mood turned somber again soon enough. There was no word about Digs, or Fred, Sarah or Molly. Quiet tears fell at several tables, but Kimbie began to sob, and couldn't stop. She had never held out much hope for those who slept below deck. She knew Digs and Fred too well to believe they had not died fighting. She didn't want to think about Sarah or Molly. About any of them, really, but she had started to deal with that already, as best she could. Her sobs were clearly something else.

"It's okay. I'm okay," she said, when people tried to comfort her. But when she noticed that Mel McRae was on one knee beside her, smiling, with tears streaming down his face, she grabbed his neck — as carefully as she could. She hugged his neck for a long time, just held on, and cried.

The prosecutor and a tireless court stenographer took depositions until almost 10 p.m. The prosecutor spent the night at the hotel and was up early, going over his notes, writing more questions. The stenographer returned at 8:30. The last of the depositions was finished right after lunch.

They were now free to go, but first they were debriefed and encouraged not to talk to media about what had happened. If they wanted, they could stay another night at government expense. If not, the government would help arrange flights. Ground transportation would be provided to the Orlando or Tampa airports.

67
Unpleasant, but necessary

Armed with phone numbers and names from the airlines and from Kimbie, the prosecutor called Sarah's sister, Molly's parents, and Fred's. Kimbie borrowed Sherry's now-recharged phone and made calls of her own. Julian insisted there was little he could say. That wasn't the point. Nothing she or anyone could say would be much help, but she needed to try. Pete probably couldn't express his condolences right now, so she would. It also crossed her mind that somebody might want to sue somebody. The prosecutor advised her not to say anything about fault or blame, but did not try to stop her from making calls she felt she needed to make.

It turned out that the families had been contacted by the Coast Guard the evening before, late. The families had been told that their loved ones had been reported missing at sea. They had been asked, just to be sure, if they had been contacted by Sarah, Molly or Fred. They had not. Kimbie told Sarah's sister how much they all liked her, how much they had learned from her, and how sad everyone was. She could not offer much hope. Obviously distraught, the sister could barely speak at first, then asked question after question, for most of which Kimbie had no answers. Finally, the sister thanked her and they said goodbye.

She told Molly's parents how their daughter had loved swimming with dolphins, how happy she had been in the days before the pirate attack, what a big help she had been on the boat. How much she and everyone, especially Bridget and Digby, had liked Molly. Kimbie's voice broke when she offered to send the mask the dolphin had retrieved for Molly. It had been found on deck. She choked up trying to tell the story, so Bridget took over. She sat with Kimbie when she called, because Ping wouldn't. Bridget cried too, but told of their swim together. She would remember Molly's wonderful attitude. Struggling for composure, Molly's parents said they would appreciate the mask, would treasure it. Thanked them both. Their daughter had not let anyone but her grandfather call her Molly for years, they said. They seemed touched by that most of all.

Kimbie told Fred's mother what a good guy she had raised, how much she and Captain Pete and Dr. Ping had depended on him. She all but extended her sympathy, but somehow she could not speak in the past tense. His mother sounded sad, but was poised, and thanked her. Fred's mom told Kimbie to take care of herself. The prosecutor had said they all had been through a terrible ordeal. Obviously grieving, she remembered to ask Kimbie to "please" give the captain her best wishes for a full recovery. Said her son admired Pete a great deal.

Kimbie did not know if Digs had any close family, though she half-remembered he might have mentioned a sister. She hoped Pete had an address or phone number, but feared he didn't. The prosecutor said the boat's log and maintenance records were missing, and no address book had been found.

By late afternoon, nearly everyone was booked on flights, either that night or the next day.

Nearly everyone. Ping had no place to go. Kimberly still had her tiny apartment in San Juan. The rent was so low she paid it six months at a time. But she didn't mention it to Ping. She had barely spoken to him since the afternoon before the pirates. It seemed like a long time ago.

In her head, she had gone over her last conversation with Pete a dozen times. He had wanted her to have a stateroom of her own. Regardless of what Julian Ping might think. Then they would talk. It seemed like a dream now. Had he really said that?

That conversation, which seemed so brief when she tried to recall it, had marked a change. Pete had hinted at a future for the two of them. They had almost whispered to keep from waking anybody, or being found. She had liked talking to Pete like that, more than a little. Neither had seemed to want it to end, but they were both practical people, and morning would come early. When she got to the stateroom, she was relieved to find Ping asleep. She slipped into bed without waking him, and smiled to herself. Pete had said he looked forward to seeing her at breakfast. She had looked forward to it too. The pirates smashed all that. Or so she thought, until the federal prosecutor got that phone call.

The way Ping had acted when the boat was captured had been awful, but it was almost understandable. They were all afraid. His attitude after they were rescued, she couldn't understand at all. Not in any way that let her see Julian in a good light. His odd mixture of indignation and arrogance annoyed her, but his unwillingness to accept any responsibility for the welfare of the passengers made her furious. Considering all that had to be done, she ignored it, stuffed it. She had too much to think about to deal with that right now. Julian's cavalier attitude about the deaths was troubling too, but she decided that was personal, his own business. His casual, almost indifferent approach to the loss of everyone's belongings could not be ignored though, or his disregard for the remaining days and meals the passengers had booked and paid for. Those things made her crazy, until she took charge. The passengers saw this and appreciated her for it.

The Coast Guard found a satchel of valuables, digital cameras, laptops, jewelry, watches and wallets, in the captain's stateroom. Pictures were still in the cameras. The lead prosecutor decided that allowing the owners to take their personal items would not hurt the government's case, as long as everything was inventoried and signed for. He had an evidence technician photograph and inventory everything, and download copies of all the digital images found in cameras, for possible use at the trial. Digital images of happy, smiling Digs, of Fred, of the captain, Molly and Sarah, were hard to deal with when they popped up on the tech's laptops. But the pictures were cathartic, too. People cried. They told stories and hugged each other. Sherry had taken a wonderful picture of Kimbie being silly with Pete, and promised to send it to her. The evidence tech overheard, and a short time later handed her a nice print in a clear folder. Kimbie gave the khaki-clad young woman a hug, hugged the picture, and showed Sherry, who tried to tip the evidence tech. The young woman said Kimbie's smile and hug were more than enough thanks. Kimbie was turning into a hugger.

She asked for ground transportation to Gainesville, where the captain was in the hospital. When Ping tried to say she did not need to go, she turned away. He retreated to the motel room he had expected them to share. The Zinsers decided to go with her to the hospital. The Marshal arranged for a rental car, and they set off.

The night before, after the depositions stopped, nearly everyone had wandered down to the bar. Kimbie did too, but slipped out alone with a glass of wine and found a place to sit and look at the water. At about 2 a.m., a security guard found her, hugging her knees and crying. Everybody at the marina knew the story, so when she told him who she was, and that she didn't want to go back to the room, and why, he took her to the night clerk. The clerk gave her another room and a toothbrush.

While Ping was being deposed the next morning, Kimbie got her few things out of his room, and that was that. Ruth went with her. It took about two minutes. She changed in Ruth's room and napped in the back of the rental car most of the way to Gainesville.

68
Deep-fried monkey

Pete's forehead, nose and right eye were bandaged. Bandages wrapped around his whole head. Any skin that wasn't bandaged was blistered and smeared with ointment. His lips were cracked from sun and salt water. So were his knuckles, and one side of his face, but those places did not need stitches, the nurse said. He had stitches across his nose, though, and on his brow and temple. The doctor said the gash on his brow would probably leave a scar, and the nose might need further surgery. A small plate doctors had inserted into his head might need more attention too, but probably not.

Kimbie gently held one reddened hand and kissed his cheek, ointment and all. The face she made from the taste made Pete almost laugh, or at least chuckle, but laughing also made him wince. He hurt, that was obvious, but could not take his one good eye off her.

When Kimbie shared what little she knew about the boat, he listened, but could not quite seem to take it in. After attempts at small talk, the Zinsers asked if they could pray.

"Sure," he said. Pete closed his one uncovered eye when they started, but opened it again and looked at Kimbie, whose eyes were closed. He had never seen her like that, so serious, and so pretty. Her hair was pulled back in a scarf Ruth had given her. She opened her eyes, saw him, and smiled. They were still looking at each other when Ruth finished the short prayer John had started. The Zinsers prayed for healing and restoration, help and comfort and peace.

Pete thanked them and exhaled as if he had been holding his breath for a long time. He asked about Digs and Fred, but had trouble understanding the answers. Nobody really knew what had happened, but it didn't look good. Seeing his sorrow and frustration, they stopped trying to explain. Pete told them he had feared everyone was dead, when he came to his senses a little. "I asked God to help you all, to help me too," he said. "I remember that. I guess he did."

John and Ruth smiled. Kimbie tried.

But Pete could not seem to hold things in his mind very long, and the subject receded. They talked about nothing for a few minutes. Kimbie found herself chattering about the nice nurses and the TV remote, until Pete asked her about Ping.

She swallowed hard and set her jaw, looked him in the eye and said, "He's gone." When Pete looked concerned, she said, "Oh, he wasn't hurt or anything. I just told him to eat dirt and die." She smiled the biggest smile she could, and tried to wink. Couldn't.

When John failed to suppress a snort, and Ruth flashed an impish smile, Pete still looked puzzled. He tried to smile, but it hurt, so nobody was sure about his reaction. He was in intensive care, post-op, after all. The visit had to be cut short.

Two hours later, a nurse came to the waiting room. Pete was awake. One of them could go back in for a few minutes. "You go, dear," Ruth urged Kimbie, who needed little encouragement. She went in, sat down, took his hand, kissed it, and they didn't talk at all until the nurse came for her.

John and Ruth got a room in the med center's hotel, but Kimbie spent the night in the waiting room. The nurses brought her a pillow and blanket, and showed her how to make a big recliner more comfy. They gave her a washcloth, soap and toothbrush. Exhausted, she actually slept, with her knees pulled up into her extra-large grey Florida State sweatshirt. The nurses, every one a proud UF grad, teased her just enough to make her smile.

Pete had a good night, the nurses said. He was a tiny bit better, but was still in serious condition. Before she saw him a nurse warned Kimbie to prepare herself, because he didn't *look* better. Sure enough, he looked worse, but she found that if she just looked at the one green eye that was uncovered, the way she had the night before, she could handle it. She didn't want to cry in front of him.

His face seemed more swollen, but had fresh and slightly smaller bandages. Some skin had turned almost black, and he was redder most places, but the nurses said that was normal. She was allowed to help with his breakfast, and was pleased when he had a good appetite. Seeing him eat boosted Kimbie's spirits enough that, when he asked, she conceded that he looked "Pretty grody." But she squeezed his hand gently and smiled as she said it.

After breakfast, she went to the Zinsers' room for a shower and change of clothes, and came right back. Ruth and John sat with her in the waiting room. They brought coffee, newspapers, water, fruit, yogurt, candy, flowers, anything they could think of. Ruth read quietly, but talked when Kimbie wanted. John read newspapers and chatted with others in the waiting room. He struck up a conversation—in Spanish—with the family of a young boy who had been hit by a car. He faced a long recovery but would be okay, the nurses said. John was able to communicate that in a way that helped. He and Ruth took the family to the cafeteria for lunch, on them, "so I can practice my rusty Spanglish," John said. One day-shift nurse spoke Spanish, but nobody on the evening shifts did, so John became the nursing station's liaison.

That evening, Estil Potter, Pete's friend from the Coast Guard, showed up. In the waiting room, Potts told them he had requested a day of leave, but instead had been sent by his boss from Key West to St. Petersburg, the sector headquarters, to pick up a piece of equipment. Lt. Commander Harris had suddenly decided the station could not wait another week for that particular item. She told Potter he could take his own car, and allowed more than enough time for a side trip to Gainesville.

By then, the nurses were letting Kimbie stay with Pete longer. They could see the good effect her visits had. Boyish, friendly Potts, in uniform, flirted with the nurses until they let him go in with her. In fact, they walked him in.

Pete gave a "thumbs up." Potts grinned at Pete and the nurses, who smiled and left. "I'm glad to see you're still among the living, ol' buddy."

"Just barely," the much-bandaged patient said.

"More than you deserve, most likely," Potts said, and smiled. Kimbie was startled, but Pete almost laughed. It was the closest to a real laugh she had heard from him here. Pete nodded agreement too, even though it was obvious that nodding—like smiling—hurt.

"Hurts to laugh," he said, but he actually laughed again, with his one uncovered eye squeezed shut. "Better than crying," he said, and chuckled again. And winced.

Pete asked why his friend was in uniform. Potts said he had been sent on a special re-supply mission after requesting leave. "The boss lady said, 'Potts, I can't spare you right now. I need you for a high-priority re-supply, from central stores, St. Pete.' I saw what she was up to, so I told her St. Pete could overnight her anything that wouldn't wait for the regular shuttle. Just to see." Pete nodded. It didn't hurt as much as last time.

"She just said, 'Fed-Ex won't do. I need you to verify it's the right stuff.' And smiled this big ole smile. You can't argue when she does that." Potts said he wasn't expected back until the end of the next day.

"She said to call if anything would prevent a timely return. I think my old eyes rolled back in my head about then," he said, as Pete laughed and grimaced, then quietly laughed a little more.

"Sounds like a good boss."

"Sure 'nuff. Tough too, when it matters. She *is* good. And pretty."

Pete's one eyebrow moved. "She even said to 'give Captain Gordon my best wishes for a speedy recovery.' You don't *know her*, do you?" Potts put stress on "know her," and watched Pete squirm.

Pete carefully shook his head, no. He looked at Kimbie, and shook his head again.

Kimbie was not sure what to think. It showed.

Potts saw he had gone too far. "Ms. Barone, I should not have done that," he said, contrite. "Commander Harris don't know Pete at all. She thinks she owes me for helping her when she was new on station. I was just teasing my old buddy, 'cause I'm glad he's okay. Even if he doesn't look the best I've ever seen him."

Kimbie relaxed. "No harm done."

Potts exhaled, relieved. Then he added, deadpan, "If I had said what went through my brain when I walked in, I would have said he looks like a deep-fried monkey." Kimbie schooled her face not to react. She also tried to come up with a better description—couldn't—and laughed in spite of herself. It had been a while since she had laughed, too. "The nurses said not to let him have any mirrors," she said, and smiled. This time she could wink.

They all laughed, Pete the longest. Potts asked Pete if he had talked to his mom. He hadn't. "I guess I forgot. Stuff came up …."

Potts just nodded. Pete told what he could remember about his short encounter with the pirates, which was almost nothing. "But I think I shot a guy, Potts. He was trying to steal my boat. I'm pretty sure I did."

Potts nodded. "Mostly I remember swimming," Pete said. "Didn't know why, just kept on." Kimbie touched his hand. "I figured I could swim for a day and a night, maybe another day," Pete said. "My head was bad. I saw sharks that turned into dolphins. Go figure."

"I've seen that, lots of times," Potts said, and smiled. Kimbie nodded agreement.

"The Coasties who got me off the sandbar looked like babies."

"Tell me about it," Potter said, really laughing. "They look like that to me too, bro."

"They said teenagers on jet skis found me. I saw a kid on a jet ski, playing with dolphins, after I was picked up. I swear, I think dolphins found me. I almost think they carried me. Seemed like it. My head was not right at all."

Kimbie hadn't heard that before and asked questions. Pete's memory about the events just before and after the pirate raid was dreamlike. But he could remember other things.

When Potts started telling Kimbie about serving with Pete, Pete's memory seemed fine, and he added details. He told Potts things he never had about the fish camp. As Kimbie listened, her mouth dropped open at times.

Potts listened carefully. Pete told how he had learned something each time he was turned down for a loan, and went from bank to bank. "On my umpteenth try, they went for it."

"I never really understood how you did it," Potts said. "I was afraid for a while maybe you might have done something funny. Non-regulation. You know?"

Pete nodded. Turning to Kimbie, he said, "We saw so many guys go bad. Dumb ones, sure, but a few guys who had a lot going for them. I probably don't have to tell you." Kimbie smiled.

"I still said you were a fool to sell."

"You were right," Pete said, sounding like he meant it. "No points, but you were right."

This relieved Potts in some way. Pete's old friend was able to convey his allayed concerns to Kimbie with smiles, nods and short, affirmative comments—"See there, Miss Kimbie?" This relieved some of her anxiety. They both had been worried about Pete's mind, it seemed, though she had not wanted to say so, not to anybody.

When there was a lull, Potts said, "I figured you could drown-proof for a couple days if you had to, but ... I prayed, Bro."

Pete looked thoughtful. "Thanks," he said, quietly. "I prayed too. I didn't know which way was up, which way to shore, but I prayed too. When I was up against it." He shivered.

Potts saw, nodded.

Kimbie saw too. She didn't know what to say, but took Pete's hand and held it. She had to admit, if only to herself, that when the pirates had come back, she had been certain she would die. She thought about whether she believed there was a God, and hoped. It wasn't a prayer exactly, but she had thought to herself that if God was real, this would be a real good time to show up. She hadn't thought about that again, though, until now.

Part of her brain said she had just been trying to deny reality. Maybe. But when she had been sure they were all going to die—they hadn't. The odds against it—intervention by dolphins—and a submarine, after all—were too amazing to be ... what? Plausible? Realistic? But here they were.

"You're still here, ol' buddy," Potts said. "You'd best remember that." Kimbie decided she needed to remember too.

"Yeah," Pete said. He felt tears well up. There they went. He wondered if they showed.

Pete had to be in a lot of pain, Kimbie thought, seeing his one visible eye brim over. The nurses said his pain meds would help him heal faster. But he didn't seem high. He wasn't loopy or anything. He couldn't remember some things, but he was himself.

He was more open and accessible than she could remember, too, except the night before the pirates, for that hour. She was pretty sure he didn't remember sitting up on the bridge, talking to her, after she fell asleep up there. He hadn't mentioned it. She wanted to, but hadn't. She hoped *that* memory would come back.

"You want to call your Mama?" Potts asked. When Pete said yes, Potts handed him his cell phone, and brought up Mary Gordon's number. Pete looked at it a minute. Kimbie couldn't believe she hadn't rounded up a phone herself. Nobody had gotten phones back, except Sherry, who never lost hers. Kimbie had learned—and told Pete—that his mom had been contacted by the Coast Guard, and knew he was okay, but she hadn't given it another thought after that. Turned out that Lieutenant Commander Harris had arranged for Potts to make the call to Mrs. Gordon.

"It was a treat, telling her everybody said you were okay, sure enough," Potts said, "but she'll feel a lot better hearing your sorry old voice." Potts beamed. "Course, I hadn't seen you myself, but I told her what I knew, 'bout the kids finding you, what the rescue boat guys said, what the doctor at Yankeetown said and all. She found out you were okay before she knew for sure you were in trouble, so that was good. She'd been worried though, more than usual, is what she said. You got a good Mama."

Pete nodded. He felt tears well up again. It was a regular thing. He almost never cried, but lately tears came at the drop of a hat.

The call was short. Pete told his Mom he was "banged up some," but nothing was broken that wouldn't heal. He reminded her of some youthful injuries and compared this to them. His mom said she was coming to see him in the morning, but he asked her to wait, since he was feeling better than the day before. She said she was glad to hear his voice, and glad he had people with him. Pete put Potts on the phone.

"My ol' buddy looks crummy right now, Mom Gordon, that's a fact, but Miss Kimbie and the nurses are gettin' him squared away." Potts actually winked at Kimbie when he said that, and she smiled.

After reassuring Mom Gordon a bit more, Potts told her to take her time and not rush up to Gainesville. "They tell me he's going to be real purty in a few days, but I got my doubts," Potts said. "No offense, ma'am, but Pete wadn't that good-lookin' even when the Coast Guard was in charge of him," he said. "Not like yours truly."

That made her laugh, but Mom Gordon said she would have to see for herself, as soon as her friend could come with her. Maybe the day after tomorrow, since Potts thought that would be okay. She thanked Potts for getting to the hospital, and told him to stop on his way back if he could, or on his next trip up I-75 to Tennessee. "You're one of my boys, and my boys are welcome anytime, Potts honey. I'll feed you too, even if it's just peanut butter."

Potts reminded her that she had cooked him plenty of good meals, never peanut butter. "But hey, can I sleep on your couch tonight? Maybe you can make me a sandwich for the road." Mom Gordon said that would be wonderful, and to wake her if she was asleep. Potts said he would. Pete said good night and they hung up.

Pete was touched that Potts had made the trip, but now he was worn out. Trying to sound upbeat for the phone call had taken the last of his energy. He slumped when his Mom hung up.

"One less thing," Potts said as he took the phone. Pete smiled.

When Potts got up to leave, Kimbie hugged him, kissed his leathery cheek and thanked him for coming. "Thanks for getting Pete to talk so much," she said. "We've been too easy on him, I think." She hugged him again and smiled so much that Potts turned to Pete. "Keeper," he said, behind his hand.

Turning back to Kimbie, he said, "Get him to tell you about how I almost kept him from qualifying for diver," Potts said, making a funny, embarrassed face. "Or not. Just keep taking good care of my ol' buddy, Kimmie Barone," he said, using the version of her name that Pete had used once that evening. She smiled and said she would. Kimbie looked at the ceiling for a second, blinked back tears, felt her face flush. Blushing wasn't very much like her, but everything, it seemed, had changed.

The Zinsers walked Potts to the elevator. "I like that boy," Ruth said when they rejoined Kimbie in the waiting room. John said they had hugged like old friends when they parted.

69
Mourn, heal, mend, plan

The Bertram was Pete's actual residence, where he lived, and Kimbie's too, more or less, except for the apartment in Puerto Rico. But the boat was not Pete's residence of record. Besides, he was in no shape to reclaim it, just yet. It was still in federal custody, so to speak. It took every string Kimbie could pull to have it released.

First, Pete designated her as his "authorized agent" concerning the boat, in writing, notarized, from his hospital bed. His honorable service in the Coast Guard helped. Potts asked his commanding officer what she could do. Lt. Cmdr. Robin Harris made her personal interest a matter of record, and asked for updates. Potts and others who had served with Pete did the same. The chief U.S. Marshal in Tampa, whose sailboat was his pride and joy, was sympathetic. Phone calls from Sarah Cale's former employer helped too.

Kimbie called the law firm before Pete was found, to find out how to reach Sarah's family, and wound up talking to one of the partners. Guarded at first, he warmed as they talked. When problems with the boat surfaced, she called him again. He would see what he could do, "out of respect for Sarah." It didn't hurt that Pete's mom called a retired nurse friend who happened to be her congressman's aunt.

Something worked. Kimbie's phone calls began to be returned. Various officials assured her that things were moving. One prosecutor mentioned "your attorney's concerns." She got updates from the lawyer, but never a bill. He sent his best when the boat was released. He knew. But the wheels of justice grind slow.

Pete developed an infection. His doctors kept him in the hospital ten more days to get it under control. Tests and therapy followed. The doctors did not think he had suffered permanent damage, but warned it might be months, even years before he would be "one hundred percent."

Pete's balance was not what it had been. For weeks, his head swam when he stood. He only fell once, but sometimes felt he was about to. He blacked out the single time he actually fell. More tests. More worry. Kimbie and Pete would have worried more, but a kind nurse with decades of experience gave some advice. Balance problems often go with head trauma, she said, but not to worry. "It nearly always gets better, by itself. Give it time." That helped. A stairwell near Pete's room was seldom used. He began to climb it. Five flights, four or five times a day, a hand always on the rail. That helped too.

His recall of events just before and right after the pirates was still missing, or confused. He was told this would most likely come back, in time, and not to push it too much. So when he could not remember something, Pete relied on Kimbie's memory.

She bought him a hickory cane with a big brass knob. It made him smile, and he used it. "Makes you look dashing," she said.

When he got out of the hospital, with the boat still impounded, Pete moved in with his mom. Kimbie rented a car and took him to Mom Gordon's neat little mobile home on Charlotte Harbor. From there she planned to go see her own parents. Pete asked her to take his truck instead of the rental. A friend had checked everything for Pete and gassed it up. Mom Gordon followed her to return the rental car. They talked about Pete all the way back. Mom Gordon patted Kimbie's arm as she drove. Kimbie put her half-empty suitcase in the little green truck and drove away with a big smile and a wave.

70
Time to rest

Since college, Kimbie had not seen her parents often. It was never convenient. Other things came first, but she called. Before the pirates, it had been a while. Naturally, they were concerned after the attack, and wanted to see her. But since she was staying with the Zinsers and working on getting the boat released almost full time, she talked them out of it. "I'm fine," she said.

But she wasn't fine. She was exhausted mentally and emotionally, even physically. She felt crummy. Beat up. Frazzled. When she decided a visit home made sense, she was anxious. She called to ask if she could come and "just take it easy for a week or two." Ruth held Kimbie's hand, literally, while she made the call. Her parents were pleased, and relieved. They offered to come get her, or send a plane ticket. She declined, but thanked them. They told her not to worry, just come.

When she drove to their home in central Florida in Pete's little pickup, they were more than pleased. She did not mention Julian, or Pete for that matter, except to say he had insisted she use his truck. Her Mom had fixed her favorite foods, plus a big pot of homemade chicken soup. Her Dad had rearranged his schedule for the whole day, just to be there when she arrived.

They fussed over her, told her how good she looked. She knew it wasn't true; her nose was raw, her throat was sore, her eyes were red, with circles under them. She had not swum in a month, and felt flabby. Ruth's scarf only partially hid her almost-dirty hair, but she smiled and said thanks.

Her Dad parked the pickup where it wouldn't be in the way. He remarked on how well-maintained it was, recent oil change, good tires, started and ran just right. After a late lunch, they wanted to talk, but after about twenty minutes, she needed a nap.

The nap, on her old bed, without even turning down the covers, lasted until her Mom lured her out of bed with the offer of fresh coffee or tea, hot or cold. Hot tea and a shower made her feel better, but she was still pooped. After more chicken soup and polite, careful conversation, she went to bed, under the covers this time.

Her room had been redecorated. It looked like a nice hotel room. Like a guest room, with her high school graduation picture displayed on her nice old dresser. Her same comfy bed hid under new linens. Almost everything was unfamiliar, but pretty. In the closet she found sentimental stuff that had once made the room truly hers, and some clothes from college. She retrieved a pair of jeans that still fit, T-shirts, a teddy bear and another framed picture with friends and SCUBA gear. Her hair was long in the picture, straighter and more blonde than white, but not much else had changed. She hoped she still had that bikini.

Her dad's routine was breakfast out, with his cronies. He volunteered at a park most mornings, and went to the library most afternoons. Unless he had a project, he usually didn't come home until supper, much as before he retired. She and her Mom had time to catch up.

After a week of sleep, rest, walks and good food, she felt better. She read for hours, talked with her parents, called Pete every evening. Not much else. One morning she woke up and realized she had energy. After breakfast she fired up her dad's string trimmer, edged the lawn and cleared a neglected corner between a big flowering bush and the garage. A flat stone, big as a kitchen table, was almost hidden by sandy soil and creeping grass. The grey-green stone triggered a happy memory, one she couldn't quite put her finger on.

Pete's truck had not moved since she arrived, so she drove it downtown, had it washed and stopped at a big home improvement store. Wandering the aisles she almost tripped over a heavy box. A park bench. The picture on the box looked nice, her parents' yard needed a bench, and the price was right. So she had them load it in the truck and picked up salads at her mom's favorite deli on the way home.

After lunch, the box wouldn't budge. So she cut open the end and pulled out one piece at a time and carried the parts to the flat stone she had uncovered. Her mother watched, concerned. It took half an hour to move the pieces and arrange them, another hour to put the bench together with tools she found in Pete's truck, behind the seat.

The cast iron sides of the bench were pale green and smooth. The wood slats glowed golden in the sun, nicer even than the picture. She followed the instructions, especially the big exploded drawing. Once the parts were all together, she tightened everything one more time and dragged the bench to the edge of the stone. It looked like it had always been there.

She put the tools away, washed her hands with the garden hose and went to take another look. The bench transformed the shady corner, and completed the yard somehow. She was almost afraid to sit on it, but when she did, it felt solid and comfortable. It wouldn't even wiggle. So she curled her feet up.

When she awoke, her parents stood over her, holding hands, with looks on their faces she had not seen in a long time.

"Do you remember your swing set?" her mom asked. "It was the same color. Your sandbox was right here by the stone. Your Daddy put your swing set just out past it."

"I remember! I loved it." She hugged the memory as she hugged her knees. "I used to sit in the swing and think. I'd forgotten." She yawned and stretched and smiled. Her father had a far-away look, and a half-smile. They were remembering, all of them.

For the rest of the visit, she hung out on the bench and sipped her mom's iced tea. She had a lot to think about. Pete. Nearly dying. Being alive. God. The rest of her life. Next week. Pete. Stuff like that.

She stayed almost three weeks. She had come here because she was exhausted, and the first week she had worked hard at just resting. The second week she exercised and walked in the mornings, but went to bed early, usually right after she called Pete. She only ventured out a few times to see old friends, or their parents. She got a new cell phone. Talking to Pete on the bench was her favorite part of the day. The third week she went to the city pool. The water made her miss the boat and miss Pete.

Kimbie and her Mom had some nice chats on the bench. They took their coffee out there in the mornings. She tried to tell her Mom about Pete, but couldn't get much to come out except how nice he was, how smart, what a good captain and diver he was, his injuries, and how glad she was that he was better. His shiny little mist-green pickup in the driveway spoke for itself, though. Her mother said her dad loved the bench, and loved that she had done such a nice thing, out of the blue. Which was obvious. She found him sitting out there a few times. She sat on his lap once, but they were both more comfortable with her leaning against him, not talking much.

One evening, after Kimbie reported that Pete had felt good enough that day to go fishing, and thought he might be ready to snorkel soon, her dad said he was glad. He tried to say he was glad they both were doing so well, but choked up. She hugged him, and said it was okay. That she was okay. Tears fell and she held his hand. He just smiled and did not try to speak. She had not told them that one of the girls who died had slept that night in what had been her berth. She did not talk about that, but she thought about it. A lot. She had felt guilty for surviving, at first. Sometimes she still did. It was tough to look at a pretty sunrise or sunset for a while. Ruth had helped by reminding her it wasn't her fault. Not in any way. The blame was with the pirates. Pete said he was thankful she had been right where she was. Lately Kimbie had decided to be thankful too. She had decided to try to make her life count, at least in part for Molly and Digs, who had believed in her. Maybe someday she could tell her parents all that, but not yet.

The next evening her dad surprised her with a quart of toffee mocha almond, her favorite ice cream. She was amazed. He just smiled. The three of them ate it together at the kitchen table. They laughed a little, and talked about long ago. She knew they wanted to know her plans, but Kimbie had no definite plans that she could talk about. Nothing beyond helping Pete get back in operation. They already knew that.

The night before she left, her parents let her take them out to eat. They went to an Italian place they picked, and had a nice evening. They shared a bottle of wine and laughed a little. When friends of theirs stopped by the table, her dad introduced her with obvious pride. He said they were going to miss her when she left again. Thinking about that later, she realized she would miss them too. Somehow they had never meant more to her than they did now.

The morning she left, her dad skipped breakfast with his pals. After they loaded her two nearly-full bags in the little truck, he hugged her. He seemed not to want to let her go. She understood. Then he said, "Thank you for coming home to rest, Kim. I'm glad to see you looking so much better, and feeling better. We both are. And thank you for the bench. That was a wonderful thing to do." They walked to the truck, where her mom hugged her again, and said she would miss her. Her Mom said she hoped it would not be too long before they saw each other again. Her Dad nodded.

Kimbie managed to say she had enjoyed being with them. That she appreciated them letting her just rest, and have the time she needed. Her Dad said he hoped she would be able to come back, soon. "You know our home will always be your home too, Kim. We love you. We'll always love you."

Kimbie felt tears well up as she stood on tiptoe and kissed her daddy on the cheek. "I know," she said, "but thanks for saying it. I love you guys too."

He smiled but didn't speak.

Kimbie called Ruth as she drove back. "I know you prayed, even if you didn't say so," Kimbie said. The visit had been sweet, she said, the best ever. "And I got so much rest! Thank you for encouraging me to go home and just chill." Ruth was pleased. Back home in California, she urged Kimbie to keep in touch.

71
All squared away

Pete's mom wanted Kimbie to call her Mary, and stop on her way back. Mary put her in the room Pete had been using. He moved to the couch in the small living/dining room, though when they got up the next morning, he was asleep on the glider on the screened porch.

Mary's trim little mobile home was surrounded by flowers and flowering bushes. The trailer park was right on the water, and her spot was about fifty yards back. Pine trees gave shade, needles carpeted the walking trail along the water, and the two women tried to get to know each other. They knew it was important. Kimbie stayed only one night, but when she left, Mary told her she was welcome back anytime. "Next week even, if you don't have anything holding you. And plan to stay a little longer." She held both of Kimbie's hands and kissed her on the cheek. They smiled, cried, laughed, and hugged. Pete leaned on his cane. He was surprised to see tears, but pleased overall, though he did not quite know why or what to say. Kimbie kissed him on the cheek, after she dried her eyes. Then she took off for Miami to talk to a favorite professor. Pete made it clear she would take the little green truck. He gassed it up before she left.

With the boat still in limbo, she came back. Sitting in Mary's breakfast nook they drew up a business plan. One of the first things Kimbie did after returning from her parents' was to formally dissolve her relationship, business and otherwise, with Julian Ping. She did not want or need her furnished apartment in San Juan anymore, and dangled it. He had been crashing with friends, trying to get back with his ex in Australia, but was at loose ends. Puerto Rico sounded good, for now. Once he got there, Ping agreed to ship the few things she wanted to her parents' home. Eventually, he actually did. Her parents called and said the boxes were in a closet, unopened, no problem. She asked her Mom to please open them, carefully, without Dad around, maybe in the garage, with rubber gloves. She knew Ping. Her Mom laughed.

Back in Tampa, assured that the boat would be released "within days," she spent one night at the hotel by the marina where the *New Delphi* should have been, then a friend of a friend offered her couch.

When federal marshals at last gave her custody, she asked around the marina for moral support. The harbormaster went with her. He went below first, radioed his office and blocked the passageway to the crew berths. The diesels started without major problems. When they got to the marina, he and another guy worked for several hours. She cleaned the galley and aired out staterooms while she waited.

"The Coasties did a good job, it's not that," the harbormaster told her. "I just wanted to do something for Pete, and for you." She could not have stopped him, so she gave him a hug. When he let her inspect, everything was shipshape, and smelled of fresh paint and Murphy's oil soap. She left the portholes and hatches open for a few days. It would be okay.

That afternoon she moved back into the stateroom she had shared with Ping. It was the smallest, and next to the captain's cabin. When she found some of Ping's underwear in an overlooked compartment, she carried the bundle at arms' length to the dock, dropped it in a garbage can, swiped the dust off her hands, nodded for emphasis, and smiled all the way back to the boat.

Being in possession of Ping's dive gear, some of his scientific equipment (and a box full of notebooks) put her in a good negotiating position. She and Pete had always kept track of the money, so she started making phone calls. It took a week but she paid all the joint debts that Julian and Pete had, with approval from both of them, and many thanks from Pete. She also paid herself the back pay she was due.

Julian did not object. He came away with some cash, no debt, bills all paid and what she could find of his stuff (except for those tiny shorts). She sent him copies of bank statements, itemized accounts and receipts, and reminded him about his rent-free deal on her former apartment for the next several months. Pete had said she was being more than fair. In the end, Ping must have thought so too. Pete got a check from him, to square an earlier dive gear sale, and a note. It wished them well. That was a surprise. Pete called Ping to say thanks. Kimbie smiled and put the check in the boat's operating fund.

News coverage had made them "famous" for a week or two, but it was old news now. The cameras had showed sad, tired survivors, Bridget and Sherry hugging and trying not to cry, a short statement by Chip and mug shots of the pirates. Nobody gave interviews, and the next day no one was findable, except Pete at the hospital. The hospital put out a brief statement, and that was that. It was ancient history now, as far as the public was concerned, but Pete's return was big news around the marina.

When she brought him down from Port Charlotte, friends at the marina had a little party, with huge Cuban sandwiches, chips and salsa, beer and plenty of teasing. Guys who had been sweet and helpful while Pete was gone, who had never said anything the least bit out of the way, now teased her without mercy. She smiled and laughed and hugged a few of them. Things got quiet when the harbormaster said he missed having Digs around. Pete had to threaten a few people with his cane to liven things up. It helped when the harbormaster said the floor was open for anybody who wanted to talk about how much they missed Ping. Kimbie nearly choked, and everybody but Pete laughed. Pete bit his lip, but looked pleased.

Friends razzed him about the cane, but were glad to see he could get around well with it, especially on the boat, where there was usually something to hold onto. He exaggerated his need for the cane, made a joke of it. The truth was, he still needed it ashore, even if it did not show that often. He had always done better on boats.

When the last of their friends left, Pete and Kimbie sat on the afterdeck, sipped beer and watched the sunset. They cried again for Digs and Fred. The week after the Coast Guard called off its search, Kimbie and the harbormaster had arranged a simple memorial for Digs at the marina. He seemed not to have any family. Pete was still in the hospital, but the guys put a picture of Digs in the office window and spread the word. A dozen people came.

The harbor chaplain read a prayer for those lost at sea. He had not known Digby well, he said, but the presence of his friends said good things about him. He commended Digs for bravery in his last hour, mentioned Fred, Sarah and Molly by name, and prayed for the safety of all who make their living on the water. A harbor cop played the Navy Hymn on his guitar. Birds and boats were the only other sounds.

Kimbie tried to say how happy Digs had been when dolphins brought so many groupers to the boat that he couldn't haul them in. How Digs had held everyone spellbound when he told of his boyhood around Crystal River. She said Pete had told her he had never sailed with anyone he trusted as much as Digs.

Several who came were people Digs had helped, with money until payday, friendly advice, an extra hand, an eye kept while they were away, or an attitude adjustment. A sailboat owner, known to be wealthy, said Digs had offered a word of encouragement when he really needed it, and he would never forget it. On the other end of the income scale, a self-described "marina rat" who hired out on various boats said Digs always seemed to know when he was living on Ramen noodles. It was uncanny, he said, how Digs would invite him aboard for chow or send "leftovers" at those times. Kimbie knew Pete accepted Digs' habit of hospitality as a matter of course, and she said so. (She didn't mention that Ping grumbled.)

When the short little service was over, people hung around. Several thanked Kimbie for arranging it. Everybody said to tell Pete they were pulling for him, to get better quick.

She sent flowers in Pete's name, her own and Ping's, to the funerals for Sarah and for Molly, but didn't try to go. She also sent Molly's dive mask, along with a two-page note it took her all day to write.

Fred had family in Maryland and Maine, it turned out. His memorial took six weeks to arrange. Pete and Kimbie went, though he had not been out of the hospital long. His doctors did not want him to travel, and forbid flying, but there was no talking him out of it. He would take a train if he had to, or a bus. Kimbie made a bed of pillows and blankets in the back of a big rented Ford. Pete slept most of the way. She decided she really hated I-95.

They checked into a hotel with a view of Baltimore harbor, ordered room service and looked out at the lights on the water.

Fred's family was well-to-do, as Pete had suspected. His parents, sister and grandfather appreciated the effort they had made to attend. Pete's face still looked bad, and he leaned on Kimbie when he walked. Fred's mother, who had been poised and gracious on the phone, tried to thank them, but couldn't finish. She let Kimbie hug her as she sobbed. Then she hugged them both for a long time. They all cried. In the end, there was nothing to say except … so sad, so young, so awful. Such a good guy. We'll all remember him.

After the service they crossed the Chesapeake Bay and headed down the Eastern Shore and into the northern neck of Virginia. They breezed through Hampton Roads and Norfolk after rush hour and stopped at a motel on the Outer Banks of North Carolina. The only room available had one king-size bed. Kimbie collapsed on it after supper and a shower. Pete spent most of the night on the balcony in the breeze, looking out to sea, but he was asleep beside her when she woke up. She watched him sleep in the early light for ten or fifteen minutes before she eased out of bed. An hour after they returned to the mainland Pete fell asleep again. She got back on I-95 and they didn't stop except for gas, coffee and one good meal until they reached Mom Gordon's.

On the afterdeck of Pete's now-nameless boat, on their first night aboard, they sat in a corner of the built-in, wraparound couch. He took her hand. She snuggled against him. It felt nice. They watched the sunset until it was gone.

"Do you remember?" he ventured. Kimbie assumed it was another hitch with his memory.

"Maybe," she said, helpful.

"I hope so." He turned to face her, and watched her expression. He could turn his head now. "Do you remember up on the bridge, before the pirates? When we talked?"

She took a deep breath and smiled. "Yes. You said ... um ... you looked forward to breakfast."

He smiled and looked relieved. "Mmm. I did. Yeah. That too. I remember that too. I hadn't thought about that part until now." He smiled. "So you remember. Good."

She could see he was thinking, remembering.

"Okay," he said, as if something was clear now. He nodded, took a deep breath, exhaled. "Okay. Good. That helps. I decided that night ... that evening ... Well, it's more like I realized ... that I'd made a mistake when I didn't try to take you away from Ping, the first time I saw you."

She smiled. "I don't know if it would have happened, then. You were a boat captain, a nice cute one, but ... Julian's cute too, and I had this heroic vision of him. Plus, he was my employer."

"I know. You remember us talking, then?"

"Which time?"

Pete shook his head, smiled and let go a frustrated grunt. "On the bridge, when I found you asleep."

"Sure." She was serious, intent. Pete exhaled. Inhaled. She continued. "I do. I thought about what we said as I went to sleep. Then the next day ... I was afraid ... that ... that I would never see you again. I think I held my breath most of that day. I mean it. It was like I couldn't *get* my breath. Like the universe had kicked me in the belly, played this awful trick. It was really selfish, I guess, self-centered, but I thought it."

"It was no trick. But I see what you mean. You thought about what I said?"

She nodded. " 'Course I did. I thought things finally were going to be right. Then everything turned awful."

Pete was quiet for a moment. "Not everything."

She smiled. "No, you survived."

"I did. You did too."

She snuggled closer. He pulled her to him, gentle. "When you came to the hospital, I knew things were different, better, but I didn't know why. I didn't remember us talking, but I sure was glad to see you. I couldn't remember much at all, or think much." He frowned, but let it go.

Kimbie shivered. "Your memory scared me. I was afraid to ask you much, at first." She looked at the water and focused on the smallest light she could see, way across the bay. In the direction the sun had gone, out under the big bridge, maybe in the Gulf beyond it. "I did a lot of thinking in that raft. I pretended to be asleep so I didn't have to talk. I thought I had lost you. I was afraid I had lost you right after you told me how you felt. I wished I had said more. I hoped, but by morning I didn't have much hope left. Then, when those guys came back, I was sure I was going to die too, with nothing much accomplished. No doctorate, no rose-covered cottage, no kids. No you. When we were rescued I still thought I'd lost you. I kept asking myself, why? Why did I live and not you? Why me and not the others? Like I couldn't wake up from a bad dream. We hadn't said all that much, but ..."

"Enough. I leveled with you," he said. "You almost leveled with me too. I thought you were pleased, I remember that. We agreed to stop selling ourselves short, remember?" She nodded. "I still had some convincing to do, but I was hopeful. I really was looking forward to seeing you at breakfast."

"I was too," she said, but thoughts of the rest of that night made her shiver. He leaned forward, looked into her eyes in the fading light, touched her cheek. She snuggled even more and he leaned back. "I'm looking forward to breakfast tomorrow, too. To the whole day."

"Me too." He breathed in the warm smell of her and felt content. "I thought I had lost you too. You, everything. My whole life."

"You thought about me?"

He nodded. "Mmmhmm. I did. I hoped you were okay, I hoped everybody was, once my brain started working. Semi-working. I couldn't remember what had happened though. It was like trying to remember a dream when you can't. But I remembered you, prayed for you. For you and everybody. I prayed that you would be okay. I asked God to help all of you. Me too. And you lived. You're alive."

Kimbie thought about that. It touched her to think Pete thought about her, hoped she was all right, even prayed, when he didn't even know if he would survive himself.

"You've got your stateroom." She could see his face from the marina lights. He was smiling.

"I wondered if you would remember that."

"I didn't at first. But it worked out, huh?"

She bit her lip.

"Why didn't Ping stay?"

"I made him see that he needed to move on. With almost no words."

Pete was silent a moment. "Did you really tell him to eat dirt and die? I didn't know what to think when you said that. Maybe I don't want to know."

She almost giggled. She wasn't sure herself why Ping had left without her having to yell and throw stuff. He could be so obtuse. "Not in so many words. I just had nothing to say to him. At all. Even before I knew you were alive, I didn't want to talk to him. Not in the raft, not later. I only said what I had to say to him. I spent half the night on a bench at the marina, alone. Thinking about stuff, about you. Crying. A security guard found me. The desk clerk gave me a room by myself. Julian didn't look for me, either. It wouldn't have mattered if he did though. I had already made up my mind, if he had. Which he didn't."

He smiled again and exhaled. It wasn't a sigh, but he sounded tired.

"Sleepy?"

"Partied out."

She understood. He had to be more tired than she was. The trip down, the nice little party and the move back aboard. She smiled, kissed his scar, and helped him get to his feet in the darkness.

They stood, arms around each other, shoulder to shoulder, and looked at the water.

"I'm glad you're here," he said. "I'm glad you're alive, glad *we're* here. It feels good."

"It does. I like being here with just you." She inhaled the cool air and the smells of the bay, and knew she meant it.

They went forward, through the salon, locking up and turning off lights as they went. They held onto each other until they came to her stateroom door.

They each thought about going to the other's room. Without words though, they each decided it would not be a good idea, not right now.

He woke with the sun, went on deck, looked around, stretched, realized his cane was in his cabin, smiled, started coffee in the galley, went back to his cabin and shaved. He tapped on her thin teak door, asked if she wanted coffee, heard a mumble that sounded positive, went to get two cups. He brought them to her stateroom, slow and careful. He was cheerful, eager for whatever the day might bring. He sat on her bed while she had her first sips, under the covers, yawned and stretched. *I like the way she smells in the morning, that is a fact.* They talked about breakfast until she sent him out so she could put on the first bikini of the day.

She fried an egg for herself, boiled two for him and made toast. He poured O.J. and a bowl of Cheerios with granola, raisins and a banana. She cut up strawberries for her yogurt. Gave some to him. They finished each other's sentences, ate and cleaned up. Then they sat back down, to figure out what their options were for the day. They could not stop smiling.

72
Just to steal a nice boat

They had to rearrange their light schedules a few times over the next few months to appear before federal magistrates and meet with prosecutors. Kimbie shuddered the first time she saw the pirates in court, but got over it. In time she could glare at the defense table, now and then.

Pete's testimony was almost a formality. As owner and captain of the pirated vessel, and the victim of attempted murder, he had to take the stand. But Pete still could not remember much about what happened that night, not in the right order, not in a way that would hold together under questioning. Even the day before the attack was fuzzy. He remembered things a few days before the pirates, though. For some reason he also remembered talking to Kimbie on the bridge. And he remembered everything since waking up in the hospital, but had almost no recall of the attack.

He had trouble separating what he remembered from what he had been told. The prosecutor set up an opportunity for Pete to say so, on the stand. One of his doctors testified on video that this was common with severe head trauma.

Pete said he had heard shots, but couldn't place them on a time line. When questioned as to whether he had shot one of the pirates, he said, "Probably," and nodded his head affirmatively for emphasis. He looked like he was still thinking about it.

In response to a question from the U.S. Attorney, Pete said he could have shot Teddy Barfield through the cabin window, if Teddy had been there that night. It was his window. He could not remember a hole being there before. But he also testified that he really wasn't sure. He could recall crewing with Teddy as a teenager. He was sorry if Teddy was one of the pirates, as the two defendants alleged, and sorry that the pirates believe Teddy to be dead. Pete also said he had not seen Teddy in at least five years, unless Teddy was in fact on his boat that night. The last time he was certain he had seen Teddy was in Fort Myers. They had run into each other, joked and talked briefly as old shipmates, asked about each other's family and parted on good terms. Pete said he bore Teddy no ill will, though he also testified that he had little trouble believing Teddy could have been involved in "shady stuff. Trouble always found him."

The defense attorneys had tried to have Pete charged with the murder of Theodore Wilson Barfield, even without a body. The U.S. Attorney argued that this was an attempt to confuse the issue. Four people were dead. Ample evidence of their presence existed, including witnesses and photos taken the day before their deaths. They had definitely been aboard, though their bodies were still missing and would likely not be found. As to whether Barfield had been present, the court had only the words of the two accused, who had been caught about to attempt eight additional murders. The prosecutor asserted that the defendants may well have killed Mr. Barfield themselves. If Barfield had in fact been aboard the yacht with the pirates in the middle of the night, the owner and captain would have been within his rights to defend his boat against an act of piracy. When Claiborne's attorney called Teddy's death "cold-blooded, barbaric," Judge Arthur looked over the top of his glasses at the defense bench for what seemed like a long time. The assistant U.S. attorney made notes. The defense lawyers conferred and said nothing further about Teddy Barfield.

Pete could remember straining to see shapes against the little lights in the passageway and salon. He could not remember how he had been injured. A doctor testified on video about Pete's injuries, and said they were consistent with the kind of trauma that could be inflicted by a blunt instrument. Similar injuries are often fatal. The doctor said he was hopeful for a full recovery, considering Pete's progress, though he could not be certain.

Pete's cane—and apparent need for it—spoke volumes. He gripped the witness box rail with his free hand as he negotiated the two steps up, and tried to move naturally. He still feared his balance could fail him. Even with the cane, he sometimes had the sensation he was about to fall. Not as often as before, but it almost happened as he left the stand. He lost his balance and pivoted wildly for a second.

Pete recovered and tried to make light of it, and walked across the well of the court without problems, but he was embarrassed, and it showed. The judge told him to take his time and to "Hang in there."

Pete stopped, turned and nodded. "Thank you, sir. I'm working on it."

Kimbie had to testify for hours. The prosecutors had prepared her, and so had the deputy marshal. They had asked her questions they expected, and answered her questions. Preparation paid off when a taxpay-er-paid federal defender, appointed to represent Aldo Salazar Gilliamet, sneered about her "arrangement" with Dr. Ping. When he asked whether she had a "similar arrangement" with Pete, her temper flared. The pros-ecutor objected quickly, pointing out that Ms. Barone was not on trial. The prosecutor also noted that numerous witnesses could testify that she would not have been available to testify, if Mr. Gilliamet and Mr. Chandler had had only a bit more time.

From then on she kept her emotions mostly in check. She explained that Ping had been one of her favorite professors in grad school, then became her employer and colleague, when she was his research assis-tant. "For part of that time, I guess you would say I was his girlfriend," she said, but she had not seen him since the day after the attack. On the other hand, "Pete Gordon is my business partner, my best friend, an honorably discharged Coast Guard veteran and former rescue jumper and diver, a licensed and respected boat captain and a person I would trust with my life." When the defense lawyer asked another question that implied a sexual relationship, the prosecutor's objection was instant and strong. The judge agreed and warned the federal defender against further questions of that type. After that it was only grueling. She gritted her teeth and got through it, even smiled.

Claiborne Chandler's lawyer, retained by his family, was a partner in a large firm with offices in Tampa, Tallahassee and Miami. He and others in the firm were on friendly social terms with both the prosecutor and the judge.

Smooth, about 40 and handsome, the attorney at first was solicitous. He tried to create the impression that Kimbie might not fully understand the legal system. That this was all new to her (outside her experience, despite her degrees), but he was going to help. At first, his line gave Kimbie a little trouble. After one patronizing question, she turned to the judge and asked, "Your honor?" When the judge told her to proceed, she asked, "How much latitude do I have in answering a leading question like that?" The judge told her to answer truthfully, but also asked the defense lawyer to reframe the question.

After that, she didn't hesitate to ask the judge questions. She even asked the pirate lawyers questions. When she called them "the pirate lawyers" the judge smiled and didn't reprimand her. Her questions ir-ritated Claiborne's attorney, but the judge continued to allow them.

It became clear that the judge liked her spunk. She was pretty, with that deep tan and almost snow white hair. Those bright eyes seemed to take in everything. She looked demure in her white sundress and jacket, an outfit she had bought for a mandatory faculty tea and worn maybe twice. But when pushed, she pushed back. One of the ladies in the District Court Clerk's office told her the dress and little jacket were "just right" for court. She went shopping and found another much like it, pale green. Her eyes were pale green too, and the defense table did not like the way they glinted.

During a break, a bailiff who was a semi-retired lawman was overheard to say, "I don't think she'd lie to save her neck, and she won't take much guff, either." Kimbie never flirted with the judge, but she paid close attention, and sometimes smiled at his folksy, plain-spoken directions. She liked the dignified, common-sense way Judge Arthur ran his court. She had never paid a lot of attention to the law, except environmental law, but prepared for the hearings as she had prepared to defend her master's thesis in grad school. She made outlines and tried to anticipate what she would be asked. One of the prosecutors told her she had worn him out with her preparations, but it was a compliment.

The Zinsers testified with good effect, as did Mel McRae, who flew down from Chicago. Mel took everyone out for an expensive dinner of stone crab that evening, and told them he had wanted the satisfaction of looking the pirates in the eye. Everybody's story more or less jibed. It appeared to the prosecutor that, after the inevitable appeals, Claiborne Chandler and Aldo Salazar Gilliamet would do time. One deputy clerk guessed they might face as much as fifteen years.

Claiborne's chestnut hair did not completely hide his scar, and on the third day he began to slump in his impeccable suits. Salazar, who wore a different sport shirt with the same linen sport coat each day, never slumped.

The jury, mostly working-class and multi-racial, seemed to like Kimbie's lack of pretense. Some of them obviously liked the way the plainspoken judge kept the smarty-pants defense lawyers on a short leash.

They were each convicted on multiple counts. Though they had been caught red-handed, in front of numerous witnesses who were their intended victims, even in front of U.S. Navy personnel, each of their lawyers made smooth and immediate statements of their intention to appeal. From the first day of the trial, each had tried to shift as much guilt onto Ricky as innuendo and implication would carry. In his summation, Claiborne's lawyer had tried to portray Ricky and Teddy as hardened criminals whom his client feared. Salazar's lawyer played along.

Despite that, Judge Arthur sentenced Claiborne and Salazar to four consecutive ten-year sentences, each, for either murder or being an accessory to murder, plus a total of thirteen years each for multiple counts of attempted murder or being an accessory. Convictions on related offenses—kidnapping, piracy, theft, vandalism, destruction of property—added more time. Federal sentences are not subject to parole or probation, so they each faced fifty-three years in the penitentiary. The prosecutors were stunned. They had not expected half that. Salazar's lawyer spoke the word, "Excessive."

The appeals process would start immediately, but the way the court's calendar worked, the next hearing would be at least six months away. On the pink Tennessee marble steps, Pete leaned on his cane with both hands and told a TV crew he hoped the outcome would make anyone think twice before attempting piracy. Asked if he was satisfied with the sentences, Pete paused and said, "I wish you could ask my old friend Digby Smith, who died trying to protect us. Or my late crewman, Fred Gold, a fine young fella just starting out in life, or Ms. Sarah Cale, who had almost worked her way through law school at night, or young Molly Molinari, who wanted to be a scientist like her hero, Miss Barone."

Kimbie hugged Pete's arm when he said that, though tears threatened. She looked the soul of reason and sweet propriety in her white sundress and jacket. She too was asked if the sentences seemed appropriate.

"I don't think so, no. Not considering they killed four decent, honest, good people—friends of ours—just to steal a nice old boat." She dabbed the corners of her eyes. "No I don't. Those killers still get to feel sunshine, read books, drink coffee, even eat ice cream. I think it would be more appropriate to feed them to sharks."

She said it as calmly as if it had just occurred to her, because it had. But her eyes flashed. The reporter, a man a head taller, drew back. Pete had to look at the sky and take a deep breath. Kimbie smiled. She took Pete's arm and they helped each other negotiate the rest of the pink marble steps.

73
Up one coast,
down another, home

The dolphin pod left the warm, blue-green Gulf, with its many lights, its big brown dead place and tasty fishes. The pod did not go toward the deep place to the west, and instead hugged the shallow coast toward the sunrise and swam south. They rounded the tip of Florida and followed the lights and the warm Gulf Stream north, stopping to eat at places they had visited as long as they had been a pod. They stopped at the Outer Banks, where strong tides nurture tiny, strong-smelling marsh creatures, and regularly sweep them into the sea. Tasty fish eat those creatures. The dolphins ate the tasty fish.

They rode the current past the big bay that men call Chesapeake, with its broad beaches, strong surf and lights.

They ventured out of the current and into the bay, but not far. The food was not to their liking. A few of the youngest ones became ill, and the pod had to rest to let the aunts tend them a day, or a few days. But no one died, or became sick enough to need help breathing. Sores got no worse, or better.

The pod let the stream from the Gulf carry them north to better water, far from shore. They encountered whales that told them about a place even farther north. The whales had gorged on masses of tiny fish, among other mostly tiny things. The pod liked the way the whales' eyes gleamed, and the contented way they spoke about the place they had fed.

The pod swam well out from the New England coast, a day's swim out, but still encountered too many boats, and fewer fish than they would have liked. Some of the young ones were listless. One or two of the old ones too, so the pod rested for several days, until they were all able to continue.

At last they left the sour taste of land behind.

Off Greenland, they found the familiar cold, thick water from the icy north that pours down through the narrows to meet what is left of the Gulf Stream, where the cold water from the north helps the current turn toward the rising sun. They found the sardines the whales had said would be there, and feasted. They ate fat, rich, oily sardines, bigger ones than the ones the whales had liked, for days, and then weeks, until everyone in the pod was more sleek than usual, and happy.

The water was less salty than they remembered, but that seemed to be a good thing for the small fish. They stayed until every dolphin was tired of the rich fare, and tired of the cold water that was not quite salty enough for good buoyancy. Chobeem had told the small ones they would grow tired of sardines, but they had not believed it was possible. He had laughed. Now they knew. When the time came to leave, they were ready.

They let the warm top of the stream help carry them east again, toward the sunrise. The current was weak, but it was a current, and at last they came to the rocky coast men call Iceland. As they usually did, the pod turned south, across the current that still carried warmth, as the song they had sung a thousand times said it always had.

Hundreds of miles south, the pod again felt the familiar coldness of water up from the deep, the same cold fresh water they had first enjoyed off Greenland. Water from the icy end of the world, Chobeem said. The oldest ones, Chobeem and Chax and a few others, had probed this current once, diving a long way down into its cold darkness. They had seen strange fishes and creatures that seldom—if ever—venture up into water warmed and lit by the sun. Creatures that make their own light, that do not look like fish or man or anything else. Timid creatures, fearsome creatures, some too beautiful and a few almost too strange to look at, much less eat.

The pod rode the cold current until it had lost most of its strength, near the rocky green islands where men have always built and loved boats, and spent a day with dolphins much like them, adventurous, rough and friendly. They swam without turning toward Gibraltar and the big, blue, busy eastern bay of the green ocean. They let the current carry them to the Canary Islands.

There, as the long song has long said, close enough to smell the fragrant coast of Africa, men have learned a bit about dolphins. The men's whistles are crude, but they can whistle about as well as they can swim, that is, a little. The young in the pod had been raised on stories about this. When they heard these men for themselves, what they heard was as funny as they had been led to expect, and as touching, and pleasant. The dolphins laughed, but they also appreciated the effort. The pod tried to talk back to these men, and rested in the pleasant islands for several days, swimming only enough to eat and play and tussle with the local dolphins, a friendly but possessive and loud bunch.

When Chax and the leaders saw it was time, they swam west and stayed north of currents they knew would take them the wrong way for this swim, toward Africa. They swam a day and a night and a day without a stop. The farther they went, the less they needed to turn north.

The swim was easier then. They found their way to the big grassy sea that men call Sargasso, with its odd creatures that swim near the surface. They collected and fed near the seaweed gyre that, although it is not a whirlpool, is still a current, one the dolphins could feel.

By then they had been away from familiar waters so long that they were less interested in things that are different. Now they longed for the familiar, warm, shallow western bay of the green Atlantic, the hook that men call the Gulf of Mexico. Their desire to get back was as strong as the drive that had urged them to start this swim. So they made their way across the warm Sargasso Sea and showed only passing interest in its strange creatures, until they again found the path that now carried only hints of the flavors of Africa.

For weeks, the pod edged across the current, riding it, swimming into the setting sun each evening, needing no encouragement to swim a long time each day. When they reached the northern coast of South America, they almost relaxed. They began to savor everything, as a sailor takes long, deep breaths when he nears his home port. But they did not stop.

As the current pushed them along in the sea that men call Caribbean, their urgency left them. They swam among islands that the old ones knew well. They were as good as back. They had had an adventure. They felt the good tired of accomplishment that comes as the end of a long swim nears, and anticipated the comfort of the familiar, the sounds and sights and flavors of home.

They were ready to be back. The entire pod had survived. Most had been ill at least once, but none had died. They were grateful and glad. They had been threatened by orcas once, and by sharks several times, without coming to harm. Men had gawked, or chased them, or tried to feed them odd things. They had tried to talk to the men in the Canary Islands, who had tried to talk to them. They had swum days out of the way to avoid fishing fleets, or nets, or bad places in the water, on the advice of whales, gulls and terns. They had taken the home-waters advice of other dolphins too, home-loving dolphins that may never take a long swim. It was remarkable that they all had made it. They talked and sang about it.

Without so much as a pause to wonder if it was the right thing to do, they had herded many fish along the paths of the seas. A few times, they had driven fish out of the paths—to food, or away from danger. They had pushed fish along—and eaten some. Fish of types and tastes and habits that the young ones had never tasted or even heard about.

Now they had. Now they knew. Now they had been on a long swim. Some pods never take a long swim, never venture far from home at all, but this pod's song told of other such swims. They would take more if they could.

Now this swim was part of this pod's song. It marked the time after the pod had helped good men. Bad men had tried to kill those men for no reason the pod could see.

The Creator of the seas and skies had allowed Chax and the pod to help, and they had. Then they had gone on a long swim, feasted on sardines, enjoyed colder and warmer waters, seen and tasted and heard amazing things, and shown the young ones that the old songs are true.

Now they were back. They were ready to be back. It was time to rest.

The End

Acknowledgments

Many people have helped this book come together,

First and foremost is my wife, Jeanie, who has been my encourager, best friend, best critic and editor. Learning to trust her judgment has been the lesson of this book and yet another lesson of this stage of my life. She is a blessing. I love you, Jeanie.

My daughter Maggie read an early draft and championed one character in particular, Popper. "Some little child is waiting to read about Popper," she said, more than once. Thanks, Mags. I love you.

Thanks also to Alice Loftin, who has thought deeply about books and writing and what is worth writing, and has encouraged and helped. Thank you for your friendship.

As a practical matter, neither this book nor the one before it would have come together without Rick Phillips, book-builder extraordinaire. Rick anticipated problems I didn't see coming, and showed smiling patience when I dithered and second-guessed. He went the extra mile, several times. Thanks to you Rick (and Donna) for your friendship.

Poet Suzanne Underwood Rhodes read an early draft and offered valid criticism and encouragement. My friends Wally and Jan Boyd read it and cheered me on. My cousin Shelly Scott, a voracious reader, wanted to know more about the bad guys. In time, so did I. Thank you all so much.

Wanda Morgan, over a long lunch, pointed out that I seemed to be trying to write three books as one. Thank you, Wanda.

My sister, Ellen Yancey Jeter, has long been my defender and encourager. Thanks, Elgin, for so many things. My "adopted" sister, Teresa Davenport, offered encouragement and the threat of bodily harm when I did not move fast enough. Thanks, brat.

Retired U.S. Navy Master Chief Petty Officer Stan Simmerman read parts of an early draft and kept me out of as much trouble as he could. Salty submariner Stan knew procedures and terms that I didn't, as a none-too-salty topwater sailor. And then some. Any submarine errors are entirely mine.

Several sailors at the U.S. Coast Guard sector headquarters at St. Petersburg, Florida, and the small rescue boat station at Yankeetown were gracious in answering questions and showing their boats. Again, any errors about the Coast Guard are mine.

The late Milton Santini is the reason this book was begun. Milton and his brother caught the original "Flipper" in shallows near the Everglades. The first Flipper was a smart female he named "Mitzi." Our paths crossed on the docks at Goodland, Florida. Milton let me hang out and pick his brain about dolphins and his life as a fisherman and dolphin catcher and trainer. Trying to ask better questions started me reading about dolphins, looking for them, watching them, wondering about them and sometimes chasing them. I remain fascinated to this day.

Books by the late Dr. Kenneth S. Norris of the University of California, and by Sylvia Earle, Randall Wells and most recently Maddalena Bearzi have informed and inspired me

Dr. Earle once said that if you study fish long enough and close enough, even the most common of them shows individuality. Not dolphins, fish. That made me think. She has done as much as anyone to raise awareness about degradation of the ocean habitat, and is a hero of mine.

Dr. Wells is one of the world's leading experts on dolphins and his books are informative, as is a visit to the Mote Marine Laboratory at Sarasota where his work is based. *The Bottlenose Dolphin; Biology and Conservation*, which he co-wrote, is excellent and comprehensive.

Dr. Bearzi's book, *Dolphin Confidential: Confessions of a Field Biologist*, is a charming, readable introduction to dolphins and marine biology, and an eye-opening update on the declining state of the ocean, as of 2012. It was featured by National Geographic in 2015.

I don't know if any of these scientists would endorse the conversations that the dolphins in this book have, or what these dolphins do. Perhaps not. However, all of these experts (and many others) have led me to conclude that dolphins are highly intelligent creatures who (or if you prefer, which) have shown they can communicate with each other in a variety of ways. They must be saying *something*. I just put words in their bubbles.

With all that said, I believe God created dolphins, and me, and can communicate with any of us, as he chooses. So I would also like to thank God for life and breath and the desire to try to communicate, however imperfectly, with my fellow creatures.

Tom Yancey
Tusculum, Tenn.